I0600197

Love of the Bladed Dove

A Drakaren Novel
Alexia Gray

Copyright © 2025 by Alexia Gray

Alexia Gray asserts the moral rights to be identified as the author of this work.

All rights reserved. This book or any portion thereof may not be reproduced, stored in a retrieval system, or transmitted, in any form or by any means, electronic, mechanical, photocopying, recording or otherwise, without prior permission of the publisher.

First printing, 2025

Print paperback ISBN 979-8-9989675-0-4

Print hardcover ISBN 979-8-9989675-1-1

Ebook ISBN 979-8-9989675-2-8

This novel is entirely a work of fiction. The names, characters and incidents portrayed in it are the work of the author's imagination. Any resemblance to actual persons, living or dead, events or localities is entirely coincidental.

CONTENT AND TRIGGER WARNING

This story isn't all ballgowns and banquets.

This story contains emotionally intense material that may be triggering to some readers, including sexual violence, captivity, and scenes of physical and emotional trauma. You know- the kind of stuff that buries itself deep then claws its way back to the surface to haunt you when you least expect it. Fun, right?

If any of that feels like too much, just close the book and walk away. No shame- some chapters aren't meant to be faced before snacks, sleep, or a good cry. This story will still be here when you're ready.

With love, lavender, and a very sharp dagger,

-Alexia

BY FLAME, BY ROOT, BY GOD AND STAR—
CALERIA SHALL RISE, OR PERISH WHOLE.

To my husband- my muse, my menace, my favorite bad decision. Thank you for being the sarcastic asshole that I fell for, the master of our chaos, and the soul I'd find in every world. I love you.

Chapter One

Layla.

The blade pressed cold and sharp against Layla's throat — a steel whisper daring her to breathe. One inhale, even a shallow sigh, and it would drink from her neck like it longed to. Her sword lay only feet away, lost in the blur of the last clash. Close, but useless. The fear clawed its way up her spine, ruthless and loud, but Layla caged it. She would not falter. Not now. Not today.

Do not defeat yourself. Sir Charles' voice echoed in her mind, not as advice, but as a command etched into her soul. She moved with the grace of a ghost wind — swift, silent, certain. Her fingers found the hilt of the dagger at her waist as her body spun backward in a practiced blur.

The sword's edge sang through empty air where her neck had been. A heartbeat later, her feet landed firmly.

She flipped the dagger, blade first in her grasp and released. The weapon soared, slicing through the space between predator and prey, burying itself deep into the man's right bicep. A grunt. A clatter. His sword fell with a ringing clang, followed by the dull thud of hilt against stone. Layla's eyes locked onto his.

Even wounded, Sir Charles instincts flared. She watched as his left hand darted toward the blade now impaling him. A mistake. She lunged.

Snatching her second dagger from the sheath at her back, she closed the distance. Her left hand gripped his wrist as her right drove the blade toward his gut, stopping just before the tip pierced skin. Her breath hitched as the realization of what she had just accomplished hit. Triumph welled as she watched the familiar brown eyes stare down at the poised steel taut against his abdomen, then up to her.

"You're learning," Sir Charles said, pride glinting through his pain. "Now go get dressed before your mother comes and slits both our throats." A laugh escaped her lips before she could catch it, sharp and genuine. The image of her regal, dagger-terrified mother wielding a blade was as absurd as it was delightful. She released his wrist, stumbling back with a grimace as her gaze caught the dagger still lodged in his arm.

"I'm sorry for the wound," she murmured, guilt pulling at her gut.

"Never apologize for defending yourself, Princess," he said with a gentle firmness. "War is coming, you must learn to survive, so that our kingdom's future can too." He added, glancing at the bloodied blade, "I just pray it never comes to this." He met her eyes again, his stare unwavering, etched with a quiet resolve. She nodded, not because she believed

Welcome to Caeleria

A land carved by war, ruled by blood, and watched by gods long forgotten.

Where the wind speaks of battles yet to come, and the rivers carry the names of the dead.

Here, loyalty is a blade's edge, and destiny is a crown dipped in fire.

Enter, and remember- nothing in Caeleria is ever truly lost.

Not love.

Not power.

Not vengeance.

Chapter One

Layla.

The blade pressed cold and sharp against Layla's throat — a steel whisper daring her to breathe. One inhale, even a shallow sigh, and it would drink from her neck like it longed to. Her sword lay only feet away, lost in the blur of the last clash. Close, but useless. The fear clawed its way up her spine, ruthless and loud, but Layla caged it. She would not falter. Not now. Not today.

Do not defeat yourself. Sir Charles' voice echoed in her mind, not as advice, but as a command etched into her soul. She moved with the grace of a ghost wind — swift, silent, certain. Her fingers found the hilt of the dagger at her waist as her body spun backward in a practiced blur.

The sword's edge sang through empty air where her neck had been. A heartbeat later, her feet landed firmly.

She flipped the dagger, blade first in her grasp and released. The weapon soared, slicing through the space between predator and prey, burying itself deep into the man's right bicep. A grunt. A clatter. His sword fell with a ringing clang, followed by the dull thud of hilt against stone. Layla's eyes locked onto his.

Even wounded, Sir Charles instincts flared. She watched as his left hand darted toward the blade now impaling him. A mistake. She lunged.

Snatching her second dagger from the sheath at her back, she closed the distance. Her left hand gripped his wrist as her right drove the blade toward his gut, stopping just before the tip pierced skin. Her breath hitched as the realization of what she had just accomplished hit. Triumph welled as she watched the familiar brown eyes stare down at the poised steel taut against his abdomen, then up to her.

"You're learning," Sir Charles said, pride glinting through his pain. "Now go get dressed before your mother comes and slits both our throats." A laugh escaped her lips before she could catch it, sharp and genuine. The image of her regal, dagger-terrified mother wielding a blade was as absurd as it was delightful. She released his wrist, stumbling back with a grimace as her gaze caught the dagger still lodged in his arm.

"I'm sorry for the wound," she murmured, guilt pulling at her gut.

"Never apologize for defending yourself, Princess," he said with a gentle firmness. "War is coming, you must learn to survive, so that our kingdom's future can too." He added, glancing at the bloodied blade, "I just pray it never comes to this." He met her eyes again, his stare unwavering, etched with a quiet resolve. She nodded, not because she believed the gods would answer that prayer, but because believing anything else would break her.

Sir Charles pulled the dagger from his bicep without flinching. The wound wept red and Layla swallowed hard. The battlefield felt closer now, no longer a nightmare in the distance. She absentmindedly watched as he cleaned her blade on his shirt before offering it back, hilt-first. She took it with a respectful nod and returned it to her waist.

"Put those thoughts aside tonight," he said softly. "I shouldn't have spoken of the war." Layla's jaw tensed. *There it was again.* That subtle dismissal—quiet and well-intentioned, but unmistakable. *He shouldn't have spoken.* Because she was a woman. Because war, bloodshed, and strategy were matters meant for men. Not for her ears.

In Graystonia, women were raised to be ornaments of virtue, not weapons of will. They were trained to bear heirs, not bear arms. A queen consort, not a sovereign. They were expected to smile politely at banquets, nod quietly through council meetings, and disappear when talk turned to policy or war. Power was spoken in deep voices around heavy tables while women waited in silk, ever graceful, ever silent. To lead—to *rule*—was not theirs to imagine, let alone pursue.

"I appreciate your honesty," she replied, words smooth and steady, a fragile thread wrapped in sincerity. Her smile was soft, practiced. "And thank you, Sir Charles. For everything." His shoulders eased at her words, unaware of the tension hidden behind her gaze. He offered a weary smile in return as she politely changed the subject. "Will I see you tonight?"

"You will, now get going." He winked, waving her off like an impatient uncle. Layla turned and ran up the stone steps, away from blades and blood, toward her own battlefield.

The castle corridors whispered of duty and preparation. Maids fluttered around her like nervous birds, giving her the same half-disapproving, half-knowing glances. *A princess running with weapons strapped to her hips, how scandalous.* Layla offered her best fabricated smile as she passed them, the weight of decorum pressing against every movement. *Tonight will decide your entire future. Please do not dally, my dear Layla...* Her mother's voice rang like a bell of doom in her mind as she skidded to a halt before her chamber door. Brass turned, and the door swung inward into her sanctuary.

Her private bedchamber greeted her like an old friend, familiar and gentle, unchanged by war or expectation. The last of the summer heat drifted through the open balcony doors, thick with the scent of sun-warmed stone and distant hearth fires. It brushed against her face, rustling the sheer curtains in playful swirls—like a lover whispering daring secrets. The Lammas celebration stirred beyond the castle, its laughter and music rippling across the rooftops in distant echoes.

Lammas. The end-of-summer festival devoted to *Serelai, the Gilded Bloom*—the goddess of harvest and abundance, whose blessings had made Graystonia the most fertile land on the continent. It was said that Serelai once walked the valley barefoot, and where her feet touched, crops bloomed wild and wheat turned to gold. For centuries, the people had honored her with feasts, bonfires, and fresh-baked bread—offerings of gratitude for her quiet favor.

Though Serelai had never spoken, never shown her face, her hand was evident in every golden field and heavy-laden orchard. And it was whispered that other kingdoms—those who had forgotten her name, abandoned her rites—had seen their lands wither. Soil gone dry. Seeds refused to root. To forget Serelai was to invite blight. To honor her was to ensure another season of bounty.

Layla and her sisters had once adored Lammas. Bonfires in the palace courtyard. Bread baked with their own hands. Running barefoot beneath starlight, their giggles mixing with the melody of a thousand others. There had been joy in honoring such a generous, radiant goddess, but there had also been joy in simply being girls. Girls allowed to dance, to laugh, to live. But not this year. Not when everything joyful felt wrapped in mourning. Not when her future, and her kingdom's, was being decided behind closed doors. There was no room left for starlight and flour-dusted hands. Only strategy. Sacrifice. Survival. She was no longer the girl who once danced barefoot for Serelai. The world was no longer letting her be.

With a sigh, Layla's gaze flicked to the bed—neat and untouched. Her favorite novel lay on the pillow, waiting like an old escape route. For a heartbeat, her fingers twitched to grab it, to fall into another fantasy world and not face the weight of reality. But not tonight. She turned toward the washroom and exhaled as tension unwound from her shoulders. The tub was already drawn, steam curling upward in fragrant spirals of lavender and vanilla. As always, Marilla had anticipated her needs.

Marilla—sweet and steady, with soft brown hair always swept back in a proper bun and a gentle sort of command that could quiet tempests. In her mid thirties now, she'd been with Layla for over ten years. She was more than a handmaid, more than a companion even. If Layla was being honest, Marilla was her dearest friend. There had always been a pleasant ease to her, one that softened the edges of even the worst days, but she never failed to keep Layla firmly on track and more or less on time.

Layla slid out of her sweat-dampened shift, letting it fall to the stone floor, and sank into the bath. The heat coiled around her limbs, drawing out the ache she hadn't admitted to anyone. Her hair floated around her in a chestnut halo. For just a breath, the world stilled. Then the thought returned. *Tonight, I must find a husband,* she could put it off no longer. It hit harder than she expected, like a cuff to the gut. Her hands curled around the edge of the tub, knuckles white with the effort to remain composed. She closed her eyes, taking in deep breaths as the panic rose. Her mother's voice rang louder now. But she was quickly yanked out of her fear filled thoughts as the door creaked open behind her. Layla stiffened, only to relax slightly when she heard the familiar footfalls. *Marilla.*

Relief softened her shoulders for half a breath... but the quiet comfort didn't last. Her thoughts returned the moment she looked up. The weight. The expectation. The helpless knowing of what tonight would require. Layla watched Marilla's every movement with a bittersweet mixture of gratitude and dread as she bustled into the washroom, humming softly under her breath. Tonight was once a night filled with celebration, light, and laughter. But not this year.

This year, Layla was expected to secure the future of a kingdom. She would be paraded like an heirloom before foreign sons and lords, all under the pretense of festivity. Her father's armies would soon march to war, and if he didn't return, Graystonia would need a male heir. A king—by blood or by marriage. Because even as the eldest, she would never sit on the throne. Not as a daughter. *Not as a woman.*

"You wouldn't be rushing if you ever left the training court on time," Marilla said without looking. Layla ducked under the water to avoid answering and to steal one more moment of refuge. "You know you need to hurry, My Lady," Marilla continued, folding Layla's discarded gown. "The festivities have already begun. Everyone's expecting you."

"My *husband* is expecting me. That's what you were going to say, wasn't it?" Layla quipped. Marilla gave a patient, practiced look. She knew Layla's resentment. She knew her fear. Still, she said nothing. "I know what's expected of me," Layla muttered, voice hoarse. "I just... need one more moment."

She gave Layla one look, took in the flushed cheeks and tense shoulders, and offered a small, knowing smile. "I'll give you one more moment," she said gently, placing a folded towel nearby. "But only one. Queen Raynera is already sharpening her tongue."

Layla sighed, then stood. Water slid from her skin in rivulets, the cool air rushing to meet her like a warning. She shivered. A battle was coming. Not with swords or blood, but with shackles. Shackles that were velvet wrapped and gold-stitched, beautiful but binding none the less.

She stood before her full-length mirror, her shoulders bare in a thin linen shift exposing the curves of her rounded breasts. Her skin glowed in the late sun pouring through the balcony, painting the stone walls in gold and flame. The tapestries hung around her, telling tales of kings, not queens, who shaped Graystonia. Layla stared into her reflection, into the familiar hazel eyes... but they didn't look like hers tonight. They looked hollow. Trapped.

The corset gripped her torso like armor worn inside out. The gown — emerald green and threaded with gold — was breathtaking. Beautiful, yes. Regal, certainly. But it wasn't freedom. It was a promise, a price really. She felt like a painting. But Layla forced her chin up anyways. *Tonight, I am the future of Graystonia.* Marilla stepped back to admire her work, pride lighting her face. Layla smiled. Small. Faint. But there.

"Thank you," she whispered to Marilla before she watched her handmaid slip out into the hall leaving her that moment.

Alone now, Layla slowly approached the door. Her hand gripped the knob. Her face settled into a serene mask of royalty even as her mind screamed and heart thundered. She would face the men who saw her as prize, not person. She would do her duty.

As the ballroom doors opened before her, music swelled and sweet perfumes rushed her senses. All eyes turned to the Princess of Graystonia, flawless, composed, radiant. Layla took a breath. And stepped into war. She would not let them see her nerves, she would wear the mask they all so dearly approved of.

Upon her approach, Queen Raynera watched her like a hawk—every step, every breath, every blink under scrutiny. Layla knew the look on her mother's face well. It was the silent appraisal of a woman who had spent her life mastering grace under pressure and expected nothing less from her daughters.

As Layla reached the head table, her mother offered a single, subtle nod of approval. That was all. But it was enough. *Thank the Gods,* Layla thought, allowing herself the briefest exhale. Tonight would be difficult enough without falling short in her mother's eyes.

Sliding into place next to her two sisters, Layla took in the Queen's appearance. Raynera wore a deep green gown nearly identical to her own, though her bodice shimmered with heavier gold filigree, and her sleeves billowed like silken wings. The Queen of Graystonia wasn't just regal, she was radiant. In Layla's eyes, no woman alive had ever matched her mother's beauty. Her long blonde curls were arranged in effortless perfection, cascading like liquid light down her back. She didn't walk, she glided. Everything about her exuded power tempered by poise and strength softened by grace. Layla had often thought her mother looked like something out of legend, an angel carved from starlight and steel. And Ciana was her mirror image.

Nineteen and luminous, Layla's younger sister- Ciana, turned heads with barely a word. The same golden hair, the same honey-hazel eyes flecked with gold, the same glowing presence that made others pause. The suitors were already circling- ambitious, desperate, eager. And Aerilynn, the youngest at seventeen, had inherited the golden hair too, but paired it with their father's deeper skin tone, sun-kissed and warm like the southern fields. All three sisters bore their parents' hazel eyes, but Layla alone was different. Her hair was a deeper chestnut, wavy and heavy like her father's. Her eyes were shadowed hazel, darker around the edges, not glinting like gold, but catching light like bronze. She stood out in ways she didn't always understand, and had long since stopped trying to.

As she settled into her seat between her mother and Ciana, Layla's attention drifted to her father sitting on the other side of her mother. King Aiddeon sat straight-backed, but tension coiled through his shoulders like drawn bowstrings. His voice was low but sharp, directed at the man beside him—Sir Charles, his most trusted commander.

"We know an attack is coming," the King murmured, his tone low and tense. "I should've canceled tonight. If I'm wrong... we're risking lives."

Sir Charles didn't flinch. "With respect, Your Majesty, you're not wrong. And I believe the risk of losing Her favor outweighs the threat beyond our gates."

King Aiddeon exhaled sharply, eyes scanning the ballroom. "I haven't forgotten what tonight means. I just question whether our people should be gathered so openly when danger is this close."

Sir Charles leaned in, voice quiet but firm. "And I would never question your vigilance, My King. But you know as well as I do—we are the last kingdom still in Serelai's grace. To forget Her, even for one night, is to invite blight upon our fields and famine upon our children. She has blessed these lands for centuries. We give thanks, not just for tradition... but to ensure our future."

Layla's gaze dropped to her wine glass, fingers tracing the delicate gold leaf pattern. Her father knew all of that—of course he did. No one revered Serelai more deeply. But he also carried the lives of everyone in this room like armor on his shoulders. That he feared for them, even knowing the cost of silence tonight, only proved what she already believed: he wasn't just a king. He was a great one.

Sir Charles softened. "Just for a few hours, let me handle whatever needs handling. Let your people see that this night still matters to you—that the Goddess is still honored, and tradition still holds. You've borne enough weight for a lifetime. Tonight, enjoy the fire. The laughter. Let them see their king is still with them... unshaken."

From the corner of her eye, Layla watched her father's posture ease, if only slightly. Sir Charles always knew how to bring him back from the edge. She was grateful for that. Aiddeon had been under unbearable pressure in recent months. She saw it in his face, in the tired way he moved. He needed this night, *deserved* it.

Her mother reached over and placed a hand on his forearm, a touch so gentle and familiar it was almost holy. Aiddeon turned to her with a smile that lit up his entire being. They were a love match and anyone who looked at them could see it. Layla had always known that her father ruled a kingdom, but Queen Raynera was his world. She, Ciana, Aerilynn—they were the rest of it. And that love, that rare and sacred bond, was why her parents had never rushed her into marriage. They had wanted her to choose love. Real love. Like theirs. But love was a luxury now. Alliances needed forging. The kingdom needed protection. The crown demanded sacrifice. And so the dream died—quietly, nobly. Layla felt it leave her like breath from the lungs. A dream briming with love, possibilities, and promises slipped away. And in its place rose the quiet weight of responsibility. She adjusted her shoulders, sat taller, and pulled her mask of serene composure back into place. Then she looked up, scanning the grand ballroom. A battlefield in silk and gold.

WITH BLESSINGS, WE RISE;
WITH STRENGTH, WE CONQUER

GRAYSTONIA

Chapter Two

Layla.

I t wasn't long before a suitor approached the table and asked for her hand to dance. Layla had known his name, station, and family before he even opened his mouth. That was her responsibility, her burden. It had been drilled into her since she could walk in heels and hold a curtsy: *know their name, know their bloodline, know what they want from you.* Her mother made sure of it.

"Alexander Morringar," she recalled silently. Son of a sergeant in her father's personal guard. She had met him before, briefly, and always in the most formal of settings. Never like this. Never with music, candlelight, and expectations thick in the air. He was about six feet tall, with neatly trimmed stubble, sun-kissed skin, short blond hair, and deep blue eyes. Not unpleasant to look at, not at all. But he never made her pulse quicken, never left her with a thought that lingered after he was gone. Still, tonight demanded an open mind, and that had to begin somewhere. *Why not with him?*

"May I have this dance, Princess Layla?" he asked, offering his hand as he bowed with effortless grace. Layla looked to her mother first. Always to her mother. The Queen's slight nod was her signal. Only then did Layla return her gaze to Alexander, meeting his with the softest of smiles.

"You may," she replied with practiced warmth. She rounded the table and took his outstretched hand. His palm was rough- evidence of sparring, of swordplay, of following in his father's foot- steps. That's how things worked in Graystonia. Sons became their fathers. Daughters became their mothers. Deviations were rare, even frowned upon. But at least his grasp was gentle, appropriate. He didn't grip too tightly. He understood who she was.

The ballroom was alive with motion, couples dancing in syn- chronized elegance beneath the flickering chandeliers. Alexander led her through the crowd with careful precision, their path carved with quiet authority. At the center, they bowed and curtsied in time, then joined the waltz in step with the others.

His questions were polite. His answers were thoughtful. He asked about her sisters, her day, her hobbies- topics rehearsed a thousand times in drawing rooms and etiquette lessons. Layla played her part. She smiled. She asked him questions in return. But the conversation lacked the color of passion, the heat of curiosity. There was no spark. No pull. No danger. And certainly, no magic.

As the music ended, a second suitor appeared- Elric, then another, and another. They came like waves- polite, charming, and forgettable. Layla's cheeks ached from holding the same smile. Her feet throbbed in her shoes. And yet her heart remained unmoved. Not one glance, not one word had stirred her. Not even a flutter. It was frustrating and yet oddly comforting. Perhaps it was easier to feel nothing. But even that thought frightened her. *What if I can't feel it at all?* She wondered, the truth catching in her throat like a thorn. The thought of falling in love terrified her, but so did the possibility that she never would. Then, as another dance concluded, a deep voice cleared its throat behind her, low and vaguely familiar. Layla turned.

Ryker Jameson. Her breath caught. Lord Jameson's eldest son. The heir to the largest holding at court, and a man whose family wielded real power. She had heard whispers of him, his discipline, his reputation, his influence. But seeing him now... He stood tall, perhaps six-two, with dark, tight curls cropped close to his head and deep brown eyes that held both sharpness and warmth. His jaw was strong, his face clean-shaven. His frame, wrapped in formal attire, still hinted at the raw strength beneath. Broad shoulders. Solid arms. The kind of man who looked like he belonged in both a ballroom and a battlefield.

"May I have this dance, Lady Layla?" he asked. His voice was steady, but something about the way he looked at her- the way his eyes lingered, made her stomach flutter.

She swallowed, schooling her features. "Of course, Lord Jameson."

He chuckled as he took her hands. "Lord Jameson is my father. You may call me Ryker, if you're comfortable." A genuine smile escaped her lips before she could stop it, and she had to look away to hide it. "How has your evening been so far?" he asked. His voice brushed her ear, and she felt its warmth bloom on her cheek.

"I've had the privilege of meeting many wonderful members of our kingdom," she replied, voice poised, polished. Not a lie, but far from the truth.

He laughed softly. "Ah, yes. I've seen the line forming. Many men chasing the favor of a very beautiful lady." She turned away, feeling the blush rise again. Compliments were common in her life, but this one felt... different. Less performance. More intent.

"I'm surprised to see you here tonight," she said, surprising herself with her directness. "Last I knew, you were training to be an officer of the guard." He looked at her, something like surprise flashing in his eyes. She wasn't supposed to know that. Daughters weren't told about armies, or war, or how close the danger truly was. She was meant to smile, to wait, and remain blissfully unaware of it all.

"Yes," he said, nodding. "I should be sworn by year's end." There was pride in his voice, earned pride. She admired that and she appreciated that he didn't ask how she knew. He simply continued, "My father requested I take leave for Lammas so I could attend with my family." Layla offered a soft smile. *How nice,* she thought. *Time with his family, in the middle of such a demanding year. That must mean something.* But Ryker wasn't finished. "My father also wished for me to officially meet you, Lady Layla." Their eyes met again, and the warmth she'd been holding at bay threatened to rise once more. Then it hit her. This wasn't coincidence. This was strategy. A setup. *Of course.* Of course, his father had arranged it. Of course, Ryker was here not simply to enjoy the festival, but to court her—to be seen with her, to make an impression, to offer himself up for the crown. Even *he* had been pulled from officer training just for this opportunity. To be the future king.

The warmth that had begun to thaw her quickly turned cold. She didn't know why it bothered her so much, only that it did. The very idea of being chosen, not for love, not for who she was, but for what she represented... it made her feel small. Powerless. Layla smiled through it. Mask back on. Chin lifted.

They danced, and though the conversation continued, the spark did not return. Something inside her had shuttered again. By the time the song ended, she gave Ryker a polite curtsy and retreated to her mother's side. She took a large gulp of wine, letting it burn its way down her throat. She had known tonight would be difficult, but she hadn't expected *panic*. And she hadn't expected this—how final it would feel. Whatever last threads of hope she'd held onto—for choice, for a love match, for something more than duty—were gone. That much was clear now.

As Layla moved the food around on her plate without eating, her mind swirled. She thought of each man. *Alexander. Elric. Ryker.* And all the others. None of them stirred the deep thing inside her. The quiet part that wanted more than duty. More than alliances. Ryker made the most sense. She could see it. She told herself she should be grateful. He was kind. He was handsome. He had let her knowledge of his training slide. He hadn't mocked her. Perhaps, in time, he would even allow her to learn more. *He would make a strong king.*

But really, none of what was expected of her tonight should have come as a surprise. She'd known this was coming for weeks—ever since the war council began, ever since the guest list for Lammas had shifted—from the joy of old friends to a lineup of eligible sons and power-hungry lords, all eager to stake their claim. But still, she couldn't quite believe it. That this was truly her fate. That by night's end, she would be expected to report her choice to her parents. And if they approved, the engagement would be set, her future sealed beside a man she barely knew, all for the good of the kingdom. What she couldn't fully accept was the possibility that her heart may forever remain still. That duty would be all she'd ever know. And sadness settled in her stomach like a stone.

Across the room, she spotted Ryker in conversation. He laughed at something. Then he glanced her way and smiled, a smile that reached his eyes. She returned it, softly, as she begged the miniscule spark to return, but it was ash and her shoulders slumped. She tried to convince herself: *There could be worse men. He is strong. Loyal.* He might even let me be part of more than just the crown. *This could be enough.* But the hollowness inside her deepened. A quiet ache she couldn't ignore.

Still staring at him while deep in her thoughts, she watched as Ryker's smile faded. His body stiffened in alarm. His eyes shifted, not toward her, but toward the opposite direction. Layla sat up straighter, her chest tightening. *What does he see?* she wondered. She craned her neck, eyes scanning the crowd. But something in her bones had already begun to whisper. Something was wrong.

Layla watched as Ryker's head whipped back toward her, his eyes wide, wild. A flicker of terror sparked in his face the moment his gaze connected with hers once again. Then, without hesitation, he ran. He ran like a man possessed, shoving bodies aside with a seemingly singular intent: reaching her. She stood frozen for a breath, her pulse roaring in her ears, then the room erupted into shrieks. Shrieks of fear. Of chaos. Of death.

Around her, the impossible unfolded: bodies dropping, thudding onto the marble floor. Pools of red spread like ink through the ballroom. And not just any bodies, Graystonian Guards. Her guards. Their throats were slit, clean and fast. Layla's breath caught in her chest. Then instinct overtook her. She grabbed the knife from her plate, the familiar weight grounding her for a moment, and bolted from her seat. Her eyes frantically scanned the sea of panic. *Where was her family?*

There. Her mother stood some distance away, dangerously close to the heart of the mayhem still erupting across the ballroom. With both arms wrapped tightly around her youngest daughters, anchoring them behind a marble pillar, using her own body as the only barrier between them and the violence. But no guards. No steel. No shields. *Where the hell are their damn guards!?* Layla's mind screamed as she tore across the chaos toward them. Two Graystonian bodies lay in her path, their eyes were still open, but lifeless. Blood pooled beneath their necks in wide, glistening circles. Her stomach twisted, but she didn't stop. She couldn't. Her eyes stayed locked on her mother and sisters— alive, for now.

Then she saw him. A man, someone she didn't recognize, was closing in on them. His attire mimicked Graystonian nobility, but Layla *knew.* She had spent her life memorizing faces, families, bloodlines. This man wasn't one of them. He wasn't *theirs*. A predator among lambs. Layla skidded to a halt and centered herself. Her grip tightened. The knife hummed in her hand—an extension of her will. Then she released it. The blade sliced the air like a whisper of justice and struck. Right in the outstretched arm of the stranger. He staggered back with a roar of pain, blood spurting from his wound. Layla was already in motion, closing the distance to her family before he could, but he turned and lunged for her before she could reach them. His hand closed around her forearms with bruising force. Even with blood pouring from his gash, he was strong. Too strong. He wrenched her around and yanked her against his chest.

"Stop fighting, you little bitch. You're coming with me!" he hissed, hot and foul against her ear. *Like hell I am!* She slammed her elbow back hard into his ribs. He yelped, his grip faltering just enough. Layla twisted free and dropped low, her eyes locking on a serving tray nearby. She snatched it, and without pause, swung. It cracked against his skull with a sickening *thud* and she watched him collapse.

Layla stood panting, heart hammering. There was no time to process what she'd done. She had to *move*. She looked toward the pillar again, her family was gone. Panic surged through her veins. She spun in frantic circles, scanning the pandemonium. What remained of the ballroom was a hellscape. The gilded elegance of the evening had shattered-replaced by screams, blood, and the clang of steel. The guards—what few remained—were fighting at the ballroom doors. Her father among them, sword flashing as he battled to protect his people's escape. Ryker was nearby, fists flying, fighting off two enemies with raw fury.

Finally, her eyes found them. Her mother. Her sisters. Farther across the ballroom now, heading toward the east wall. Her mother was trying to lift Ciana off the floor but seemed to be struggling. Aerilynn stood beside them, seemingly paralyzed in shock. Tears streamed down her face as she watched the horror unfold. Layla ran.

"It's my ankle!" Ciana cried as Layla closed the distance, her face twisted in pain. Layla dropped to her side, a rush of relief flooding her as her hands moved instinctively to help. Together, she and their mother pulled Ciana upright, her weight sagging heavily between them, arms looped over their shoulders for support. Ciana turned her head, her tear-filled eyes locking onto Layla's, wide and terrified. Layla met them with a firm nod, fierce and steady. They were going to get out.

"Mom! Who is this? Who is attacking us?" Layla demanded as they stumbled toward the northeast exit, the only escape untouched by blood. Her mother's face was stone and shoulders rigid, tight as a bowstring.

"Bartoria," she spat. Layla's blood went cold but before she could react, a hand landed on her shoulder. She spun, ready to kill, ready to die before she let them harm her family.

"Princess—it's just me!" Sir Charles said quickly, hands raised. Relief cracked through her like a lightning bolt. "Please let me help." He moved in without hesitation, slipping one arm beneath Ciana's knees and the other behind her back. With practiced strength, he scooped Ciana into his arms. She sucked in a breath, clinging to his shoulders as her injured ankle finally hung free, no longer bearing weight.

"Sir Charles!" her mother demanded. "Where is the King?"

"He's with the last of the guards, Your Majesty. I'll get you out, then go back for him." Layla nodded. Then turned to Aerilynn.

Her sister still stood frozen, shoulders rigid, tears tracking silently down her cheeks. She stared ahead, unmoving—eyes wide and unblinking, as if her mind couldn't catch up to what was happening around them.

Layla stepped in close and grabbed her arms. "Aerilynn," she said, her voice unsteady but unwavering. "You have to move." Aerilynn didn't respond. "We need you. I need you."

Layla seized Aerilynn's face with shaking hands. Forcing their eyes to meet, refusing to let her sister drift further into shock. "Move. Now," she pleaded, much more forcefully this time. Finally, Aerilynn blinked. Her lips parted in a soundless breath as she gave a small nod, allowing Layla to quickly pull her into a tight embrace. The embrace lasted only a second before Layla shoved Aerilynn forward- away from the chaos and towards the others.

Then Layla turned. She couldn't bring herself to leave without a final glimpse of the only home she'd ever loved. the only place she'd ever known. But the ballroom held no trace of her home now, only the echo of carnage. Blood slicked the marble floors. The scent of blood and scorched stone burned her nose, the air thick with the clash of steel and screams of the wounded. And now she saw them—truly saw them. Bartorian soldiers, their noble finery a disguise, their blades already dripping red. They had hidden in plain sight,

Her gaze found her father—fighting, relentless, surrounded. His back pressed to the last standing guard as they held the line with nothing but fury and steel. That sight caused her instincts to flare. Layla swiftly spotted a nearby table. *Knives.* Not proper weapons, but enough.

"Stay with Sir Charles!" She said, as she turned to dart away. "He'll keep you safe. I love you!"

"What?! No! What the hell are you doing?!" Aerilynn shrieked, reaching for her. Layla slipped free of her sister's grasp, snatched the knives, and surged forward before Aerilynn could stop her. *These aren't daggers, but they'll have to do.* She moved like a shadow, weaving through pillars and bodies, heart pounding, breath shallow. The crowd was distracted enough that no one saw her coming.

She stopped, took aim and released. The knife struck true, embedding in the shoulder of a Bartorian about to strike her father. The soldier stumbled, and in that half-second, the King turned and cleaved his head clean off. No sooner had the head landed than her father's eyes whipped around to find the source of the hurled blade. They quickly landed on Layla.

"Layla, no! Run!" King Aiddeon roared across the battlefield that had once been a ballroom. She froze, the force of his voice ricocheting in her chest, but she didn't obey. She couldn't. She swore she saw something flash in his expression- *was it surprise? Agony? Fear?* He turned back to his opponent, his sword already mid-swing. His sweat-soaked chestnut hair clung to his brow in thick strands. Steel clanged and rang through the air like thunder. The chaos was deafening.

Layla scanned the fight, heart pounding against her ribs as she searched for her next shot. Her hands wavered, but she locked her arms tight, steadying herself against the surging tide of fear. Another Bartorian came charging toward her father. She took a breath, cold and clean like mountain air, and released the next blade. It struck the man in the thigh. He screamed and dropped to one knee, just as her father gutted his current opponent with ruthless precision and spun toward the next, finishing the kneeling Bartorian with a brutal swipe of his sword.

Watching him in motion was like watching a storm made flesh. Even drowning in fear, Layla couldn't help but marvel at him. *That* was her father. A true warrior. A true King.

She tore her eyes away for a heartbeat, glancing toward the ballroom's center and her breath caught. *Ryker*. She watched in horror as his body crumpled forward- his knees giving out, then he collapsed as a Bartorian slowly withdrew a blood-slick sword from Ryker's gut and shoved him to the floor like he was nothing.

"No!" The word tore from Layla's throat, raw and helpless. She bolted toward him but her feet left the ground before she made it a foot away. An arm wrapped around her chest, hard, slamming her back into a massive body. Her arms now pinned to her sides. A human vice gripped her, yanking her away from everything. She screamed and thrashed, clawing for any movement she could find. She forced her hand, still clasping a knife, just far enough away, then plunged the blade into the man's thigh. A howl erupted behind her ear, hot and foul—but he didn't loosen his grip. She struck again with her final blade. The man buckled slightly forward with a grunt, but his arms only cinched tighter. He was a mountain of muscle, and she was drowning in panic.

Her mind raced. Her chest burned. *Fuck. This isn't good. This is bad. This is so—* Her eyes collided with her father's. He turned toward her, mid-swing, and in that moment, everything slowed. His expression cracked. Just for a second. Just long enough for her to see what lay underneath the warrior's mask. Then rage bloomed across his face. And with that rage, he charged. Sword raised, eyes burning, cutting through Bartorians like they were nothing more than paper before flame.

Layla kicked and bucked, desperate for another inch of movement as her father closed the gap with terrifying speed. Every heartbeat a battle cry as the seconds slowly passed. One man, three enemies down in seconds. Her father moved like a god. Then, without breaking stride, he dropped to one knee, spun, and sliced through the ankle of the man holding her. The Bartorian's grip around her instantly shattered. Layla fell to the floor with a gasp, finally drawing a full breath. Her father was on her in an instant, dropping beside her.

"Layla! Are you hurt?!" he demanded, frantically scanning her limbs, his hands flying over her arms, her shoulders, searching for wounds.

"No," she stammered, barely able to speak. She did a quick check herself, mind buzzing. No blood. No pain. Nothing, *thank the Gods.*

"Thank the Gods," he echoed, his chest rising and falling like thunderclouds, eyes already scanning their surroundings again. "Listen to me," he said, voice steely, fast. "Go down this hallway. Head to the castle's west wing. Find the library. Behind the west bookshelf, there's a hidden tunnel. It'll take you directly out of the castle. Get to the old oak tree on the edge of the forest. You know the one. Your mother and sisters will meet you there." He lifted her to her feet like she weighed nothing, and then spun around, ending the life of the crippled Bartorian loudly writhing in pain with a swift thrust to the chest. The man choked. Blood spilled from his lips. Then silence.

"No! Father, wait, I can help! Let me stay!" Layla's voice broke as she reached for a weapon, anything, but she was out of knives. Her entire body was shaking, not from fear, but from something deeper- *purpose.*

Her blood roared with it. "I *need* to help. I *have* to." Her father turned, seized her shoulders. The fire in his eyes was unwavering.

"No." His voice was pure command. "That's an order." Layla froze. Her heart cracked under the weight of it.

"But—"

"I said *go*!" he growled. "Now, Layla! That is a royal command from your king!" The sheer force of it slammed into her. The fire inside her flickered—then faltered. Terror seeped back into her limbs like ice. Fear for him. Fear for her family. Fear for her kingdom. For the future. She opened her mouth, trying to argue, but her words dissolved. She had never felt so small, and yet so full of something too vast to name.

"Damn it, Layla!" he shouted, shoving her toward the hallway. "GO *NOW*! That's an order!" She stumbled back, the door swinging open behind her. And in that final moment, she saw it- her father, all alone as Bartorian soldiers encircled him. The last of the Graystonian guards lay dead only feet away.

"GO!!!" he screamed back to her now, not taking his eyes off the enemy as they closed in. Tears blurred her vision, but she turned and ran. She ran like the halls themselves were collapsing behind her. Every step felt like betrayal. Like failure. Like she was leaving her heart behind in that blood-soaked ballroom. But she ran. She ran because he ordered her to. She ran because if she didn't, his sacrifice would be for nothing. She ran because she had to survive. And because one day... she would *make them pay*.

By the ancient edict of Graystonia's forebears,
the throne shall forever be claimed by the blood
of men. It is through their strength and lineage
that the kingdom endures, for only the man's
hand is fit to bear the crown. Let it be decreed:
The mantle of power is his, and his alone.

-BY DECREE OF THE CROWN OF GRAYSTONIA.

Chapter Three

Layla.

Layla reached the library within heartbeats, her chest heaving, lungs scraping for air. She slammed her shoulder into one of the towering oak doors, forcing it open with a groan that echoed louder than she liked. The familiar scent hit her instantly- dust, leather, parchment. A sacred perfume of old stories and forgotten time. For a split second, the weight of the room struck her like a ghost. She had loved this place. A fragment of memory surfaced: herself curled into the plush maroon couch, legs tucked beneath her, a stolen book in hand, devouring stories by candlelight long after she was supposed to be asleep. Her heart ached with the simplicity of that stolen peace. But the memory was a luxury she couldn't afford. Not now. *Focus,* she told herself. *Survive.*

There were only three escape tunnels hidden within the castle, known solely to the royal family. She darted toward the western wall, weaving between shelves of ancient tomes and towering scroll cases. Her eyes snapped to the deep red tapestry, its embroidered depiction of their sacred forest shimmering faintly in the moonlight that spilled through the stained-glass dome above. It hung like a silent sentinel between two great shelves- elegant, beautiful, and completely deceiving.

With an unsteady hand, Layla reached out and yanked the tapestry aside, revealing the narrow opening hidden behind it: a sliver of shadow, stone steps barely visible in the dark below. She pressed herself against the cold stone behind the tapestry, her breath held hostage in her throat. The woven forest scene swayed lightly in front of her, giving her the barest glimpse of the library she had once cherished. The place where she had spent countless hours, safe and invisible between shelves and pages, now desecrated by the sound of foreign boots on marble.

The doors flew open with such force the echoes cracked like thunder through the vast room. Bartorian soldiers stormed inside, their voices sharp and guttural. Layla's entire body stiffened.

"Check everything. Don't leave a corner untouched," one barked. She bit her lip so hard she tasted blood. *Please, Freyric—just this once,* she begged silently, sending a quick prayer to the God of Luck.

Through the thin slit in the hanging tapestry, she watched one soldier march perilously close to her position. He scanned the northern bookshelves, then turned toward her wall. His eyes flicked briefly across the tapestry but didn't linger. She sent another prayer up thanking Freyric as the guard kept moving.

She waited, not wanting to make a sound and draw their attention. One heartbeat. Two. Ten. Then, muffling her breath with her sleeve, she turned, crouched low, and gripped the sides of the hidden entrance. The narrow passage gaped beneath the stone, a spiral staircase descending into nothingness. One last glance. She dared it. Just one. The library she loved- the maroon couch, the towering shelves, the stained-glass dome above, all stood silent under the weight of invasion. Her home, her history, her joy. All of it was crumbling. And her father was not behind her. *He's still fighting.* Her throat tightened as she tried to convince herself the thought was true. Then she slipped into the tunnel.

It was darker than she remembered. The air was damp, thick with the smell of dust and earth. The stone steps beneath her feet were uneven and narrow, spiraling down into pitch black. She kept one hand on the wall, the other clutching her dress to avoid tripping as she descended fast—half-running, half-falling. She'd only been in this tunnel once before, many years ago, when her parents brought her down late one night under the guise of a lesson in royal duty.

"Every heir must know the way out, in case the worst ever comes," her father had said, his voice low but firm. Her mother's hand had rested on her shoulder the whole way down. She'd barely been twelve. It had felt like a story then. A secret passage meant for queens in fairytales.

Now it was real. Now it was war. Muffled shouts echoed behind her—closer now. And then: metal scraped against stone. Footsteps. They had found the passage. *No, no, no!* Panic spiked in her veins as she pushed harder, faster, barely catching herself as she stumbled on the last turn.

Then moonlight. A faint, silvery glow was bleeding through cracks at the bottom of the stone passage. The exit.

She threw herself at the heavy stone threshold. It didn't budge. *Move Damn it!* She pushed again. Nothing. Her palms scraped against the rough stone, and a cry of frustration tore from her lips. The footsteps behind were louder now, rushing down the staircase. Layla snarled in defiance and shoved her full body against the stone. It groaned beneath her weight. Her muscles screamed. Her whole body shook. Her hands ached from the pressure. *MOVE, DAMN YOU!* Finally, a sudden *shift*. A pocket of air. A breath of wind. The door creaked open just enough, and she threw herself through it, landing hard on her hands and knees. Fresh air hit her face like ice. The stars above glimmered through the canopy. The moon was full, high and bright and she was out.

She staggered to her feet, heart pounding, ears ringing. The tunnel exit was nestled at the base of a sheer cliffside that few would ever guess held such a secret. She didn't even pause to look back, not to check how close they were behind her. She just ran, legs burning, lungs on the verge of collapse. Her feet slipped on the wet grass, but she didn't stop. She kicked off her shoes mid-sprint, the soft slippers useless on uneven ground. Cold earth met her bare feet, grounding her, propelling her forward.

Thirty yards of open pasture stretched before her, then the tree line. The woods were close. But so were the Bartorians. A shout rang out behind her. They were through the tunnel. She could hear the boots again. The harsh language. Layla ran harder, faster than she ever had. Her body had no strength left, but her fear didn't care. Her will to survive didn't care.

As she reached the edge of the trees, she dared a glance over her shoulder. A dark wave of enemy soldiers spilled from the secret tunnel like a plague. *Gods help me,* she thought. *I reeeally need to stop looking back.* Branches tore at her arms as she dove into the forest. The shadows swallowed her whole. With a sharp inhale, Layla forced her anxiety down, locking it away just enough to keep her legs moving. The forest loomed before her like a living wall- dense, dark, and unknowable. She sprinted toward it, praying to any god that might still be listening. *West. Just keep going west.* The great oak stood somewhere in a clearing that way. Her father had said they would meet there. Her family would be there. *They had to be.*

Branches tore at her dress and skin, and roots threatened to pull her down, but she pushed forward. She didn't dare look back again. Let the Bartorians get lost in the blackness behind her. Let them vanish like the nightmare they were. Still, as she ran, her mind worked frantically to gauge her surroundings, but it was impossible. Trees twisted above her like the ribs of a beast. The night masked everything, and the speed at which she was moving made any kind of navigation futile. She had to trust instinct, faith, and memory.

After what felt like an eternity, though it could have been hours or minutes, her legs finally began to falter. Each step dragged heavier than the last. Breath ragged and chest burning, Layla slowed to a staggering stop. Her eyes scanned the forest for any semblance of shelter. Somewhere, anywhere to hide. The forest floor crunched beneath her as she moved, each step painfully loud in the otherwise dead silence.

The heat of the day had faded, replaced by a cool breeze, but her body didn't register it. Her gown clung to her with sweat. Her muscles screamed. Her lungs felt carved from stone as she spotted a chestnut tree—tall, wide, and climbable. If she could get high enough, maybe she'd see the clearing. Maybe she'd see the oak.

She staggered toward it and leapt for the lowest branch. Her arms trembled violently from exhaustion, but she forced herself upward. She wrapped her legs around the branch, hauled herself onto it, and kept climbing. Again. Again. Every limb felt like fire, but she climbed until the branches grew thin and brittle beneath her weight. *There, safe enough.* Hidden in the dense canopy, she slumped against the trunk, chest heaving. Her entire body shuddered from the exertion.

Time passed. Maybe minutes, maybe longer, until her breathing finally slowed and lungs eased. Layla swept her gaze across the forest floor, searching the darkness for the slightest shift, the faintest stir of danger. But no one came. No footsteps. No Bartorian assholes gleaming in the moonlight. She was safe. For now.

So, with careful effort, she rose to stand on the narrow branch, one hand gripping the trunk to steady herself. Her legs wobbled beneath her, fingers still twitching from the sprint, but she forced herself to focus—eyes scanning the treetops, searching. The clearing had to be close. Somewhere beyond the tangled canopy waited the Great Oak, their meeting place. Their refuge. That thought steadied her more than the bark beneath her palm.

The Great Oak... larger and older than any tree in the forest. Its limbs stretched wide and protective, its roots buried deep in the bones of the land—and deeper still in the memory of her childhood. Nothing grew near it. No vines dared climb its bark. Even nature, it seemed, remembered what it was. And so did she.

As her gaze strained to catch a break in the canopy, a half-forgotten tale rose from the corners of her memory. Something her handmaid once whispered when she and her sisters lay curled on a blanket beneath those sacred branches.

"It was not planted by hand, but by heart," Marilla had said once, her voice as soft as the breeze that stirred the summer grass. Layla had been a young girl then, soon after Marilla had first started tending her. The memory continued as Layla recalled being curled between her sisters on a quilt beneath the Great Oak. Sunlight spilled through the canopy above them, dappled like gold coins across their faces. Marilla had sat cross-legged beside them, her brown hair twisted into its usual bun, though a few strands had escaped in the heat. Her eyes—kind, thoughtful, not yet lined from years of watching too much and saying too little—had held something deeper that day. Something like *memory*.

"The God Eliryn," she began, *"was not a god of war or sky, nor of stone or sea. He was the God of Endings. Of dusk and harvest. Of farewells. And he knew all too well what it meant to lose what one loves most."* The girls had gone still, even the ever-squirming Ciana. Layla remembered holding her breath. *"He fell in love with a mortal,"* Marilla continued, her voice laced with sorrow and awe. *"A woman who laughed with her whole soul ~~ ' ` ~ed even the heavens to follow her heart. But mortals are fragile ~~ds... gods are bound by time in ways we cannot understand. '—by sword or sickness, no one remembers—Eliryn did not*

37

rage. He wept....And where his tears fell, the oak grew. Tall, proud, and alone. No other tree dared grow beside it. Not out of fear—but reverence." She had paused then, brushing a leaf from Aerilynn's hair. *"The Great Oak stands where the god knelt. Some say if you listen closely in the hush between heartbeats, you can still hear her name on the wind. Sealed into its roots forever. But what matters most,"* Marilla had added gently, tucking a curl behind Ciana's ear, *"is what came after."* Layla had blinked up at her, wide-eyed.

"The world was different before that love, before that grief. Eliryn's sorrow ended an age. But his love... his love began a new one. That tree marks the place where the old world died—and something new was allowed to bloom. They say it is blessed. That those who seek its shelter with true hearts may find not just peace... but purpose." Marilla had smiled then, warm and wise, looking at each of them in turn. *"So, when the world feels like it's ending, little ones, you come here. Because this tree doesn't just remember loss. It remembers beginning again."*

Layla had never known whether it was truth or fable. But standing there now, with blood on her hands and terror in her throat, she wanted to believe it. She needed to. Because if the tree was born of grief and love and gods, then maybe, just maybe, it would protect her again.

As the memory of Marilla's voice faded, so too did the comfort it brought. The past slipped from her fingers like mist, and new fears crept in to take its place. Her breath caught as her mind began to spin. *What if I ran too far?* Her pulse thundered. *What if I crossed the border into Antonin territory?* Her stomach turned at the thought. The Antonins. Her people's enemies long before she was born. After the Southern War, Graystonia had claimed part of their land, and the hatred between them had only grown. Her father had always told her the war had started like all wars do, land and power, but the wounds never closed. The Antonins had never forgiven. And if one of *them* found her out here, alone... unarmed...Layla's hand clenched around a rough strip of bark. The only options were madness. *Go back? Risk capture by the Bartorians. Keep going? Risk death by Antonin hands.*

"Shit," she whispered, barely audible as her shoulders slumped against the trunk. Her thoughts wouldn't slow. She tilted her head back to look at the moon, its light cutting through the tree branches like a judgment. *I must be deeper into the forest than I thought,* she reluctantly began to acknowledge. She was lost, and navigating in the dark would be suicide. She had to wait. Regain her strength. Figure out a plan.

Her limbs were already going slack, her body begging for rest. As much as her mind screamed to stay alert, to stay ready, her body was done arguing. With a deep sigh, she let her eyes close for just a moment, just long enough to quiet the storm inside her. But before sleep could claim her, Layla whispered into the night—quiet, raw, meant only for the Gods.

"Goddess Serelai... thank you...for all you've given. For the fields. For the harvest. For the beauty of our land." Her voice faltered. "I'm sorry tonight wasn't what it should've been. That blood stained your celebration. But I hope... I pray... it's enough. That you'll still hear us... That you'll still bless us." A soft breeze stirred the canopy above her, brushing her cheeks like a mother's caress. The scent of wildflowers threaded faintly through the leaves—out of place in the thick woods, and gone just as quickly as it came.

Layla drew in a sharp breath. Her chest rose and fell, too fast, too sharp. *She heard me...* The thought echoed, disbelieving. *The goddess heard me.* It was impossible. The gods didn't answer—not like this. Not to mortals. And yet... they had. She had.

Warmth flooded her chest, so sudden it made her sway where she sat. For one brief, flickering moment, she let herself believe it. Hold it. That the goddess had listened. That the old stories weren't just stories. That maybe—just maybe—Graystonia still had her blessing. And that meant something. Even if the kingdom was still in danger. Even if Layla didn't know how to save it, only that she had to try. That she had to live.

She breathed in again, steadier this time. The moment was sacred—but it couldn't last. She was still alone in the woods. Still hunted. Still needed. She let the awe settle deep in her bones and locked it there, a quiet promise she wasn't entirely alone. But belief wouldn't carry her home. She had to move. She had to survive. She had to reach her family. She had to protect what was left. Because without that, none of it—no prayer, no sign, no blessing—would matter. This night was meant to honor the goddess and shape her future. Instead, it had been swallowed by blood.

And as the night air cooled her sweat-soaked skin, and her muscles gave out beneath her. Layla—Princess of Graystonia, survivor of bloodshed and steel—surrendered to exhaustion and fell into an uneasy sleep, hidden among the branches of a silent tree.

FROM THE BLOOD OF WARRIORS
OUR STRENGTH FLOWS ETERNAL

ANTONIN

Chapter Four

Theron.

E ach morning, before the first blush of dawn kissed the treetops, Theron Drakaren rose. Like clockwork, he embarked on his territory patrol, a daily ritual carved into the fabric of his life as head warrior of the Antonin tribe. The eastern stretch of the border was always his-dense forest, silent and veiled in the light of dawn. It took nearly half the day to complete the circuit, but Theron didn't mind. The solitude suited him. Out here, with only the rhythm of his boots and breath, he didn't have to be the unshakable pillar his people demanded. Out here, he could just be a man with a blade and a duty.

The path was well-worn beneath his feet, moss-covered roots rising like old bones through the soil. The morning air was crisp and damp; every surface gleamed with dew. Beams of tentative sunlight broke through the thick canopy above, lighting his path in scattered golden shards. It was peaceful- the kind of peace that felt like a secret in a world built on tension and survival. But today, peace felt like a lie.

His mind was still knotted with what he and his scouts had seen in Bartoria the days prior. They had returned just the night before from a scouting mission, dispatched by his mother, the queen, to verify the growing unrest in one of the borderlands. Rumors had been spreading that King Ivar, the vile Bartorian ruler, was looking to expand. And if that expansion pushed south-west, it would mean Antonin lands.

Theron had witnessed the truth for himself, and it had made his blood boil. Bartoria was a corpse of a kingdom, decaying from the inside out. Beyond the gilded walls of the capital, the rot was everywhere. The slums reeked of death- bodies left to rot, stripped of dignity and forgotten. The living were little better. Women and children, gaunt and hollow-eyed, wandered the streets like ghosts, ribs protruding through torn rags. And the guards... They didn't protect. They pillaged. Theron could still hear their laughter echoing off crumbling walls, their hands taking whatever they pleased—coin, food, flesh.

He clenched his jaw. The screams haunted him most. It had taken every shred of control not to leap from the shadows and strike them down. His blade had ached to be drawn. But orders were orders- observe only, no engagement. And Theron never disobeyed a command, especially not one from his mother.

When he'd returned the night before, the rage still burned in his blood. But rage had no place in his report. He gave it plainly, without flourish, each brutal detail sharpening the lines of the queen's face. She had ruled their territory for five years with a blade's edge—cold, precise, and unyielding. From her, Theron had learned the long game. The patience of a predator. How to wait, watch, and strike only when the outcome was certain. Not because it was easy, but because it was necessary. And necessity always came before desire. Even when every part of him had wanted to paint Bartoria's streets red, he hadn't. Because he was a warrior. Because he was her son. Because duty came first. Always.

After his conversation with the queen had ended, sleep abandoned him. Slipping through his grasp like smoke no matter how still he lay. Theron had tossed and turned on the rough cot, its bear hide stretched tight over bundled branches, every movement stiff with unresolved outrage.

His hut—simple but solid, its walls packed with mud and timber, its seams lined with hide—offered warmth but no solace. The thick bison fur folded neatly in the corner waited for the frost of winter, and all Theron could do was stare at it aimlessly as he waited for the sleep that never came. By morning, the fire inside him still crackled, banked just beneath the surface, waiting to be unleashed.

As he continued on his morning patrol, he tried to shake the memories loose, focusing on the subtle movements in the underbrush and the calls of waking birds. Hoping the brisk walk of duty, the simple act of doing something, would simmer that anger. But it didn't. And all he knew was that if Bartoria brought war to Antonin, Theron would be ready. And this time, he wouldn't be observing.

As Theron refocused on the rhythmic stillness around him, a sudden rustle broke through the serenity, a sharp disturbance in a nearby chestnut tree. Instinct surged through him. In one fluid motion, he stepped silently behind a pine, fingers tightening around the hilt of his sword. Every muscle in his body coiled with readiness, his senses honed to a razor's edge.

Peering around the tree's rough bark, he allowed his eyes to adjust to the dappled light piercing the forest canopy. What he saw next was not what he expected. A woman, clad in a deep emerald gown, was descending the tree's wide limbs with the grace of someone desperate, not practiced. Confusion flickered in Theron's sharp gaze. No one should have been this deep into their territory, especially not alone. Not unarmed. *Not dressed like that.*

As she reached for a lower branch, her dress caught, and in an instant of unintentional exposure, the hem pulled upward- far too far- until the fabric was tangled above her hips. The sight it revealed was... distracting. Impossibly so. Theron blinked once, then again, trying, and failing, to ignore the view: porcelain skin kissed by morning dew, the perfect curve of her ass silhouetted by sunlight. The moment hovered between obscene and divine. He dragged in a breath through his teeth. *Gods, what a view.*

Then—*thud.* She fell hard, gracelessly, into the mud below with a muffled grunt. Theron winced in reflexive sympathy. He took a step forward, but she sprang to her feet faster than expected. He immediately melted back into the covers of tree and brush, swift and silent. She began stripping off the soiled gown with a frustrated efficiency, revealing a white shift clinging to her curves. It was soaked, nearly transparent from dew and sweat. Revealing perfectly large and inviting breasts that he couldn't look away from. Her long, curling chestnut hair sticking to damp skin. She looked both wild and regal- like a forest spirit caught between fleeing and fighting.

Theron bit down, his jaw tense as desire warred with duty. His body reacted before his mind could wrestle back control, the heat rising, unmistakable and unwanted. This woman was trouble- an outsider, possibly a spy, or worse. And yet his thoughts betrayed him, imagining her curves pressed against him, his hands spanning her waist, her thighs clenched around him like a vice. He forced the fantasy away, furious with himself. *Focus, warrior. This isn't some tavern seduction—this is a breach of the border. She is a threat.* He exhaled sharply and ran a hand through his damp hair, realigning his thoughts. It's time to act.

Without a sound, Theron advanced, gliding through the under-brush with predatory ease. She hadn't noticed. He closed the distance-one step, then another- until he was just behind her. She turned, not seeing him before it was too late as she promptly collided with the wall of his chest. She staggered back with a startled gasp, her eyes lifting slowly to meet his. Wide, hazel eyes framed in panic. And something else.

"You don't belong here," Theron growled, voice low and edged with authority. He stepped forward deliberately, letting his towering presence loom over her like a stormfront. Her lips parted, but no words came. She tried to look past him, scanning the trees, searching. *For allies? Or an escape route?*

"Is someone with you?" His tone sharpened, demanding. Yet she remained silent. "Tell me now," he warned, menace curling around every syllable. "This is your only chance." Then he saw it before it happened—the tightening of her shoulders, the flicker of rebellion in her gaze. She swung, but he caught her wrist easily. She gasped, surprised. He swiftly seized her other arm before she could react further, holding her in place with firm, unshakable control. "Stop," he commanded, his voice a growl of restraint. He brought her closer, his face inches from hers now. Her breath hitched, but her eyes met his with defiance rather than fear. *She's got fire,* he thought, not without a thread of admiration.

"Who. Is. With. You?" he demanded again, drawing each word like a blade. She didn't answer. Instead, she tried to headbutt him. He pulled back just in time, the attempted strike missing him by inches. He chuckled, the sound dry and unexpected. "Spirited," he muttered, more to himself than to her. Her stubborn silence made it clear, he would get no answers here. *Fine.* He spun her around, seizing her by the shoulder. With precise force, he propelled her forward, back in the direction of the village. Fortunately, he hadn't made it too deep into the borderlands yet. Still, the fact that she'd gotten this far without detection disturbed him. He'd need to interrogate the guards and possibly himself, later. To no surprise, she resisted, planting her feet in the dirt and pounding against his grip.

"Unhand me now!" she cried.

"Come. Or die." He didn't yell. He didn't need to. His voice, calm as steel and just as cold, held all the threat in the world. She paused, staring at him, weighing her options. *Good. She wasn't a fool.* Her fists stopped flying, though her eyes burned with resentment as he resumed the march. Theron glanced down at the woman beside him- barefoot, mud-splattered, fierce-eyed. He wondered, for the first time in many moons, just what the gods were playing at.

As Theron marched steadily back toward the heart of the Antonin stronghold, he noted with faint relief that the woman, though clearly reluctant, did her best to keep pace. Occasionally, he glanced down, observing the tension etched across her features. Her expression was not one of panic, but calculation. She was thinking- possibly strategizing her next futile escape attempt.

She was tall for a woman, he guessed around five-foot-seven, but her frame was slender, almost fragile when compared to his broad, battle-hardened form. If she tried to fight him again, he wasn't sure whether he'd laugh aloud or simply shake his head. Still, he gave her credit- she had the fire to try.

Theron kept his thoughts to himself as they traveled, but unease began to stir in the back of his mind. *What would his mother do with her?* Queen Okteria Drakaren was no brute, not to her own people. But when it came to outsiders? Trespassers? Theron had seen firsthand what her wrath looked like. And it wasn't loud. It was quiet, sharp, and absolute. He cast another sidelong glance at the woman just as her body shifted. Her fingers curled into a tight fist, and she began to draw her arm back. *Not this time.* In a single, seamless movement, he swept his left arm around her waist and hoisted her over his shoulder. With his right, he secured her legs against his chest, iron-willed and immovable. She wriggled, fists beating weakly against his back, but her strikes were wasted against the wall of muscle that bore her weight.

A low chuckle rumbled from his chest before he could stop it. Her persistence was—if nothing else—admirable. He paused only to remove the blades sheathed at his back and repositioned them along his front, safely out of reach. She may not have landed a punch, but he wasn't about to underestimate her a second time.

As he carried her, his senses sharpened. At this proximity, her scent enveloped him-delicate, intoxicating: lavender and vanilla. It caught him off guard. Some of his favorite herbs—ones he'd ground with his own hands to treat the wounded. Lavender reminded him of summer in the wilds, of peace before battle, of simplicity. *Get your head straight,* he told himself again. *She is not a damned flower. She is a trespasser.*

The forest path gave way to a more worn trail. The edge of the Antonin tribe's settlement rose ahead of them like a fortress carved from nature itself. The trees thinned slightly, revealing the woven structures and open-circle training grounds that marked their home. Two warriors stood watch at the threshold, where wild gave way to worn earth and structure. Theron gave them a curt nod. They didn't move to stop him. None ever would.

"Inform the queen. An immediate gathering is required," he ordered without slowing. One of the young guards took off at a sprint, disappearing into the heart of the settlement. As Theron pressed deeper into the village, all eyes turned to him and the woman hanging over his shoulder. A ripple moved through the people like wind through leaves: curiosity, concern... and something darker. It had been years since an outsider crossed into Antonin land and lived to speak of it. Longer still since one had been carried into the tribe by its head warrior.

The Antonin people were born of the forest. Men and women alike were taught from their earliest days to survive, to fight, and to honor the land that gave them breath. They worshipped Varyn, the God of Blood and Valor, in all things. they bled for him in battle, whispered to him before every hunt, and taught their children that valor was sacred. They took only what they needed and wasted nothing. Their way was simple, ancient, and unyielding. "Antonin" meant *one with the trees*, and it was a name earned through discipline. Though every member was trained for combat, few women joined the ranks of the active warriors. Those who did were forces of nature. Chief among them was Queen Okteria.

As they neared the central gathering ground, known simply as *the Circle*, the crowd thickened. Word had spread fast. Warriors from every division emerged to see what had drawn their commander from his patrol. Then Theron's instincts tensed. The men weren't looking at the woman over his shoulder with suspicion. They were looking with hunger. His jaw locked as he realized the thin white shift she wore was still damp from her fall, clinging to every curve with an unintentional allure. She was virtually bared to the eyes of men who had not seen a stranger in years.

A surge of something feral had torn through him the moment that she had slammed into his chest and looked up at him—bruised, trembling, yet still burning with defiance. Now, with her in his arms and his men raking their eyes over, it hadn't faded. If anything, it burned hotter. His grip tightened on her thighs, fighting for control, and he shifted her subtly, shielding more of her from view without even thinking.

Antonin women never needed his protection—they were warriors born. Even the broken women of Bartoria hadn't stirred this instinct in him. But she had. A fragile outsider with fire in her gaze and no strength in her bones. She wasn't his. She wasn't his to protect. And yet the need to shield her clawed at the core of him, loud and unruly. *For Fucks sake,* he needed to get his head on straight.

As they reached the Circle's core, Theron promptly bent and released her. She hit the ground before him with a soft grunt and a thud. He winced, just slightly. He hadn't meant to drop her that hard. Not really. But he had *meant* to get her off his shoulder and out of sight.

Every muscle in his jaw tensed as he stood over her, watching as she scrambled to push herself upright. Then, instinctively, he lifted his gaze. His eyes swept over the warriors assembled—men who were still staring too long, too openly. Theron's expression darkened as his gaze swept the warriors. Most had the sense to look away. The few who didn't, met a stare sharp as flint. His fists clenched at his sides, tension still thrumming in his blood as he forced it down. There wasn't room for whatever this was. Not now. Not here.

Queen Okteria ascended the stone platform at the head of the Circle, her commanding presence needing no introduction. She was flanked by the tribe's fiercest warriors, save for one—her eldest son, Theron himself, who stood below, shoulders square and blade ready. As head warrior of the Antonin tribe, his place in their hierarchy was unquestioned. No one matched his skill in hand-to-hand combat or his ruthless precision with a sword. He had never tasted defeat—and he never intended to.

Beside the queen stood Kain, Theron's younger brother. Though he shared the same sharp jawline and chiseled features, Kain stood slightly taller, his long, sun-bleached hair brushing past his shoulders, green eyes glinting with mischief. His build was leaner, his body a weapon of agility rather than brute strength. And though Theron could easily overpower him in a close fight, he couldn't deny that Kain's bow was deadly—his arrows landing silent and precise from distances most warriors wouldn't dare attempt. But for all his talent, Kain's loyalty was... flexible. While Theron lived by discipline and duty, Kain indulged in defiance. He questioned their mother's every decree, contributed only when it suited him, and spent most of his time bedding women or loosing arrows at trees out of boredom. Theron didn't bother hiding the disdain in his glance but looked away before it turned into a glare.

Queen Okteria stood tall atop the stone, her presence as formidable as any battle-forged leader. With hair dark as tree bark after rain, cascading over thick, muscular shoulders and golden skin that shimmered in the sunlight. She looked every inch the warrior-queen, one who had seized her crown in the midst of heartbreak, yet never once faltered. Her green eyes, matching Kain's, narrowed sharply the moment they landed on the foreign woman. The crowd stilled. Twenty paces from the stone, the trespasser stood alone in front of Theron. He observed as his mother's posture shifted subtly—shoulders straightened, chin tilted. He recognized the stance. Predatory. Regal. Ready.

Her eyes pierced the stranger like blades. "Why are you here?" Queen Okteria demanded. Her voice cut through the Circle like steel drawn across stone, each syllable laced with restrained fury. Theron inhaled through his nose, already predicting where this was going. His mother had been on edge for weeks—preparing, waiting. The looming threat of Bartorian aggression had agitated her more than she let on. Now, this woman, this near-silent trespasser, had dared to enter their sacred lands. *To beg? Or deceive?* He looked down at her. But something had changed. Gone was the startled, wide-eyed girl from the forest. In her place stood a woman with her spine straight and chin lifted.

"I... I am..." she began, faltering slightly. Theron tensed. *Don't fall apart now.* Then she found it, the composure, the strength. "I am Layla Eradellian, Princess of Graystonia. I am here to seek your alliance with my people... against the Bartorians."

The Circle fell into stunned silence. *Princess...Graystonia...* The words struck like twin arrows. Theron's mind reeled—trying to fit this broken, breathless girl into the image of a sworn enemy's heir. The forest around them felt suddenly too quiet. Then the rest hit him. *The Bartorians attacked them? Not us?* Relief surged so swiftly through his chest it nearly stole his breath. His people were safe. His stronghold unburned. *For now.* But standing before him, draped in dirt and blood, was not just any survivor. She was Graystonian Royalty. A woman born of the very kingdom that had carved Antonin land from their maps during the Southern War. An enemy by blood. A symbol of everything they had lost. And yet here she was—shaken but unbroken, begging for unity where there should have been only fire. That, somehow, shocked him more than anything else.

Her voice rose again. "Last night, the Bartorians launched a surprise attack. They've taken the city. My home. My people are dying, and we cannot withstand them alone." Theron's face remained unreadable, but inside, his instincts continued to clash. He had trained his whole life to face war—but never wanted one for his people. And now, this woman stood here, a survivor of what he feared most. His relief was tangled with pity he didn't want to feel for her. He lifted his gaze to his mother.

Queen Okteria's eyes sparkled—not with sympathy, but something far colder. *Delight.* A slow, cruel smile touched her lips. *Damn,* Theron thought. *She's enjoying this.*

Okteria descended one step on the stone, her voice loud, sharp. "Ah. So, you don't want alliance. You want my army. You've already lost, what could you possibly offer me now?"

The princess didn't flinch. "My father has always respected your borders. He has never harmed your people. He is a just king. He—"

"Is likely dead," Okteria cut in, amused. "Or cowardly, sending his daughter in his stead. Either way, irrelevant."

Theron noticed her instantly go rigid before responding with only a hint of disdain. "This is a war against cruelty. The Bartorians will not stop at us. Once we fall, they'll come for you."

"Let them," the queen snapped before turning away. "And when they arrive, we'll do what we always do: spill their blood into our soil, let it feed our roots, then burn their bones to ash." Theron's fists tightened at his sides absentmindedly. The queen stopped her decent away, glancing over her shoulder with a final, poisonous smile. "Tell me, little princess... have you lived a good life? Because a swift death would be too kind. I intend to bring a century's worth of Graystonian sins down upon your shoulders. You will die slowly, knowing you failed. Starved, forgotten. Alone." Then she nodded—just once, to Theron. *Dump her in the pit.* Was the unspoken request. He inclined his head in silent obedience.

As the crowd murmured and dispersed, Theron took the princess by the wrist and led her through the heart of the village. Warriors returned to their tasks, many smirking as they passed—their hatred for her people deeply embedded in their bones. The scent of smoke, leather, blood, and bark filled the air, rich with the work of hunters and smiths. Theron kept himself between her and the others, blocking their stares from the soaked dress still clinging to her skin. He told himself it was decency. That it meant nothing. But the truth gnawed at him. He was leading her to their prison—to starve, to disappear. *So why the hell did it matter who saw her?*

Soon they approached the pit—a hollowed-out prison carved straight into the earth, its only barrier a heavy, cross-hatched iron grate. The packed dirt walls were damp and uneven, as if the ground itself had been forced to swallow whoever was thrown inside.

He waved over the nearest guard. "Tynan," Theron barked. "Stand watch. No one enters unless commanded." Tynan smirked at the woman, then gave Theron a curt nod before he moved to open the hatch, dragging the heavy slab aside with a grunt of effort. Theron reluctantly released her wrist. Tynan immediately grabbed her and led her toward the pit's edge. Without hesitation, he shoved her in. She landed hard with a cry, her body crumpling to the dirt floor far below. Theron clenched his jaw until the muscle in it pulsed. Then, without a word, he turned and walked away. But the image of her remained—chestnut hair tangled, dress torn, pride bruised yet unbroken. She was meant to die down there.

Slowly. Quietly. And yet, a part of him—one he didn't understand and didn't ask to feel—hoped she wouldn't.

Layla.

Hands shoved her back, and she plummeted. Layla hit the packed dirt with a bone-jarring thud, pain erupting in her knee as it took the full force of the landing. A breathless gasp escaped her lips. Above her, the bald-headed guard loomed, his smile cruel, his eyes devoid of sympathy. Without a word, he reached up and dragged a heavy iron grate across the opening, slamming it shut with a finality that echoed through the small space like a sentence passed. The sound of boots walking away somehow struck her harder than the fall. She was in. And she was alone.

Layla scrambled to a sitting position, scanning the small enclosure with wide, burning eyes. Her pulse thundered in her ears. She could see no other shapes, no shadows moving in the corners. No other prisoners. No waiting executioners. *Thank the Gods,* she thought, releasing a breath she hadn't known she'd been holding. But the relief was fleeting. There was nothing in this pit. No straw bedding, no bucket, no food. Not even a stone to sit on. Just four tightly packed earthen walls and the scent of dust, death and iron. The air felt heavy. Dead. As if hope itself didn't bother coming here.

She sat back and began checking her limbs. Her wrist still throbbed from her earlier fall in the forest, but it wasn't broken. Her knee was bruised and raw, but she could stand. She'd had worse. Her body would hold. It was her mind she wasn't so sure about.

Her hands shook as she brushed dirt off her palms, but she forced her breathing to steady. She wouldn't cry. She couldn't cry. If she let that dam break now, she didn't know when—if—she'd stop. And she'd be damned if she let the Antonin bastards have the satisfaction of seeing her unravel. *Think, Layla.*

She pressed her hand against the wall nearest her. The surface was bone dry, packed so tightly it might as well have been stone. Her fingers dragged over the grit, nails searching for any imperfection, any seam to dig into. *Nothing.* Not even a crack to whisper through. She cursed herself again for leaving her shoes behind when she fled. At least they might've given her a heel edge to dig with. She needed a plan. Fast.

The thought of her mother and sisters hiding at the Old Oak made her chest ache. *Were they still there? Had they waited, had they run? Were they even still alive?* She shoved the thought down. Hard. There was no time for grief. No time for fear. If she didn't escape, there'd be no one left to rally the survivors. No one left to fight for Graystonia. Her people needed her. So she strained her ears, trying to pick up any sound from above. The bald guard-*Tynan, he had been called-* wasn't visible from her angle, but occasionally, she could hear his voice rising in conversation with others. She pressed herself to the back of the pit and stared upward at the grate. Ten feet, maybe more. She could reach quite aways with a jump. But the walls gave nothing. Not even a whisper of footing.

Night had fallen. The stars offered the faintest silver glow, filtering through the slats above. She sent a desperate prayer to Tychic, the God of Strength, and Feyric for luck once again. *Let him be asleep up there. Please... just give me this.* She scuttled to the northwest corner. Earlier, she'd started digging with her nails, carving a tiny foothold into the wall. It was barely an inch or so deep—just enough for the tip of her big toe. It wasn't much, but it was all she had. She pressed her toe into the makeshift crevice and braced herself. *One breath. Two.* Then she launched. Her hands scraped against the dirt wall, searching for purchase—anything to cling to. Her fingers clawed the air, but there was nothing to catch. Her foot slipped, and she crashed to the ground in a tangle of limbs.

"What the hell are you doing down there?" Tynan's voice boomed down. She scrambled backward into the darkness, heart hammering. She didn't answer. "Just so you know," he drawled, his face now just barely visible in the moonlight, "if you try any shit, I'm allowed to kill you... However I see fit." He leaned down slightly, grin wicked. "So please... try something."

Layla's stomach turned. The sick satisfaction in his voice was more revolting than the threat itself. She curled into herself, pressing close to the earth as if it could swallow her whole. Her arms wrapped around her knees, and she clenched her jaw. She needed a new plan, because one way or another, she wasn't dying down here.

By divine command of Serelai, Goddess of Abundance and Renewal, the people shall offer their gratitude and gifts in reverence to the land, upon the sacred solstices. Through offerings of harvest, of gold, and of their heart, the kingdom of shall remain blessed. Let it be known: to honor Serelai, at these times is to ensure the prosperity and flourishing of the realm.

-BY DECREE OF THE CROWN OF GRAYSTONIA.

Chapter Five

Layla.

Three days had passed. Three days since she woke in the branches of that damned tree, her world turned upside down, her home burning behind her—and now this pit. This cursed pit. No food. No water. No sunlight beyond the slivers that pierced the grate overhead like mocking fingers of hope. Time had twisted into something meaningless. Her lips were cracked. Her throat, dry as ash. Even lifting her head from where it rested against the packed wall took effort she could barely muster. And still, her mind wouldn't quiet. Between bouts of restless sleep and hallucination, memories crept in—soft at first, then sharp as blades.

"A woman's weapon is her presence," her mother's voice whispered, too close, too clear. *"History and strategy are for kings and generals. Not for daughters of the realm."* Layla blinked hard, trying to banish the echo. *"Smile, even when you want to scream. That's how a queen commands a room."*

Other voices followed—tutors, instructors, stewards of etiquette over the years and silence. *"You must be pleasant, not powerful... A husband leads, a wife supports... You are to be graceful, obedient, and wise enough to keep your mouth shut."* She curled tighter in the dirt. Those teachings had once been gospel. She'd worn them like velvet—lush to the eye, but heavy and suffocating beneath the surface. Now they felt like chains, rusted and cold.

But one voice had always cut through the rest. Her father's. *"If you had a brother, this wouldn't fall to you,"* he'd said once, jaw tight with something like guilt. *"But you don't. And one day, you'll bear the heir. If anything happens to you, Layla... the line ends."* So, once a week—beneath the judging eyes of courtiers and the quiet disapproval of her mother—he trained her. In the courtyard, not hidden, but never praised. He trained her how to move. How to block. How to survive. And if he was away, Sir Charles carried on the lessons without question.

But what good had any of it done? No one cared how she smiled or how poised she was at the bottom of this pit. And her training? *Clearly useless.* Useless against hunger. Against silence. Against the dark. None of it had prepared her for this.

And yet... something in her spine refused to bend. Refused to let her wilt like the polished princess all of those instructors had so badly wanted her to be. She wouldn't give up. She would get out. She would find her family. She would save her kingdom.

A shuffle of boots overhead snapped her back to stillness, to the present. Voices. Two of them.

"Tynan, who forced you on such a miserable position?" One asked, smooth and rich, his tone wrapping around the words like silk over steel. The sound of it made her eyes flutter open. Something about that voice felt *dangerous*—not cruel, but quiet and deliberate. Almost amused.

"Who do you think?" Tynan's harsh voice answered with a sneer she could practically hear.

"Ahh, yes. How is our little prisoner?" the velvet voice asked, tone light but weighted with curiosity. Layla stayed still. Wanting to see who the voice belonged to, but knew she couldn't see anyone or anything from down here. All she could do was listen. *Velvet Voice. Was this her captor?* The man who had carried her like she weighed nothing, while her traitorous body had burned with confused desire and resentment at his touch. She hated him. She hated all of them. But she still remembered the heat of him. The restraint. The way he had tried, however subtly, to shield her from the gazes of the tribe.

"She hasn't tried shit with me here. Wish she would, so I could be the one to slit her throat," Tynan laughed sharply. A cold coil of dread wrapped around Layla's spine.

Then Velvet Voice responded, his words a whisper barely louder than breath: "You know... you could always *say* she tried something. No one would question it. And you'd be remembered for it." Layla's breath caught. Her heart slammed against her ribs. *No. No, no, no.*

"You're a good man," Tynan replied with a sick grin in his tone. He was going to do it. He was going to kill her—and no one would stop him. "When did you get back?" Tynan asked after a moment.

"Just now," the man replied, casually. "She was right. They took the castle."

They took the castle. Layla's eyes snapped open and pulse surged. She pressed herself up weakly against the wall. *My home...* Tynan just grunted in response. Her mind spun, the dry haze of hunger momentarily cleared by adrenaline. *Someone else knew. Someone else believed me.* But was that what this was? Confirmation? Or the prelude to her execution? Then, something hit the dirt beside her. She jerked back as her eyes strained... An apple. It rolled slightly across the ground before settling in the dust. Dirt clung to its bruised skin. Layla stared at it like it might vanish. She didn't dare move. Didn't trust it. *Why would they feed me now?* She squinted upward, expecting Tynan's ugly face to leer down at her. Waiting for the joke. The cruelty. But nothing came. No gloating. No mockery. Just the soft sound of footsteps retreating. Still, she waited. Then finally crawled.

She dragged herself to the corner, her body shuddered from the effort. The apple waited for her like some impossible miracle. She picked it up with shaking fingers, turned it slowly in her hand, checking for cuts, for poison, for anything that might reveal the trick. Just a bruise. Just fruit. Just... *hope?* Her hunger shattered every doubt and she bit into it. Sweetness exploded in her mouth. Her entire body shuddered with relief. The apple's juice ran down her chin as her eyes squeezed shut, overwhelmed. It wasn't much. But it was enough. Enough to survive a little longer. Enough to believe she might still find a way out. And deep in her gut, Layla knew—whoever *Velvet Voice* truly was... this was not over between them.

Theron.

"Are you sure starving her to death is the best plan?" Theron asked, sharper than he intended. The words left him too quickly, they were urgent, almost reckless. He cursed himself the moment they echoed off the wooden walls of the queen's hut. Queen Okteria turned from the table at the center of the room and leveled a slow, appraising gaze at her son. Her expression was unreadable, but her silence was never idle. She was measuring him.

"This isn't like you," she said, her tone smooth and quiet. Dangerous. "Do you know something, Theron?" He straightened immediately, shifting his posture into neutral discipline. His expression closed off like a fortress gate.

"No," he replied with calm precision. "I just feel it's... wasteful. Our people are eager. They hunger for retribution." The words tasted bitter, even as he spoke them. What he didn't say was that the image of the Graystonian princess-alone, starving, half-conscious in that pit-was clawing at him more than it should. He'd seen death. Dished it out by the blade. He'd never flinched before. But this... this wasn't death. This was something slower, crueler. And for the first time, it felt like it was rotting something inside him.

From across the room, Kain leaned lazily against a timber beam, arms crossed, eyes glittering with amusement. Theron didn't even have to look to know the smirk was there. "Well, *I* never thought I'd see

the day," Kain drawled. "Big brother's questioning the queen herself."
Theron ignored him. Okteria turned her attention back to the map, fingers tracing lines and borders that had long since ceased to be diplomatic. Now they marked bloodlines. Graves.

"I'm just saying," Kain continued, clearly bored. "If the idea is to kill her, at least let the warriors have a little fun with it. A trial by fire, maybe. Let her bleed in the Circle. Starving her is so... quiet."

Theron saw the way their mother's eyes flicked upward, how a smile ghosted across her lips. *Damn it.* Kain knew exactly how to play to her appetite for public spectacle. And worst of all, it worked. Theron's stomach twisted. Something in him recoiled at the image. Layla-no, the *prisoner*- brought out into the Circle for sport, for public humiliation, for execution. That wasn't justice. That was theater. And he couldn't let it happen. Not because she was noble or because she was beautiful. Because something in her—delicate yet unyielding—spoke to something buried in *him*.

"If she lives," Theron said, forcing his voice into neutrality, "we can use her as leverage. A bargaining chip." Okteria's gaze snapped to his. There was nothing hidden in her face now, just annoyance and the slow flicker of suspicion. She never hid what she felt. She *wielded* it.

"Why would we need leverage?" She snapped. "Graystonia has already fallen. The Bartorians have done what we should've done years ago." She stalked toward him, the full weight of her queenly authority coiled in her stride. "And thank Feyric that they brought her right into our hands. The last spoiled relic of a dying house. We can kill her slow or fast. That is *my* decision. Unless..." Her smile widened, smug and sharp. "Unless you're *challenging me*, Theron?"

Her words hit like a thrown spear. Silence fell. Even Kain's lazy smirk froze at the edges. Theron didn't blink. Didn't move. He stared back at her with steel in his jaw but nothing in his face. This wasn't a challenge. He knew the line, and he hadn't crossed it. But he had *approached* it, and they both knew it. He didn't speak. He wouldn't justify himself. But the heat in his chest, the one he couldn't quite name, was alive and pulsing.

Okteria's nostrils flared before she turned away, brushing the conversation aside like it was beneath her. "That's what I thought." She waved her hand, dismissing them both like a final decree. "Get out."

Theron dipped his head, controlled and formal. He pivoted and walked out into the moonlit clearing without a word. Kain followed, boots crunching on the hardened earth behind him.

"I like this side of you brother," Kain teased, practically humming. "Never seen you push back before. Was she a good lay before you dragged her in?" Theron stopped cold. A slow, dangerous turn brought him face-to-face with his brother. Kain grinned. "There it is. Knew you cared."

Theron's fists clenched, wrath coiling beneath his skin. Kain clapped a hand on Theron's shoulder, voice low and triumphant. "Interesting." Was all he said before Kain turned and walked off into the dark, leaving Theron standing alone beneath the stars. He breathed slowly. Deeply. He wanted to hit something. Or scream. Or march back into the pit and drag her out himself. But he didn't. He just stood there, staring at nothing, the forest trees seemingly whispering around him. *Why her? Why now?* He had no answers. Only a growing, burning certainty that what they were doing was wrong. And that if he didn't act soon... it would be too late. Yet he knew he couldn't. He must obey.

Layla.

Night crept in, pressing against the iron grate above her like a weight. The stars were barely visible, just slivers of distant light, but Layla hardly noticed. Her mind spun endlessly, tangled in the threads of what *Velvet Voice* had said that morning. *"They took the castle."* Not the city. Just the castle. That meant the Bartorians hadn't charged through the gates with fire and war, they'd slipped in. From the inside. Which could only mean one thing. *There's a traitor in Graystonia.*

Layla clenched her jaw as a dull heat flickered in her chest, chasing away some of the chill. Someone from her court had betrayed them. *Her* family. *Her* people. And they would pay. But vengeance required survival. And right now, she wasn't sure she would make it through another day.

Her limbs were weak, her head light. The apple she'd devoured earlier that morning had kept her going, but every joint in her body ached, not from injury—but from thirst. A cruel, wringing dryness that left her tongue thick and her vision hazy. She had enough strength left to think, but barely. Her thoughts spiraled between questions and survival plans, none of which gave her any comfort.

Then-footsteps neared from above, forcing her focus vaguely to the presence once again. Her heart thudding painfully in her chest as her frayed nerves flared.

"Twice in one day. What's this about?" Tynan's voice cut through the stillness. His tone was sharp with suspicion. Layla strained upward, trying to see beyond the angle of her pit, but darkness swallowed everything outside her small world.

"Figured you might want to slink off for an ale," came that smooth, unshaken voice. *Velvet Voice.* Layla went utterly still.

Tynan laughed, pleased. "Good man." His boots thudded against the earth, growing fainter. Then-*creak*. The grate shifted slightly open. A moment later, something hit the ground beside her with a dull thump, and the grate slammed shut again.

"Drink. You're going to need your energy for tomorrow," Velvet Voice said from beyond her view. His voice was quieter than before. More clipped. Layla's eyes darted to the bundle on the floor of her prison. She didn't move. Her lips were cracked, and her throat begged for moisture, but her instincts refused to yield to trust.

"Oh yeah? And why's that?" she rasped, surprised by how raw her voice sounded in the dark. A pause. Then—

"You're going to fight to your death." She froze. Her mouth parted in disbelief. Her heart jolted once in her chest—then kept thudding, louder, harder. His voice softened, turning almost ghostly. "Don't lose."

Then, footsteps. "Thanks, man," Tynan called out as Velvet Voice's own footsteps faded into the night. Layla was alone again. But everything had changed. Her fingers trembled as she stared at the small bundle lying in the dirt. Her brain screamed caution. *This could be a trick. Another test. A poison.* But her body overruled her thoughts.

She crawled over silently, like prey avoiding a predator. When she reached the bundle, she untied it with care. Inside, she found a small leather pouch, a chunk of meat and another apple. She lifted the pouch first, bringing it to her nose. *Water.* She could've cried. Layla took a cautious sip, then more. It wasn't much, but it felt like life itself. Cool relief spilled down her throat and across her chest. Her limbs warmed, if only slightly. She cradled the pouch like a sacred relic, holding it tight against her stomach. Her gaze shifted back to the piece of meat and apple. *No tricks. No poison.* She was sure of it now. He was helping her. *But why? Who was he? If he was her capture, why would he help her now, after delivering her to this hell?* Whatever the reason, she didn't have time to puzzle it out. Because tomorrow... she would be thrown into a fight she hadn't asked for, with warriors who would take *joy* in spilling her blood. Layla leaned her head back against the wall and breathed deeply, letting the water settle in her bones. She was going to fight. And she was going to **live**.

FROM THE BLOOD OF WARRIORS
OUR STRENGTH FLOWS ETERNAL

By the sacred decree of the ancient ones, the blood of warriors flows eternal within the hearts of the Antonin. Obedience, duty, and loyalty are our sacred virtues. We are bound to protect the members of our tribe and its sacred lands, to serve with unwavering strength and unity. To falter is to dishonor the blood that runs through us. Let it be known: the tribe's will is the will of the gods, and through loyalty, sacrifice, and devotion to the land, we are made strong.

-FROM THE OATHBOUND LAW OF THE
ANTONIN FLAME

Chapter Six

Theron.

Like all others in the Antonin tribe, Theron woke before the sun. It was not out of habit, it but instinct. The kind bred through decades of ritual and discipline. When the air still held the chill of night and the forest whispered beneath the weight of ancient roots, that was when Antonin warriors rose.

Theron sat up on his cot, exhaling slowly as the familiar weight of the day settled over him. His hut was humble by choice- made of tightly bound branches, brush-packed walls, and a ceiling woven so thick with thistle and pine that only slivers of morning light pierced through. No furniture beyond the cot. No keepsakes. No distractions. His sword, polished and battle-worn, rested upright by the wall near his gear. A small bowl of fruit sat untouched at the floor. That was all. While others in the tribe filled their homes with carved tokens and stories etched in wood or bone, Theron preferred efficiency. Clean. Cold. Controlled.

He stretched slowly, his neck cracking on each side. Normally, his sleep was dreamless and uninterrupted, his mind a silent weapon just waiting to be unsheathed. But lately? Lately, everything had shifted causing restless sleep, if any at all.

He laced his leathers in silence, tugging the cords tight across his thick thighs, then pulled on his armor. Every piece strapped into place with practiced ease. The heat already clung to his skin, and he hadn't even stepped outside. But he would rather sweat than feel unready. Still, his mind churned- unsettled, unwilling to quiet. And he hated it.

The woman—*Layla*. Even her name disrupted the fragile silence in his thoughts. Her claims had been verified. The castle had fallen. The Bartorians had swept through like fog and flame. Yet knowing the truth changed nothing. Not about today. Not about what he would have to witness. She was going to die. And he would have to stand there and let it happen.

Theron stepped outside. The forest greeted him like an old companion, cool air brushing over sweat-dampened skin. The light beyond the treetops was still blue with night's end, the sun just starting to breathe over the horizon. He walked toward the Circle, steps steady, calculated. Queen Okteria was already there, flanked by warriors. She turned her head slightly as he approached.

"Inform them they will get their vengeance today. No other news from the Bartorian front." Her tone was smooth. Calculated. Theron nodded once.

"I'd like to stay," he said simply, as if the words meant nothing. "To witness it." His mother gave him a knowing glance, sharp, reading between the lines. But she said nothing. Just turned and strode toward the stone platform that presided over the Circle like a throne. Theron continued to the head of the Circle, stepping in front of his warriors. He didn't need to shout. His presence commanded attention like thunder before a storm.

"No updates," he said. "But today, we take vengeance. Let's make our ancestors proud." His gravelly voice rumbled through the warriors gathered around. Murmurs of satisfaction, anticipation, even bloodlust, rippled through them. Faces lit up with hunger. Their time had come.

"Sparrow," Theron called, eyes scanning the group until he found his most trusted warrior. Sparrow gave a curt nod, his icy blue eyes steady above his braided black beard. Their bond welded together by wounds and will. Theron trusted him with his life. "Take my shift this morning." Another nod. No words needed. Theron turned and ended the meeting with a simple glance. They all knew what to do.

He found his mother again, still speaking to warriors, likely about the youth combat groups. He interrupted without care. "Who do you want?"

Queen Okteria didn't even blink at the bluntness. "Frea," she replied. A beat passed, and then, with a glint in her eye, "No weapons. We wouldn't want it to end *too* quickly." Theron's jaw flexed. He gave a nod and walked away, heart sinking. *Frea.* Of course. Their fiercest female warrior besides Okteria herself. Ruthless, fast, brutal. A shadow on the battlefield. She was built lean like Layla, but harder. Sharper. And unlike Layla, she had nothing to lose. Frea was beautiful, yes, but it was the kind of beauty that drew warriors to worship before they bled. Theron had never pursued her, despite the challenges fought over her attention. He didn't have the time—or the hunger—for women like her. Strong in muscle, self-reliant, carved from the same stone as him. Warriors who needed nothing. Wanted nothing. Just like he was taught to be. But today, her beauty and line of suitors didn't matter, only her blade. Layla would die and not quietly. He shouldn't care. *Rules are rules.* He had said that to himself a thousand times before. But today, the words rang hollow.

Layla.

"Let's go!" Tynan snapped, yanking the heavy grate open and throwing down a wooden ladder with a loud *clatter*. Layla stood still on the far side of the pit, her feet anchored by something heavier than fear. Her limbs screamed in protest after days of stillness and starvation. Her joints cracked and muscles yelled. "*Now!*" he barked, pointing his sword straight at her chest.

She flinched, just barely, but enough. Her ragged body dragged itself forward, unwilling but obedient, as she gripped the ladder and began to climb. The wood bit into her raw palms. Each step was an effort. *This was it.* She was walking to her death.

Tynan didn't give her a moment to breathe. His sword jabbed at her spine as he shoved her back in the same direction she had be brought from days prior. The same dirt path. The same thick air, laced with sweat, seared meat, hot metal, and worn leather. But the woman walking it was not the same one who'd been dragged here days ago. She was now more fractured, but still not yet broken.

They reached the crowd quickly. A perfect ring of Antonin warriors surrounded the Circle, everybody tense with bloodlust. Layla scanned the crowd as she was shoved forward. Their eyes were not curious, they were eager. Starvation was too slow for them. This... this was entertainment.

Tynan brought the flat of his blade hard against the back of her knees and she dropped. A searing pain flared as she hit the ground, but she grit her teeth and pushed herself back up. Every movement hurt. But still, she stood. And she met Queen Okteria's gaze. The queen's expression was practically gleaming.

"Wondering why you're here, Graystonian?" She called, her tone mocking. Layla said nothing. She kept her back straight, her jaw tight. She would not show fear. Not in front of them. *Not now.*

"As much fun as it was to know a Graystonian princess was starving in our pit, you were taking *too damn long.*" The queen rolled her eyes like this was all terribly inconvenient. "Of course one of your kind couldn't even *die* right." A few in the crowd laughed. Layla didn't move.

"I've decided to give you a chance at one of our customs. A challenge. Simple rules: you fight. You survive... Or you don't." Queen Okteria's voice rose with relish. "Usually weapons are allowed, but we didn't want to give our *dear Frea* too much of an advantage." Her hand gestured to the left. Layla followed it. There, stepping into the light, was the woman. Frea. A warrior carved from obsidian and ruin. Her movements were like the elusive forest panther- graceful, fluid, and laced with lethal intent. Her long black hair was braided down her back, and her eyes bored into Layla's, promising nothing short of brutality. Hatred poured from her like a heatwave. Layla's mouth went dry. Her stomach twisted. She didn't have the strength to fight this woman. Not like this, maybe not even on her best day if she was being honest with herself. *But you will,* she told herself. *Or you'll die on your knees.* So, with a deep breath, Layla raised her hands and slipped instinctively into the defensive stance Sir Charles had engrained in her.

"*Begin!*" Queen Okteria shouted.

Frea didn't hesitate. She lunged. Layla ducked, the punch whistling past her ear. The speed stunned her. Frea was already circling again, fluid as a predator. Layla stumbled sideways. Another blow whistled at her- *crack.* Pain bloomed in her side. She gasped, her legs faltering. Righting herself, Layla swung wildly, a desperate move. Frea slipped it easily and delivered another punishing strike to her ribs. This time, Layla crumpled forward. Then- *snap.* A fist collided with her face. Her vision shattered. She went down, dirt rushing up to meet her. Black crept at the edges of her sight. *Get up! Get up!* She pushed herself to her knees—but it was too late. Frea spun. Layla saw the boot coming only for a second before it collided with the side of her skull. Then- nothing.

She awoke on dirt. Again. The cool, familiar floor of the pit. Her current sanctuary but also her tomb. Her body was fire and lead. Her head rang with an unrelenting pulse, each beat a war drum against her skull. She couldn't see from her left eye. Her ribs howled every time she tried to inhale. It was night again. She'd been unconscious for hours, if not days. *At least I'm alive,* she thought bitterly. She leaned back against the wall, chest heaving, pulse roaring. She didn't know how long she could keep surviving this.

"You alive?" came that voice. *Velvet Voice.* Laidback. Low. Like this was just another night around a campfire. She squinted toward the sound, pain lancing through her face. She didn't respond. Didn't have the strength for snark or questions. "You need to figure out some new moves if you're going to win *tomorrow,*" he said casually, like they were discussing breakfast plans. *Tomorrow?* Her stomach lurched. Her skin went cold. She felt the vomit surge, clamping her jaw tight to fight it back. *Another fight?* Her mind spun, trying to calculate how she could possibly recover in time. The answer was: she wouldn't. Not without help. Not without *something.*

The grate above shifted open again, and she tensed. A soft *thud*—then it closed. She opened her eye slowly. Another pouch. Her shaking fingers reached for the pouch, opening it to find the now familiar items, water, meat, and an apple. She pressed the cool leather of the water pouch to her bruised face and exhaled. She didn't understand him. This man. This voice. He delivered her to death—and then gave her the means to delay it. *Was it guilt? Or strategy? Or something else entirely?* She didn't know and honestly she didn't care at this moment. She needed a plan. She couldn't survive another day reacting. If she wanted to live, she needed to become something else. Not a princess. Not prey. A *fighter.*

**BY FLAME, BY ROOT, BY GOD AND STAR—
CAELERIA SHALL RISE, OR PERISH WHOLE.**

THE LAW OF DIVINE SOVEREIGNTY

*No mortal shall claim godhood, nor raise their
name above them.* To defy the gods is to forsake
the land itself. Crops shall rot, rivers will bleed,
and the stars will turn their backs on the earth.

- THE HIGH LAWS OF CAELERIA

Chapter Seven

Layla.

Layla had drifted in and out of a hazy, aching sleep all night. The darkness was her only company, except for the constant pulse of pain behind her eye and the occasional rattle of her ragged breath. Her brain had felt waterlogged, her thoughts sludgy and fragmented. But still, she had clung to one thing: *A plan.* A bad one. A desperate, probably-fatal plan. But it was hers.

So when the sun bled gold over the trees and the grate groaned open again, she didn't shrink. Not when Tynan threw the ladder down like a weapon. Not when his sword hovered behind her like a promise. She climbed. Slowly. Every rung another protest from her body. Every breath a rasp. Her limbs quaked under the strain. *My family needs me,* she repeated in her mind like a chant, a shield against the pain. She didn't speak. Didn't falter as he shoved her through the settlement. Her bare feet stumbled more than once, tripping over loose earth, but she kept moving. Tynan's sword sliced shallow lines across her back with each misstep, but she gritted her teeth and pushed forward. She would not die crawling.

By the time they reached the Circle, her legs were barely holding her. When he finally pulled the sword away, she crumpled. Not in surrender, but in refusal. *You don't get to knock me down again.* She chose to fall. And then, she stood.

Slowly, excruciatingly, she rose to her feet. Every bruise screamed. Her ribs lit with fire. But she stood tall, chin raised, eye zeroed in on the queen atop the stone. Queen Okteria's smile was all venom and delight. Layla knew the odds. Knew her death was a near certainty. But there was something else buzzing in her chest now. Not fear. *Resolve.*

And so she spoke. "I challenge..." Layla's voice cracked. She paused, swallowing against the desert of her throat. "I challenge... *him.*" She pointed to Tynan. Gasps rippled through the crowd. Tynan blinked, momentarily surprised then grinned like a wolf who'd just been handed a lamb. Queen Okteria tilted her head, eyes narrowing.

"You think you're calling the shots here?" she asked, voice low and dangerous.

Layla didn't look away. "If I competed in a challenge yesterday," she said, teeth grounding slightly, "then I don't see why I can't call one today."

A murmur of amusement swept the gathered warriors. The queen stared down at her in silence, calculating.

"For my freedom," Layla added, cutting through the noise. "I challenge for my freedom." Okteria's eyebrows rose, lips twitching in bemusement.

"You want out of our prison?" she echoed, mocking. "Your *freedom*?" More laughter followed. The queen shrugged, dismissive. "After yesterday? I wouldn't care what you asked for. You're not going anywhere but the ground."

Layla swallowed the rising wave of nausea, keeping her spine straight, even as her legs trembled.

"Any other ridiculous requests before you die?" the queen added, gesturing flippantly.

"Yes." Layla forced the words out. "Weapons." That broke the crowd entirely. The laughter was louder this time, genuine disbelief. *The prisoner wants weapons.* She might as well have requested a crown. But she didn't care. She needed a fighting chance, even if it was a small one.

Through the laughter, her one good eye found him. Her captor. The one who had carried her, imprisoned her, but also—fed her. Spoken to her. *Protected her?* He stood near the queen now, his massive frame hard to miss, wrapped in leather, muscle and steel. And he wasn't laughing. His expression was unreadable, save for one thing: His eyes. They burned into her with something that felt like—*worry?* Layla's breath hitched in surprise. Not fear. Not pity. But concern was radiating from him.

Her gaze held his, drawn to the deep blue beneath his brown-sun kissed curls like they offered shelter. For a moment, she forgot the pain.

The noise. The Circle... But as quickly as it went, it all slammed back into her as the queen's voice cut through her momentary distraction.

"If you want death that quickly, so be it. Weapons it is." Okteria's voice was smooth and cold. "Who's willing to let their weapon meet Lapetic in her hands?"

Layla's blood chilled. *Oh no.* She hadn't considered this part. No one would offer her a weapon. *Why would they?* She wasn't one of them. She was the enemy. A Graystonian. A living trophy. Then movement caught her eye. A man stepped down from the platform. Blond, tall—taller than her captor even. Riddled with tattoos winding intricately across his bronzed skin. His green eyes flashed with mischief and danger. Layla stood her ground as he approached, heart pounding, and tilted her chin up defiantly to meet his eyes.

"So," he said casually, raking his gaze down her battered form, "what's your weapon of choice?"

She narrowed her eye, ignoring the wave of fresh heat that spread across her cheeks. Her body may have been wrecked, but she wasn't blind, he was undeniably beautiful in a cruel, serpent-like way. But his smirk made her want to punch him. Then, to her shock, he pulled a sword from his belt and two daggers from his thigh and held them out toward her. An offer. She blinked, stunned. *What game was this?*

Layla hesitated for only a breath before her instincts kicked in. She reached out and took the daggers with both hands, leaving the sword behind. Her grip tightened around the hilts, reacquainting herself with the feel of steel in her palms.

She noticed his smirk widen before he returned his sword to it's sheath and turned to walk away.

"Good luck, little dove." He said casually over his shoulder with a wink.

Dove? she almost gagged at the name. She also attempted to ignore the chuckle from the repulsive blonde man as he swaggered way. But it caused Layla's rage to flare—pure and hot—driving out the remainder of her fear and focusing on steaming anger. But she knew in this moment, anger was good, and she could use it.

Layla turned her attention back toward her opponent in the Circle. Tynan was already waiting, sword in hand, grinning like this was going to be fun. Layla focused on adjusting her stance, daggers poised, the burn in her ribs now a dull background roar behind the pounding of her blood. She could do this. *She had to.*

"Begin!" Queen Okteria's voice sliced through the tension like a blade.

The command hadn't finished echoing when Tynan lunged forward, sword raised high, teeth bared in something between a grin and a snarl. Layla didn't think. She *moved.*

With a flick of her wrist, she released one of her daggers in a desperate throw, straight at his face. The blade sang through the air, silver against sunlight, and missed. Barely. It shot past his temple and buried itself in the ground somewhere behind him. *Shit!* He was on her now.

She dove to the side, heart racing like a war drum. His sword slammed into the ground where she'd been, the impact jarring the earth beneath her ribs. Adrenaline tore through her, pushing the pain down, stuffing it into a box she'd deal with later, if she lived long enough to have a *later.* She scrambled up, barely on her feet again when the blade came for her. Another sweeping arc. This time, it kissed her left bicep. The searing pain of it lit her nerves on fire.

"Holy fuck!" Her arm went numb instantly from the deep gash. She stumbled back, her breath ragged and sharp. Blood poured down her arm, soaking the fabric of her shift. Her hand spasmed, the dagger it held slipping from her grip and clattering to the ground. *Not now. Please, not now.* Tynan saw it. Saw her eyes flick down toward the fallen blade. And he smirked right before he charged again. Layla didn't wait to think. Instinct screamed. She *dropped*, flat to the dirt, just as his sword came down. The blade passed so close she felt the air shift above her spine. *Keep moving.* She rolled, her arm shrieking as she pushed herself toward the blade she'd dropped. His feet thundered after her. She spun onto one knee and grabbed the dagger. Tynan roared behind her, his sword rising again for the final blow...but she was quicker.

She drove the dagger *up*. Right into his throat. The world instantly went still. He stopped. His eyes went wide. A single, choking breath gurgled from his mouth as blood began to spill down his chest, splattering across her. His blade slipped from his grasp and landed with a soft *thunk* beside her. Layla didn't breathe. She couldn't. He fell to his knees. And then forward, face-first into the dirt beside her. Dead.

Her breath came in short, uneven bursts. Her ears rang. It was over. She had *won*.

The pain in her bicep roared back with a vengeance, snapping her out of the daze. Her gaze lifted slowly to the queen. Okteria's expression was thunderous. Her lips were tight, her fists clenched at her sides. Her eyes sparked with unspoken vengeance.. *No. This isn't over.* Layla's gut twisted. She didn't know what to expect—*vengeance? A second fighter? An arrow to the heart?* Time moved strangely.

She saw him, *her captor*, step forward and lean toward the queen. Whisper something in her ear. Something quiet. Measured. The queen's mouth tightened. Her gaze flicked between them. Then, she nodded. He jumped from the stone, landing with the grace of a god, and began walking toward her. Layla's eyes found his. She couldn't read them. Not warmth. Not cruelty. Just... intensity. Something cold slipped down her spine. She turned back to the queen, throat dry, heart pounding.

"Congratulations, Princess," Queen Okteria said, the words spat like acid. "Your freedom is yours. You no longer will stay in our prison." Layla let out a breath she hadn't realize she'd been holding. She'd done it. *She'd actually done it.* Her legs buckled slightly as she tried to rise, the world tilting. Blood loss on top of everything else was stealing her balance. But she stood. Somehow. Then—

"Oh, but Princess," the queen added, almost purring now. Layla froze. Her gaze snapped up. "Don't think you're leaving." Her stomach dropped.

"But you said—" Layla began, voice hoarse, but Okteria raised a single hand and silenced her.

"I said," she repeated, eyes narrowing, "you could have your freedom... *from our prison.*" The words landed like a blade in her chest. "That's it."

The finality of it was worse than any cut. Layla's knees gave out. She collapsed back to the ground, shattered. Her arm screamed in agony. Her vision swam. Her ribs ached with every shallow breath. She wasn't going home. She had won the fight—and lost the war. Still a prisoner. Just not in a pit. The sour tang of vomit burned the back of her throat as despair clawed its way back in. Her head sagged forward, resting on her arm as blood dripped onto the dirt. *I'm not getting out of here.* But even as the tears threatened, they didn't fall. Because one thought came louder than the others. *You're still alive.* And as long as she was breathing, she would fight.

Theron.

Theron knelt without hesitation, slipping his arms beneath the woman who had no business still being alive and lifted her with care that surprised even him. Her frame was light, far too light. Blood clung to her skin, soaked into what was left of the shift she wore. Her head fell against his chest, cheek pressing into the bare skin above his leathers. She didn't speak. Didn't move. But he felt the tremors beneath his hands—constant, violent shivers wracking her from within. Her one open eye stared blankly forward, glazed with pain and something dangerously close to hopelessness. Tear tracks streaked the grime on her face. *She should be dead. Gods, by every measure, she should be.* And yet—she wasn't. She had fought, and by some miracle, won. The shock of it clung to him, fierce and quiet, surrounded by a warmth that could only be described as relief.

When Tynan had crumpled in the dirt, her blade buried deep in his throat and blood spilling across the sacred Circle, Theron had known exactly what would follow. He saw it in his mother's face—the shift from stunned silence to something far more volatile. A vein pulsed in her temple. Her eyes burned with pure hatred as one hand curled at her side like she might draw her own blade. So he leaned in and said the first thing that came to him.

"Let me get her out of your sight." It wasn't a solution, just a temporary diversion. But Okteria gave him a nod. Not forgiveness—just a reprieve. A sliver of time. How much, he didn't know.

The crowd parted as he passed, their stares a mix of stunned silence and thinly veiled contempt. He was still carrying a captive, after all. But no one dared stop him. Still, he held her tighter. She wasn't in chains. She wasn't rotting in that pit. And whatever she was now... he wasn't sure. He only knew she needed mending, if only until the queen passed her judgment.

He strode through the village, jaw tight, steps unwavering, until he reached the mending hut—the one place no one would question him. A space where she could sleep, undisturbed, for a few stolen hours. It was the only thing he could offer her. He didn't pause. Just shoved aside the woven hide flap and stepped into the warmth inside. Eir turned at the sound. Her sharp eyes widened at the sight of what he carried—but only for a breath. Then her hands were already in motion. Years of service had trained her well: tend first, question later.

She gestured to the larger of the two cots. "There." Theron laid Layla down with gentle precision. Her body tensed as he lowered her, a faint whimper of pain slipping from her cracked lips. *She still didn't look at him. Didn't have the strength to, maybe? Or maybe she didn't want to...* He let his thoughts fade as he straightened, deciding at that moment he wasn't going to step outside. He folded his arms, boots rooted to the floor, eyes never leaving her as Eir got to work. Eir didn't ask him to go. She simply moved around him. He appreciated that.

The elder worked methodically cleaning away the bloodied mess across her skin, dabbing salves into open wounds, wrapping her arm tight to stop the bleeding. Layla's body winced beneath every touch, but she didn't cry out. Not once. It was only when Eir asked her to drink that she reacted. Theron saw it. That flicker of fear in her eye. *Distrust.* And he didn't blame her. Still, she took the medicine. Seconds later, her body slackened, and her breathing deepened.

The potion had done its job, drawing her under and Theron finally exhaled. He hadn't even realized he'd been holding his breath. She looked... different like this. Her face softened. The furrow in her brow melted. Her lips, parted slightly, trembling no longer. For the first time since she'd stumbled into their territory, she looked at peace. He hated how much he liked seeing her this way. And when Eir finished, she stepped back and washed her hands in the bucket near the door. Then, silently, she gathered two small bowls and handed them to Theron.

"She'll sleep most of the next day," she said quietly. "Salve for the bruises. This"—she nodded toward the darker bowl—"for the pain. When she wakes, you'll need to help her apply it." Theron dipped his head in acknowledgment. "She's yours now," Eir added softly. Not as a declaration of possession—but as a burden. As a responsibility. Then she turned and left, giving them privacy.

The moment the door flapped shut behind her, Theron sank to the floor beside Layla's cot, back resting against the hut's wooden wall. The weight of the day- the blood, the defiance, the impossible victory-pressed in from all sides. He let his head fall back, eyes closing for just a moment. *What now, Theron?* His mother would not let this go. He knew her too well. Layla may have survived the Circle, but she hadn't escaped the queen's wrath. Not by a long shot. And yet—he'd bought her time.

He opened his eyes and looked at the woman sleeping beside him. Bruised, broken, and bloody... but still alive. Still *fighting*. He'd let her sleep here until night fell, then slip her past curious eyes and unspoken questions. Somewhere quiet. Somewhere she could rest, maybe even begin to heal—if only for a while. Just until the weight of his mother's judgment came down like an axe. He wasn't even sure if he was doing it for her... or for himself.

By the ancient decree of Graystonia, all shall
uphold their duty to the kingdom above all else.
Loyalty to the crown, the land, and the people
is sacred, and no act of dishonor shall be
tolerated. To serve the kingdom with integrity is
the highest calling, for through service,
Graystonia endures.

-BY DECREE OF THE CROWN OF GRAYSTONIA.

Chapter Eight

Layla.

L ayla jolted upright, panic tightening her chest as the outlines of the unfamiliar crowded her vision. Her breath hitched, heart pounding as she strained to see through the dimness. Relief washed over her in a hesitant trickle when she realized she could see out both eyes. Barely, but it was something. Then she saw him. Her captor. Sitting not more than a few feet away, legs crossed at the ankle, silent, watching her.

She scrambled backward until her spine met the wall of the hut, breath shallow, instincts flaring. He didn't move, didn't speak. Just watched her. There was no cruelty in his expression, no amusement either. But there was no comfort. Only unreadable stillness. As the seconds stretched, and no harm came, her fear settled into wary awareness. Layla's eyes darted around the small hut. It wasn't the healer's, no warm hearth, no gray-haired woman with soft hands and kinder eyes. This one was cramped, bare. A cot. A single bowl. No windows. Just a woven hide hung over the doorframe.

Their way of life was so different. Rough. Sparse. Efficient. A constant reminder she was deep in the belly of enemy lands. Movement snapped her focus back. Layla watched as he stood slowly, his frame stretching to impossible height in the confined space. She shrank instinctively. But he stepped closer and then dropped to one knee in front of her. His sea-glass eyes didn't hold the sharpness she expected. They flicked to the floor, where he picked up a familiar bowl- salve, it looked to be the same kind the old healer had used. He extended it to her. Layla hesitated, but eventually reached out, their fingers brushing for just a moment. The spark that jolted through her fingertips made her stomach clench. She looked up sharply, both confused and furious with herself for the reaction.

"Use this for the next few days," he said, his voice gravelly and low, too low for this tiny hut. It rippled over her skin like a command and a caress all at once. She hated that her body responded before her mind could stop it.

"I'll be alive for the next few days? That's shocking," she replied with as much sass as her broken body could muster, trying to hide the waver in her voice. His jaw flexed, the faintest crack in his mask. But his silence returned like a wall. Ice-cold. *Right. That answered that.* Her stomach turned. She looked at the bandage wrapping her stitched bicep. Her head didn't hurt nearly as much. The medicine had worked. Her bruises had dulled to a deep ache rather than a scream of agony. *But what was the point in mending her?* She was still a prisoner. The reminder caused her to set the salve aside.

Without another word, he rose and dipped out the door. "Don't let anyone in. I'll be back," he said to someone outside. "Sparrow. Watch my hut." Footsteps shifted. Then stilled.

Layla sat frozen, eyes fixed on the hide-covered entrance. *Run,* her instincts whispered. But logic was louder. She wouldn't make it ten feet, not like this. Her entire body sagged, the fight momentarily draining out of her. *What now?* She gripped her bicep gently, grounding herself, blinking away the heat stinging her eyes. She didn't want to cry. She couldn't. She was a princess—trained to endure, to survive the worst with her head held high. And this... this was not the end. Not yet. She was still breathing. Still alive. That meant she still had a chance. She reminded herself of that truth as she shoved the hopelessness back down where it belonged. She couldn't let it take root. Couldn't let it win. When the moment came, she'd run like hell. So she drew a breath. Then another. She could do this. She had to.

A few minutes later, the hide lifted and he dipped back in. *Theron,* she thought. She didn't even know how she remembered his name. Probably from that awful whisper of a woman, the queen. He stepped inside, dropped a bowl beside her, then leaned against the opposite wall. She watched him pick up a piece of meat from his own bowl and bite into it. He chewed slowly, never breaking eye contact. Layla's nose twitched at the scent of food. Her stomach growled violently. She looked down, meat and corn. Her mouth instantly watered.

"Eat," he commanded. She hesitated. Just for a moment. The food hadn't killed her yet. And the way he stared... he didn't seem the type for trickery. Just bluntness. Brutal honesty. She could work with that. She picked up the meat and took a small bite. The flavor exploded across her tongue and she couldn't stop the small, relieved moan that escaped her lips. She finished the meal quickly, grateful but still tense. Unsure of what came next.

He tossed her a water pouch. She nearly wept at the sight of it. Layla downed it quickly, greedy for the cool liquid. When she finished, she sat the pouch down gently on the ground and exhaled. Her body hummed with warmth and, for the first time in what felt like forever, a shred of comfort.

"Thank you," she whispered. She didn't expect a response. He just watched her, always watching it seems. The silence wrapped around them, heavy but not hostile. She wanted to ask him what came next. What he wanted. What the queen wanted. But something in his demeanor said now was not the time. Or maybe... maybe he didn't even know himself. Her eyelids drooped. She fought it, but her body demanded rest. Real rest. So she curled back up on the cot, arms wrapping instinctively around herself. She'd survived another day... She was still alive... For now.

Hours had passed by when Layla's eyes fluttered open again. She blinked through the pitch-black haze of the hut, her breath catching as she sat upright. It took her a moment to register where she was. Realizing she was still within the confined space of her captor's dwelling. Her body was stiff, sore, but less agonizing than before. She glanced to the side—and froze. He was there. *Theron.* But not looming, not watching. Asleep. He sat slumped on the floor, legs outstretched, head tilted back against the wall. His chest rose and fell in a steady rhythm.

A silent thrill of adrenaline surged through her. Her heart thundered in her ears. He was asleep and this was her chance. *Now or never.*

Moving inch by inch, Layla slid her legs off the cot and pushed herself upright. Her eyes never leaving the sight of him. Her bare feet kissed the packed dirt floor without a sound as she tiptoed to the entrance. Carefully, she pulled back the hide with slow, practiced fingers. Moonlight filtered through the trees in scattered patches, offering just enough to see as she leaned out.

Warriors lingered near a fire thirty yards away, laughing, drinking. Their attention nowhere near the hut. She turned her head once more to glance back at Theron. He hadn't stirred. So she slipped out. Skimming the hut's outer wall, she crept to the back where trees loomed. Her heart thudded louder with each step.

Once within the cover of the forest, Layla broke into a run. She didn't care where she was headed. North, south- it didn't matter. Anywhere was better than here. Branches snapped beneath her feet. Wind lashed her skin. Her lungs burned. But it didn't matter. Freedom. She could finally taste freedom....

A hand yanked her backward so hard her feet left the ground as her right shoulder slammed into the trunk of a tree. Scorching pain tore through her bicep and down her side. Her scream caught in her throat as she took in the sight of the man before her. It wasn't Theron. It was a stranger. An Antonin warrior she hadn't seen before. With short dark brown hair, black eyes, and a menacing smile carved across his face like a scar. His body pressed against hers, pinning her to the bark.

"How am I so lucky," he purred, hot breath curling against her cheek, "to look up from the fire and see a little white nightgown slip away into the trees?" His eyes raked her body. She fought to turn away, heart seizing in her chest, but his hands were clamped tight on her arms. She couldn't break free.

He leaned closer, nosing down her neck. She shuddered in revulsion and fought against him harder. Her body screamed from the effort. "This is going to be fun," he whispered with sick delight, and true terror surged.

But that terror unlocked something within her and her training kicked in. Sir Charles's lessons echoed in her mind as she struck forward with her knee, catching him square in the groin. He yelped, doubling over causing his grip to loosen. She followed with a sharp upward knee to the face. A crunch echoed as his nose exploded in a spray of blood. She ran. Or tried to. Her wounded arm screamed as he snatched it, dragging her back before she could escape. He hurled her against another tree. Air left her lungs in a sharp gasp. She couldn't breathe. He slammed his forearm across her chest, pinning her.

"You're not going anywhere, you little Graystonian bitch!" He shouted, spit and blood flying with the words. One hand pinned her as the other tore at her nightgown. She screamed and shoved against him, clawing and crying, but it was no use. He was stronger and fueled by rage. Tears blurred her vision as he struck her across the face and the world went sideways. *No. Not like this. Please not like this.* Layla's head lulled as she squeezed her eyes shut.

Then, the weight vanished. His grip. His breath. His body—gone. She collapsed to the ground in a heap, sobs racking her as confusion and fear collided. Blinking through the tears, she saw them—two bodies, one atop the other. A blur of fists. A roar of pain. Then silence. Her attacker crumpled, and the other man stepped into view. Massive. Unrelenting. A silhouette carved from night. *Her captor... Theron.* He had come for her.

Layla's breath hitched violently. She scrambled back across the floor, instinct overriding reason. Her limbs quivered, her palms slick with cold sweat. *What now?* The last time she'd seen him, he had brought her food. Sat silently nearby while she ate. Taken her to be mended with strange, unspoken gentleness, and then let her sleep while he stood guard. And now, he stood above her —Antonin, like the others. A man of war. A man of *this* place. Her heart thrashed wildly in her chest. She didn't know what he was going to do. After what she had just endured, how could she trust *any* of them?

She stared up at him, half-expecting violence, betrayal, anything but what came next... He didn't speak. Didn't ask. Didn't offer false comfort. He simply bent down and lifted her into his arms and Layla reluctantly sagged against him, too dazed and broken to resist. Her tears streamed freely now, soaking into his leathers. Her bruised body shuddered in his grip. She expected harsh hands. Cold indifference. But instead... he held her gently like before. As if she were made of something delicate. As if she mattered.

She dared to glance up at his face. His jaw was clenched tight, his brow drawn in unspoken torment. His grip was strong—but careful. Protective. And despite everything, despite the pain, the terror, the betrayal of her body and dignity—something inside her sparked with desperate relief. He had come for her. He had saved her. And behind them, the man who had tried to break her whimpered on the ground, broken and bleeding. Theron didn't look back. And Layla, shattered but breathing, let him carry her into the night.

Back in the safety of the hut, if such a word still held meaning. Theron dipped through the hide flap and gently set her down on the cot like she might shatter. He dropped to one knee before her, eye-level with her once more. Layla's breath caught in her throat at the intensity of his expression. Fury still swam in his piercing blue eyes. But now, something else had overtaken it. *Concern?*

He stared at her bleeding arm, his brows furrowed so tightly they nearly touched. Then his eyes slowly drifted upward, and for the first time, he seemed to register the new damage to her face. His jaw clenched. A muscle ticked. Without a word, he reached up and brushed his calloused fingers to her swollen cheek. Layla winced, a quiet hiss escaping her lips from the contact, but she didn't pull away. His hands were rough. Worn. Lined with the kind of strength that came from war and wood and weather, but they were warm. So warm. That warmth curled into her skin, melting past the bruises and bone and straight to something far more fragile. She absentmindedly closed her eyes. A breath she didn't know she was holding slipped free, shaky and exhausted.

It made no sense, but for the first time in days, she felt safe. When she opened her eyes, she found his gaze still fixed on hers- softened now, no longer hard or unreadable. Something almost reverent lingered there. And then, like a gust of wind slamming shut a door, he pulled his hand away and stood, turning his back on her. Her stomach instantly dropped. Utterly confused, she looked down and understood.

Her shift was barely hanging on, the last remnants of fabric bloodied, torn, and twisted around her waist. Her chest was entirely bare. She sucked in a sharp breath and grabbed at what was left, clutching it to herself as humiliation surged like a tidal wave. He glanced back over his shoulder just as she managed to pull the fabric up high enough to cover herself.

"Wait here," he said gruffly, disappearing through the hide flap. Layla huddled on the cot, heart racing. She stared at the empty space he'd just filled, fear slowly crawling back into her lungs. *What if someone else came in? What if the other man found her again?* But barely a minute passed before the hide flap lifted, and Theron stepped back inside. He held a bundle of folded leather garments under his arm.

"Dress." His command was short and clipped. He placed the clothes beside her and didn't move. Layla blinked. *Was he... going to just stand there and watch?* She looked from the pile of clothes to him, and back again. When she stood, clutching her tattered shift to her front, he still didn't budge and her pulse spiked. But then, thankfully, understanding seemed to dawn in his eyes. With a low grunt, he turned his back and Layla exhaled in relief. She unwrapped the last of her ruined shift and let it fall in a heap on the floor. Her skin prickled in the cool air, goosebumps rising. She worked quickly, rifling through the clothes. The skirt was simple, fitted around her waist and layered in strips of hide. The top—some kind of leather corset—was more of a challenge. It strapped over one shoulder and laced at the back. Layla tried and failed to secure it herself. Her bleeding arm made the task nearly impossible.

"Um..." she whispered, her voice barely audible. "Can you... please help me?" Theron turned at the sound of her voice. His eyes moved from her to the corset she clutched helplessly to her chest. Without hesitation, he stepped toward her, his massive form consuming the space between them. She tilted her chin up as he looked down at her, those impossible blue eyes holding her captive. Gently, he took the strap from her shoulder and tied it into place, his fingers grazing her collarbone.

"Turn," he murmured. She obeyed. His hands were sure and steady as he laced the back, pulling the cords tight. The top cinched around her ribs and lifted her breasts higher, more than she was used to. When he finished, his hands lingered for just a breath, then fell away. Layla turned back to face him, cheeks flushed with heat. He didn't look away, not this time. Instead he reached down, tore a strip from what was left of her shift, and wound it tightly around her bleeding arm. His touch was efficient, focused, but careful.

"Eir will re-stitch you in the morning," he said roughly. "This will work 'til then." Layla swallowed, her throat dry.

"Thank you," she whispered. He didn't move. Didn't blink. Just stared at her so fiercely it was as if he were trying to memorize her. Brand her into his vision. Her breath caught as her body reacted, tight, tense, and wanting. Wanting something she didn't understand. *What is happening to me?* She broke the gaze and turned away, trying to suppress the flutter in her chest, the ache under her skin. Theron stepped back, retreating to his usual place against the far wall, arms crossed, jaw hard. Her shoulders sagged slightly in... *disappointment? No. No, that was insane.*

She dropped onto the cot, confusion clouding her mind. Then she remembered the other warrior. The hands. The weight. The helplessness. Her head jerked toward the entrance of the hut. Fear slammed back into her like a slap. She must have made a sound, or maybe he sensed it, but Theron stood straighter.

"No one will come in here," he said darkly, voice full of gravel and heat. "This is mine. No one touches what's mine." Layla's heart stopped at the admission. She stared at him, breath lodged in her throat. *Did he mean the hut? Or... her?* She couldn't ask. She wasn't sure she wanted to know.

Let bone crack and blood spill, but no soul may
be severed from the tribe without the queen's
command. Death among the Antonin is not a
right- it is decree. Only within the Circle may
fate decide otherwise.

-FROM THE OATHBOUND LAW OF THE
ANTONIN FLAME

Chapter Nine

Theron.

Theron hadn't slept. Not truly. Not since the moment he found her. He sat in silence, his eyes flicking over to her again. She lay still, almost too still, her chest rising and falling with slow, deliberate breaths. But her eyes were wide open, unfocused, fixed on the ceiling above her as if she were trying to find some escape in the wood and shadows. He knew she wasn't resting. No, she was likely trapped in the prison of her own mind, reliving every gut-wrenching moment of the night before. And he—he was the one who had failed to stop it.

The knot in his stomach hadn't eased. If anything, it had festered and grown, wrapping tight around his insides like a serpent. Seething anger, guilt, loathing, all of it boiled just beneath the surface of his skin.

How could I have let this happen? He hadn't just failed his duty as a warrior. He had failed her.

The memory struck with brutal clarity—the empty cot, the cold imprint of where she should have been. Panic had slammed into him like a hammer to the chest. He'd shot upright, already reaching for his sword, heart pounding with the certainty that something was wrong. He had torn out of the hut without hesitation, instincts clawing their way to the surface, feral and blinding. The moment the scream had sliced through the darkness—*her* scream—something inside him had snapped clean in half.

He had run like a man possessed, trees whipping past in a blur, branches clawing at his skin as if the forest itself tried to hold him back. But all he could see, burned behind his eyes, was her. And then he'd reached the clearing.

He'd seen Visen—*that bastard*—hovering over her, ripping away what little remained of her dignity, his hands where they never should have been, his body poised to destroy. The rage that had filled Theron then hadn't roared. It *burned*. White-hot. Silent. Absolute and deadly. He hadn't hesitated, just barreled straight into Visen with the full force of his rage, knocking him off her and into the dirt. The look on Visen's face—a flicker of recognition, followed by pure terror—had done nothing to quell the need for blood. Theron had let it consume him.

Blow after blow, fist after fist, until Visen's face was pulp and his own knuckles throbbed with pain. And still, it hadn't been enough. Nothing would be. But then he had looked up, looked at *her*. Shivering. Mud-streaked. Tear-soaked. And recoiling... from *him*.

She had reacted as if he were no different than the monster he'd just torn from her. Crawled away as if his hands could hurt her too. And that had shattered him. He had stepped forward slowly, carefully, gathering her into his arms with a reverence that contradicted the blood staining his skin, and thank the gods she hadn't fought him. Just sobbed against his chest, too broken to speak.

He'd walked them back in silence, the weight of her small frame anchoring him, grounding him. He hadn't spared Visen a second glance. Because he knew, if he looked back, he wouldn't stop. *No one touches her again. Not while I breathe.*

Morning broke around them in a soft haze, but the calm did nothing to soothe him. His body ached from staying motionless throughout the night, the tension gripping his muscles like iron. He rose stiffly, stretching as quietly as he could, but she noticed. He could feel her eyes watching him, hesitant but curious. Her cheeks were bruised, both now, the color deepening in cruel contrast to her skin. He had to look away. He wasn't worthy of those hazel eyes, not after what she'd endured. Not after what he had failed to prevent.

A soft cough just outside the hut drew his attention. Theron stepped to the entrance and pulled the flap back slightly. A bowl waited on the ground—fruit, bread, a strip of dried meat. He hadn't asked, but someone had known. Likely Sparrow. He bent, picked it up, and returned to her side.

"Eat," he said, his voice rougher than intended, but gentler than usual.

She obeyed without a word, snatching a piece of bread and tearing into it with quiet desperation. He didn't eat. Couldn't. He needed to face his mother. To figure out what came next. But part of him didn't want to leave her side. Not even for a moment. He lingered at the entrance, then glanced back.

"Come," he ordered, prepared to march off again. But her voice stopped him.

"Layla..." she whispered.

He froze. Then slowly turned to her, surprised, catching the defiance now back in her stare.

"My name," she said again, stronger this time. "It's Layla." He met her gaze, something tugging deep in his chest and he nodded.

Come... Layla," he said, softer now. He already knew her name—but hearing it aloud, speaking it himself, struck something deep. It settled in his mind like a brand as he led the way.

As they approached the Circle, the dying moonlight etched faint lines across the awakening encampment. His thoughts drifted briefly to the night before, and a fresh wave of fury welled up. He remembered bursting into Frea's hut, interrupting her mid passionate ride atop Kain without an ounce of shame...

"Leathers. Now." He demanded. Frea hadn't even pretended to be embarrassed, simply pointed.

Kain, of course, had to add, "enjoying the show, brother?" He didn't respond. Just took the damn leathers and ran.

Now, seeing Layla in Antonin leathers? *Gods.* They clung to her body in ways that made his blood simmer. The top barely contained her generous breasts, and the skirt—if it could even be called that—left her long legs and perfectly rounded ass far too visible for his peace of mind. She looked like a warrior goddess. Strong. Wounded. Infinitely untouchable. *And his....*No. Not his....*But his to protect.* Or at least, that's what he wanted. What he would do, if it were up to him. He had spoken the words. Claimed her safety. Declared her protected. And if it were his decision alone, he would honor that vow until his last breath.

But it wasn't his decision. Not fully. The queen's orders still stood above his own wants, no matter how fierce the need had grown to shield Layla from everything and everyone. Lost in his thoughts, he momentarily glanced down and noticed she was barefoot. *For fucks sake!* He cursed silently. He hadn't thought of everything. That would be fixed. Immediately.

Today, he would face the queen. He would do his duty. But gods willing, he'd find a way to keep Layla safe—even if he had to fight for it. And Visen... if the bastard so much as looked at her again, Theron would put a blade through him without hesitation. But first—first, he had to make sure she never looked at him with fear again. That, more than anything, was what he couldn't bear. Not from her. Not from *Layla.*

He shook his head. *The gathering.* Right. He had to focus. He was the head warrior. The one they looked to for leadership and control. But ever since she'd fallen into his world, his thoughts had been anything but controlled. Layla—gods, even her name was a distraction—was taking up far too much space in his mind. And the worst part? He didn't want her to leave it.

As they began to weave through the crowd, the warriors' glances shifted in their direction. Some confused, some assessing, some even admiring. But no one dared question him aloud. Still, Theron saw the silent curiosity in their eyes, why she was in tribe leathers, why she was at his side. *Let them wonder. Let them burn with questions they'd never be brave enough to ask.*

When they reached the front of the Circle, Theron came to a stop beside Sparrow. Without a word, Sparrow turned his head slightly, their silent language clicking into place. Years of battle, of blood and brotherhood, had taught them to speak without sound. Theron looked down at Layla. As if sensing his gaze, her eyes met his—wide, cautious, intelligent.

"Stay with Sparrow," he murmured low. She glanced between them, uncertain, her hesitation clear. But after a moment, she nodded. That small gesture gave Theron the tiniest breath of relief. She'd be safe. Sparrow would make sure of it. He turned toward his true challenge now- his mother.

Queen Okteria stood near the stone ledge that overlooked the Circle. She'd been watching them. The look she gave Layla was nothing short of venomous. But when her gaze met Theron's, her face twisted into false warmth, a deception only a child of hers could see through.

"Theron," she purred, her voice velvet over steel. But her eyes slid back to Layla like daggers.

"What exactly are your plans for Lay—the prisoner?" He quickly corrected himself. Forcing his voice to stay even. Okteria was slow to answer, as always when she wanted to wield control. Finally, she turned back to him, her words acid-dipped.

"She may no longer be our prisoner, but she will be our slave," she said coldly. "As her kingdom crumbles, she will labor as a reminder of our victory. Every day she breathes among us, she will prove that Graystonia is no more."

Theron's stomach turned. A tight, furious knot tangled in his gut. *A slave?* He wanted to scream. To roar. To shove the word back down her throat. But he clenched his jaw and let the fire burn inward. His fists curled at his sides.

"I want confirmation that the Bartorians have taken the city," she added, flicking her wrist like the conquest of a nation was nothing. "Send a group. And teach the girl our food. If she runs... she'll wish she were dead." And just like that, the conversation was over. Queen Okteria turned away, leaving a trail of bitterness in her wake. Theron closed his eyes and exhaled a slow breath to keep himself from exploding. Then he turned to address the warriors, shaking the tension from his arms like a cloak he couldn't shed.

"Routes remain the same," he barked. His voice rang sharp across the Circle. "Kain—you're leading the group to Graystonia. Confirm the state of the city." He knew without looking the kind of expression that order would put on Kain's face. Surprise, likely followed by that ever-familiar smirk. He *always* sent Sparrow. But Sparrow had a more important duty now- watching Layla. Protecting her. He wasn't leaving her unguarded again. As he scanned the warriors, Theron's gaze landed on Visen. The sight of him was both satisfaction and poison. Visen was barely recognizable, his face a patchwork of swelling, bruises, and blood. Two blackened eyes. A broken nose. A split lip. Theron's knuckles still ached from the memory. But it wasn't enough. *Not nearly enough.* If tribe law didn't forbid him from executing a warrior without trial, he'd have gutted the bastard himself.

Out of the corner of his eye, he caught his mother watching him. Her smirk was all-knowing. She hadn't missed the tension, the bruises. She didn't need to ask what had happened. But Theron had no intention of offering explanations. If anyone tried to dig, they'd find nothing but silence and a death glare.

He tilted his head toward a nearby warrior. "Garrun. Take my eastern route." Then to Sparrow: "Get some sleep. I want you on guard tonight." Sparrow gave a short nod—nothing more was needed. His eyes flicked to Layla, then back to Sparrow. He understood where exactly he was needed tonight. With those orders done, Theron gave one last sweeping look at the gathered warriors, jaw set. "You have your orders." And with that, he turned on his heel and walked away—no further words, no room for questions.

As the group began dispersing, Theron headed back to her. She had been watching him intently. There was something in her eyes—something questioning, something almost trusting. He hated how much it affected him.

"Come," he said simply, leading her toward Eir's hut once again. At least Eir's would be quiet.

As they dipped back within the comfort of Eir's hut. He could see the older woman preparing her tools inside. When she saw them, the reopened gash across her arm, the new bruises and cuts across Layla's face and body. Eir didn't say anything once again. Just simply gestured to the same cot as yesterday. This time Layla didn't waver to accept her assistance. That was until Eir offered her the same drink as yesterday.

"No thank you," she said softly, yet firmly. "I will endure."

Theron turned slightly at the tone. There was strength in it. He respected that. Eir didn't argue, only began to clean the wound, then handed Layla a piece of bark when the time came. Layla gritted through the stitching without a sound, and Theron felt something strange rise in his chest. *Pride? Guilt? Maybe both.* He should've thought to clean her up himself, but it hadn't occurred to him. He wasn't used to caring for others. Only commanding them.

When they left for Illyada's hut, Layla looked cleaner, her eyes brighter, despite the bruises. The image of her yesterday, bloodied and sobbing in the dark, still haunted him. Illyada was already elbow-deep in dressing a deer when they approached. Her blade slicing effortlessly through muscle and hide. She was the tribe's best chef. A warrior in her own right, but preferred to slice up animals over others when she had the choice. She paused only briefly as they approached, waiting for instructions. Her strength and silence were things Theron respected.

She wouldn't question this task, and more importantly, she wouldn't mistreat Layla.

"She's yours during daylight," he told Illyada. "Train her well." Illyada gave a single nod, no questions asked. Theron looked at Layla, just once, but it was enough to make something tighten in his gut. He stepped in, close enough to catch the scent of her skin—clean now, soft and earthy, but still laced with that same trace of lavender he'd caught the first day she fell into his path. He leaned in, his lips brushing her ear, his voice low enough for only her to hear.

"Don't run," he whispered—more plea than command. Then he turned away before the temptation to stay could override his sense. He needed to move. To breathe. To do something. His blood simmered beneath his skin, too hot, too volatile. The loathing festering in him over Visen, the confusion twisting his thoughts every time Layla looked at him like he mattered—it was too much. He had to do something or he would snap. Just then, his gaze caught on Kain near the trees, streaked with mud like the rest of the scouts. His brother stood tall and smug, arms crossed, bow slung over his back.

"Kain, just scouting, nothing more." Theron barked.

Kain raised a brow. "Just scouting?" he repeated mockingly. "Funny. I thought you came over to ask about last night." Theron stiffened. Kain leaned in, whispering with a wicked grin, "You know, I didn't know watching was your thing, but hey no judgement. Whatever gets you off."

The snarl that escaped Theron's throat was involuntary. He shoved Kain backward with force. Kain just laughed, throwing his arms up.

"Relax. I'm going. Scouting only. I swear."

He gave that mischievous wink that told Theron that Kain was not going to follow a damned word he commanded. But Theron turned away before he did something he couldn't walk back. Theron knew he needed to work off some of this anger, fear, and, if he was being honest with himself, sexual frustration. His body was coiled tight, his mind chaotic. So he sought out the one thing that always grounded him—Not war. Not bloodshed. But controlled, focused combat. He desperately needed that. Needed the violence with rules, the fight with purpose.

He found Xaden by the outer ring of the Circle—seated on a sun-warmed boulder, sharpening his blade as if he had all the time in the world. The rhythmic scrape of stone over steel was the only sound between them for a moment. Xaden looked up, his dark eyes sharp and knowing, catching the storm raging behind Theron's usually unreadable face. A slow, cocky grin crept across his lips. He knew that look. Everyone did.

"You need to hit something," Xaden said, rising to his full, imposing height. Nearly as tall as Theron, Xaden's frame was broad, sculpted muscle wrapped in skin the color of rich onyx. His coiled dreads were pulled back into a knot at the nape of his neck, and his tight, well-groomed beard framed a jaw sharp enough to wound. Tattoos snaked over every visible inch of his arms and collarbones, ancient Antonin markings that told stories only their warriors would ever understand. Unlike most, Xaden wore his lethality with a smile, a charismatic ease that made people forget just how many men he had laid in the ground. Brutally skilled, impossibly fast, and never afraid to finish a fight he didn't start.

Theron gave a silent nod, already stripping off the outer vest of his leathers. "Circle?"

Xaden motioned to the packed earth sparring ring with a flourish. "After you, Commander." Wordlessly, they stepped inside. Around them, warriors paused mid-task, falling into stillness as instinct kicked in. The Circle wasn't a place for wasted movement and these two weren't men to spar lightly. Even with Sparrow or Xaden, Theron rarely unleashed his full strength. And when he did, it was never for practice—it was because his demons demanded an outlet.

They entered the ring, dust swirling around their boots, the stones marking the perimeter already scuffed by countless battles. There was no need for formality. No salutes. No words. Two blades rang free in unison. They circled once, and then steel met steel with a force that rang across the compound. The crowd halted as the echo cracked through the air. Xaden slid back, feet sure and deliberate, absorbing the blow with fluid grace. But Theron didn't relent. He came at him like a storm unleashed—shoulders tight, jaw clenched, every muscle in his body screaming to move, to strike, to punish. To punish himself.

Dirt kicked up around them, swirling with every strike. The clang of steel, the thud of boots, the rasp of breath—each sound a drumbeat in Theron's ears. Xaden moved like wind, agile and sharp, always just out of reach. But Theron pressed forward, relentless. A tempest given form. He wasn't sparring. He was punishing himself.

Since he'd stayed hidden in the shadows in Bartoria, watching broken women and starving children suffer—*not at the hands of invaders*, but from the very men meant to protect them. Guards who laughed as they stole, as they took. Their fear wasn't of strangers. It was of their own.

He hadn't drawn his sword. He'd followed orders. Like always. Always follow, never question. Always obey.

Then there was Layla. From the moment he'd watched her fall into that pit on the first day, her body crumpling like a broken bird. He hadn't moved. Hadn't fucking moved. Just stood there like some stone-hearted brute while they tossed her in like an offering to rot. And last night? Last night had nearly torn him apart.

Seeing her collapsed at the base of the tree sobbing, arms wrapped around herself as if she could hold the pieces of her body and mind together. Blood splattered all over her. Bruises already blooming like ink across her skin. Her face was dirty, lashes clumped from sweat and tears. And when her eyes finally lifted to meet his... Gods. That look. She stared at him like she didn't recognize him. Like he was just another monster. Another captor. Another man who would hurt her and walk away. And it broke something in him. Because that was the same look he'd seen those days ago from those Bartorian women and children. It was the look of the hunted. Of the discarded.

So now, as he slammed blow after blow at Xaden, he wasn't fighting for skill. He was trying to burn that look out of his memory. He was trying to bleed the guilt from his bones. Because if she ever looked at him like that again— He didn't think he could bear it.

He let out a guttural yell and slammed his weight forward, battering Xaden's defenses. Their swords clashed. A battle of strength now. Xaden held his ground, muscles straining as his boots dug into the dirt. He leaned in close, his voice low and even, not the least bit winded.

"You keep fighting like that, you'll break something," he said with a smirk. "Might be me. Might be you. But something's giving out." Theron growled in response and shoved harder.

"Say what you need to say, brother," Xaden said. "Or swing until your anger burns itself out. Either way, I'm not the one you're mad at." Theron's blade quivered in his grip. Not from fatigue. From fury. From grief. From everything he hadn't said when he should've.

"She's not yours to save. Stop punishing yourself."

Theron froze, just for a breath. That's all the opportunity Xaden needed, he swept Theron's feet out from under him. Theron landed hard on his back, breath knocked out of him. He stared up at the open sky, his chest heaving. *Fuuuuuck.* He decided to just lay there for a moment, grounded by the pain, before he slowly sat up. Xaden offered a hand and Theron took it. No more words were needed. He didn't thank Xaden. He didn't have to. He just stood up and took his stance. Blood pumping, lungs burning, sweat coating his skin, his mind was just a little clearer but he needed more. He had failed Layla once. He wouldn't again.

Layla.

Back at Illyada's hut, Layla stood awkwardly, trying not to breathe through her nose. The stench of blood, earth, and animal musk saturated the air. A massive deer hung from a thick wooden branch nearby, its body gutted open, entrails dangling. Several smaller creatures were piled on a long wooden table next to it. Knives of all sizes gleamed under the late morning sun, their sharp edges catching the light like tiny promises. Layla swallowed hard. She clutched her stomach, praying the small breakfast she'd eaten earlier wouldn't betray her. Her gaze wandered to the neat row of knives. They ranged from finger-length to forearm-sized. Something in her sparked—a *flicker of hope? Of escape?* Her hand twitched before a firm voice cut through the air.

"Graystonian." Layla's eyes snapped up. Illyada stood near the table now, wiping her hands with a stained cloth. The woman's muscles flexed beneath her sleeveless tunic, and her red hair was tied up in a loose braid that draped over one shoulder.

"I saw that look," Illyada said, not unkindly. She stepped closer and placed a hand on her hip. "You think one of those blades is your way out? Touch one without my say, and I'll have to stop you. That's not a threat. Just a truth." Layla gave a tight nod and lowered her gaze. Still, the knives shimmered in her peripheral vision. *So close.*

Illyada let out a short breath, less a sigh and more like an exhale of understanding. "I'm not here to make you suffer more than life already has. You got handed a shit deal, and you're standing by my hut because of it. I won't pity you, but I won't be cruel either." Layla blinked. That... wasn't what she expected.

"Now," Illyada continued, tying an apron around her waist. "You're here to work. If you're going to survive in this tribe, you pull your weight. You stink of perfume and politics, so I doubt you've cooked before. Am I right?" Layla stayed silent at first, then shook her head. No point in pretending.

"Didn't think so. Doesn't matter. I'll teach you. Not out of charity, but because we don't waste hands here. And we sure as hell don't waste meat. Grab that bowl under the deer, scoop out the rest of what's inside, and bring it over. Then we sort organs."

The deer's insides were steaming in the morning chill as Layla worked her hands through slick organs and ropes of sinew. Blood painted her forearms up to the elbow. Her hair stuck to the sweat on her neck, yet she didn't care. It was disgusting, exhausting, but oddly satisfying—because for once, she was doing something, not just enduring.

A slow crunch broke the rhythm. The sound of teeth sinking into an apple. Wet. Purposeful.

"You missed a piece," a voice drawled behind her—low, smug, and entirely male. "Unless you were saving the liver for me. How romantic."

Whoever it was, whatever new asshole thought he'd try his luck today, he wasn't worth her time. She was elbow-deep in blood, sore from head to toe, and had well and truly reached her limit with men and their mouths. So she said nothing. Didn't even look at him. Praying he would just go away.

The sound of another bite and more chewing continued.

"Didn't think doves played with entrails," he murmured as she heard him near, voice curling around her like tendrils of smoke. "You wear the mess well though... Kind of makes me wonder what else you'd look good covered in."

Disgust curled through her. *Was there no end to vile men and their imaginations?* She was already bracing for the worst as she finally glanced toward the voice, glare set and tongue sharpened.

Gods. It was him. The tall, sunlight-haired brute from yesterday. The one who had offered her his daggers with a leer that had made her skin crawl and her stomach flip in equal measure. He stood at the edge of the clearing, half in shadow, apple in hand, watching her like she was dessert he hadn't yet decided how to devour.

Their eyes locked and he smiled. Slow. Wicked. Inevitable. And then he moved—each step deliberate, a predator circling his prey not to strike, but to savor.

Layla rolled her eyes, not hiding her disgust in the least before she returned her attention to the carcass before her. "Gods, it's you."

"I get that a lot," he said without shame. "Usually right before I'm asked to stay." She didn't dignify that with an answer.

She felt him more than heard him close the distance between them. Once he was standing directly behind her, she quicky realized she didn't like the feel of him towering over her. So Layla promptly stood up, emanating confidence as she crossed her arms over her chest and glared up at him. He was now so close that she could smell the apple on his breath and the leather at his collar. His green eyes roved her face...then lower.

"I've been picturing you just like this," he went on, voice dropping, "elbow-deep in blood, cheeks flushed, mouth set in that little scowl you think makes you look scary... You don't by the way. You just look like sin served rare."

Layla's scowl deepened, but she didn't let his words affect her. She wouldn't give him the satisfaction. "I'm sure I'm not far off in guessing most women find you as revolting as I do."

His smirk deepened, slow and self-assured. "Maybe," he said, taking another bite of his apple, letting the juice run down his fingers. "But most of them don't stop at just looking." He winked at her. Clearly trying to get under her skin.

He stepped in, close enough for her to feel the heat coming off him as she had to tilt her head completely up to even still see his face. "What about you, Dove?" His voice dipped, rough velvet. "You curious?" That wolfish grin back on his face as his eyes dragged over her like a physical touch. "Because I sure as hell am curious about you."

"Curious? Ha. Please. I don't waste my time on mangy mutts." She gave him a slow once-over, her gaze dripping with judgment.

His grin only widened. "Careful, Dove. This mangy mutt might just bite."

"I'm counting on it," she said coolly, as she dropped her gaze to her nails, pretending her blood covered hands were so interesting at this moment in time before peering up through her lashes. "Bite me, and I'll shove that apple so far down your throat, you'll be coughing up seeds in the afterlife."

His's eyes twinkled, and then he barked out a laugh. The sound so rich as it burst from his chest. "Spirited. No wonder my brother can't stop brooding."

She stilled. "Your brother?"

He leaned in with a conspiratorial whisper, his breath warm against her ear. "You didn't know? Theron. My big, broody, bashful brother. Son of our ever-terrifying queen." Layla blinked, stunned. Th warrior leaned back, giving her a slow once-over. "Careful, Dove. You're surrounded by more wolves than you think."

He tossed the apple core into the brush and turned, already striding off with that maddening ease. Just before the trees swallowed him, he glanced back over his shoulder, winked, and whistled low. "See you around, little one."

Layla stared after him, her whole body pulsed—not with fear, but with blazing rage. She didn't realize she was gripping the deer's organs in her hands until they squelched.

Illyada's voice snapped her out of it. "Looks like someone got under your skin."

Layla exhaled sharply and shook her head. "Like a tick," she muttered.

Illyada laughed as she dropped a squirrel's head into the stew bucket. "You'll get used to him....Now, back to work."

"Doubtful." Layla muttered before dropping back down to continue to work on the deer.

The hours passed in blood, sweat, and heat. Layla learned far more than she ever wanted to about animal guts. She'd hunted before, sure, but she never touched what came after the kill. That had been servants' work. Here, it was survival.

By midafternoon, her skin was sticky, her muscles sore, and her pride battered. Sweat dripped from her temple, only to be smeared around her face with bloody hands. She caught her reflection in a bowl of water—feral, red-streaked, and somehow... hardened. Then she saw him. Her giant. *Theron.* He walked up the path shirtless, sweat glistening across his chest and arms. The intricate tattoo on his left shoulder wrapped down his arm and across his pectoral like a woven flame. His abs were chiseled, his expression unreadable. Layla's eyes snapped away before she let them drop too far down his body.

She hunched over a rabbit, pretending to focus as footsteps approached. As she heard him slow to a stop, she hesitantly peeked up. He stood in front of her now, holding up a pair of worn leather boots.

"Here," is all he said as he handed them over to her.

"Oh... uh. Thank you," she murmured. Their eyes met. Blue crashing into hazel. His intensity made her stomach twist, and for once, it wasn't nausea. He nodded once and turned, walking away without another word. Illyada chuckled from the squirrel she was skinning. Layla's cheeks instantly flushed crimson as she tried to shake the warm feeling off.

Layla's head jerked up. "What?" Illyada just laughed and shook her head.

Layla looked back down at the small boots in her hands, still warm from his grip. Her fingers tightened around them slightly, heart thudding louder than she liked. That small act—simple, thoughtful—shouldn't have affected her like this. But it did. It stirred something dangerous in her chest. *Confusion? Weakness?* A trembling hope she had no right to feel. He was the enemy. She had to remind herself, force herself to remember that Theron wasn't just some mysterious, brooding warrior who'd saved her. He was *Queen Okteria's son*. Son of the woman who had stolen her freedom, and now kept her caged like livestock while her people were scattered, likely slaughtered or worse. He bore the blood of the very line that is aiding in destroying her life. So why did his touch feel like safety? Why had his voice, commanding yet soft, made her want to obey, just for a second?

She looked up in the direction he'd walked, catching the broad line of his back as he disappeared between the huts, and it stung. He wasn't cruel like the other brother, whose smugness oozed like spoiled wine. Theron had carried her. Protected her. Given her boots so her feet wouldn't bleed. But kindness didn't erase allegiance. Just because the wolf didn't bare its teeth didn't mean it wouldn't still bite.

Her grip on the boots tightened. No matter how tender his voice, how intense those eyes, or how her stomach fluttered when he looked at her like that- he was still the son of her enemy. And she couldn't afford to forget it. Not now. Not when her kingdom still needed her. Not when she still had to escape.

BY FLAME, BY ROOT, BY GOD AND STAR—
CAELERIA SHALL RISE, OR PERISH WHOLE.

THE LAW OF BALANCE AND BLOOD

*Where one kingdom rises, another must fall. So
it has been o it shall remain.* Caeleria does not
permit eternal empires. Greed begins ruin,
Harmony is bought in sacrifice.

- THE HIGH LAWS OF CAELERIA

Chapter Ten

Theron.

After a brutal day of sparring and drills, all Theron wanted was an ale and a few hours where no one expected him to command anything but his bed. But first, he had to fetch Sparrow and... Layla. He hated how that thought sent a charge through his chest.

Theron walked the worn path between the huts, nostrils flaring as the rich scent of Illyada's rabbit stew hit him. As he neared her post, his gaze instantly found Layla, crouched near the tree where the deer had been hung earlier. She was elbow-deep in blood and entrails, her arms smeared with gore and her hair stuck to her face in sweaty strands. Still, she looked fierce. Alive. Tempting. She turned to stand, and their eyes caught—just for a breath—and he swore something flickered behind hers. *Was that... joy?* Then it vanished, replaced by that tight, guarded wall she wore too damn well.

"Come," he said. She bent over to grab a bowl, and his body betrayed him- again. That leather skirt was far too short, the curve of her thighs testing every shred of discipline he had left. He clenched his jaw, trying to think about anything other than how good she looked even when covered in blood and gods know what else.

Illyada gave him a knowing look and arched a brow. "She needs to help me set the tables first. Then she's all yours." *Yours.* Theron didn't like the possessiveness that word stirred inside him. Or maybe he did. He leaned against a tree and waited, arms crossed, keeping his expression unreadable. When Layla finished and approached, still avoiding his eyes, Illyada handed him two bowls of stew. He grunted his thanks and turned with a flick of his head. She followed in silence.

As they reached the communal tables, the usual bustle of evening mealtime surrounded them—clinking bowls, roaring laughter, the screech of children darting between fires. Theron usually ate fast, drank faster, and retired to the quiet of his hut. But tonight felt different. He gestured for Layla to sit beside Sparrow, who looked up from his drink and gave her a polite nod. Theron dropped into the seat across from her and studied her subtly over the edge of his bowl. She wouldn't meet his eyes. *Was something wrong?* He shook the thought away as he noticed the stares around them. Not everyone approved of a Graystonian sharing their table- least of all the drunken warrior slurring two seats over.

"And now the Graystonian whore's eating with us?" Visen sneered, too loudly. "What's this tribe coming to?" The second he heard it, Theron saw red. He was up and across the space before anyone else could move, grabbing Visen by the collar and slamming him down onto the table. Dishes clattered. Ales spilled. Conversations stopped.

"I should've killed you last night," Theron growled. Then came the blade. He rammed the tip of his knife into Visen's gut, just enough to twist it and cause agony without killing him. Visen choked on his own scream as Theron cut off his air with a hand around his throat. Blood pooled across the table. Silence echoed around them, save for the squelch of pain and Theron's labored breathing. When Visen finally passed out cold, Theron dropped his limp body to the dirt.

"We do not disrespect women," he barked. "Get him out of here."

Two warriors moved to drag Visen's body away as Theron returned to his seat and downed what remained of the ale before him.

"I mean that one was mine, but sure," Xaden drawled, plopping into the seat next to him. "You can steal my drink and my dramatic entrances. No big deal." Theron shot him a glare but said nothing. Xaden smirked and leaned forward, eyes twinkling as he looked to Layla. "That must've been a hell of a show for someone like you, huh?"

Layla glanced up, arching a brow. "Someone like me?"

"I mean, you're not exactly from around here." Xaden chuckled and took a long swig of a new ale. "Sorry. That sounded worse than I meant it. I just mean—here, respecting women isn't optional. It's law. Shit like what he said doesn't get put up with around here." He shrugged then went on slightly more chipper, "My name's Xaden by the way."

Layla let out a cold laugh and stirred her bowl. "Oh, is that what this is? Respect?" Her voice dripped venom. "Guess I missed that memo somewhere between being left in a pit to starve to death, forced to kill a man just to survive, and ending up elbow-deep in deer intestines." She paused as she lifted her spoon. "And just when I thought the welcome couldn't get any warmer, your friend over there assaulted me under the stars last night. Truly—" she looked up, deadpan, "—I've never felt more cherished."

Sparrow choked on his ale.

"Oh and nice to meet you Xaden." She said with feigned politeness.

Xaden blinked. "For Fucks sake," he muttered as his eyes went wide to her admission. His fork hovered midair as he glanced from Layla to Theron. Theron hadn't moved, but he was practically vibrating with tension, his knuckles white around his mug of ale, clearly about to crush it.

Xaden leaned back with a dry chuckle and acted as though he was deep in thought stroking his chin. "Noted. Next enemy princess we capture- we'll skip the pits and fists, and go straight to wine, silk robes, fine furs. Wouldn't want anyone thinking us savages." He winked at her as the mock sincerity broke through her nerves.

Layla's mouth parted slightly before she threw her head back and laughed—truly laughed. The sound was unexpected, bright and un-guarded. Theron loved it. He could've lived in that sound, if only it weren't born from the nightmare she was recounting.

"Thank you," she said, still giggling as she shook her head. "I would've much preferred that kind of welcome."

As Layla finally calmed herself, she swiped a mug of ale and took a long drink. Theron blinked. Xaden blinked. Even Sparrow looked vaguely impressed.

"Well then," Xaden said, slowly grinning. "Didn't have you pegged for the ale type. You might survive here after all."

Layla wiped her mouth with the back of her hand. "Yeah, I would have much preferred wine but when you're with savages..." She shrugged her shoulders and took another gulp.

Her raw retelling struck Theron like a fist to the ribs. His throat tightened. She wasn't just talking about Visen—she was talking about all of it. About him. About the night he'd captured her, and every moment since. She was suffering because he'd brought her here. Because he hadn't stepped in when he should have, even when his instincts screamed at him to act. Because he always followed orders.

Theron's fists curled beneath the table, knuckles white. He stared down at his untouched bowl, unable to look at her—unwilling to let her see the maelstrom unraveling behind his eyes. Guilt twisted low in his gut, sharp and relentless. Without a word, he stood, pushing back from the table with enough force to make the wood shudder.

"Let's go," he snapped. Layla blinked but rose without protest. Sparrow silently stood as well, falling into place behind them.

As they passed through the rows of huts, Theron kept his eyes forward but his thoughts knotted tight. Something had been weighing on her all evening. The sharpness in her voice, the hollowness in her stare—it had started before Visen's taunt. He wanted to ask. To help. But the words caught in his throat like thorns. Deep down, he knew he didn't deserve her explanation. Not after what she'd endured. Not after the part he played. So he didn't dare press her. They reached his hut, Sparrow falling back a few paces. Theron turned to him.

"Watch the hut tonight." Sparrow nodded once, arms folding across his chest as he leaned against the outer wall. Theron lifted the hide and gestured for Layla to step inside. Layla immediately walked over and sat on the cot, her shoulders slumped as she stared down at her feet, seemingly lost in a world far from this one. No sharp words. No fire in her eyes. Just a heavy, echoing silence that wrapped around her like a second skin.

Theron lingered near the wall, his jaw tight. He would never take a cot from a woman, especially not from her. So the ground would have to do. He reached up and unfastened his leather armor, peeling it away with a quiet exhale. The hide shirt followed, damp with the sweat and weight of the day. As he stripped it off, he caught the slightest flicker of movement—Layla, peeking up through her lashes, momentarily drawn from her trance. Her eyes dipped to his chest, lingering, before she blinked and looked away just as quickly. Theron swallowed hard. *Keep it together.*

He crouched beside the cot and bundled the shirt beneath his head. The cold earth beneath him was a welcome contrast to the fever that licked at his skin whenever she was near. A chill against the heat she stirred without even trying. The muscle in his body began to ease, tension slowly uncoiling from his spine as he listened to her move—slow and hesitant—before she finally settled into the cot.

Theron stared up at the hut ceiling, tracing the faint beams of moonlight like they could spell out the answer to the turmoil brewing in his chest. He'd done worse things in war. Captured worse men. Followed harder orders. But none of them lingered in his thoughts the way *she* did. *Layla Eradellian.* The woman he had unknowingly dragged from her fallen palace. The woman who, despite everything, made him want to question orders for the first time in his life. And yet, he couldn't. He was a soldier forged by obedience. And now, he was the weapon that had carved her life apart.

Theron shifted on the floor, his jaw clenching as guilt curled through him again like smoke. She was here—injured, humiliated, alone—because of *him*. Because when he'd found her climbing down from that tree covered in mud and royal blood, he hadn't given a second thought to his duty in that moment. He'd done what he was trained to do. Except now, every time he saw her, that decision haunted him a little more.

"Try to sleep," he muttered after a long stretch of silence, his voice rougher than he intended. He wasn't sure if she heard him. Her breathing had evened, and he hoped she'd found some small pocket of rest in this nightmare of a place. He watched the soft rise and fall of her chest from the corner of his eye, the moonlight casting her face in a silvered glow. She looked almost peaceful now. *Almost.* Theron closed his eyes again, willing his mind to settle. But it didn't. Instead, images flared behind his eyelids—Layla, crumpled on the forest floor... Layla, trembling in his arms... Layla, smiling softly at Illyada before catching his eye and dropping her gaze...The light dimming like she remembered exactly who he was. *The queen's son. The man who stole her freedom. The man who couldn't stop thinking about her even though every part of him screamed that he should.*

In the dead of night, Theron's instincts flared to life, tearing him out of his dreams. A soft broken cry ripped through the silence of the hut like a dagger to the gut. His eyes flew open as he shot upright, one hand already on the hilt of his sword as his pulse pounded in his ears. The moonlight cast pale streaks across the floor, just enough for him to scan the room and locate the source of the sound. *Layla.* Still in the cot, but not at peace. Her body jerked and twisted beneath the thin blanket, breath ragged as muffled whimpers escaped her lips. She was dreaming- no, *reliving.* Theron knew that look. Knew that sound. Knew that kind of haunted. His grip loosened from the sword as he moved closer, crouching at her side with careful, practiced steps. His fingers hovered above her arm for a moment, uncertain, then rested lightly against her skin.

"Layla," he said, voice low but steady. She didn't wake. Her brow furrowed, a soft gasp catching in her throat as her legs pulled tighter under her. Theron leaned in closer, his hand giving her arm a small shake. "Layla." This time, firmer. Her eyes shot open. She jolted upright, crawling backwards against the cot as if trying to make herself disappear into the wood behind her. Her chest heaved, eyes wild, the raw edge of panic still alive in them. She stared at him as though unsure whether he was friend or foe. His heart cracked under the weight of it. Then, gradually, she blinked. Recognition flickered there hesitant, then full.

"Theron," she breathed, her voice soft and quivering, like she couldn't quite believe he was real. He let out a slow exhale, every muscle still strung tight. She relaxed against the cot with an audible sigh, rubbing her face and pushing damp hair away from her eyes. "Sorry," she muttered, glancing away. "Must've had a nightmare. I didn't mean to wake you."

Theron said nothing at first, just studied her face. The way the moonlight hit her cheekbones, the exhaustion etched into every line. Gods, she'd been through so much. And it was *his* tribe, *his* command, that put her here. That had taken her.

He nodded once. A quiet, almost reverent motion. Then he stood and walked the short distance back to his place on the floor, sinking down onto his bundled shirt. His hands went to his hair, fingers dragging back through the strands as he fought to calm himself. He could feel her eyes on him, even before he turned to meet her gaze. There they were—those eyes he could lose himself in, watching him like she didn't quite know what to make of him. He held her gaze, just long enough to feel his heart twist in his chest again. *What was she doing to him?* She was a prisoner. She was Queen Okteria's leverage. She was Graystonian. And still... he wanted nothing more than to protect her. He couldn't explain it or the war going on within him constantly throughout this past week. The war he never saw coming.

"Theron..." her voice came again, quieter now. He turned his head slightly, facing her. "Thank you," she whispered. "For what you did earlier." Theron didn't move, didn't speak—just gave a small nod. Because if he tried to say anything else, he might confess to everything he wasn't ready to admit, everything he still didn't completely understand. So he just closed his eyes as he acknowledged that he was so completely *fucked*.

Layla.

Layla couldn't fall back asleep. The nightmare had jolted her violently from the fragile thread of rest she'd managed to cling to, and now it was gone entirely—scattered into the black corners of the hut like ash. Her chest still heaved with remnants of panic, the raw ghost of the dream clinging to her like a second skin.

She had been back at the castle. Not as it was the night of the invasion, but eerily still. Silent at first, that unnatural kind of silence that presses into your skull and sets your teeth on edge. She recalled that she had moved through the halls, barefoot, weightless, as though her feet barely touched the ground. And then, just as she had reached the long dining hall—the one where they'd shared royal banquets, birthday feasts, and endless political performances—the fire had begun. It had erupted everywhere.

Flames had crawled along the mahogany walls, surged up the heavy curtains, and danced across the vaulted ceiling like they'd been summoned straight from the bowels of hell. The air had thickened with smoke. The stone floor beneath her had pulsed with heat, slick with melted varnish. She hadn't been able to breathe—every gasp had scorched her lungs, fire clawing down her throat. But the fire hadn't been the worst part. It hadn't been the destruction. It had been her family.

Her mother had stood at the head of the table, clutching her two younger sisters to her chest, screaming Layla's name again and again.

Their dresses had been smoking, the flames licking hungrily toward their feet as they scrambled back. And her father—gods, her father—had been trapped in the corner, blade in hand, held behind a wall of roaring fire. Their eyes had caught across the blaze, his filled with helpless torment and a silent, desperate plea. She had tried to run. She had screamed at herself to move. But her limbs had betrayed her. Her body had turned to stone. And then the fire had reached her.

First the hem of her emerald dress, then her arms, her legs, the heat racing up her body, devouring everything in its path. She had opened her mouth to scream, but only smoke had poured out. The fire had consumed her, and still, she had seen them. Her sisters' shrieks had turned shrill, inhuman. Her mother had sobbed her name. Her father had bellowed like a man being torn apart. She had burned. Helpless. Useless. Watching everything she loved turn to ash.

And then, Theron. His voice. His hand. The deep rumble that shook her awake like a thunderclap. She remembered gasping for breath as she stared into his face, dripping with sweat, her pulse racing with terror. She hadn't expected to feel relief at seeing him, but she had.

Now, hours later, Layla lay motionless on the cot, her eyes pinned to the rafters above her, listening to the quiet rise and fall of Theron's breath. He had saved her. *Again.* Her gaze shifted to his sleeping form. Even on the ground, he looked like something carved from stone-solid, unmoving, reliable. It wasn't fair. None of this was fair. That he could be *this*- kind, gentle even, in rare moments- and still be one of *them*. Still be the reason she was here. Still be the son of the woman who held her in chains without even touching her. The same woman who had issued a silent death sentence to her kingdom.

Layla's stomach turned with nausea that had nothing to do with the stew earlier. She couldn't forget who Theron really was. No matter how soft his voice had been when he'd said her name. No matter how gentle his hands were when they roused her from darkness. He wasn't on her side. None of them were. And if she ever wanted to see her family again—if there *was* a family left to save—she would have to act.

She turned her thoughts toward Illyada's hut. The knives laid out in rows. She remembered seeing one particularly small blade with a black handle. Sharp. Light. Easy to hide. *That one.* Tomorrow, she would take it. Discreetly. Illyada was tough but not infallible, there would be a moment. Plus Layla had nimble fingers, always had. The question now was what came after. *Would she kill someone to get out of here?*

Her gut twisted as her mind echoed with the image of Sparrow's kind face, who now stood guard outside this hut. His quiet, steady presence beside her lately. His attempts at gentleness. His clear loyalty to Theron. *Could she kill him if she had to? So that she could slip out tomorrow night while Theron was sleeping?* The rational part of her, the queen-in-waiting, the strategist, told her yes. If it meant getting out, reaching her people, finding her mother, her sisters, *her father*, then yes. She could do anything. But the girl inside her, the one who had never killed another living soul until that horrible day with Tynan. That girl wasn't so sure.

Layla turned onto her side, wrapping her arms around herself tightly. She thought back to the blood on her hands that day. *What would it be like this time? Worse?* She stared at the wall in front of her, muscles taut, her nails digging crescents into her forearm. Her heart hammering even in the stillness. *You can do this,* she told herself. *You must do this.* And she would. Because if she didn't, her kingdom would be nothing more than ashes and screams in a nightmare that she would never wake from. But gods help her, it was going to destroy whatever piece of innocence she had left. She closed her eyes, but sleep never came.

Theron slowly stood and stretched, the early morning light catching on the ridges of his muscled torso. Layla, still wide awake but feigning sleep, let out a deliberately timed yawn and sat up slowly. Brushing her hair from her face as if she'd just stirred too. She watched as Theron bent to retrieve his leather armor and shirt from the ground, shook them out, and pulled them on with deliberate ease. The movements pulled every muscle in his arms and chest tight. She didn't mean to watch, but she couldn't seem to look away. And gods help her, *it was a really nice view.*

Once dressed, Theron grunted and gestured for them to go. Layla followed silently, her limbs stiff with exhaustion. As they emerged from the hut, Sparrow stood exactly where they'd left him the night before—posted by the entrance, waiting with quiet patience. She glanced at him-still, silent, loyal- and a pang of guilt flickered through her chest. If her plan worked, he might be the first casualty. She reminded herself why she had to do this. *Her people. Her kingdom. Her family.* Still, it hurt more than it should have.

The three made their way to the morning gathering. As they stepped onto the main path, Layla felt the weight of every eye on her. Same as yesterday. Same judgment. Same distrust. She held her chin high and kept her spine straight. She wouldn't let them see her shrink.

Sparrow's arm reached out in front of her, and she stopped beside him once again. Clearly, this was her place during these assemblies. She obeyed without argument, eyes scanning the crowd until they landed on Queen Okteria, perched with calculated poise and that same expression of cold satisfaction. The queen's lips twisted ever so slightly. Layla could only assume she found satisfaction at the sight of Layla's blood-smeared face and filthy clothing. The message was clear: *Good. Let them see what you are now.* But Layla wasn't going to give her the gratification. She wasn't going to try to hide. She was going to stand tall as ever.

Theron stepped forward. "No news. Go on," he said simply, then turned without another word. Layla blinked, startled by how brief it was. Then again, he didn't seem like the type to waste words.

He swiftly escorted her to Illyada's station without ceremony, nodding once before striding off toward the training grounds. Illyada barely looked up from the massive turkey sprawled across the table. She pointed a bloodied blade toward a bowl of innards for Layla to start sorting.

Layla sighed and stepped up. Her stomach turned at the sight and smell, but she just took a deep breath and got to work. Still caked in yesterday's grime, she must have looked feral. Face streaked with dirt and blood, hair sticking in messy clumps around her cheeks. But no one had said anything. And she hadn't dared ask for water to wash. Until Illyada dropped a wooden bucket of clean water beside her with a soft grunt and handed her a rag.

"Here. So you can clean off," Illyada said without fanfare, then turned back to her chopping.

Layla stared down at the clear water like it was holy. She blinked, overwhelmed by the simple kindness. "Thank you," she said softly, genuinely, turning to face Illyada fully.

Illyada didn't look at her though, just got straight back to work. "The queen wanted to see you humiliated. Bloodied. Letting you stay filthy was the easiest way to keep her content. But I figured one day was enough." Layla almost laughed. *Of course.* Strategic cruelty, disguised as obedience. *Clever.* She crouched and scrubbed herself raw, relishing the feeling of blood and dirt sliding off her skin. When she stood again, damp and cleaner than she'd been in days, she gave Illyada a small but sincere smile. Feeling a bit lighter as she returned to the task at hand.

"I know you probably think she's a monster," Illyada said, not unkindly. "Okteria may have married into the title, but make no mistake—she rules in her own right. No one dares question her. She's not cruel without cause, but she's unflinching. A force of nature when it comes to protecting this tribe. She upholds the law because the law keeps us alive. Survival, order, loyalty—that's what matters to her. And she's never hesitated when hard choices had to be made."

Layla simply blinked at her, not sure why Illyada was even telling her this. But a knowing question at been eating at her that she desperately wanted to know the answer too. "But... how is that allowed? For a woman to rule alone?" Her voice caught on the word queen, like it didn't belong on her tongue—like it defied everything she'd ever been taught.

Illyada blinked, clearly confused by the question. "How does she not?" Layla stared. Illyada shrugged. "We bleed just the same. We fight just as hard. Sometimes harder. Don't mistake gentleness for weakness. The queen commands because she's earned it. Because no one leads like she does."

absorbed the words, each one unsettling something inside her. She thought of her mother—stern, cold, loyal to her king above all else. She thought of herself. Of what might've been, if she'd been born on the other side of the border. She let her mind continue to wander.

"And her sons?" Layla asked, voice quieter now. "What can you tell me about them?"

Illyada softened, just a touch. "Theron was raised by the late king, King Aric. Trained to follow orders without hesitation. Duty. Loyalty. Discipline. That was carved into him from the time he could walk. His father taught him that protecting the tribe comes before everything. That obedience keeps people alive. He's deadly, yes—but never without cause. He waits for the order. Then he acts."

Layla's breath caught as the memory of Theron's ferocity slammed back into her. She had seen Theron fight—twice now. Once in the forest, when Visen had assaulted her. Theron had come out of nowhere, a storm of fists and vengeance, beating Visen nearly to death. And then again at dinner, when Visen had dared to mouth off. Theron hadn't hesitated then either. And yet, outside those violent bursts, Theron was composed. Controlled. Always standing just a little too straight, jaw clenched, voice low but sharp. Like his entire existence had been trained to obey—bound by duty, carved into discipline. Every breath he took was permissioned by something deeper: loyalty to his tribe. Orders first.

Everything else second. Now, Layla saw it more clearly. That restraint wasn't quiet. It was dangerous. And somewhere beneath her ribs, something like awe twisted—sharp and uninvited.

"So all the warriors here are like him?" she said, masking it with sarcasm. "Stoic saints with blades for hands and a moral code carved in stone?"

Illyada chuckled. "Most of them."

Layla arched a brow. "What about the other brother, the one with the apple and the oversized ego?"

Illyada snorted. "That would be Kain." She paused and shook her head slightly. "And believe it or not, there's more to him than sarcasm and swagger. Though he does enjoy getting under people's skin."

Layla rolled her eyes and muttered, "He's exceptional at it."

"That he is," Illyada said, her smirk softening. "He's... different than Theron. Raised by the queen more so than the king. It is my opinion that she taught him how to bend rules, to read between lines instead of charging through them.... Don't let the grin and attitude fool you—he cares more than most. And he'll break every law we have if it means doing what's right." She paused, her voice dipping lower. "And he'll smile while doing it." The clear admiration was there in her tone as Illyada spoke of Kain. Which thoroughly confused Layla with the image of him that was already being created in her mind.

But Layla allowed this new information to shine a sliver of light on a possible different view of the repugnant man. Her thoughts drifted—unbidden—to that moment in the Circle. When everyone else had stayed still, silent. And he had stepped forward. Not with pity, not with mockery—but with quiet resolve. Offering her his daggers. His sword.

Giving her the chance to fight. Still, that didn't mean she liked him. Or trusted whatever game he was playing beneath that smug grin.

She exhaled slowly, pushing the memory aside. "He's still vile," she muttered, more to herself than to Illyada, and went back to work like the conversation hadn't shaken her more than she cared to admit. Illyada burst into laughter as she turned and made her way toward the vegetable garden behind him.

Layla softly laughed in response, but the conversation vanished from her mind in an instant as she watched Illyada walk away. Her stomach flipped. *Finally. A chance.* Her eyes darted to the now unguarded knives along the prep table, heart pounding with sudden urgency. She carefully tracked Illyada's steps, waiting—watching. When Illyada completely turned toward the forest's edge to gather ripe tomatoes, Layla moved. One smooth sidestep. A quick grab. The smallest blade slipped into her palm, then disappeared into the waistband of her skirt. She turned to check if she'd been seen—And that's when the Bartorian guard exploded from the woods.

Illyada barely dodged the first strike, stumbling back as the man's sword tore through the air. His second swing caught her arm, slashing it open. Blood bloomed along her sleeve. Illyada reached for her sword, but the Bartorian was faster. His blade crashed against hers, sending it flying to the dirt. Layla's heart stopped. Without thinking, she whipped the stolen knife up beside her cheek and hurled it. The blade spun through the air and struck the guard square in the eye. He dropped instantly. Illyada turned in stunned silence, her eyes wide, locking with Layla's. Layla gave her a nod in response, right as six more Bartorian guards burst from the trees.

Illyada snatched her fallen sword and charged the nearest enemy. Layla grabbed two more knives from the table and threw them with deadly precision. One caught a man in the chest, the other in the neck. She turned to grab another blade and help Illyada finish them off. But before she could throw it, an assault of Antonin warriors rushed past, slamming into the enemy with a brutal clash of steel. In moments, it was over. The clearing was littered with dead Bartorian soldiers. Layla stood frozen, her breath coming hard, the final knife clenched in her hand. She calmed enough to quickly slip it into her waistband with a flick of her wrist before someone noticed.

"You!" A voice roared. An Antonin warrior she didn't recognize stormed toward her, sword drawn, violence in his eyes. "This is your fault!" He raised his blade, pressing it against her throat. Before she could react, Illyada's voice cut through the air.

"Stop! She saved me. Don't harm her, or you deal with me." The man instantly faltered at her words before glancing at Illyada's bloodied arm, then back at Layla. Confusion flickered in his eyes but he reluctantly lowered his sword. Then spat at Layla's feet before stalking away. Layla realized she'd been holding her breath and exhaled shakily.

"Come," Illyada said, gripping her wrist and tugging her down the path. "We need to tell the queen."

They approached a modest looking hut nestled off the main path. Layla's eyebrows rose. *This was where Queen Okteria lived?* It wasn't grand.

It wasn't guarded. It looked like every other hut in the village. Layla's opinion of her shifted ever so slightly. *Everything Illyada had said about her and now this?* The queen wasn't what she'd expected at all. The flap opened and Queen Okteria stepped out. Eyes narrowing the moment she saw Layla.

"We've been attacked," Illyada said plainly.

The queen's focus snapped to her. "Explain."

"Seven Bartorian guards came at us by my hut. Layla killed three of them, we got the rest." Okteria stared, clearly caught off guard. Then her gaze swept back to Layla. Suspicion. Disgust. But maybe, just maybe... curiosity.

"Are there more?"

"Not that we could see," Illyada said. "Xaden took a small unit to sweep the perimeter. He's waiting on orders." The queen gave a curt nod and disappeared down the path. Layla exhaled.

"What now?" she asked.

Illyada shrugged. "Now we get back to work. If they need us for anything else, they'll let us know."

The quiet between Layla and Illyada became something almost sacred. Not warm, exactly—but understood. There was a mutual respect in the silence that passed between their steady hands and shared rhythm over the prep tables. Illyada had saved her in a way, and Layla had returned the favor. The debt was even now. And maybe, just maybe...In some small way, Illyada had started to see her.

The mid-afternoon sun slanted down through the tree canopy, filtering dappled gold over the mess of bloodied feathers and animal hides. Layla worked without complaint, her hands sure and practiced now. Every time her fingers brushed another knife, she remembered the one hidden in her waistband. A cold weight against her hip. Her escape. Her guilt.

She shouldn't feel guilty. But she did. Even after killing three Bartorian guards, her enemies, there was a tight ache in her chest. Not regret. Not fear. Just the stark realization that every time she wielded a weapon now, it meant something irreversible. It meant someone didn't get to go home. Didn't get to live. She supposed that's what made her different from the Antonin. They wielded death like it was another tool on their belt. She wielded it like a last resort.

Illyada, sensing her mood perhaps, finally broke the quiet. "You think too much."

Layla blinked, glancing over. "Excuse me?"

Illyada didn't look up. "When you kill, you hesitate. I can see it. You're not soft, but your heart still makes noise. One day, that will get you killed... or save you. Not sure which."

Layla frowned. "I don't want to become numb to it. To killing."

Illyada paused her knife mid-slice and finally met Layla's gaze. "Then don't. But be fast enough that it's them who bleed, not you."

Layla stared at her for a moment before nodding. "Fair enough." The conversation ended as quickly as it had begun. But the moment lingered, threaded into something that might one day resemble trust.

Not long after, Xaden sauntered over, dirt-smudged and grinning, clearly just returned from the forest perimeter.

"Well, well," he drawled, throwing an apple up and down in one hand. "Look who's still alive. Thought for sure you'd die this time."

"The gods can't seem to agree on how I should go," she said, washing her hands in the bowl nearby. "Guess you all are stuck with me until they decide."

Xaden chuckled and leaned one elbow on the prep table, clearly watching her. "So... what's the deal, Princess? You planning to assassinate us one by one with those dainty little knives? Those throws were wicked."

"Wouldn't you like to know," she replied coolly, finally glancing at him with a mock-sweet smile. "Don't worry, I saved your death for last. You seem like the type to make it long and dramatic."

Xaden laughed loudly at that. "Damn. You're almost Antonin already."

"Careful," Illyada muttered without looking up, "I might start liking her." Layla's lips twitched in a faint smile. Despite everything, despite the blood on her hands, the knife in her waistband, the constant ache of worry for her family, she wasn't entirely alone here. Somehow, amid the gutting tables and wary glares, she had carved out the tiniest space of acceptance. Not safety. Never that. But maybe something close to survival. She'd take it. For now. Because tonight, she would escape. She would find her family. And nothing, not kindness, not camaraderie, not even the flicker of warmth she felt when Theron looked at her like she was more than a pawn, would stop her. But still, part of her whispered: *You don't have to hate them all to save your own.*

By the ancient rite of blood and bone, every
child born of Antonin blood shall kneel before
the fire at the age of five and offer their oath.
From that day forth, they are no longer merely
flesh- they are warrior. Bound by duty, forged
in strength, and pledged to the tribe above all.
To refuse the oath is to sever one's blood from
the line of warriors, and to dishonor the very
breath of the gods. Let it be known: the blood
oath is not a choice. It is the first act of
devotion, and the sacred beginning of a life
given to tribe and blade.

-FROM THE OATHBOUND LAW OF THE
ANTONIN FLAME

Chapter Eleven

Theron.

Theron was deep in training, demonstrating hand-to-hand combat techniques to a group of young warriors, when Queen Okteria approached. The moment he caught the tension in her expression, his body stilled. Something was wrong. He stepped away from the circle, wiping sweat from his brow as he met her gaze.

"The Bartorians attacked. Our people are safe," she said curtly.

His shoulders straightened, muscles going rigid. "Where?"

"Near Illyada's hut. Only seven of them. All dead. There may be more hiding in the woods." *Illyada's hut.* His stomach dropped. *Layla.* He clenched his fists to keep from bolting. Okteria said *our* people were fine. *Did she mean Layla too?* He wouldn't dare ask. Not in front of her.

"You need to sweep the woods. Take a team, scout, and report back. Whether they came for her or not, they crossed into our home. I won't tolerate it. Kain will return soon with more information, but until then, we act." Theron nodded. Orders were orders. Even when every nerve in his body screamed to go to Layla. He turned and moved swiftly through the village, selecting his most capable men with practiced efficiency.

At Sparrow's hut, he leaned in. The warrior was asleep but snapped upright the moment Theron entered. "Find Layla. Stay with her," Theron ordered. Without a word, Sparrow was up and out of his hut, heading in the opposite direction. Theron let out a breath. At least she wouldn't be alone...If she was alive that is.

Theron led a group of eight seasoned Antonin warriors to the forest's edge. In silence, they covered their faces and arms in mud for camouflage. Theron marked his face with three thick streaks, melting into darkness without effort. His ink-covered skin cloaked his form, turning him into a wraith among the trees. They spread into a wide formation, keeping twenty feet of distance between each man, and advanced southeast, toward Graystonia.

Hours passed. The forest pressed in around them, thick with silence and tension, but no more Bartorians appeared. Finally, Theron signaled the return. It was nearly midnight when they stepped back into the torch-lit village.

He found Queen Okteria near a small fire, warriors clustered around her in quiet conversation. She turned as he approached.

"We swept to the territory line and back," he reported. "No signs of more enemies. Kain might be facing resistance, though."

"He'll manage," she replied, already turning her focus back to the flames, no doubt plotting her next move. Theron held back a frown. Kain was capable, yes, but unpredictable. Chaos seemed woven into his footsteps, as if it was born to follow him.

"Get some sleep," Okteria said, waving him off. "We'll wait for Kain's report."

Theron didn't need to be told twice. His feet carried him swiftly toward his hut, weaving through fires and warriors still abuzz with the night's events. Tankards clanked. Stories grew wilder. He passed Sparrow leaning against his hut, watching the tree line with silent vigilance. Theron gave him a nod and stepped inside.

Layla sat up the moment he entered. Her wide eyes scanned him, *checking for injury?* Relief quickly washed over her as her features softened.

"Are you okay?" she asked, her voice quiet but full of concern. He nodded, scanning her in return. *No blood. No bruises. Nothing broken.* Only then did his chest unclench.

With a sigh, he dropped to the ground beside the wall and let his head fall back. The tension finally began to unwind from his muscles. After a few moments, he opened his eyes and caught her staring, but not at his face. His lips curved slowly. Her gaze flicked up. She blinked, startled to find him watching as color rushed to her cheeks.

"I... I was staring," she stammered, gulping. "At your sword." His brow quirked in amusement. She instantly panicked. "No! Not *that* sword—your *actual* sword. The one by your hip! I was looking at the craftsmanship... In the moonlight... That's all." Theron chuckled, a low, warm sound rumbling from deep in his chest. A real smile tugged at his lips. For the first time in hours, days even, he felt something close to peace. *She was safe.* That was all that mattered.

Layla.

Wow, do I love his smile. The sound of Theron's laugh lit her chest like a torch. It was deep, rare, and devastatingly warm. Layla couldn't tear her eyes from him as he settled against the side of the hut, looking bone-tired and battle-worn. She'd never been so relieved to see someone before. Just hours ago, she'd been convinced she might never again.

When he'd charged into the hut tonight, her breath had hitched. He was safe. He was alive. A fact that made her chest ache with something dangerously close to... joy.

She lay back on the cot now, exhaling softly. The tension in her muscles melting now that she knew he was all right. But her moment of relief quickly soured as her thoughts turned back to her plan. She was supposed to escape tonight. To run. To save her family. Yet after today's attack, the tribe was more restless than she had ever seen them. From the sounds of it outside the hut, they'd be up all night with sharpened blades and narrowed eyes. There was no chance of slipping away unnoticed.

Frustration and despair coiled tight in her chest, thick and suffocating. Another day lost. Another day her family might suffer. Another day her kingdom was left in ruin. A single tear slid down her cheek, warm and uninvited. She quickly rolled over to face the wall, not wanting Theron to see her cry once again. He already had too many pieces of her she hadn't meant to give. Thankfully, sleep eventually claimed her.

By morning, the camp buzzed with a strange stillness, everyone waiting for the scouting party—waiting for Kain. At the gathering, no new information was shared. *Nothing.* That silence was louder than any declaration of war.

Back at Illyada's, Layla was knuckle-deep in another dismembered squirrel when a sickly, pungent odor crept through the trees. The stench of rot. She turned her head instinctively, face twisting in revulsion.

"They're burning the bodies," Illyada said flatly, not pausing in her cutting. "The Bartorian guards." Layla followed the dark smoke curling into the late morning sky. She didn't feel the need to mourn, to cry.

Let them burn. Those men helped destroy her home, take her people, strip her of everything she loved. They deserved the fire. And part of her—maybe the deepest part—hoped they felt every second of it.

As the sun began its descent, Layla scrubbed her arms furiously in the water bucket Illyada had filled. But no matter how hard she scrubbed, the stench of death clung to her like a second skin. She finally sat back, defeated, her arms red and raw. She reeked of decay and disgust. Her head dropped just as Theron came into view.

A flicker of warmth spread through her chest, immediately dampened by the realization: if she escaped tonight, this might be the last time she saw him. She didn't know how that made her feel. Just that it hurt more than it should. Theron gave his familiar grunt—her silent signal. Illyada handed them both a slab of roasted meat, and they made their way toward the communal tables. The last rays of light filtered through the trees as Layla took her usual place beside Sparrow, eyes low.

Xaden barreled toward them like a charging bear. "Well, I'll be damned! The knife flinging badass herself!" he bellowed, entirely too loud for Layla's liking. She blinked, unsure if he was joking or just drunk.

"Me?" she asked, incredulous.

"Who else?" Xaden gestured to her like she was a prize stallion. "You took down three Bartorian soldiers- with cooking knives! If I hadn't seen it with my own eyes, I'd say someone was full of shit!" Layla chuckled despite herself. Praise for her knife skills wasn't something she was used to, especially not from warriors. Her chest warmed, pride blooming like fire. Xaden shoved a tankard of ale toward her.

"To the woman who saved Illyada's ass—and our tastebuds in the process! Cheers, princess!" Ale sloshed across the table as he raised his tankard. Layla laughed, genuinely this time, and tapped her cup against his. For the first time since her capture, she felt... welcomed. Xaden's humor, Sparrow's occasional smirk, even the banter—it was the closest thing to normal she'd felt in weeks.

By her second, or maybe third ale, Layla found herself gazing at Theron again. He sat across the table, quiet as always. Her eyes traced the ink that curled around his powerful arms. Each line of muscle, each symbol etched into skin, pulled at something primal inside her. Her gaze drifted lower... to those hands. Broad. Calloused. Capable. She imagined them on her and quickly squirmed in her seat. Then she realized—he was watching her, watch him. Over the rim of his tankard, his eyes collided with hers. Not casually. Not politely. But unapologetically devouring her. She froze, caught in the heat of it, pulse thundering as she waited for her him to look away. To stop staring at her like that, but he didn't stop.

"Well?" Xaden's voice snapped her attention away just as Sparrow nudged her with an elbow. Layla blinked and turned, cheeks aflame.

"I—I'm sorry. What was that?" She stammered. Sparrow and Xaden shared a knowing laugh.

"I was asking," Xaden said, leaning forward like a curious drunk child, "where the hell did you learn to throw knives like that?"

Layla chuckled, flustered. "My father. King Aiddeon. He believed the daughter who would one day marry the future king and bear the heir, should know how to defend herself. God forbidden someone ever try to harm me." She gave a knowing glance around the table. The ale giving her the giggles at how ridiculous it was now to say that allowed. "Sir Charles, our Head Guard, helped train me." She finished, a fond smile on her face at he memories of training with her father and Sir Charles.

However, at her words, the mood around the table shifted. Sparrow stiffened. Theron's shoulders tensed. Xaden, oblivious, grinned and clapped the table.

"Well, sounds like dear old dad did something right. Remind me never to stand across from you at the practice ring." Layla laughed softly, grateful for the recovery as she noticed the change in everyone else's demeanor. Her eyes hesitantly drifted back to Theron, just in time to catch him rising to his feet. Their eyes connected again. He tipped his head ever so slightly toward the path. An invitation to leave with him. Her heart pounded. She didn't know why she felt this was something special, intimate even. When he escorted her everywhere most days these feelings made no sense. Yet she couldn't help the nervous knot forming in her stomach.

She turned to Sparrow and Xaden. "Thank you for the laughs, Xaden. Goodnight."

As she stood, Xaden called out, "Goodnight, princess. I plan to keep my heart intact by staying on your good side!" He waggled a small dagger in the air, and Layla burst into laughter before following Theron into the trees.

The tankards of ale still buzzed faintly in her veins but the soft breeze was clearing her foggy brain slightly. Her thoughts and emotions

were everywhere as they walked, but one question kept trumping everything else on her mind in this hazed state.

"Theron..." Layla's voice was tentative as they walked side by side,
the moonlight speckling the forest floor in ghostly patches. Her hands
aimlessly fidgeting before her. "Is there any way I could... wash?"

Silence.

She winced, instantly regretting it. *Of course not. What prisoner
asked for luxuries? What captive deserved comfort?* She bit her lip and
kept her gaze fixed on the dirt path beneath her boots.

"I know I probably can't," she added, her voice barely above a
whisper. "It's just... I'm disgusting. I can't even stand myself anymore."

Still, no answer.

Her chest tightened, the liquid courage doing nothing to dull the
humiliation surging through her. She risked a glance up—only to find
him no longer walking. He had stopped in the path, his broad back
rigid. The silver light kissed the sharp angles of his shoulders, the coiled
tension in his frame. Slowly, he turned his head, casting her a look over
one shoulder. His expression was unreadable, his eyes shrouded in the
dark—but something flickered there. As if he was weighing something.
Something he wasn't sure he had the right to give. Something she wasn't
sure she had the right to ask.

"Come," he said simply, then turned off the path and headed into
the trees. Confused but hopeful, Layla followed, quickening her pace
to stay close. The forest thickened around them, cloaked in dusk, her
heart thudding louder with every step. He wouldn't hurt her. *Would he?
Surely not. ...Right?* Still, a voice in the back of her head whispered: *Dirty
is at least still alive...* She kept walking anyway.

Eventually Theron slowed, and Layla's breath caught as she glanced past his shoulder, not at all knowing what to expect in this part of the forest. Well away from the main hub of their village. She was met with a vision pulled from a forgotten dream. A crystal-clear pond stretched before her, rimmed in silver by the rising moonlight. Fireflies danced over the water's shimmering surface like drifting stars, casting glimmers of magic into the night. A soft gasp escaped her lips. It was stunning. Ethereal. The kind of place songs were written about. Had she stumbled upon this pond as a free woman, she might have considered it her favorite place in all the kingdoms. But she wasn't free. And that truth twisted like a knife in her gut.

Theron stopped ten paces from the edge and turned toward her, his expression still so unreadable, especially in the dark. "Don't try anything," he said, voice rough but calm. Then, without another word, he turned his back to her. A silent offering of privacy.

For a heartbeat, Layla stilled. The pond beckoned her, but it was the gesture that sent a strange warmth trickling through her chest. She rose on her toes and leaned toward him. "Thank you," she whispered, soft as the breeze, then padded to the edge of the water.

She kicked off her boots and reached for the laces of her leather top. The material fell to the ground with a soft thud. Her skirt followed, and then she stood bare beneath the moon. She paused, casting one last glance over her shoulder. Theron hadn't moved. A mix of relief and disappointment fluttered in her chest. Part of her wanted him to look. Part of her wanted to want him to. She quickly blamed those thoughts on the ale and slipped into the water with a hiss of breath.

It was cool, but not cold—just enough to send a shiver up her spine as she submerged, scrubbing frantically at her hair and skin. She worked the blood, ash, and grime from her limbs as though she could also strip away the weight of the last few days. When she emerged, breathless and cleaner than she'd been in a week, she felt like herself again... almost.

The air bit at her damp skin as she stepped out. Water traced rivulets down her curves as she moved. Layla swiftly gathered her clothes and slipped into her skirt. She reached for the thick leather top and hesitated. There was no way she could lace it herself...*well probably not....* Clutching it tightly to her chest, she turned toward Theron. He still faced the trees, motionless as a statue.

"Um... Theron?" She called, her voice soft and apprehensive. He shifted, glancing over his shoulder just barely, clearly trying to respect her privacy. "I—could you help me again?" She asked, holding up the top so he'd understand. Theron turned fully now. His eyes dropped to the garment pressed against her chest as his jaw tensed. The muscle on the side of his neck flexed as his gaze slowly dragged upward to meet hers.

Gone was the familiar glacial blue in his eyes. What looked back at her now was molten and dark, burning with something far more dangerous than annoyance or irritation. He didn't speak. Instead, he moved toward her, slow and deliberate. Layla's breath caught as she turned to offer him her back. Her heart pounded as she felt the heat of him at her spine in and instant. Then—his touch. Barely there, like a whisper of wind against her skin. His fingers brushed her neck as he swept her wet hair forward over her shoulder, letting it fall in damp waves across her chest. Goosebumps erupted down her arms. He didn't say a word as he laced the top, but she could feel every measured breath he took behind her. The leather tightened slowly, cinching against her breasts, each pull of the cord making her gasp softly. His hands grazed her shoulders, feather-light but searing. Her nipples tightened against the cold leather.

Theron's breath brushed her ear. "Turn," he murmured.

Layla did—slowly. Her chest brushed against his abs as she faced him, forced to look up to meet his gaze. He was so close, towering over her. Every part of her buzzed with awareness of him. He reached for the warrior strap, hands skimming up her arms until they hovered near her throat. Her heart skipped in response.

Theron lifted her heavy hair and let it fall again in a single sensual motion, fingertips dragging down her spine as he fastened the strap in place. Every inch of her skin burned with his nearness. And then she felt it. His hardness—pressed against her stomach. Bold. Unapologetic. Layla's breath hitched. Her thighs squeezed together instinctively, trying to quiet the pulse of aching want that bloomed deep inside her.

Theron's hands slid down, brushing her bare sides—touching the soft skin between her skirt and the cinched leather top. His calloused thumbs rested against her hips as he looked down at her like he was drowning in her. Everything inside her said *yes*. She parted her lips and nodded—wordlessly begging him to kiss her. To end the agony of this tension they kept pretending didn't exist.

Then— "Ahem." The sound shattered the moment like a stone through glass. Layla and Theron snapped their heads toward the voice. Kain. *Of course it was Kain.* He stood a few yards away, arms crossed, a smug smirk tugging at his mouth.

"Am I interrupting something?" he asked, absolutely delighted to be doing just that. Theron's hands fell from her hips as he stepped back, his jaw tight with frustration. Layla was still breathless, her body burning and unsatisfied.

"Mother sent me to find you," Kain continued, keeping his eyes on Theron. "She says we've got a lot to discuss."

Layla watched Theron nod curtly. He strode past her, the fire in his eyes shuttered. Kain glanced over his shoulder and caught her stare—then winked. Layla's cheeks flushed, not with embarrassment this time, but frustration. She followed them in silence, the ache between her thighs a cruel reminder of what *almost* happened. And what, gods help her, she was starting to *want* to happen far too badly.

WITH BLESSINGS, WE RISE;
WITH STRENGTH, WE CONQUER

By sacred order of the crown, honor is not a possession, but a legacy. It is earned through duty, upheld though loyalty, and passed from blood to blood. Let it be known: the child shall rise by the grace of their family's devotion, or fall beneath the shadow of its disgrace. In the service of the realm, a name endures. In betrayal, it is broken.

-BY DECREE OF THE CROWN OF GRAYSTONIA

Chapter Twelve

Theron.

Theron begrudgingly followed Kain back toward the village, Layla trailing just behind them. Every step was a cruel reminder of how close he'd come to losing himself in her—how her soft breath, her parted lips, the way she'd looked up at him with absolute surrender... Gods, he'd been seconds from kissing her. From pressing her against a tree and letting go of every rule, every shred of duty. And then Kain. *Damned Kain.* His groin still ached from the denial, a dull throb that mocked his restraint, but the moment was gone. The mission ahead demanded his full attention now. War didn't wait for lust. Or love.

Sparrow waited near the outskirts of the camp, arms crossed, his posture relaxed but Theron could see it in his eyes. He knew. Kain must have run into him first and gleaned the story. Of course Sparrow would've known Theron would want to hear from Kain the moment he returned. Still. *Couldn't the bastard have taken just a little longer?*

Theron cleared his throat and tipped his head toward Sparrow as he passed, a silent order. *Stay with her. Don't let her out of your sight.* Sparrow nodded without a word and moved toward Layla. Theron didn't dare look back at her. He couldn't. Not now. One more second of her gaze and he might've turned around, dragged her back into the trees, and kissed her like he'd been dying to since the first time she screamed at him. *Focus.*

He walked beside Kain in silence, tension thick between them. He could feel his brother watching him—smirking. Probably thinking the whole thing was hilarious. Theron didn't return the glance. Didn't need to. He could hear Kain's barely-contained laughter rumbling away. *Fucker.*

They promptly reached Queen Okteria's hut. She stood just outside it like a carved statue of war, flanked by the warriors who had returned with Kain. Her eyes were sharp, her body still, and Theron could feel her impatience radiating off her like heat from a forge.

"Speak," she commanded the moment they were within earshot.

Kain stepped forward, the air seeming to thicken with the weight of his arrogance. Theron stood beside him, shoulders squared, curious to hear exactly what the state of Graystonia was when Kain found it, and more importantly, how he left it.

"Well," Kain began. "Good news and bad news. The Bartorians still only hold the castle. The Graystonian army is rallying around the capitol. From what we gathered, most of their guards were outside the gates when the Bartorians launched a surprise attack during some royal event.

The entire thing reeks of betrayal—someone on the inside let them in." Kain shook his head in clear disproval before continuing. "They want the soldiers and the people to surrender. With the Graystonian king dead, and no male heirs, they're trying to claim the throne."

Queen Okteria scoffed and flicked her hand. "Foolish men, thinking a woman can't rule a kingdom." Theron glanced at her but said nothing. His thoughts had already turned to Layla but then he realized....

"How did you get all this information?" he asked Kain, already dreading the answer.

Kain smirked as a damned mischievous twinkle appeared in his eyes. "One of the Bartorian guards was... very forthcoming."

Theron's jaw clenched. "For fucks sake, Kain."

"What?" Kain shrugged. "He talked, didn't he?"

Theron stepped toward him, voice like thunder. "You tortured him?"

"Enough," Queen Okteria cut in. "We need to know why they attacked us. If their only goal is to seize Graystonia, why come here?"

Kain opened his mouth, confusion written all over his face, but Xaden spoke first. Stepping from the shadows near the fire to answer Kain's unspoken question. "They attacked yesterday. Seven of them, near Illyada's hut. They're all dead now—mostly thanks to Illyada... and Layla."

Theron's head snapped toward him. "Layla?"

Xaden blinked then chuckled. "You really weren't listening at dinner, were you?" Theron's fingers curled into a tight fist as he impatiently ignored the gentle taunt.

"I already told everyone," Xaden continued, talking directly to Theron more so than Kain at this point. "Layla nailed one of them from forty yards with a kitchen knife. *In the eye.* Dropped him like a stone. She got two more before I got there. Poor bastards came hunting a princess—got a dagger-slinging badass instead."

Theron stared down at the ground, trying to make sense of it. *Layla—fighting like that? Killing like that?* It didn't match the image he carried in his mind. The girl he protected. The one who tensed when he raised his voice and clutched his shirt when fear overtook her. The one he'd watched sleep, chest rising in fragile rhythm, as if a breath too loud might shatter her.

And yet...

She had killed Tynan. He couldn't deny that. But if he was honest, he'd chalked it up to panic and luck—a desperate swing in the dark, not skill. She wasn't trained. She wasn't hardened. She was... Layla. A girl who needed protection. At least, that's what he kept telling himself. But now, that story was starting to crack. And he wasn't sure whether the shift unsettled him—or intrigued him.

"She might've been their target," Kain added. "If they were trying to wipe out the entire royal line, they would've come for her next."

Theron's thoughts came back to the present as he noticed Queen Okteria's eyes flare at Kain's thoughts. "Perhaps that's true," she said coolly. "But their reasoning no longer matters. By stepping onto my lands and attacking my people, they made us look weak. Unprepared. That is unacceptable." Her voice sharpened. "I assume a substantial force remains stationed in the Graystonian castle to hold it?" She turned to Kain. He gave a single nod, confirming her thoughts.

"Then we strike there. Not to save Graystonia—but to gut Bartoria's plans from the inside. We'll cut their force down where it's entrenched and send a message to the entire realm: I don't care what crown they serve—trespassers will bleed for it. Let them cower behind their northern walls where they belong."

She paused, letting the weight of her words settle like a blade pressed to a throat. "We leave in two days." She promptly turned and disappeared into her hut without another word.

Theron stayed where he was, arms loose at his sides, thoughts churning. It was happening. Real war. Not a raid. Not a border skirmish. A full siege—the kind that could become the catalyst for the very conflict they'd long feared would engulf the continent.

And the last time an enemy had dared cross into their territory, it hadn't been met with mounds of corpses or scorched earth. His mother had chosen restraint—vengeance, yes, but tempered by politics over war. He knew she'd regretted it ever since. Bartorian blood had been owed for a long, long time.

His feet carried him down the familiar path toward his hut, but his mind—his heart—was somewhere else entirely. Five years hadn't dulled the memory of that blood-soaked day by the river. It still lived beneath his skin, sharp and raw. Time hadn't softened the grief—it had only taught him how to bury it deeper.

He had been walking beside his father—King Aric of the Antonin. A warrior. A legend. A man carved from stone and shadow. Aric had ruled their people for as long as Theron could remember, with fire in his chest and justice in his blood. His sword had never left his side, as if even the gods feared what he might do with it.

Theron had idolized him, trained under him, bled beside him. He had spent his entire life studying the man's every move—learning, emulating, striving to become the warrior and leader Aric was. He never imagined that day would be the last.

They were returning from a northern scouting mission, just the two of them and a small escort, crossing the Thornveil Run River. The trees had thinned into jagged rock, the land falling away into a sheer cliff. The river below had been high—thundering, wild, hungry. It masked the danger that was unknowingly all around them. The snap of a branch. The whisper of boots in the brush. Then the first arrow struck the warrior closest to Theron, burying itself in his throat as chaos erupted.

Lumiren soldiers, cowards, swarmed like vermin from the undergrowth. Interlopers crossing Antonin land under Bartorian sanction—or so they would later claim. What followed was a storm.

Theron's blade found flesh again and again. His instincts took over, honed and lethal. Blood sprayed his face. His sword arm moved faster than thought, every strike a blur of muscle and steel. A Lumiren lunged, screaming. Theron sidestepped, drove his blade into the man's ribs, and shoved him off the cliff's edge—already turning, already hunting for the next threat.

Then he saw him.

Aric stood just twenty feet away, felling enemies like a god of war—until a flash of steel cut into his leg, dropping him to one knee. It happened too fast. Another soldier surged forward and drove a blade into Aric's chest. Deep. So deep. Blood sprayed from his mouth as his body convulsed.

Theron had roared, sprinting forward as if sheer will could stop time. But the sword twisted, and Aric crumpled, the strength leaving him all at once. The Lumiren turned, smirking—Theron's blade took his head clean off. The body fell beside the king it had slain, but vengeance tasted like ash. Theron collapsed beside his father, hands pressing into cooling flesh, pleading—begging—for life to return. It never did.

The battle ended minutes later. They won—if it could be called that. Theron hadn't celebrated. Hadn't even stood. He just knelt there as the river roared on.

When they returned home, Queen Okteria wasted no time. She demanded blood. A debt owed. Kain delivered it himself—an arrow straight through the heart of the Lumiren king's eldest son. A message that echoed across kingdoms. The Lumiren king had wept. Pleaded ignorance. Swore it would never happen again. Lies. Every word. Theron still remembered the cold calculation behind his eyes.

Next came Bartoria. Okteria and Theron stood before their high council, demanding answers. A Lumiren sword had pierced her husband's heart—by way of Bartorian lands. And still they denied. No orders. No permissions. No alliance. No fault. The queen left with her chin high and her wrath buried—but never silenced.

Theron had known what she was doing. She was choosing politics. Choosing to mourn with her sons rather than force the tribe into open war with the North. The death of the Lumiren prince was a message—brutal and final. A blood-for-blood sacrifice meant to satisfy justice. It was a hard choice. The wise one. But it wasn't the typical Antonin one. And yet... they accepted it. They accepted her.

"We have the blood of a prince," she told Theron afterward, her voice forged from ice and iron. "Let it be enough. For now." He hadn't argued. He hadn't had the strength. He was supposed to become king that week. The tribe had waited. The council had prepared. But Theron refused.

"I am a weapon," he told her. "Let me be one." And Okteria, burning with grief, had agreed. She would rule and he would remain what he had always been—a shield for his people. A sword for their enemies. But deep down, Theron had known the truth. He had never felt worthy to rule. Not like his father. And wasn't sure if he ever would.

And now, with war again looming, Theron couldn't stop the ache in his chest. He missed him. Gods, he missed him. His voice, his laughter, the way he never wavered even in the face of death. Theron had never needed his counsel more than he did now.

He stopped just outside his hut, staring at the hide that covered the entrance. He could still feel the weight of it all pressing against his ribs. And now Layla. Her father—the king of Graystonia—was dead. Just like his own father. Her home overrun. Her family likely gone. Her pain... it would mirror his. He hadn't even told her yet. The woman he couldn't stop thinking about. The one whose body had nearly pressed into his just hours before. Whose scent still lingered on his skin. Who had apparently thrown knives like a goddess of war and then whispered his name like a prayer.

His hand clenched the edge of the hide, fingers digging into the leather. His heart beat like a drum inside his chest, a sound only he could hear. And for the first time since meeting her, he was afraid to see her eyes because he didn't want to be the one to shatter them.

Theron ducked beneath the hide and stepped into the quiet of his hut. The flickering moonlight cast soft silhouettes along the walls, and there—sitting upright on the cot—was Layla. Her eyes snapped to his the moment he entered, filled with a desperation that pierced straight through him.

"What did you find out about my family?" she asked, her voice already trembling. "Are my people okay? Please... please tell me." Theron froze mid-step. His gaze dropped to the dirt floor between them, jaw tight, chest constricting with the weight of the truth he couldn't speak. Orders were orders, no information outside the command circle, not until the official gathering. *No exceptions.* He had abided by that law his entire life. But this was Layla. And his silence was a betrayal all the same.

Her breath hitched. "No... no, no. Don't do that. How many people have we lost? Is it my sisters? My mother?!" Her voice climbed, panic lacing every word. She stood now, eyes wide with raw fear. Theron couldn't bring himself to lift his head. Couldn't find the words. Every instinct in him screamed to hold her, to fix this, but how did you fix the destruction of a world?

Then her voice cracked, nearly splintered. "It's my father, isn't it?!" Her cry hit him like a blade to the gut.

Slowly, he lifted his gaze. She deserved that much. The moment his eyes met hers, whatever fragile hope she had been clinging to, splintered, She saw it all in his face—grief, sorrow, guilt. He didn't need to speak, the truth was etched into the very core of his eyes...And then, she broke.

Her legs gave out, and Theron surged forward, catching her just before she hit the ground. She sobbed, loud and unrestrained, as her fists curled against his chest. He lowered them both to the floor and wrapped his arms tightly around her, cradling her like she was made of glass. Her cries echoed through the small space, ripping him apart one piece at a time. Theron pressed his cheek to the crown of her head, eyes closed, jaw clenched against the powerless anguish building inside him. He couldn't bring her father back. He couldn't silence her sorrow. All he could do was hold her. Shield her. Anchor her. And he did. For as long as she needed.

Minutes bled into an hour before her sobs began to fade, her body growing heavy with exhaustion. When she stirred, gently pulling away, Theron loosened his hold. He didn't want to. Gods, he didn't want to.

But he let her go. She stepped back, wiping her swollen eyes, her face pale and hollow. Theron's heart ached at the sight.

"Sleep," he said softly, his voice barely above a whisper. She hesitated, then gave a tiny nod and curled onto the cot, curling into herself. Her gaze was vacant now as if she had nothing left to feel. Theron turned away, forcing himself to give her space. He tugged off his vest and rolled it beneath his head as he lowered to the ground. The moment his body touched the floor, he felt the overwhelming pull to reach for her again. To hold her. Protect her. Tell her she wasn't alone. His muscles twitched and his fists clenched. He couldn't do that. Not when she needed something no arms could provide. But what he could do—what he *would* do—was make the bastards who caused this to suffer.

He stared up at the ceiling of the hut, rage simmering beneath his skin like a second heartbeat. Death would become his offering. His promise. Every Bartorian responsible would bleed. For Layla. For her family. For the silent scream now carved into her soul. He would become vengeance incarnate. And no one would be left standing. Now to only convince his mother...

Layla.

Layla rolled onto her back, the cot's rough fabric scratching at her damp skin, but she barely felt it. She didn't feel much of anything now. Her chest ached, but even that pain was muted, distant, like it belonged to someone else. *Her father was dead.* The words reverberated through her skull, an endless echo of finality. Her father—the strongest, kindest man she had ever known—was gone. Murdered by Bartorian hands. And she hadn't even been there to fight beside him. To protect him. To say goodbye.

Tears threatened again, but her eyes were dry. She had cried herself empty. Instead, all that remained was a strange stillness—numb and cold, like winter settling into her bones. She turned her head and glanced over at Theron, now asleep on the ground beside her, his broad chest rising and falling in steady rhythm. He'd held her through the storm, his silence saying more than words ever could. For that, she was grateful.

He was a good man. And that made everything worse. Her stomach twisted. Because she was going to miss him. Her heart already did. But she couldn't let that stop her. Not now. Not when her people—her sisters, her mother, her kingdom—might still be alive and waiting for her. Depending on her. Layla turned back to face the ceiling. She needed to leave. Tonight.

She counted the seconds. The minutes. Giving Theron time to drift deeper into sleep. She waited until his breathing evened out, slow and steady, the weight of exhaustion finally claiming him. Then she moved. Slowly, quietly, she reached into her waistband and closed her fingers around the small knife hidden there, the hilt warm against her palm. It had been a lifeline once. Now it would be her ticket home. And maybe... Sparrow's death sentence.

The thought made her stomach roll. *Sparrow. Loyal. Quiet. Watchful.* He'd never hurt her. He'd never done anything but follow orders. But if she was going to escape, he was the obstacle between her and the forest. Her hands slightly shook as she tightened her grip on the blade. *Do it for your sisters,* she told herself. *For your mother. For Graystonia.* She sat up, slow and soundless, and glanced toward Theron. Still asleep, *thank Freyric.* She stood from the cot as lightly as she could, every muscle tense as a drawn bowstring. Her bare feet touched the dirt floor without a sound. The knife tight in her quivering fingers. She inched forward, careful to move around Theron's form without waking him. One step. Another. She kept her gaze flicking between the flap of the hut and the warrior lying still at her feet. *Just a few more steps...*

"What are you doing?"

The voice—low, rough, laced with sleep and suspicion—froze her blood. Layla stopped mid-step. Her heart thundered in her chest as she dared a glance down. Theron was no longer asleep. His eyes were open now, dark and locked on hers. No trace of drowsiness remained. Only something sharp. Controlled. Dangerous.

She didn't answer. Couldn't. She gripped the knife tightly, her breath catching as she watched him rise, slow and fluid, like a predator narrowing the distance to its prey. The small space between them vanished in a single step. He stood before her now, towering and unreadable. She couldn't run. Not with him standing in her way.

"I asked. What are you doing?" He was still mostly in shadow, but she could feel the heat of his gaze scorch across her skin. Her mind panicked. She couldn't think, couldn't speak. But then something surfaced. A memory. Her mother's voice, soft but pointed: *"Men are ruled by many things, Layla. But desire is always at the helm. Learn when to use it."* Before she could second-guess herself, her eyes dropped from his eyes to his lips. She rose onto her toes, leaning forward to close the now miniscule space between them, and pressed a kiss to his mouth. A short, startled kiss—but a kiss nonetheless.

She stepped back, heart racing. "I... I'm sorry. I just—sorry." She couldn't meet his eyes now. Her cheeks burned with the shame of her impulsiveness, her recklessness, but before she could turn away, his hands were on her, cupping her face and tilting it up.

His lips met hers again, but it was no tentative graze this time. This was fire. His kiss was demanding, ravenous, like he'd been starved and she was the only remedy. His arms wrapped around her, dragging her flush against his body. She gasped against his mouth as heat flared through her chest, her stomach, her thighs. His presence consumed her. She let go of the blade and it fell unnoticed to the ground. All her plans, thoughts, everything went out of her mind as she was engulfed in this moment with him. She kissed him back with the same desperate hunger, wrapping her arms around his neck as his mouth claimed hers again and again. When his hands slid to her lower back, drawing her hips forward, she felt the undeniable evidence of his desire pressing into her. Her pulse roared in her ears.

His name left her lips in a breathless whisper. In one swift, fluid motion, Theron lifted her, his strength effortless, and her legs wrapped around his waist. He carried her to the cot, his mouth never leaving hers. The moment her back touched the familiar rough fabric, Layla was all sensation. The warmth of his hands roaming every arch and curve of her. The crush of his body above hers. His lips tracing fire down her jaw, to her throat, and lower still. She had never felt so... alive.

His hand slipped under her top, cupping her swollen breast, squeezing gently. The tips of his fingers rough but reverent. She shivered. Her skin tingled in his wake. Each slow movement of his body against hers sent a surge of need pooling low in her belly. She wanted more. Gods, she wanted everything. But—

"Theron... I..." Her voice was barely audible. Still, it was enough. He stilled. Every muscle in his body tensed above hers. She didn't know how to say it. Her breath caught in her throat as embarrassment flooded her. "I... I haven't—" she began, faltering.

But Theron's expression changed. She saw it instantly—the recognition, the shift. He didn't need her to finish. He pulled back. And in the next breath, he was gone.

Layla sat up, stunned. She stared at the empty doorway, the hide swaying behind him. The heat that had consumed her moments before drained from her body like a receding tide. Gone was the fire. Gone was the man who had kissed her like she was the last thing worth fighting for. She looked down at herself—flushed, shaken, half-undressed—and felt the familiar sting of shame crawl up her throat. She pulled her clothes back into place with trembling fingers. The ache in her chest was no longer desire. It was rejection. Confusion. Hurt. *What just happened? Had she pushed him too far? Had he not wanted her anymore after realizing she was inexperienced? Or was it something else entirely?* She curled into herself, pulling her knees to her chest, tears stinging the corners of her eyes once again. This night was supposed to be her escape. Her beginning. Instead, it had turned into another wound she didn't know how to stop bleeding from.

BY FLAME, BY ROOT, BY GOD AND STAR—
CAELERIA SHALL RISE, OR PERISH WHOLE.

THE LAW OF ETERNAL OATHS

An oath sworn beneath open sky of Caeleria
binds soul to bone. Whether whispered in love or
roared in vengeance, a broken oath shall
fracture the spirit beyond healing.

- THE HIGH LAWS OF CAELERIA

Chapter Thirteen

Layla.

Layla woke with a rage so sharp it nearly choked her. It pressed hot and wild in her chest, a tempest of fury at the Bartorians, the Antonin warriors who'd stolen her freedom, and most of all—at Theron. That last one she hated the most, because it shouldn't matter. Not compared to everything else. And yet, her stomach still twisted at the memory of his hands on her skin, the heat in his eyes... the shame that followed.

She had kissed him. She had started it. But he had been the one to push it forward, one step, then another, until she was burning for him. And then, as soon as he realized what she was—what she hadn't done—he'd abandoned her like she'd repulsed him. The humiliation made her skin crawl. Maybe he only wanted women who already knew what to do. Maybe he'd known all along that she was untouched. It wasn't exactly uncommon in Graystonia for noblewomen to wait until marriage unless they were careless or lowborn. She had never been either. But maybe most of all… her rage was grief in disguise.

Her father was gone. She hadn't even gotten to say goodbye. She wanted to scream, to claw her way home. To be with her family. To protect them. To grieve beside them. But she was here. In this cursed village. In Theron's hut. And he hadn't even returned last night. She'd waited. Foolishly. Hoping he'd come back, offer some pathetic attempt at comfort, even an awkward glance or grunted apology. But he hadn't.

Dawn crept in through the slits of the hide, and Layla knew she had to find out what today would bring. The other warriors had returned. She needed to know everything about Graystonia, about the city, about whether her mother and sisters still breathed. She needed a new escape plan.

The hide lifted, and Sparrow's voice cut through her thoughts. "Come on." He didn't look in, didn't offer an explanation, just the command. Layla followed, ignoring the way her stomach clenched.

As she straightened outside, movement from the neighboring hut caught her eye. Kain emerged, casually adjusting himself. She caught his gaze just as a tall, raven-haired woman stepped out after him. Frea. *Of course*. Layla watched with thinly veiled disgust as Frea dragged a hand down Kain's backside before walking off. Kain smirked at Layla, his eyes gleaming with wicked amusement, and winked. Her jaw dropped. *Seriously? He's screwing the same woman who nearly killed me?* She rolled her eyes and turned back to Sparrow, grinding her teeth. The last thing she wanted to think about was Kain having sex. Or Theron not having it with her.

They walked in silence to the morning gathering, her ire ebbing as nerves took its place. Her fists clenched at her sides. She needed answers.

As they neared the gathering, her eyes betrayed her—scanning the crowd until they landed on Theron near the front. Her breath caught before she could stop it. He didn't look at her. Not once. It hit like a punch to the gut. Her cheeks burned, and she hated herself for caring.

"The Bartorians hold the Graystonian castle—but not the city," Theron's voice rang out, calm and cold. "They want the territory. They think by claiming there's no male heir, they can force the army to surrender. But after stepping onto our lands and attacking our people, this is no longer about strategy—it's about message." He looked over the crowd, his gaze resolute. "We strike tomorrow. Not to save Graystonia—but to crush Bartoria's plans where they stand. We take back the castle. We kill every soldier arrogant enough to cross into the South. Let them learn what happens when you provoke the Antonin. We do not forgive. We do not forget. Prepare yourselves. Tomorrow, we march to war."

Layla's mouth fell open. *They hadn't taken the city? The people... her mother, her sisters—could still be fighting. Could still be alive.* She moved without thinking. She shoved forward, weaving through the crowd, momentarily forgetting her embarrassment, her fury, everything but the desperate, blinding hope that surged in her.

"Take me with you!" she shouted. Theron didn't even glance at her. The only indication that he had even heard her was that his jaw flexed and he brushed her off with a grunt. Like she was nothing more than a damned gnat to him now.

"No! You will listen to me!" she snapped, grabbing his arm. "I know secret tunnels. Ways into the castle that no one else does. I can get you inside. But only if you take me." She stood tall, defiant, daring him to deny her. He turned at last. His eyes met hers. Something flickered there—something unreadable—but it was gone before she could grasp it.

"Let's take the little dove," Kain interjected, appearing seemingly out of nowhere with a lazy grin of his. Casually draping an arm around Theron's shoulder like they were all friends and weren't talking about the future of her kingdom. "If she dies, I call that a win-win." Theron's entire body went taut. His fists clenched, jaw rigid, eyes narrowing like he was holding back the urge to murder Kain on the spot.

"No," Theron growled, dark and low.

But then Queen Okteria stepped forward, her gaze calm and calculated. "We take her. Use her knowledge. And if she dies... make sure she has been of value to us first." Just like that, her life was no longer her own. *Again.*

"Don't worry, brother," Kain said as he turned to go. "I'll train our little dove today so she has a fighting chance... Not like I need the time to practice anyways."

"You're not touching her," Theron snapped, pushing Kain off him, who only laughed and walked off.

Layla's heart pounded. She turned back to Theron, her voice calm despite the storm inside her. "I can fight. I can help. Even if I have to do it beside him." She waved in the direction of Kain's back as he continued to walk away.

Theron exhaled through his nose, slow and sharp. "You're coming," he muttered. "But you will not be near the battle. That's final." He turned on his heel before she could respond and began striding toward Illyada's hut without so much as a second glance. Layla scoffed. Indignation surged through her, sharp and cold. *What was his problem? Did he hate her now? Because she dared to want him? Because she wasn't seasoned in matters of intimacy? Because she wasn't like the presumable many women before her?* She wanted to scream at him. Ask if he thought she was disgusting. If her inexperience was that revolting. But she didn't. She bit her tongue so hard it nearly bled. She would see her family again. That's what mattered.

She followed Theron and Sparrow to Illyada's hut, watching as Theron gave a curt nod to Illyada and immediately walked off with Sparrow like she wasn't even there. Not a glance. Not a word. Layla clenched her jaw. Her chest was too tight to breathe. *Fine. Two could play that game.* She stomped over to the workbench, snatched up a rabbit, and began gutting it with far more aggression than necessary. She didn't care that blood spattered her hands. She welcomed it. Let Theron play the cold-hearted warrior. She was a fucking queen's daughter. And tomorrow, she'd prove it.

"Jeez, what did that poor rabbit ever do to you?"

The familiar velvet voice pulled Layla out of her thoughts like a splash of cold water. She didn't look up. She didn't want to. Not now. Not when her fury had nowhere to go but the unfortunate rabbit guts beneath her bloodied hands. She knew that voice. *Kain.* Of course it would be him. Freyric thought he was being funny today by sending Kain to her while she was in this mood. Layla focused harder on her work, slicing into the sinew as if ignoring him might make him disappear.

"Oh fine. Ignore me," he sighed dramatically. "Then I won't spar with you today to prepare for battle. I'm sure you already know everything there is to know about fighting." Layla's eyes snapped up to meet his, and there it was—his ever-present smirk, cocky and knowing.

"Well, come on then... or do you want to keep torturing that poor bunny?" He arched a brow and gestured to the butchered remains in front of her. Layla turned instinctively to Illyada, who gave a small nod of approval. Without another word, Layla tossed her blade on the table and rounded it quickly, stopping just short of Kain's side. A nervous but excited energy starting to radiate through her now. *She was going to get to train.*

"Come on, Little Dove," he said with a grin as he draped an arm over her shoulders. Layla immediately ducked out of his grasp and sent him a glare sharp enough to draw blood. He chuckled, unfazed. "This is going to be fun."

As they neared the Circle, several warriors were already at work, swords clanging against one another, the air thick with heat and grit. Layla's shoulders relaxed slightly when she noticed Theron was nowhere in sight. *Good.* She wasn't ready to see him. Not after how he was acting.

"Let's see how handy you are with a *sword*," Kain said, stretching out the word with an eyebrow wiggle that made her roll her eyes.

"You're disgusting."

"Thank you," he said cheerfully and tossed her a blade.

Layla caught it, though the weight threw her off balance for a second. "Uh, I don't think I'm supposed to have one of these." She stated as she nervously looked around at the other warriors. Expecting someone to come stomping over and take it from her.

"No sword, no more Little Dove." He took a fighting stance, ignoring her hesitation. Clearly unconcerned that he just handed their captive a true weapon.

"And stop calling me that," she grumbled, gripping the sword and squaring her stance. The name made her feel small, fragile—neither of which she had the luxury of being anymore.

Kain lunged, fast and without warning. Layla dodged just in time, the steel singing as it missed her by inches. She stumbled, her pulse spiking. He came at her again, fast and relentless. He didn't ease up. Not even a little. On the third strike, she tripped and hit the dirt hard, the wind knocked from her lungs.

"I'm not Theron," Kain said, towering over her. "I'm not going to baby you. If this is all you've got, you're going to be a liability tomorrow." Layla pushed to her feet and lunged at him, anger burning away the last of her hesitation. She went on the offensive, striking again and again, but he dodged each blow with infuriating ease. Her arms ached. Sweat soaked her back. But she didn't stop.

"You're trying to wound me," Kain said, more serious now. "But you're not trying to kill me." Layla froze.

"You have to kill, Dove. If you hesitate in battle, you die. Or worse—your family does. Do you understand that?" His tone wasn't mocking now. It was something else. Something earnest. She looked into his eyes and nodded once. "Good," he said. "Then stop wasting time. Kill me."

They trained for hours. He barked corrections, gave her advice, and pushed her harder than anyone ever had. By the time she nearly dropped the sword from her sweat-slick hands, he raised a hand and called for a pause. He grabbed two water pouches from nearby, tossing her one. She downed it gratefully, her chest rising and falling like a battle drum. It was the first time in days she felt truly strong.

"Sword," he said, holding out his hand. Reluctantly, she handed it over.

"Oh... are we done already?" She asked, surprised to hear the faint disappointment in her own voice. He didn't answer right away. He turned from her, sliding off his leathers and sweat drenched tunic The muscles in his back rippled with the motion, and despite herself, her eyes traced the beads of sweat rolling down the ridges of his torso. Her cheeks flushed hot, and she quickly looked away. But when she glanced back, he was already looking at her. That smirk again ever present. *Damn it.* She braced herself for the taunt, but he only shook his head and laughed.

"If you want to be done, fine," he said. "But I figured we could see how skilled you were with your hands."

Layla groaned at the innuendo. "You're unbearable." But she dropped into a stance anyway as he laughed.

They went at it again, bare-handed this time. She didn't land a single blow. He was faster, stronger, more experienced. When he finally waved her off, she was panting and sore.

"Don't underestimate your abilities or overestimate your strength. That's how you get killed," Kain said, the usual smugness softened by sincerity. "You're too weak to wield a sword and don't have the skills yet to properly win in hand to hand....But a knife? That you can wield. I've seen it." Before she could respond, he handed her a dagger.

She took a step forward, reaching for the offered dagger, eyes fixed on his. Then, with a flick of her wrist, she grabbed a second dagger from his thigh and pressed it to his abdomen, just hard enough to nick the skin. His eyes widened, then narrowed with what could only be described as pride as a real smile spread across his face. A quiet moment passed between them. The kind that hummed with respect and something else—something unspoken.

"What the fuck is this?!"

Layla jumped. Theron's voice tore through the air like thunder. She turned and saw him stalking toward them, rage carved into every line of his face. Only then did she realize just how close she was to Kain—still holding the blades, his sweat still glistening between them. She took a large step back. Kain remained unfazed, still looking down at her, his familiar smirk back in full force.

"Thank you, Kain," Layla said softly. "I mean it." He winked, then bent to grab his leathers, tunic, and sword before starting to walk away.

Kain!" she called out, holding up the daggers. "Here—"

He glanced over his shoulder. "Keep them, Dove. You'll need 'em." And with that, he walked away, leaving her standing there between fury and fire. Between two very different men.

Theron.

Theron hadn't seen Layla all morning, and that absence clawed at him more than he cared to admit. The air was thick with the storm rolling in, and a strange pressure had been building in his chest since dawn. He'd spent the better part of the morning sharpening blades and checking supplies, anything to distract himself from the fact that he was still horrified with himself for pushing her too far last night.

But when he finally spotted her in the Circle, locked in heated sparring with Kain, his blood ignited.

He watched as she lunged toward his brother, a fierce determination in her stance that Theron hadn't seen before. She was drenched in sweat, hair clinging to her temples, and yet she moved with silent precision, swift and striking. Theron's eyes narrowed. *What the hell is Kain thinking*? She's not supposed to be out here.

Theron's nostrils flared as he stalked toward them, a violent tension tightening beneath his skin—not just at Kain, but at himself for not anticipating something like this. Kain never followed rules, never cared who he dragged into his chaos. And Layla? She should've known better. She was too valuable, too untrained, too... fragile.

But as he closed in, the clouds tore open, spilling a torrent like nature's own outcry. Rain came down in thick sheets, soaking him to the bone within seconds. He didn't care. He no longer focused on his disdain for his brother but on the woman who was now clearly pissed at him just feet away. He rubbed the back of his neck with one hand, taking a deep breath as he closed the distance between them. She lifted her chin as he neared, but didn't say a word. But that boiling anger seemed about to burst from within her.

"I just don't want you getting hurt any more than you already have." He fumbled with the words, but they were the truth. He only just wanted her safe.

"He was helping me. Teaching me. Why the hell is that a problem!?" She hissed. Rage seeping out with every word.

"You don't need it! I will keep you safe!" Theron responded. Layla's face shifted from indignation to bewilderment. Then he noticed her shoulders soften and her eyes shut for a moment before kindness met his gaze.

"I appreciate you wanting to keep me safe. But I can defend myself. Kain really gave me some great pointers with a sword..." Theron started shaking his head and cut her off before she could continue. He didn't need Kain getting her killed.

"A sword is awkward in your hands. You're too small. You will lose balance too easily...You will die." Theron pleaded with her. Wanting her to hear him. He didn't want her to go tomorrow with some obscene thoughts Kain had planted and get killed in battle because of it. He wanted to protect her.

As the rain came pouring down, he could still see the deep hatred back in her eyes bearing up at him. Not at all what he hoped. Then Layla truly surprised him.

She whipped out one of the small knives he had seen Kain just give her. Confusion danced across Theron's face as she threw the dagger at a nearby tree—*no, not at the tree*—a squirrel darting up its bark. The blade found its mark mid-climb. The animal dropped with a thud. Theron froze. *What in the name of the gods...*

He looked back at her—chest rising furiously, drenched in rain, eyes blazing with challenge. She held his gaze, her body shivering, not with fear or cold, but with what he would guess was *adrenaline? Anger? Pride maybe?*

"A sword is not the only way to win a fight," she said, voice cutting through the storm like lightning itself. Then she turned and stomped away.

He didn't even realize his mouth had fallen open. It snapped shut the moment he regained sense of where he was. Without a second thought, he took off after her.

She charged into the hut just ahead of him, shoving the hide flap aside with more force than necessary. He followed a step behind, ducking in after her. As his eyes momentarily adjusted, then he took in the sight before him-Rain clung to her like a second skin, her soaked body trailing water across the packed dirt floor. By the time he stepped inside, she was already pacing—back and forth, arms wrapped tightly around herself, as if trying to contain the fury and heartbreak threatening to rip her apart. Her hair stuck to her face in damp strands, her breaths short and sharp.

"Why did you kiss me like that if you cared that I hadn't..." she snapped, throwing her arm toward the cot. Her voice cracked as her eyes blazed.

Theron halted. Confusion spread across his face as he tried to piece together what she was saying. "Hadn't what?"

Layla sucked in a sharp breath and shook her head, looking away before she collapsed onto the cot. For a moment, she said nothing. Then her voice came again, quieter this time. "You had to have known I didn't have any... experience."

Realization struck like a fist to the chest. *She thought he'd rejected her because she was untouched? Because she wasn't experienced?* His gut twisted. Gods, he'd been such a fool. He crossed the room in two strides, slowly lowering himself to his knees in front of her. His hand came up instinctively, brushing the soaked strands of hair from her cheek. She tensed but didn't pull away.

"Layla..." he said her name like a vow.

"I wanted to," she whispered. "With you."

Theron's entire world stopped at hearing those words from her lips. Fire shot through his veins. His cock hardened instantly, pressing painfully against his pants. And yet, he didn't move. He waited—just long enough for her eyes to flicker to his lips. Then he surged forward, claiming her mouth like he was drowning and she was air. She gasped against him, her hands flying to his hair, pulling him closer. Their kiss was desperate, aching, needy. His hand slid down to the strap of her warrior top, quickly pulling at the cords. Then with a firm tug, it loosened. Tossing it to the ground in a glorious heap.

When he pulled away, it was only long enough to see the rise and fall of her bare chest. Her nipples beautifully perked and taunting, he exhaled a hungry curse under his breath at the sight. Theron leaned down and drew one into his mouth, letting his tongue circle and suck until her moan filled the hut. It was the most erotic sound he'd ever heard. He groaned, the low and involuntary sound escaping from his throat as one hand sliding down her ribs to the waistband of her skirt. Layla arched into him, silently begging for more. He paused only once, to make sure she was ready.

"I want you," she whispered again, breathless this time. That was all he needed.

He ripped the skirt from her with practiced ease, tossing it to the floor. She was stunning—pink, wet, trembling. Theron knelt between her thighs and kissed slowly down her body, letting his breath tease her still damp skin. When his tongue finally met her center, her back arched violently. She cried out, her fingers knotting in his damp hair as he proceeded to devour her. He didn't stop, didn't slow—not until her entire body locked up and she shattered beneath him.

When she was done shaking, he waited for her to slowly open her eyes before he stood and undressed in silence before her. She watched him, cheeks flushed, eyes wide with awe and want. His cock painfully hard now. Then Theron lowered himself over her again, lining himself at her entrance. He kissed her slowly, reverently, giving her one final chance to change her mind. *She didn't.*

With one slow thrust, he entered her. Her gasp was soft, broken. Theron stilled, letting her adjust. *She was so tight. So warm.* Gods, he could barely hold back. But he knew he needed to. So he began to move in slow, deep strokes. Each time she whispered his name, he pushed deeper, harder, faster. Then her legs hooked around his hips as her nails scraped down his back. He was plunging into her now. Wanting to hear every desire filled sound he could ring from her. When she came again, crying out with abandon, Theron followed. Pulling out just in time and groaning through clenched teeth as he spilled onto the ground beside the cot.

He immediately collapsed next to her, chest heaving, limbs shuddering. Layla turned to him, cheeks flushed, eyes glossy. And in that moment, he didn't care about battles, or Kain, or rules. He only knew that he would kill anyone who tried to take this woman from him. His Layla.

"You're mine," he growled, pulling her into his chest and pressing another passionate kiss to her lips.

FROM THE BLOOD OF WARRIORS
OUR STRENGTH FLOWS ETERNAL

The blood of the Drakaren is sacred, born to lead by the gods' degree. But blood alone does not command rule. A leader must serve with strength, wisdom, and loyalty to the tribe. Should they falter, the people may invoke the Rite of Reckoning. In that trial, truth will speak- and only the worthy shall rule. For no name, no blood, stands above the will of the Antonin.

-FROM THE BLOODBOUND OATH OF THE
ANTONIN FLAME

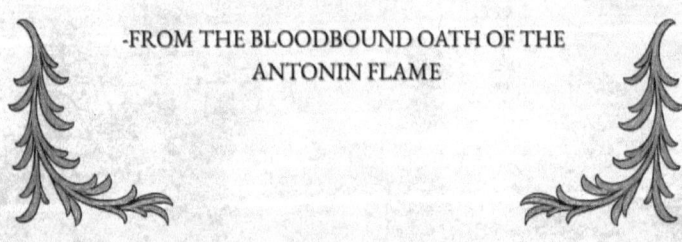

Chapter Fourteen

Layla.

Layla stirred awake, her body a tangle of limbs with Theron's, his bare skin pressed hot and firm against hers. Her cheek rested on his chest, the steady rise and fall of his breathing calming her racing mind. For the first time in what felt like ages, she felt safe.

Her lips curved into a smile before she could stop them. The warmth of his embrace, the scent of rain and leather clinging to him, the protective way his arms curled around her like a shield from the world. Every inch of it filled her with something dangerously close to contentment.

She nestled closer, her fingers grazing across the ridges of his chest. Theron stirred beneath her touch, and as she tilted her head to look up at him as his eyes opened slowly. The moment they found hers, he smiled. Not his usual tight-lipped, brooding smile, but something unguarded and real. Layla's heart squeezed. She leaned up and kissed him gently, just a small press of her lips against his. But when she started to pull away, his arms tightened, pulling her back to him. She laughed softly, the sound muffled against his neck. Theron's smile widened—but then, almost instantly, it was replaced with something deeper. His gaze darkened, molten with hunger.

He leaned in again, kissing her with slow reverence. There was a question in the way his lips moved, and she answered by parting hers. His tongue slid into her mouth, and with it, the embers that still smoldered between them flared into life. His hands drifted from her spine to her hips, gripping her there as he rolled them with ease, guiding her on top of him. Layla's breath caught as her thighs spread across his waist, her body fitting against his like it had been carved for this.

He leaned up, capturing her nipple with his mouth. His tongue circled the tight peak, teasing until she moaned, arching her back in a desperate attempt to get closer. His other hand slid up to cup her other breast, thumb rolling over her other nipple until it too ached for him.

"Gods," she whispered, the word dissolving into a whimper.

Theron's hand slid down her back and gripped her hip firmly. His other hand wrapped around his length, guiding himself to her entrance as his gaze met hers with blistering intensity, pupils blown wide, breath ragged. She bit her bottom lip and nodded. Then he eased into her, slow and unrelenting. Layla gasped, back arching, hands bracing against his chest. She could feel every inch of him stretching her, filling her completely. Her body trembled from the overwhelming pleasure as she sank down fully, letting him bury himself inside her.

Theron's hands anchored her to him, fingers digging into her hips as he began to guide her, helping her roll and rock on top of him. Every movement sent sparks racing through her, heat pooling deep within her core. She moaned freely now, no longer shy about the sounds he pulled from her.

His thumb found the sensitive bundle at the front of her center and began to circle, sending streaks of white-hot lightning through her. Her breath hitched as her hips stuttered. She gripped his shoulders and ground herself down harder against him. Theron's head dropped back against the cot, a guttural groan leaving him as he bucked up into her. Again and again, faster now, harder, deeper. Her vision blurred. Her thighs quivered around him. And when the wave finally crashed over her, she cried out, body convulsing violently with pleasure. He sat up suddenly, wrapping his arms tightly around her and pulling her flush to his chest. She buried her face into his neck as he grunted against her ear, his thrusts growing more erratic, more desperate. He growled her name like a prayer before gently lifting her and setting her down beside him. Then he turned swiftly and spilled himself onto the ground beside the cot, his body shaking from the force of his climax.

They both laid there panting. Now breathless and tangled in sweat. Theron turned to her again, wrapping an arm around her waist and yanking her to him with a possessive sound in his throat. He buried his face in her hair, and she could feel a soft smile curving on his lips as he exhaled deeply. Then he kissed her temple, and for a moment, there was only peace.

Though that peace was quickly interrupted when he whispered into her hair, "We have to go."

Layla nodded, her body still humming, and reluctantly pulled away from the warmth of his chest. She sat up, reaching for her clothes. As she slid her skirt over her hips, she could feel his eyes on her. Her lips twitched with satisfaction. She grabbed her top and pressed it to her chest just as Theron pulled on his pants, the muscles in his arms and abdomen flexing with every move. Layla's couldn't help but let her eyes linger at the amazing sight before her. He noticed. Of course he noticed. That wicked, knowing grin returned to his face, and it made her stomach somersault.

Theron walked over and gently laced her top back up, his fingers grazing her skin with such tenderness that she had to bite the inside of her cheek to keep from melting into him again. When he finished, he grabbed his leather armor, threw it all on quickly, and without another word, led them out into the early morning.

The storm had passed. The world smelled like wet earth and pine. The sky was beginning to lighten, streaks of rose and lavender cutting through the tops of the trees. Sparrow was at his post just outside the hut. The man didn't react when Theron emerged with Layla in tow. He simply fell into step beside them. Layla's thoughts tangled in a restless haze. She didn't know how to act now. She couldn't stop staring at the back of Theron's head, wondering—*Did last night change anything? Did it mean something to him? Or was it... just heat? He had said she was his—but what did that even mean?*

Whatever it was, Layla knew one thing with certainty: she didn't regret giving herself to him. Not for a moment. Because when the time came, when she returned to Graystonia, saved her family, and was bound by duty to marry a man for the good of the kingdom. A man chosen not for love but for alliance—she would still have had this.

She would remember what it felt like to want someone, not because she had to, but because she couldn't not. She would remember what it was like to burn for someone. To feel pleasure and passion so powerful it left her breathless. For once in her life, she hadn't been a princess. She hadn't been a symbol, a pawn, or a future queen. She had just been *Layla*—and she had been wanted.

When they reached the tribe, Layla instinctively halted as Sparrow did. She expected Theron to walk to the front, to give orders, to ignore her like he had so many mornings before. Instead, he turned around and faced her fully. She blinked up at him, confused—just in time for him to lean down and press a soft, unhurried kiss to her lips. The kind of kiss that said *mine* more than any word ever could.

When he pulled away, he murmured so only she could hear, "Stay with Sparrow."

And just like that, he was gone, striding toward his mother without a backward glance. Layla stood frozen, lips parted in shock. The whole Circle had gone quiet. Dozens of warriors had seen. Her face flushed hot, and she turned slowly to Sparrow, who looked at her from the corner of his eye with the smallest hint of a smirk before returning to his stoic silence. Layla stared down at her feet, heart pounding. Apparently... last night had changed *everything*.

Theron.

She is mine. The thought echoed through Theron's chest like a battle drum as he pulled away from kissing Layla—*my Layla*—in front of the entire tribe. He wanted there to be no doubt. No question. No room for misinterpretation. The warriors could gawk, whisper, or question behind their teeth, but they would never lay a hand on her now. Not without consequence.

He knew his mother would be furious. She'd see it as weakness. As irrational. As a disruption of control. But Theron didn't care. He would face her wrath head-on if he had to. For the first time in a long while, his decision hadn't stemmed from strategy or obligation. He wasn't defying orders—he simply wasn't acting because of them.

This wasn't duty. This was want. This was instinct. This was her. And it terrified and thrilled him in equal measure.

As he turned from Layla, her lips still tingling on his, and walked toward the front of the Circle, he ignored the stunned expressions of the warriors. Their silence was almost louder than any insult. But Theron kept his head high, his steps measured. What he had done wasn't a declaration of weakness. It was a warning.

He made his way over to the weapons stockpile, grabbing several small throwing knives and a thin leather belt designed to hold them securely. He needed to be prepared. More knives. More blades. More death tucked into every fold of his clothing. He also grabbed the small clay bowl filled with fresh, earth-rich, dark mud. Warrior paint. Ritual. Camouflage. Identity.

Sparrow, ever dependable, silently peeled away when Theron returned to Layla's side. She was still watching him like he'd sprouted wings and flown.

"What?" he asked, lifting an eyebrow. Her eyes didn't blink. It was like she was trying to solve him. Theron simply held out the belt and knives in both hands, an offering. Layla's mouth parted slightly as she took in the items in his hand, a beat passed before she tentatively accepted them. He watched tentatively as she tied the belt tight around her waist and began sliding each blade into its designated slit. She glanced down at her sides, where the twin knives Kain had given her were already sheathed—everything on her seemingly in its rightful place now. And yet, he caught the faint furrow of her brow.

"I thought you preferred small blades? Is that not right?" Theron said, his voice low and even, but hesitant.

"I do. I just..." She stuttered, blinking at him. "Thank you. This is perfect. Thank you," she said again, more firmly this time. He gave a short nod in response. He didn't understand her confusion, *did she think I wouldn't want her prepared*? She needed to protect herself, even if he'd do everything in his power to keep her from needing to.

But he let the questions fall away as he turned, motioning for her to follow. Not so that she could witness the ritual, he just needed her near for a moment longer. Before duty claimed him. Before war pulled him somewhere she couldn't follow.

He stepped toward the brazier that had been placed at the core of the Circle, its flames already stoked high with sacred ashroot and bone-char. The heat lashed at his skin, but he welcomed it. The altar beside it waited, stone worn smooth by generations of warriors. Upon it lay the ceremonial blade—dark steel veined with etched runes that shimmered faintly as if breathing. This was something they only did before a big battle, never wanting to ask too much of Varyn but knowing the importance of his blessing all the same.

Theron lifted the bowl of mud in his other hand, almost anxious for the next step. Dipping three fingers in and dragging them across his own eyes in broad strokes, then down the length of his unmarked arm. The motion was practiced, grounding. The cool grit of earth steadied his pulse and narrowed his thoughts. The old ways were never for show. They were meant to ready a man—mind, body, blood. But today, the markings carried more than tradition. Today, they would grant him stealth in the shadows... and strike fear into any who met his gaze.

He set the bowl of mud on the altar, fingers still streaked with grit and ash. Then he reached for the ancient blade resting beside it. Theron took it in his palm and with steady purpose, he drew the blade. The slice was clean, diagonal across the flesh of his hand. He turned his palm over the brazier and let the blood fall freely into the flames. The fire hissed, cracked— then flared with a sudden burst of deep blue before settling once more into gold. It was a sign. *Varyn saw them.*

He pressed his bloodied palm to his chest, whispering the words passed down from his father: "For blood. For tribe. For valor." The flame hissed in response, licking higher into the morning air. As he stepped back, he could feel it begin—the slow, searing stitch of skin pulling itself closed. Not by medicine. Not by time. By will. *By Varyn.* The blood stopped flowing. The wound sealed, thread by unseen thread, as if the God's invisible hand dragged a burning needle through the torn flesh, binding it back together in sacred silence. One by one, the others stepped forward. Each warrior bled for the God of Blood and Valor, and each time, the flame flared in acknowledgment—as if Varyn himself watched from beyond the veil, collecting their offerings. A chant began to rise among them, low and guttural. It was not sung, but felt—a rhythm like a second heartbeat, ancient and unrelenting, echoing through the stone and soil beneath their feet.

Theron stood still, the bowl of mud cooling in his palm, the ritual near complete. And then he saw her. Layla had stepped forward. Unbidden. Uninvited. And his breath caught.He hadn't motioned to her. Hadn't expected her to participate in this sacred rite. His chest tightened as she reached for the ceremonial blade. *What is she doing?* A flash of panic surged through him. She didn't understand. This wasn't a simple wound—it wouldn't close unless Varyn allowed it. Unless she was blessed. And if she wasn't... She'd bleed. Maybe worse.He didn't want her hurt—not like that, not at all. His mouth parted, ready to stop her. But the words didn't come. Because Varyn's flame didn't flicker in warning at her presence. It flared—high and wild—before she even touched the blade, stopping him cold.

He watched as she drew the blade across her palm and the moment shifted. The forest stilled, as if the trees themselves had paused to witness what she had done. Her blood hit the fire and the flames surged. Not just blue—but violet, edged with white, a flash so bright it stole the breath from his lungs. It roared like a scream of approval, then fell quiet again, embers pulsing like the beat of war drums. And her wound... it vanished just like all of theirs had, causing all of the warriors beside him stir in shock.

He watched as Layla blinked down at her hand, clearly stunned. Theron's gaze lingered on the rapid rise and fall of her chest that was too quick to be calm. But it didn't seem to be pain that gripped her, but awe or fear. Maybe both. *Varyn had accepted her.* The God of Blood and Valor had marked a foreign princess as one of their own. Theron's throat tightened. He stared as she pressed her hand to her chest in a shaky mimic of the vow, and Theron realized she wasn't actually mimicking, she meant it.

Sparrow reappeared a moment later, painted and composed as always. He stepped forward to complete the ritual as Layla moved to stand beside Theron once more. With steady hands and effortless precision, Sparrow moved through the sacred motions. When he finished, he set the ceremonial blade back in its place. The flame gave a brief, sharp burst of acknowledgment—then extinguished itself in a whisper.

Sparrow stepped up beside Layla, grunting to imply they were good to go. Theron barely registered him through the haze still clouding his mind. *What in the Gods had just happened?* But he just forced himself to nod. "Stick by Sparrow," he said to Layla, voice rough and uneven. "You'll be safe."

He ran a hand through his hair, trying to shake the chaos loose from his mind. There was no time for questions. No time for attempting to make sense of what he'd seen. Whatever Varyn had done—whatever it meant—the god had claimed her. Marked her like he had all of the others. And that alone should have been enough. Theron couldn't afford to dwell on why. He should be grateful. She was protected now. Not invincible—none of them were—but watched. Chosen. And that would have to be enough. Because he had warriors to lead. A battle to win. And his mind needed to be clear, his blade steady.

As Theron approached the front of the assembled cohort, he could feel the weight of his mother's stare like a dagger between his shoulder blades. But he didn't look at her. Not now. His focus needed to be sharp, honed like the blades hidden along his frame. He scanned the tribe. Each warrior now smeared in mud, armed and alert. They were ready. With a single nod, he set them into motion. They fanned out into the dense trees, heading in a southeastern path toward Graystonia. All proceeding to thread through the forest like a snake's tongue.

Theron's boots pressed into soft earth as branches bowed around him. The sunlight slipped in slivers through the thick canopy, illuminating dust and sweat in the air. It was late August. The heat was already rising, and the air clung heavy to his warriors skin. But his people would not slow. They were Antonin. They would reach Graystonia by nightfall. Then they would wait. Observe. And at sunrise—strike.

As he confidently navigated through the dense brush, he couldn't help but think that he still didn't want Layla anywhere near the fight. Varyn's blessing didn't change that. Just because the God had marked her didn't mean she belonged in the blood and chaos of war. She would point out the tunnel entrances once they were there and that would be all. He'd made that decision long ago. She didn't need to see more violence. Not again. Not if he could help it.

But even as he told himself that, the truth pressed in. He had seen a woman in need of protection. A fragile princess ripped from her palace, grieving, afraid. That was the Layla who had stirred something deep in him—something instinctive, fierce, unshakable. But now... he was starting to see what he'd missed. She wasn't just trying to survive. She was preparing to fight. There was strength in her, buried beneath the softness—steel, waiting in silence. A fire that no longer flickered, but burned with direction. Purpose. Resolve. She wasn't just a princess in exile. She was a wildfire. A warrior. And she was ready to go to war for her kingdom. And gods, he still wanted to shield her from it all. Even now. Especially now. He didn't know if she needed his protection anymore. But he would offer it all the same. Even if she never asked for it. Even if it meant standing between her and the fire she had become.

BY FLAME, BY ROOT, BY GOD AND STAR—
CAELERIA SHALL RISE, OR PERISH WHOLE.

THE LAW OF THE CHOSEN FLAME

*Some knowledge is sealed for a reason. Let none
break the ancient seals without divine
permission.* What sleeps beneath Caeleria
should never be stirred without purpose- or the
continent will weep and ruin.

- THE HIGH LAWS OF CAELERIA

Chapter Fifteen

Layla.

Layla stuck close to Sparrow as they moved through the dense forest, the damp scent of moss and bark rising from the ground beneath them. The air was heavy with tension, every twig snap or rustling leaf a potential sign of danger. No one spoke. Not even Kain. It felt as though the entire Antonin tribe was holding its breath as they carved their silent path toward Graystonia.

Her thoughts remained anchored to one thing: her family. Her mother's voice. Her sisters' laughter. The brave way her father used to stand when trouble came. She swallowed hard and forced herself not to imagine the worst. *I'm on my way to save them. I'm on my way.* She repeated it like a prayer, a mantra to ward off panic.

As the hours dragged on, her legs began to ache, but she refused to slow. She could feel they were getting close, she recognized the trees here, the shapes of their trunks, the particular tilt of the undergrowth. They must be getting close to the Graystonian border, if not already crossed. Just ahead, she spotted a familiar clearing, sunlight slipping through the canopy and striking the grass with a golden glow and her heart leapt.

Layla absentmindedly jogged toward the clearing, toward the ancient oak she had climbed a hundred times as a child. She ran a hand across its gnarled bark, its familiarity grounding her. Sparrow remained a step behind, the ever silent and watchful sentinel. She spun slowly beneath the canopy, scanning the tree line for any sign—any whisper—of her family. She knew it was foolish. They wouldn't just be hiding in the woods, waiting for her. But a small, desperate part of her still hoped.

Then—whip!

Something sliced through the air near her ear, tossing her hair aside with the breeze of its passing. A solid *thunk* followed. She turned toward the sound and saw a hatchet buried deep in the tree beside her. Her blood instantly ran cold as she turned back towards the direction it had come. Another hatchet flew from the thicket. This time, she ducked, her instincts roaring to life as she tried to locate the source. A second later, a Bartorian soldier burst from the brush, arm cocked back, another weapon ready to fly. But before he could throw it, an arrow sang through the air and pierced his skull. He dropped like a stone.

Layla whipped her head around. Instantly spotting Kain off aways to the right, lowering his bow with effortless ease. His mouth curled into a wicked grin as he winked at her, already reaching for another arrow.

Ten more Bartorian soldiers emerged, but the Antonins were ready. Kain loosed two more arrows with deadly speed. Xaden was a whirlwind of steel, carving through enemies with fluid brutality. The rest of the tribe moved like phantoms, dispatching the Bartorians before they could rally. Then Sparrow was suddenly in front of her, pressing her back against the oak tree with his body. His broad frame became a wall, his blade ready. Layla had drawn her own knives instinctively, but the fight ended before she could act. Eleven Bartorians fell in minutes.

The forest returned to silence, save for the distant chirp of crickets and the heavy breath of warriors. Layla's heart thudded in her chest, but adrenaline made her limbs steady. As they moved forward, she noticed Kain ahead, scanning the path. She strode up beside him, her voice laced with challenge.

"Strange," she said, tilting her head. "I thought you didn't care whether I died or not." Her voice dripped with mock curiosity, every word a deliberate prod.

He turned, slow and sharp, eyes gleaming beneath the diagonal streaks of war paint. His blond hair was tied back in a tight bun, sweat slicking the line of his neck. That gaze—steady, unreadable— and wholly locked onto hers now.

"Things change, Little Dove." His smile was faint but real this time. Not mocking. Not sharp. Just... honest.

She blinked, completely caught off guard by the lack of sarcasm. "Well... either way, thank you," she said softly, genuinely, before drifting

back to Sparrow's side. But the words stayed with her. *Things change....
What had changed?* But more importantly, *why did it matter?* She
glanced over her shoulder once. Kain was scanning the trees again, jaw
set, but there was a new weight behind his posture, like he was watching
her as much as the enemy. Layla bit her lip in frustration and turned
away, unsettled.

By dusk, the trees began to thin. The sky deepened to a velvety purple.
They were close. Layla's breath caught as she saw the towering trees that
lined the west side of the castle—her home. Tears stung her eyes, but she
didn't let them fall. She was almost there, and this time she wasn't alone.

Sparrow stopped, and the tribe did the same. They dropped their
packs, sitting in clusters to eat. Layla settled beneath a tree, chewing
an apple slowly, her eyes scanning every leaf, every stone, every sliver of
moonlight peeking through the canopy. Then her eyes fell on Theron.
Striding through the warriors like a force of nature, his muscles flexing
with purpose. Her pulse immediately quickened.

"Come," he said simply. Layla tossed her apple core aside and
stood, brushing her hands against her thighs. She followed without
question, Sparrow following with his usual quiet presence. Theron led
them to a small group of Antonin elites—Queen Okteria, Kain, Xaden,
and a few others. All hunched over a rough-sketched map of her home.
Theron stopped just beside them and turned to her, his voice firm yet
gentle.

"We need you to show us where the tunnels are. Now." Layla nodded. This was why she was here.

She led them swiftly to the edge of the forest, crouching low behind a thick veil of trees. The castle loomed in the distance, a brooding silhouette of stone and moonlight.

"You can't see it from here," she whispered. Lifting her arm and pointing to what looked like an ordinary stretch of wall near the cliff base below the western tower. "But right there—see the faint crack in the stone line? Press the darker block, third row from the bottom, just to the left of the ivy. It's a release. It'll open a narrow passage that leads under the servants' wing and up into the library." Theron followed her gesture with his eyes, his expression sharp and unreadable. He gave a tight nod, taking in every word.

She continued on towards the southern side of the castle. The group circled wide through the brush until they reached the jagged cliffs that rose behind the rear courtyard. Layla halted again and dropped to a crouch behind a cluster of moss-covered boulders.

"This one's harder," she warned, her voice even quieter now. "The door's halfway up the cliff face, just behind that jut of stone. You won't spot it unless you know what to look for." She glanced over her shoulder, meeting their eyes. "It's a latch hidden in the rock. You have to scale to reach it."

Theron's hand twitched at his side, like he was barely restraining the urge to stop what he knew she was implying. His jaw flexed once, tension carved into every line of his face. But he said nothing. Didn't argue. He just gave a clipped nod, trusting her before speaking through gritted teeth.

"Lead the way. We'll cover you."

With a dagger in hand, she scaled the rocks like a cat, Theron close beside, Sparrow directly below. She reached the hidden crevice and pointed, heart hammering in her chest. He nodded, mouth clenching his blade. Then they quickly climbed back down in silence.

When they reached the forest floor again, Layla let out a small laugh, breathless. Shocked she didn't slip and fall to her death on such a treacherous climb. But the relief was short lived as Theron turned on her.

"Please tell me the next tunnel doesn't require you to risk your damn life again." His voice was a low rasp, angry, yes—but laced with concern. Layla's lips twitched.

"The eastern tunnel faces the ocean. You'd need a boat to reach it." Theron just grunted at this. The tension momentarily dissipating as she could tell he was already strategizing. Already planning. But for the first time in a long time, Layla didn't feel like a prisoner. Or a pawn. Or a princess. She felt like a warrior. And whether it was with Theron, the entire tribe, or herself alone, she was going to take back her home.

Theron.

The moment Layla revealed the layout of the tunnels, the rest of the plan fell into place like pieces of a war map finally complete. Theron outlined the divisions, two main strike forces, one for the southern and one for the western entrance, each to split again once inside. A third group would remain hidden within the tree line, flanking and providing cover if needed. He gave the orders clearly, each word like a stone dropped in water. Queen Okteria stood beside him, a silent and approving force.

But just as Theron finished, Layla stepped forward, voice urgent. "I need to go with the southern group. It's the closest entrance to the dungeons, my family could be down there." Her eyes burned with determination, and Theron's chest tightened.

Queen Okteria turned slowly, the glint of venom already dancing behind her composed smile. Theron's pulse picked up. This was not going to end well.

"You thought you were going in with us?" Queen Okteria asked, her voice a smooth blade wrapped in silk. She stepped closer, chin raised, eyes gleaming like a predator toying with its prey. "Did you truly believe we brought our entire force to save your family?"

Layla stiffened, her breath catching. She glanced toward Theron—clearly desperate for contradiction, for any flicker of denial in his eyes. But it wasn't there.

He watched as Okteria's lips curved into something cold. "No, princess. You were brought here for one reason: to show us how to get in. And you've served that purpose well." She began to circle Layla slowly, the way one might appraise a sacrifice. "With your help, we'll take down two enemies in one strike—Bartoria and your precious Graystonia. A gift, really. Wrapped in silk and blood."

Layla's voice cracked. "But... you told me this was about revenge. About the Bartorians invading your lands—trespassing."

"Oh, and it is," Okteria said, almost kindly. "Bartoria stepped onto Antonin soil and dared to kill my people. They will bleed for that. Every last soldier rotting inside that castle will die screaming, and their bones will be left as a warning."

Her eyes sharpened. "But don't mistake me. That castle isn't being attacked to save Graystonia. I care nothing for your kingdom. Your line." Her voice dropped to a venomous whisper. "This is justice. A reckoning generations in the making. Your ancestors—your great-grandfather, your precious noble blood—they were the ones who stole Antonin land in the Great War. Who carved us up and forced a treaty we never asked for. They expanded their crown by gutting ours."

Layla's lips parted, but no sound came.

"I don't care that Varyn marked you," Okteria said coldly. "You still carry their blood. And that makes you a symbol of everything we were forced to swallow. So, if I have the chance to erase every last Eradellian from the realm, then why wouldn't I take it?" Her smile was too calm. "I'll let your gods ponder that question while your family burns. I'm sure Varyn will understand."

Theron took a step forward now, jaw tight. "Mother—"

"Do not," she hissed, turning sharply toward him. "You know what they did. You know what we lost."

He said nothing. He didn't know what to say, what to do...

Layla's voice, when it came, faltered for a moment, but not from fear. "This was never about stopping Bartoria... This was about destroying me."

Okteria tilted her head. "Not you, girl. What you represent. Blood for blood. That's the law of our gods, is it not?" She turned to her warriors, voice rising. "The time for mercy passed long ago. This time, we end it."

"Get her out of my sight," the Queen snapped, her smile gone. Her voice cracked like thunder. Theron stepped in, almost instinctively, his hand closing around Layla's. She let him pull her for a few paces before stopping short. She turned, voice cracking as her outrage boiled over.

"Did you know?" she demanded, voice tight, eyes blazing with betrayal. "Did you know she planned to kill my family?" Theron opened his mouth—but nothing came out. He hadn't known. Not exactly. But deep down, some part of him had sensed it. And that unspoken truth was now a noose around his throat.

"I won't let her hurt you," he said finally, his voice low. Steady. A desperate vow as he reached out to touch her face. Remind her he would do anything to keep her safe.

Layla let out a ragged breath. "Gods, Theron—this isn't about me!" Her voice cracked as she stepped out of his reach. "I'm not worried about myself—I'm worried about my family! My mother, my sisters. They're still in that castle and she plans to murder them!"

Her breath came faster now, he could see the fury unraveling into something raw and aching. "So what are you going to do?" she asked, voice sharpening. "Stand there with that damned sword of yours and watch it happen? Are you going to let it happen?"

He stared at her, body taut with tension. His mind was spinning so fast he didn't even know what to think. To do.

"If I ask you to stop it... if I ask you to protect them, too—will you?" Her voice was barely a whisper now. "Will you fight for them, Theron? Or will you kill them yourself if your mother commands it?"

He knew his silence was deafening, but he couldn't defy a direct order. That went against everything that had been engrained in him his entire life. No matter what the order was or how he felt about it. He had to obey his Queen...

He watched, heart splintering, as Layla's eyes brimmed with tears—but none fell. Instead, her lips curved into something fractured and cruel, and it broke something open in his chest.

"So then your plan is what?" she spat, the venom in her voice cutting clean through him. "Go slaughter my family and then have me waiting for you in your hut? Be your prisoner for life and hope I still want to fuck you?!"

He took a step toward her. He had no answers. He just needed her. To hold her. To keep her safe if he couldn't do anything else right. But she instantly recoiled. Like his nearness was fire. Like it repulsed her.

"Don't," she breathed. "Don't you dare touch me."

Every word that followed was a dagger, deliberate and merciless. "You may keep me here. You may force me to be your prisoner for life. But I will never forgive you for this." Then she turned—sharp, final—and walked away.

Theron didn't move. Couldn't. He had spent his life honing steel, commanding men, living by the sword and by his queen's word. His loyalty to his people had never wavered. But now, his people and his heart stood on opposite ends of a blade. He ran a hand through his hair, gripping the back of his neck until it hurt. *How could he follow through with this? How could he not?*

He turned slowly to head back to the camp. The firelit huddle of his warriors awaited, his mother's voice no doubt already dictating the final movements. Theron's steps were heavy. The only clarity he had was this: he would kill every Bartorian he found inside those castle walls. Of that he was certain. But when it came to Graystonia—to Layla's family... he didn't know. Not yet. He wasn't sure who he was anymore. All he knew was that Layla's pain had become his own, and no battle plan could prepare him for the war now waging inside his chest.

WITH BLESSINGS, WE RISE;
WITH STRENGTH, WE CONQUER

By the ancient decree of Graystonia, any who are found guilty of treason to the crown shall face the highest form of punishment. For the betrayal of the crown is the betrayal of the kingdom itself, and no mercy shall be shown. The traitor's fate shall be sealed by their actions- swift and final, to preserve the integrity and honor of Graystonia. Let it be decreed: betrayal of the crown is the death of the soul, and the punishment shall reflect the gravity of such a crime.

-BY DECREE OF THE CROWN OF GRAYSTONIA.

Chapter Sixteen

Layla.

Hours dragged by as Layla sat slumped against a tree, betrayal and heartache an inferno in her chest as the morning quickly crept in. After those moments with Theron, she'd allowed herself to foolishly hope. She had believed, just for a moment, that maybe she was no longer just a prisoner. But that fragile illusion was now shattered. Theron had chosen his mother, chosen war, chosen revenge... over her.

She stared bitterly around the forest at the Antonin warriors preparing to invade her home. The thrill of bloodlust was nearly tangible in the air, rippling off their armored bodies like heat waves. Even Sparrow, always so composed, practically vibrated with anticipation beside her. She hated the calm before the storm. Hated being made to watch her world slip from her fingers while she sat like a caged animal.

She had spent hours running through every desperate plan she could conceive: take out the warriors closest to her, somehow slip inside the castle undetected, bypass both Antonins and Bartorians, find her family, and escape with them into the city—back to her own soldiers. But each plan crumbled faster than it formed. She sighed, her head thudding against the bark behind her. She was trapped. And they were all going to die.

The Antonin warriors began dispersing, slipping into their assigned routes like ghosts in the trees. Layla's stomach twisted as she imagined the slaughter to come. That was when Kain appeared, stepping casually in front of her and Sparrow, like he hadn't just been preparing for war.

"Change of plans," Kain said, voice low. "You're leading my group into the castle. I'm staying with our little captive." Layla's eyes narrowed. Her heart rate spiked. *What is he doing?*

Sparrow blinked, his hand still resting on his blade. "I don't believe you."

Kain just shrugged, totally unbothered. "Well, Theron wouldn't say this out loud but " he leaned in slightly, "I'm kind of the better shot from a distance. You two are all about that up-close-and-personal thing. I interpreted this with his grunts, of course, but it's what his soul was saying." Layla almost rolled her eyes. Even now, Kain couldn't resist being a smug ass.

Sparrow, however, remained stone-faced. "He'd be pissed if this plan went to shit because I trusted you."

Kain shrugged. "That's between you and his soul, friend. Now go kill some bad guys." He gave Sparrow a casual salute, the smirk never leaving his face. Sparrow lingered a moment longer, eyes flicking between Layla and Kain, before finally nodding and jogging off into the woods. Kain turned to her then, and the grin he wore wasn't teasing anymore—it was determined.

"Come on, Little Dove. Let's go save your family."

Layla's heart leapt. "You're helping me?!" she asked, breath catching. "...Why?"

He turned back to her with a slight groan, clearly annoyed. "Because unlike my brother, I don't feel compelled to follow every command like it's divine scripture."

"But Theron..." Her voice faltered. "Did he send you?"

A pause. Kain's expression shifted—something almost gentle in his voice. "He couldn't say it. Not in front of them. But he knew I'd do what needed to be done." A weight settled in her chest. Theron hadn't blindly followed. He hadn't bowed to the bloodshed of her family. When it mattered most, he'd chosen what was right. He'd chosen her.

Layla nodded before quickly following Kain into the thick of the forest. They approached the southern cliffside entrance just behind a group of Antonin warriors scaling the rocks. Blending in, Layla and Kain moved swiftly, unnoticed amid the chaos. Making the treacherous climb in stealth with all of the others. When they reached the secret door, Kain leaned in, his breath barely a whisper.

"Once inside, you lead. I've got your back." Layla simply nodded in response.

They slipped into the castle. The roar of steel on steel rang out around them, Antonins clashing with Bartorian guards. The battle had already underway. Layla kept her focus. *Long corridor. Ballroom balcony. Through the garden. Southeast wing—dungeons.* She repeated the route like a mantra, grounding herself in the plan. Her grip tightened on her blades just as a Bartorian appeared in front of them. Kain's arrow hit him before Layla could even raise her arm. They kept moving.

Another hall—more blood. Layla flung a blade into the skull of a Bartorian who had pinned an Antonin to the ground. The man gave her a grateful nod and charged back into the fray. They pressed on, slipping behind a pillar near the ballroom balcony.

A warrior sprinted past, bloodied and breathless, catching sight of Kain. "They pulled the queen back to camp," he shouted over the chaos. "Bartorian blade caught her in the gut during the breach. She's alive, but pissed—won't stop barking orders from the tree line." Layla didn't slow, but the words struck like a jolt to her spine. The queen was down. Which meant... Theron was leading now. Inside these walls. Inside her home. His voice. His command. She didn't know what that meant—what he would choose to do with that power. Only that, impossibly... it gave her hope.

"Gods," Kain muttered, breathless, "that woman's made of iron." Layla nodded, driving one of her daggers into the side of a Bartorian who lunged from a blackened corridor. She twisted sharply, yanked it free, and kept moving. But her gaze lingered on Kain a beat longer. He didn't waver. Didn't let the blow of his mother's near-death rattle him. He fought with steady hands, sharp focus—like a soldier bred for chaos. *Like a son forged by a queen.*

Another enemy rushed them. Kain stepped forward, parried with his sword, and rammed his elbow into the man's face. Blood splattered. The body dropped. Then he tapped Layla's shoulder.

"Three ahead," he whispered. Her breath caught, but she nodded, daggers ready as her focus snapped back into place. Kain leaned out, loosed three arrows in quick succession—thwip, thwip, thwip. Three Bartorians fell.

"Go!" he hissed. Layla darted forward. She was immediately met with a Bartorian guard swinging wide with an axe—she ducked low as she slid past. Slashing her dagger across his thigh as she went. He howled before collapsing behind her.

She vaulted the stair rail, boots landing hard. Below, she caught an unexpected glimpse and nearly stumbled. *Theron.* He was forged fury as his sword carved through the chaos with devastating precision, each movement as fluid as it was lethal. She hadn't expected to see him here. Not like this. Not like some wrathful god made flesh. She nearly stopped to watch, heart stuttering at the sight of him—until Kain grabbed her by the collar and shoved her down the stairwell.

"Live now, gawk later."

Layla swore under her breath—but immediately obeyed, sprinting into the dark.

Layla's chest rose and fell as they reached the garden entrance. She paused for a heartbeat—too exposed, but the fastest path. Seeing no one in sight. She inhaled sharply and then they darted into the open garden. Instantly, pain exploded in her shoulder. An arrow. Blood.

"Kain—!" She winced. He immediately threw himself over her, arm wrapped tight around her as they continued their sprint. She felt more than heard two arrows thud into Kain's back. He stumbled but didn't stop. Before she could truly react, he squeezed her tighter, yanking her on.

"Keep going! Don't slow down!" Kain yelled with an edge of pain in his voice. Layla abided, not slowing down until they ran behind an archway near the entrance to the dungeons. Kain's warmth was instantly gone as she heard a loud groan. She spun around to check on him while they were momentarily safe from the aerial assault. He was leaning his shoulder against a wall. Two arrows sticking out of his back. Layla gasped in horror. Her face must have shown her concern because Kain looked at her with a pained smile.

"I'm okay, Little Dove. But if I'm going to be of any help to you, I will need you to pull these out," Kain sarcastically quipped. She couldn't believe he was joking around at a time like this!

"You want me to take them out?! Now!?" Layla exasperatedly responded. Thoroughly alarmed by the request.

"Just do it quick, Little Dove. We don't have time for this." He retorted. Still acting as though it wasn't a big deal. Layla reluctantly nodded her head and stepped forward. She slowly reached her tremoring hand for the first arrow that had pierced just below his right shoulder blade. As her fingers wrapped around the shaft, Kain let out a small groan of pain.

"Just pull it!" Kain snapped with biting humor through gritted teeth. Layla instantly yanked with all her might, ignoring her own screaming pain from her left shoulder as she did it. The arrow was dug deep but thankfully came out. Blood started pouring down his back. She looked around but there was nothing she could cover it with. *Shit, shit, shit!* Layla internally panicked.

"Just get the other one, Dove. We need to get going before our friends come down to find us." Kain tossed out dryly.

What he was saying made sense, but Layla definitely felt like she was more worried about the blood loss and injuries than he was. She shook her head and held her breath as she yanked the other arrow out of his lower back. It had narrowly missed his spine. As she tossed the bloody arrows to the ground, she looked over at his blood-soaked back in panic.

"We need to stop the bleeding!" Layla desperately rasped as she attempted to get across to Kain how pressing of a matter this actually was. He jus turned around and grabbed her wrist, pulling her to the dungeon entrance. Clearly, only one of them was concerned about it.

Kain groaned as he let go of her wrist and grabbed for one of his arrows to prep his bow. As they swiftly descended the stairs, expecting to run into a group of Bartorian guards, they rounded the bottom step and came across only one. He drew his sword out, ready to attack, but Kain was too quick. His arrow had pierced the guard's sword arm, forcing him to drop it to the ground. Kain stepped forward, now holding another arrow directly in front of the guard, aimed at the center of his skull.

"Go find your family," Kain growled. "I've got him."

"Keys," Layla demanded. The guard snarled and tossed them at her feet. She grabbed them and ran.

Cell after cell—nothing. Then the last one. A body on the floor. *Her mother.*

Crouching down beside her mother, Layla gently pulled her hair back from her face and checked the pulse of her neck. *She is still alive!!!* Layla rejoiced internally as she released the shaky breath she had been holding. She rolled her mother onto her back and froze. The woman had been beaten so badly, it was a miracle she was still alive. She was covered in only the Gods know what, atop of swelling and bruises from head to toe. Layla's heart fell to her stomach. She tried to lift her but couldn't. She wasn't strong enough and she couldn't seem to muster her mother to wake up. Reluctantly, she left her there and ran back to Kain.

"Kain!" she shouted as she sprinted back. "I found my mother—but I need you."

Kain looked up, pale and bloodied. "Where are your sisters?"

"I don't know. They're not in the cells." She turned on the guard, the sight of her mother like that reigniting the seething anger that was at a constant simmer. "Where are they?!" she shouted. He just sneered in response. Layla approached him in a blind rage as she punched him square in the face. The guard rocked backward and quickly brought his hands up to his nose, blood instantly gushing down his face.

"You bitch!" He yelled, stepping towards her. But Kain was quicker, He stepped closer, positioning the arrow only a foot front of his face now.

"Don't move another fucking inch, or this next arrow is in your eye and the following one in your dick." Kain seethed. Menace flaring from his eyes. The guard glared at him and then turned back to look towards Layla.

"They're gone, and you'll never see them again." He smirked at her.

Layla instantly lunged forward, driving her blade into his abdomen and twisting. The guard let out a loud and pained groan.

"WHERE ARE THEY!?"

"Bartoria," he groaned. "Your own Sir Charles sold them. The king made him rich." Layla's vision narrowed, not believing this. *It couldn't be true.* "We couldn't find you, so they finally sent the other two princesses off last night. Better two than zero...." The guard slurred before he collapsed.

She turned to Kain, shaking. Still not wanting to believe it. But in her gut, she didn't know how, but knew the man was telling the truth. "They're gone. My sisters—they're..."

"One thing at a time," Kain said, voice steady. "Let's get your mother. Then we find them... I promise Dove." She nodded. Layla somehow knew he meant every word. Quickly turning on her heels she showed Kain where her mom was lying in the filth at the back cell. Kain ran in and scooped her up with a deep groan.

"Kain, are you sure—?" he cut her off before she could continue.

"I've got her. Let's move."

They didn't take the garden way back—too dangerous. Instead, Layla led him to the maid's kitchen. Two Bartorians turned to face them as they entered. Her blades were flying before they could even draw their weapons. Both bodies dropped in unison.

"Come on," she whispered as she grabbed more blades off her belt and held the door open for Kain and her mother to enter. As they crossed the kitchen, they could hear commotion echoing on the other side of the far door. Layla held up a hand for them to wait.

As the silence fell beyond the door. She looked at Kain and nodded. *Time to get out. Time to survive. Time to fight for everything that was hers.*

She threw the door open with a sharp breath, blades at the ready, prepared to kill whatever enemy stood in her way. But just as her eyes swept the room and she raised her arm to strike, she halted. Not because there wasn't a target, but because of who the target was.

Theron stood alone in the center of the room, towering over three Bartorian corpses bleeding at his feet. He was soaked in blood, some of it his, most of it not. The shadows under his eyes made him look almost feral. For a terrifying second, he looked like something conjured from nightmare—a war god sculpted from stone and rage. Then he saw her. His sword dipped half an inch, and confusion shattered his hardened expression.

"What the hell are you doing here?!" he bellowed, voice sharp and stunned.

Layla's own shock fumbled her words. "What do you mean? You sent Kain to help me get my mother—we've got her, she just—"

"Kain?!" Theron snarled, stepping forward. His dark eyes snapped behind her.

Kain appeared in the dim threshold next to her, her unconscious mother wrapped protectively in his arms.

"Hey there, brother," he said casually, grinning like he hadn't just betrayed a war order.

Layla's breath caught. Her heart plummeted. "So, you didn't send him." Theron didn't answer. He didn't need to. Her jaw tightened, heartbreak hardening into venom-laced wrath. "Of course you didn't," she spat. "I don't even know why I expected anything different." Before Theron could respond, the door behind him flew open.

Xaden burst into the room, urgency crackling off him like a spark.

"They're at the gate," he said. "Graystonian soldiers. Dozens at first, now more keep coming. We don't know how many."

Theron turned sharply. "And our men?"

"Poised to meet them," Xaden replied. "They've taken position just inside the entrance. Orders are to strike the moment they breach the threshold."

The words hit Layla like ice. She shoved past the others, boots skidding on the stone as she made for the nearest window. In the distance, beyond the courtyard walls, she saw it—the gleam of armor under the rising sun. Her breath caught—Graystonia's banners rose through the trees, her army thundering forward at last. Relief swelled in her chest. They'd come. They were here. But the joy barely formed before it twisted, sharp and breathless, as her gaze snapped to the entrance—Antonin blades drawn, ready to strike. Her people were walking straight into an ambush.

She turned toward Theron, urgency surging in her veins, and closed the space between them. Her hand pressed lightly to his chest—steadying herself as her burning anger was momentarily ebbed by the sheer panic of what was about to happen to her men.

"Theron," she said, voice low, breathless. "Don't." She searched his face, desperate for the man she'd once glimpsed beneath all the armor and orders. "Please," she said, voice trembling. "You've already done what you came here to do. The Bartorians are dead. You've sent the message your mother wanted. Don't reignite a war between our kingdoms—a war that ended generations ago. Please, Theron."

His jaw clenched, the muscles in his neck pulsing, barely restrained. She could feel the tension rolling off his chest beneath her hand like a thunderstorm waiting to break.

"Take the win," she begged. "Don't lose everything for nothing. Not today.."

She looked into his eyes, pleading—not as a princess, but as someone who had trusted him. Someone who still wanted to believe there was something left of the man she thought she saw that night under the stars. "Please, Theron."

For a moment, the war god cracked. His expression softened, just barely. But she saw it. His sword lowered. Not all the way, but enough. Then he turned slightly and gave a sharp nod to his warriors, jerking his chin toward the exit.

"Xaden," Theron said, voice like steel. "Inform our men to stand down. We leave the message carved in Bartoria's dead. That's enough for now." His words weren't loud, but they echoed like a closing gate. Xaden froze for half a second, stunned—but nodded. Then turned, vanishing into the corridor with purpose.

Layla didn't wait. She ran—heart hammering, breath ragged, her hair whipping behind her like a banner of defiance. Stone blurred beneath her feet, but her mind was sharp. Theron gave the order to retreat—sparing both sides the bloodshed that would have sealed a centuries-old feud in carnage. It was the right choice. A merciful one. But it also meant he was leaving. And with that command, Layla knew she'd never see him again. Still, she didn't look back. She couldn't. Because ahead—through those towering doors—was everything she'd fought for. Her people. Her kingdom. Her chance to stop blood from spilling where it didn't have to.

And when the gates finally cracked open, Layla stood at their threshold—Kain at her heels, her mother cradled in his arms. She wasn't alone, but she had never felt the weight of her role more. Between two armies, between bloodied past and uncertain future, she stepped forward. Not just a daughter. Not just a survivor, but the only one left to lead even if the law said she couldn't. And she prayed—gods, she prayed—that her people would see her. Hear her. Follow her. And somehow, in that impossible space between war and peace... that they would."

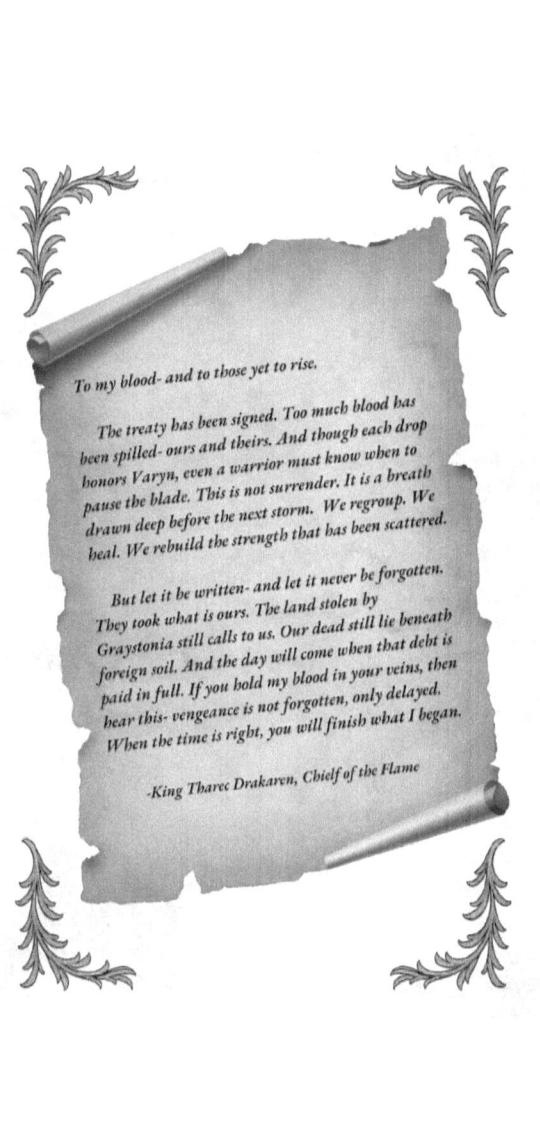

To my blood- and to those yet to rise.

The treaty has been signed. Too much blood has been spilled- ours and theirs. And though each drop honors Varyn, even a warrior must know when to pause the blade. This is not surrender. It is a breath drawn deep before the next storm. We regroup. We heal. We rebuild the strength that has been scattered.

But let it be written- and let it never be forgotten. They took what is ours. The land stolen by Graystonia still calls to us. Our dead still lie beneath foreign soil. And the day will come when that debt is paid in full. If you hold my blood in your veins, then hear this- vengeance is not forgotten, only delayed. When the time is right, you will finish what I began.

-King Tharec Drakaren, Chielf of the Flame

Chapter Seventeen

Layla.

As Layla stepped through the front doors of her home, the morning light spilled across the bloodstained stone like a quiet reckoning. Dew still clung to the grass, glinting soft gold in the rising sun—but nothing about the moment felt gentle. Not with the scent of death still thick in the air. Behind her, the last of the Antonins vanished down the blood stained halls, slipping through the hidden tunnels like ghosts retreating into legend. She watched them go—just for a moment. Then she turned. There was no time to mourn what had passed... only to face what waited ahead. And there they were. Her army. Her people.

They charged across the outer court in formation—until they saw her. And stopped. Blades half-raised, shields still braced. All poised to reclaim their home from what they believed were invaders. And in a way... they weren't wrong.

Layla stood in the threshold. Not in silk, not in the royal green of Graystonia but in Antonin leathers—rugged and worn, smeared with blood. Her face was streaked with black war paint, a foreign mark of survival. Her hair was wild in the breeze, matted and tangled, still damp from sweat and battle. She looked nothing like their princess. And everything like the wrath they deserved.

Kain stepped up behind her, silent but unwavering, the queen still unconscious in his arms. Layla didn't move aside. She didn't explain. She didn't beg. She let them see her—bloodied, branded by war, standing guard at the gates of her own home. Let them doubt. Let them falter. But not for long. Because whether they were ready or not... the crown had no one left but her. And she would wear the weight, if not the title.

"I am Layla Eradellian, Princess of Graystonia," she announced, her voice loud and unwavering. "This man is not your enemy. Kain of the Antonin Tribe helped me save our queen. He is not to be harmed."

One soldier stepped forward. A young man, probably 30, with tousled brown hair and a deep scar across his jaw.

"My Lady," he said, bowing low. "I am Sir Edwin of the Royal Guard. I'm not sure if you remember me. But I must update you at once." If he was surprised to see the princess before him dressed in Antonin leathers, her face smeared in war paint and blood, he hid it well. No flicker of doubt. No hesitation. Only duty.

"Secure my home, Sir Edwin," she stated, her voice clipped, regal.

"We will sweep every hallway and hidden chamber before the hour is done," he replied. "Any remaining Bartorians will be dealt with swiftly."

"And the city? Our people?"

Sir Edwin straightened. "The city stands. We held the line around Graystonia and her nearby villages. One hamlet was lost early in the siege—many dead, My Lady. But the rest were protected. The worst hit was the castle."

Layla nodded, grief blooming beneath her ribs but held in check. She couldn't afford to crumble now. "Very well. Kill any Bartorian still within these walls," she ordered, voice steady. "And make this clear to the Antonin stragglers: they may leave with their brethren, or they may die here. That is the only mercy I will offer."

The guard bowed again. "Yes, Princess."

Layla's gaze flicked to her mother. "Now someone bring me a physician and take us to my mother's chambers. Quickly."

A flurry of men moved at once, one soldier helping Kain carry the unconscious queen while others ran ahead to prepare the rooms. As they disappeared down the corridor, Layla stood still for a moment. Absorbing the silence that had finally returned to her home. Blood soaked the stones beneath her feet. Her father was dead. Her sisters had been sold to Bartoria. But Graystonia was not lost. And neither was she.

Once inside her mother's chambers, Layla pointed to the large canopy bed. "There," she said, her voice already tight with emotion. Kain and the soldier moved at once, without pause. They strode across the room, Kain's movements stiff but purposeful, and gently laid Queen Raynera onto the mattress. The soldier quickly exited without a word as Layla took his place at her mother's side a moment later, before absentmindedly falling to her knees. Her hands shook as she pushed strands of her mother's matted hair from her face, revealing bruised skin and fading cuts. Her gut twisting as her concern for her mother began to race. *Why hasn't she woken up yet?*

A sharp knock at the door snapped both her and Kain into readiness. He reached for the dagger at his thigh as Layla's hand went to her belt.

"It's Sir Edwin, Lady Layla," came the voice from behind the door.

She let out a slow exhale and nodded to Kain. "It's okay." Kain didn't question her, simply opened the door. Sir Edwin stepped inside and bowed with practiced grace.

"My Lady," he began, "the castle is secure. All the Bartorians have been eliminated. And..." he hesitated as he glanced at Kain, "no other Antonin warriors remained to meet their deaths."

"Thank you, Sir Edwin." Layla rose to her full height, her voice steady despite the anger coiling tight beneath her skin. "Now explain to me what the hell happened." Kain moved to her side, his presence grounding her.

The guard shifted uncomfortably. "Days ago... Bartoria attacked during Lammas. We didn't know—"

"I know," she snapped. "I was there. I watched my father give his life protecting me. What I want to know is how they got in."

"Sir Charles, My Lady. He betrayed your family. We didn't know it at first—none of us did. But after the siege began, pieces started falling into place. He manipulated the guard deployments. Moved men away from key posts. And worse... we found the documents later. Signed orders. An official seal granting Bartorian envoys access to the royal ball." He exhaled, shame heavy in his voice. "They didn't crash the gates—they were invited in. Once inside, they sealed the castle from within. We—your remaining loyal guard—held the city and villages as best we could, waiting for a signal. But we couldn't breach the walls."

Layla closed her eyes, jaw clenched. *Sir Charles.* Her father's closest confidant. A man she'd known since childhood. Trusted like family. He actually did do what that Bartorian had said.

"And how are you here now?" she asked coldly.

"When the Antonin warriors attacked the inner castle, chaos broke loose inside," Sir Edwin said, his voice measured. "In the confusion, the Bartorian guard made a fatal error. They rerouted forces inward, abandoning their hold on the gate to reinforce the throne hall."

He looked up at her, pride simmering behind the exhaustion in his eyes. "That was our moment. We were ready. We'd been watching. Waiting. We seized the gate the moment it was left exposed—we planned to take it back in King Aiddeon's name, My Lady."

Layla took a breath, forcing the emotions to stay down. She heard what she needed to know. "Place guards on this room. I want updates every hour on the city's borders. And I want a strike team ready within the day. We leave for Bartoria to retrieve my sisters."

Sir Edwin stiffened, clearly surprised by the last order. "Of course, My Lady. I'll gather our best men." He bowed again.

"Sir Edwin?" Layla added gently, stopping him before he turned away.

"Yes, My Lady?"

"Our men valiantly defended our people. Thank you. My father would have been proud." A small smile pulled at the corner of his mouth before he bowed once more and stepped out. He gestured to someone in the hall, and moments later, a man entered.

"This is Dr. Aldren, the Graystonian physician," Edwin announced. "May he examine the queen?" Layla nodded and stepped aside. She remembered Dr. Aldren from his many years treating at the castle and nearby cities. He was a good man and trusted physician. Layla released a small breath at the sight of him here to help her mother.

"Princess," Dr. Aldren said softly, "I must ask for the room." Reluctantly, Layla abided.

As they leaned against the stone wall in silence. Layla's thoughts spun out like threads, too many to follow. So she tried to anchor to just one. "Why did you help me?" she asked suddenly, glancing up at Kain just beside her.

Kain kept his eyes closed but smiled faintly. "Does there have to be a reason?"

"There's always a reason," she muttered. "Some ploy I haven't seen yet, probably."

"Probably," he echoed, the grin widening. Layla just shook her head and the silence returned.

Eventually, Dr. Aldren somberly opened the door. "My Lady…" he said carefully, "I bring grave news. The queen has been brutally beaten, and…" he looked down, clearly ashamed of what he was having to report. "She was assaulted, likely more than once. She'll live, but she needs rest, and time."

Layla stood momentarily frozen before darting past him, her knees buckling as she collapsed beside her mother, clutching her chest as the tears finally broke free.

Raynera Eradellian had never been a warm mother. She believed in honor, tradition, and sacrifice. That women were raised to birth kings—not rule as one. She had been her husband's right hand, his quiet shadow. To the world, she was beauty and grace. To her daughters, she was steel. But even steel could break.

Layla wept for the mother who never coddled her, never whispered "I love you," yet always stood tall as an example of duty, pride, and unwavering grace. *How could anyone hurt her like this?*

After some time, Layla lifted her head, wiping her tears. Her eyes drifted to Kain, now shirtless, sitting backward on a chair as the doctor stitched the arrow wounds on his back. His muscles were taut with pain, his jaw clenched. Despite everything, a sense of gratitude welled in Layla's chest. He had taken those arrows for her. For her mother.

Dr. Aldren cleaned and dressed the wounds before speaking softly to Kain and leaving a bowl of herbs beside him. Kain promptly stood and stretched, wincing as he did. He grabbed a nearby whiskey bottle, dropped into the chair, and tilted his head back against the wall, eyes closed as he took a long swig. Layla found herself watching him—his long torso, the lazy bun at the back of his head, the confident smirk that curled across his lips ...Then he cracked an eye open.

"You like the view, Little Dove?" he teased.

Layla rolled her eyes. "Thank you... for everything," she said instead. "Tell your Queen I am grateful your men left in peace. As of now, I do not consider us at war. That's mainly because of you."

Kain grinned, head still against the wall, his eyes shut once again. "You're welcome."

Layla studied him. Mildly confused why he didn't move to leave. "You can rest in a bed if you want. I'll find you one."

"Oh? You offering to join me, Little Dove? I'd be honored." He flashed a wicked grin, those green eyes flying open with piercing mischief as they snapped to hers.

Her cheeks flushed deep red. "No! I—just—ugh!" He chuckled, leaning his head back to rest again.

"I mean it," she said more seriously. "You're free to go. My men can protect my family now." He opened his eyes, and when they met hers, they didn't waver. The mischief was gone—replaced by something quieter, heavier. A steady intensity that bore into her.

"I'm not going anywhere. If you're going to Bartoria, I'm going with you." Layla's composure cracked slightly. The swell of emotion in her chest was impossible to ignore.

"...Okay," she whispered.

"Okay," he echoed, a flicker of contentment settling across his face. He took another swig, then leaned back slowly, letting his head rest as she watched sleep soon begin to pull him under.

They waited in comfortable silence until a soft knock came. Kain raised an eyebrow, but Layla motioned that she would handle it. She opened the door to a familiar face.

"Marilla," Layla breathed, throwing her arms around her hand-maiden. "You're safe!"

"And you!... Gods above, you need a bath," Marilla said with a watery laugh, her voice cracking despite the teasing. She quickly wiped a tear from her cheek, trying—and failing—to collect herself. "Most of us were in the city for the festivities," she added, her tone softening. "I suppose... the gods had a hand in that." She offered the explanation before Layla could even ask, as if trying to fill the silence with anything but tears.

Layla nodded, dazed. The words sank in slowly, but the relief was instant and all-consuming. She drew in a shaky breath, blinking hard—willing herself not to fall apart now, not when the dearest friend she feared lost was standing right in front of her. Safe. Alive.

"I brought you a gown. Go use your mother's tub. I'll sit with her." Marilla's voice was brisk, familiar—already slipping back into business as usual like she hadn't just been blinking back tears. Composed, capable, unshakable. It made Layla chuckle. Of course Marilla would be the one to think of a bath and fresh clothes when the world had nearly ended. Gods, she was so happy she was okay.

But then Marilla's posture stiffened, her eyes catching on something just past Layla's shoulder. Kain. She said nothing, but the tension was unmistakable.

Layla stepped in quickly, her voice low but steady. "He helped me. Helped the Queen. He's not the enemy, Marilla."

Marilla gave a reluctant nod before cautiously passing by Kain to sit beside the queen. Layla didn't doubt Kain's loyalty—not after today—but Marilla was different. Familiar. Gentle. The queen wouldn't startle awake at the sight of her. Kain, on the other hand... Layla nearly laughed at the image, then exhaled a quiet sigh of relief and slipped into the bathing chamber.

She shed her leathers with aching efficiency, the fabric peeling away like a second skin. Turning to the mirror, she took herself in—bruised, bloodstained, too thin. A body carved by war, not court. Her fingers brushed a cut on her collarbone, her reflection both foreign and familiar.

Princess by blood. Warrior by fire. And now, undeniably both.

Layla bathed quickly, scrubbing herself raw as she used her mother's oils—lavender and vanilla. She couldn't help but smile because they smelled like home. The gown Marilla brought was sage green, soft and flowing with an open neckline. It didn't feel like armor, but somehow, it gave her strength.

She stepped out, hair still damp, but Marilla didn't dally and took her leave. Reassuring she would be back often to check on both her and the queen.

Layla offered a quiet, sincere thanks before returning to her mother's side. She took her hand gently, eyes searching her face.

"Please wake up," she whispered.

"So, this is the Princess of Graystonia. I see it now." Kain teased from across the room. More awake now than before. Layla rolled her eyes at him.

"Don't get me wrong. You looked great in the whole warrior woman thing and this... thing." He waved his hand at her attire, "But my favorite so far is the little white dress." He winked at her with that taunting smirk. Layla just glared back at him. *Asshole.*

Shut up, Kain," Layla muttered, then straightened her tone. "If you'd like, you're welcome to use the washroom while we wait." It was a clumsy attempt to change the subject, and they both knew it. But thankfully, Kain stood and stretched with lazy ease anyways.

"I'll be quick, try not to get into too much trouble while I'm in there." Kain didn't even look at her before shutting the washroom door. Layla just shook her head in frustration at him.

Before her mind could begin to wander once again, a knock at the door caused her to start to stand. Sir Edwin again, she assumed. But just as she turned away from her mother, gently removing her hand, the tips of her fingers were squeezed and Layla's entire body went rigid with shock.

"Mother!" Layla's voice cracked, breathless with joy. "You're awake!" Queen Raynera's eyes fluttered open, unfocused at first, her face pale and worn. She blinked slowly, confusion giving way to recognition.

"Layla?" she rasped, her voice barely audible. "You're alive... Thank the gods." Her gaze softened for just a moment before her lids fluttered shut again from the weight of exhaustion.

Layla grasped her mother's hand tighter, the warmth of it anchoring her in the chaos of everything she'd endured. "I'm here, Mother. We've taken the castle back. You're safe now." But the words faltered on her tongue slightly as she took in her mother's injuries again—how broken she looked lying there, beaten, pale, so unlike the woman who had ruled at her father's side with iron resolve. The woman who had taught her that tears were wasted energy, that emotion was for the behind closed doors.

"You were hurt badly..." Layla's voice dropped to a whisper, ashamed she couldn't say it outright. Ashamed that she hadn't been there in time to stop it.

Queen Raynera's fingers twitched in Layla's hand, her brow furrowed slightly. "I know," she whispered. "But I'm alive... I'll heal." Her eyes opened once more, glassy and tired, and fixed on her daughter's with sudden intensity. "Ciana? Aerilynn?" urgency piercing the weakness in her voice. The question stabbed through Layla like a dagger. Her throat tightened. She looked away for the briefest moment, forcing herself to hold it together. When she looked back, her voice shook.

"They were taken, Mother. Bartorian soldiers, before we got here. I'm so sorry... But I swear to you, I'm going after them. I *will* bring them back." Raynera's jaw tensed, her eyes closing briefly in pain, more emotional than physical. Then she pushed against the bed, trying to sit up. "No," Layla said firmly, placing her hands on her mother's shoulders. "Please. You're too hurt. You need to rest. Let me do this for you. For them."

Raynera's breath caught in her chest, but she stopped fighting. Her eyes met Layla's again, fierce despite the exhaustion in them. For a heartbeat, Layla saw her mother, the warrior behind the crown, the strategist who'd stood beside her father as his right hand. The woman who had never told her she was proud, but had always expected her to be worthy of pride.

"I see your father in you," Raynera murmured. "So skilled. So brave. And stubborn, gods help us."" Her lips curved in the faintest hint of a smile.

A sob choked in Layla's throat as tears streamed freely down her cheeks. "I'll bring them back," she vowed again, the words raw and sacred. "Whatever it takes. I'll bring them back to you."

A soft knock echoed at the chamber door. Layla knew what it meant— it was time. She leaned forward, brushing her lips against her mother's temple. "I love you," she whispered. The words were fragile, spoken from the deepest part of her. Words she had always wanted to say—and hear—but had learned not to expect. Queen Raynera didn't say it back. She never had. But her hand squeezed Layla's once more, stronger this time, and her eyes—though tired—held an unspoken truth: *I love you too. I'm proud of you.* Then, with a final look, she gave a slight nod and let her eyes close again, surrendering to sleep.

Layla rose slowly, wiping her tears with the back of her hand. The warrior in her hardened once more. She crossed the room with steady strides just as Kain emerged from the washroom, steam trailing behind him like mist from battle. His damp hair hung limp around his face, briefly touching his collarbones. His pants hung low on his hips as he padded barefoot across the stone floor. He made no comment, offered no smirk, just grabbed for the door with quiet purpose. Clearly pretending he hadn't overheard anything, she was grateful for it.

He opened the door, posture relaxed but alert, and Sir Edwin stood waiting on the other side.

"Is it time?" Layla asked, her voice low but ready.

"Not yet, My Lady," Sir Edwin replied, shifting awkwardly. "There are... Antonin warriors at the front gate requesting an audience with you. We've disarmed them and held position, but we weren't sure how you'd want to proceed, especially with, uh..." His eyes flicked briefly to Kain, clearly unsure what lines were being drawn anymore. Layla's brow furrowed. *Antonin warriors? Here?* Her gaze cut to Kain, but he only gave a shrug, equally in the dark.

"I'll handle it," she said, her voice firm with command. "Thank you, Sir Edwin. And please alert me the moment your men are prepared to ride for Bartoria."

Sir Edwin gave a sharp bow. "Of course, My Lady." Then he turned and strode off, armor clinking softly with each step.

Without a word, Kain gathered his leather armor and bloodied shirt, his fingers moving with practiced ease as he pulled them on over his bare chest, wincing slightly. One by one, he slung each piece into place—his bow over his shoulder, the soft thump of the arrow satchel settling at his back. Ready.

They exited the chamber together, their steps synchronized in silent understanding. Down the grand hall they moved, past shattered vases and blood-streaked marble, and out through the towering front doors of the castle. Beyond the gate, three Antonin warriors stood waiting, their armor dulled by travel and bloodshed. They kept their distance, clearly respecting the boundary laid before them. But Layla's breath caught in her chest as her eyes locked on the tall silhouette in the center. Even through the distance, she knew. It was Theron.

BY FLAME, BY ROOT, BY GOD AND STAR—
CAELERIA SHALL RISE, OR PERISH WHOLE.

THE LAW OF SACRED SOLSTICES

On the solstices, all bloodshed must cease. These
days belong to the gods alone. Any war waged
during them invites divine wrath-- drought,
storm, or plague.

- THE HIGH LAWS OF CAELERIA

Chapter Eighteen

Theron.

T heron stood behind the towering iron gate of the Graystonian
castle, flanked by Sparrow and Xaden. Their weapons had been
stripped, and Graystonian guards surrounded them in a tight circle,
blades drawn, eyes wary and unwelcoming. Theron didn't flinch. If it
came to bloodshed, the three of them could cut their way through the
lot of them with brutal efficiency. But it wasn't the swords or the glares
that had his heart pounding. It was the woman on the other side of that
gate. *Layla.*

She emerged from the castle like the very embodiment of royalty.
Gone were her warrior leathers, replaced now with a green gown that
shimmered softly in the sunlight. Her hair was still damp, cascading over
her shoulders like burnished silk, and every inch of her posture radiated

power. Kain walked at her side, an unexpected loyalty that hit like a blow, but it was her eyes that arrested Theron. Eyes that once looked at him with fire and curiosity, now burned with pure hatred.

"Why are you here?" Her voice sharp and steady, cutting through the air like a blade.

Theron swallowed hard. Her anger smoldered just beneath the surface- controlled, but unmistakable. Still, he stepped forward, suppressing the instinct to bow his head like a guilty child. "May we come in and speak?"

Layla hesitated for only a moment before motioning to one of her men. The iron gate groaned as it slid open. Theron, Sparrow, and Xaden stepped forward, their boots crunching on the stone path. The guards closed in behind them, blades still drawn.

"Speak," she commanded, her voice like steel wrapped in velvet.

"We've come to help you rescue your sisters," Theron said evenly. Layla's brows lifted, then a sharp laugh burst from her lips—mocking and bitter.

"*You?* You're here to *help* my family? *Now?*" Her voice was incredulous, almost feral with smoldering resentment.

Theron didn't respond right away. The weight of her disbelief was crushing. She had every right to spit those words at him. He deserved far worse. "May we speak privately?" he asked, quieter now.

"No," she snapped. Her chin lifted in defiance. "Not hours ago, I asked you to do exactly this and you refused. You chose your queen's command over the lives of my innocent family. Over *me*." Her voice faltered just slightly on the last word. "The same queen who ordered their massacre. So tell me, Theron—what changed?"

His throat tightened. "Queen Okteria doesn't know we're here," he admitted. "We came on our own...I came on my own." He paused, searching her eyes for any trace of the woman who once stared up at him under the stars. "I was wrong. I see that now. When I realized what she planned for your family... I should've spoken. I should've fought for you—for them. I knew it wasn't right, and still... I said nothing, did nothing. I see that now. And I'm... I'm sorry, Layla. Truly." The words were foreign on his tongue—heavy and raw. But true.

Layla's expression remained unreadable. Her silence screamed louder than any accusation. Theron continued, needing her to understand. "We know Bartoria. Its terrain. Its soldiers. We've scouted their lands more recently than your men. Let us help you bring your sisters home." He could feel her gaze strip him bare. Then, slowly, she stepped forward until she stood directly before him. Despite the height difference, she looked up at him with nothing but ice and authority.

"You and your men may help," she said, voice dangerously low. "But if you disobey me once, I'll have my guards gut you where you stand." Theron couldn't stop the corner of his mouth from twitching upward at the notion. She saw it and her jaw hardened like stone. "You may help me, Theron," she added coldly. "But I will never forgive you."

Those words hit harder than any blade ever could. He clenched his fists, forcing himself to stay composed as she turned and walked away. She moved like a royal angel—elegant, untouchable, impossibly far from him now. Her gown whispered over the stone with each step, hair catching the light like flame and silk. She was fire, she was grace, and she was no longer his to protect.

Kain stepped beside him, biting into a peach like they were on a leisurely stroll through a market square. Theron didn't look at him—not yet—but the weight of Kain's hand settled on his shoulder.

"Welcome to Graystonia, brother," Kain said, voice light and taunting, but laced with something quieter. Respect, maybe even empathy. But Theron wasn't in the mood for peace offerings.

"You defied orders," he said flatly, his voice low. "You helped her. Why?"

Kain's grin barely faltered. "Figured she'd be more fun alive."

Theron turned, eyes hard. "Why, Kain? Why choose her over the tribe? Over your orders? Over our Queen?

Kain took another bite, chewing slowly. "You always did love speeches."

Theron's fists clenched, but he looked closer. Beneath the sarcasm, beneath the lazy defiance, was something steady. Certain. Familiar. And Theron—who had spent his life honoring law and silence, who had been forged by his father into a weapon of obedience—recognized what he saw in his brother's eyes: *choice.*

Kain defying orders was nothing new. He'd done it his entire life—reckless, unruly, impossible to contain. But this... this was different. He hadn't just ignored a command. He'd gone against their queen. Against their tribe. For her. An enemy princess. A girl who should've meant nothing to him. And yet—he'd chosen her.

Theron didn't understand it. Couldn't. *What was it about her that made Kain turn his back on everything? Fascination? Rebellion? Boredom?* It had to be one of those. It had to be. Because if it wasn't... If it was something deeper...something real...Theron wasn't sure which truth cut deeper.

Theron exhaled, silently shaking those thoughts from his mind. He knew Kain wouldn't give him a straight answer. He never did. And honestly, it wasn't worth the fight, the guessing, the anger—not now. Not after everything. So instead, he did what he knew he should. What he'd known in his gut since the moment he saw Kain carrying Layla's mother through the smoke and blood, defying everything to do what was right, no matter the reason behind it. What he hadn't dared to do himself.

"Thank you Kain," he said, the words rough in his throat. "For protecting her. For doing what I..." His jaw flexed. "What I should have."

Kain blinked, surprised. But then his smirk softened into something unreadable. He nodded once. Solid. No gloating. Just understanding. The silence that followed wasn't awkward. It was an unspoken truce. A shared truth. And for the first time, Theron let it stand.

Theron looked around the grand hall as he waited. Gold-trimmed columns, rich tapestries, the scent of lavender and burning oils, it was another world compared to the open, rugged lands of the Antonin. Yet despite the luxury, his only thought was of Layla. He had lost her trust, maybe permanently. The weight of that betrayal sat in his chest like stone. If he had simply stood up to Okteria, if he had *acted*, none of this would have happened. She would still look at him with those bright, questioning eyes. Not as if he were the enemy.

A short time later, Layla returned. Cloaked in dark green, she was once more the warrior. A belt of blades strapped across her chest, the same ones he had given her. And Kain's daggers at her side. Jealousy twisted in his gut again, but he pushed it away.

"We're ready," she said. "You can have your weapons back now."

She barely looked at him, but the flicker of her voice lingered in his ears. A guard approached with armfuls of Antonin steel. The warriors quickly rearmed, strapping on their familiar instruments of death. Theron breathed easier the moment his sword settled against his hip. Its weight was reassuring, solid.

"You girls ready yet? Or need more time to keep getting dressed?" Kain's voice called out. Theron didn't dignify the comment with a response. But by the gods, he was going to punch him before this trip was over.

They rode out as a group of twenty, cloaks snapping in the wind as they cut through the outer walls. Theron was given a massive black stallion.

The horse huffed at him suspiciously but warmed to him quickly, nudging Theron's hand for affection.

He mounted the beast smoothly, watching from the corner of his eye as Xaden struggled to do the same. Kain and Sparrow laughed, and even Layla cracked the smallest smile. But when her eyes met Theron's, the smile vanished. Replaced by a wall of pain so thick he felt it in his bones. He looked away, jaw clenched, breath shallow. He had shattered something in her. Maybe something in himself too. He would ride into hell to fix it. He would bring her sisters back if it was the last thing he did. And maybe... maybe she'd see him again, not as the man who betrayed her, but the one who would die to protect her.

Layla.

Layla tried her best not to laugh as she watched the Antonin warriors struggle miserably on horseback. Between the sheer panic in Xaden's wide eyes and Kain's constant, subtle grimacing, it was far too entertaining for a day that had held so much pain. If she didn't know better, she might have thought they'd never ridden before.

Xaden caught her amused glance and dramatically clutched the saddle horn. "If I fall off and die, promise me you'll tell people it was during something epic, like slaying a bear or saving a village. Not from being thrown off a damned horse."

Layla stifled a laugh, her lips twitching. "Noted."

He groaned. "Gods, give me a sword and twenty enemies over this four-legged demon any day."

She shook her head smiling then reluctantly shot a glance at Theron. Unlike the others, he looked at ease in the saddle, too at ease. *Of course he would be the one Antonin to move like he was born on horseback.* That fact irritated her more than it should have.

The air had grown noticeably cooler with the sun's retreat, and as they pressed forward, Layla realized the last day of summer had passed them by. Fall was here. Normally, it was her favorite time of year, when the leaves turned to fire and gold, when laughter filled the streets during Graystonia's harvest festivals. But now those thoughts soured instantly. She could only picture her sisters dancing barefoot in the city square, ribbons in their hair. She desperately prayed that they were still in Bartoria. That the gods had slowed the enemy's journey somehow. She whispered Feyric's name under her breath.

They rode hard until twilight bled through the trees. Layla finally tugged the reins, slowing her horse when her men signaled that the time had come to stop. Together, they veered off the dirt path into the dense forest. Soon after, the group dismounted, and the warriors tied their horses near a small creek trickling through the clearing. Water for the animals. Stealth for the warriors.

"Don't shoot, I swear I'm only planning to murder a rabbit or two," Kain quipped as he stepped toward the trees waving his bow. His voice echoed to the Graystonian soldiers who bristled at the movement. Layla gave her men a small shake of her head. "Let him go," she muttered. Ironically, she trusted him now more than anyone else from the Antonin camp.

She watched a few of her men break off to hunt while others started a fire or took up guard positions. Theron and Xaden settled by a growing flame. Xaden rubbed his sore thighs and muttered something about walking the rest of the way. Sparrow had been told to immediately rest. She didn't remember the last time she had seen him sleep.

Layla wandered toward Sir Edwin, who straightened the moment he noticed her approaching. She motioned for him to remain seated and lowered herself beside him, grateful to rest her aching body.

"Sir Edwin," she began casually, "how did you become head of the guard?"

The young man blinked, clearly not expecting the question. "I... trained under Sir Charles, My Lady. But please believe me, I had no idea what he was planning. I would never betray the crown. Never betray you."

"I know." Layla leaned back slightly, watching the flames flicker between them. "If we can't trust our own guard, we have no hope of rebuilding. I'm choosing to believe Sir Charles acted alone. If I'm wrong, you'll inform me."

"Of course, My Lady," Edwin nodded firmly. "And we will find your sisters. I swear it." Layla studied him more closely. So young, yet chosen by his peers to lead. That had to mean something. She decided she would let his actions speak for him in Bartoria. A quiet beat passed before she lowered her voice.

"Sir Edwin... should I be concerned about the men here obeying my orders?" He looked confused at first—then realization dawned, and his expression sobered.

"No, My Lady. Every man here knows you will bear Graystonia's future king, even if he hasn't arrived yet." He paused, then added gently, "But... if I may... solidifying a powerful marriage will end any whispers of doubt." Layla nodded slowly, even as the words splintered something deep in her chest. She knew this. Knew what was expected of her. A marriage—political, strategic, not romantic—was always part of the plan. But that didn't dull the pain. It made her feel yet again like a piece on a game board, valuable only for her ability to produce a son, not her ability to lead. She looked out over the darkening forest, wind whispering through the trees, firelight dancing on steel and ash. First her sisters. Then her kingdom.

Theron.

Not far off, Layla was now sitting beside Sir Edwin. Theron watched from the recesses, unnoticed. Her voice was low, her posture relaxed but alert. She was asking questions, listening, commanding gently but firmly. She looked strong. She looked *whole*. She looked like someone who no longer needed him. And maybe she never had. Still, Theron would help her find her sisters. He would see this mission through, even if it killed him. Maybe especially if it did. Because even if she never forgave him... He would spend the rest of his life proving he should've tried harder when it mattered most. Theron dropped his gaze back to the fire. Flames crackled, leaping higher as Xaden tossed a few more branches into the pit.

"Tell me," Xaden said softly, only loud enough for Theron to hear. "When this is over... what then?"

Theron didn't answer right away. His jaw tightened. "I don't know."

"You think she'll ever forgive you?"

"No." The answer came out rough. Immediate. Honest.

Xaden looked at him for a long moment, the usual teasing gone. "You should have fought for her. Fought for what you knew was right."

"I know." Theron stared into the fire, the glow painting the edges of his face in amber and shadow. "I know." He repeated. They sat in silence for a while, the fire between them and the weight of unspoken things pressing down like a second nightfall. He should've argued. Should've fought harder when Queen Okteria revealed her intentions. He'd never questioned orders before, his entire life had been shaped by obedience, by honor defined through submission to the will of his queen. But that moment? That moment had deserved defiance. He should've stood for Layla. For her Family. For what was right. Instead, he had stayed silent—and that silence had made him complicit. Now, he would carry it with him. Always.

Layla.

Kain returned to camp with three rabbits and two birds slung over his shoulder, his cocky grin preceding him. A few of her guards clapped him on the back in thanks, already moving to start plucking and roasting. Not long after, her own men trickled back from the trees, holding up a few squirrels, less impressive, but it would suffice. Dinner tonight would be meager, but no one complained. They had warmth, weapons, and a direction. That was more than they'd had days ago.

After watching Theron slip away toward the perimeter, likely to take a guard shift, Layla wandered over to check on Xaden. He sat on a log, nursing a piece of fruit like it had personally offended him.

"How are you holding up?" Layla asked, keeping her tone gentle, but her lips twitched attempting to suppress a smile. "You were less than thrilled on horseback today."

Xaden let out a long, dramatic sigh and leaned back. "You noticed, huh?" He scratched at the stubble on his jaw, glancing up at her with tired amusement. "Back in our tribe, I could fight blindfolded and drunk and still hold my own. But the second you throw me on a demon beast with hooves? I turn into a newborn deer. It's humiliating."

Layla let out a soft laugh, genuinely charmed by his honesty. He smiled at the sound. "Don't worry," she teased, patting his back, "if you fall off tomorrow, I'll make sure to tell everyone it was a reeeally big bear." She widen her arms to as far as they could stretch as she spoke the tale. They both laughed until it faded into comfortable silence before Sparrow rolled over near them, stirring slightly. Then he sat up and nodded at Xaden. It was his turn to rest.

Sparrow rubbed the sleep from his eyes as he grabbed a squirrel and an apple before plopping down beside Layla. They sat in silence, watching the fire crackle, until her eyes wandered toward Theron across the clearing. He stood with a few of her guards, demonstrating sword technique. His movements were fluid, sharp, controlled. *Teaching them?* She wasn't sure if it annoyed or impressed her more. Shaking her head slightly, she turned back to Sparrow, her fingers tracing the edge of a dagger from her belt.

"Why are you here?" she asked him, her voice low. "I mean... really. Did Theron make you and Xaden come?"

Sparrow chuckled through a mouthful of squirrel meat. "Simple, really. A few days ago, Theron told me to protect you with my life. I agreed."

Layla blinked, stunned. "That's it?"

"That's it," he said with a shrug, as if he were explaining what day it was. She stared at him, absolutely bewildered.

"You know," Sparrow continued, eyes still on the fire, "he's saved my life more times than I can count. So, maybe I'm trying to return the favor for once." Her jaw tightened. "And for what it's worth," Sparrow added softly, "he's never defied an order. Not once. Not until you. Not until today."

Layla didn't respond. Her nails bit into her palms as she clenched her fists in her lap. *But does that even matter now? That he only questioned it after the blood had already spilled?*

"Appreciate your loyalty," she said coolly. "But what he did, what he allowed to be ordered, is unforgivable." Sparrow didn't argue. He just nodded and stayed beside her in silence. It reminded her of when she was first taken. When words had failed her, and silence was all she could bear. Somehow, he'd known even then when to speak and when to just be there.

Kain appeared a short time later, dropping down on her other side with all the grace of a lazy lion, propping himself up on his forearms. He stretched his legs out dangerously close to the fire.

"You're going to burn your feet," Layla warned.

He turned his head toward her, smirking. "Worried about me, Little Dove?" She rolled her eyes, but couldn't hide the small smile tugging at her lips. They both turned back to the fire.

"You know," she said, angling her body toward him, her voice soft, "I misjudged you." Kain turned his head, eyes catching hers. In the flickering firelight, his green eyes looked molten, intense. The teasing smile curled on one side of his mouth.

"Oh, I'm sure you did," he said, his gaze drifting—not to her eyes, but slowly, purposefully, over her face and down her body. Layla froze, caught somewhere between shock and amusement. Her mouth parted slightly, but no words came. Then he looked back up, meeting her gaze again, and chuckled darkly. "You weren't *entirely* wrong though."

Was that a joke? She stared at him, caught off guard. But before she could find a retort, her attention was pulled toward Theron again. Still demonstrating, still speaking with her men. She laid back with a groan, shutting her eyes. No matter what he did—teach her guards, stand in silence, bleed for her—her anger refused to leave her body. He had broken through the walls she had built around her, made her believe, even briefly, that she could trust him. And then he'd shattered it all. But still, damn him, she felt safe with him around.

Somewhere between fury and exhaustion, Layla drifted to sleep, nestled between the very men she once saw as enemies.

She woke stiff and sore, her body already aching from the ride. The fire had reduced to embers. As she stretched, she noticed someone sleeping beside her. Not Sparrow. Her heart sank. *Theron.*

With a loud, exasperated groan, she rolled onto her back and sat up. Out of the corner of her eye, she saw Theron stir and stretch beside her, his presence as aggravating as it was familiar. *Great.* She rose to her feet, brushing the dirt from her clothes. She needed to relieve herself—and clear her head. She turned toward the trees. Of course, she heard him following.

She spun to face him. "What are you doing?"

He stopped, towering a few feet away. "Where are you going?"

"I'm not your concern. Go away," she hissed, trying not to wake the others.

"You'll always be my concern, Layla." His voice was low. Steady. Too damn calm. And his eyes, —those traitorous blue eyes, held that same look he'd given her in the hut. When he'd held her after she broke. When he'd kissed her like she was the only thing keeping him alive.

Her shoulders slumped. The resentment ebbed, if only slightly. "I have to pee, Theron. Just... go."

He didn't move. Just turned around, crossed his arms, and stood guard. Of course he did. Layla ducked behind a tree, shaking her head. He made it so damn hard to keep hating him. And that was the most infuriating part of all.

ASH AND CARRION ARE
THE SEEDS OF OUR GLORY

BARTORIA

Chapter Nineteen

Theron.

A sharp twist of something unspoken knotted in Theron's chest as he watched Kain lean in to help Layla onto her horse. The easy way she smiled at his jokes. The light touch of her fingers on his shoulder. The effortless laughter between them, like they'd known each other forever. It caused him more anguish than he wanted to admit.

All his life, Theron had been the son who did everything right. He had shaped himself into the embodiment of the ideal warrior—unquestioning, unbreakable. The kind of leader others would follow without hesitation. Whereas Kain had always been a wild card, good in a fight but impulsive and selfish. Reckless, even. *But now?* Now Layla smiled for him. She leaned into him. *Trusted him...* And for the first time, Theron couldn't help but wonder if Kain was the better man.

He tore his eyes away, fists clenched, and walked to his horse that was currently still tethered beside Xaden's. The usually chipper warrior was halfway into his saddle, muttering curses through gritted teeth as he adjusted his balance.

"For the love of all the gods," Xaden grumbled, pulling himself up with the grace of a wounded bear. "If I fall and break my neck, tell everyone it was in a blaze of glory. A duel. Something dramatic. Not death by horse."

Despite everything, Theron huffed a small breath of amusement. "A bear is no longer sufficient?"

Xaden shot him a sideways glare but grinned as he steadied in the saddle. "Just make sure it's badass okay."

The clouds above rumbled, then broke open, spilling torrents of rain that drenched them within seconds. Visibility dropped, and the road dissolved into a river of mud, but no one slowed. They couldn't afford to. Over half the day passed and the rain never let up, but still they trudged on. Theron never taking his eyes off Layla's dark green cloak. Watching for any faulter in her horses steps. Thankfully it never came.

Lightning split the sky as they reached the Thornveil Run river that bordered Bartoria. On a dry day, the current was treacherous. Now, it was a churning monster. They had no choice but to attempt the crossing. Theron's gut twisted. He didn't fear death, nor for himself. *But Layla?* One misstep, one slip under those waters, and she'd be gone. He kicked his horse forward, placing himself close behind her. The cold water surged up the legs of his mount, rising fast. Just up ahead, he stared down that green cloak. His anchor in the chaos.

The front line of Graystonian soldiers had just made it to the midpoint when the river lunged. A wall of water surged down from upstream, a muddy wave that crashed into the men and horses without mercy. Screams cut through the storm as steel clanged and hooves flailed. Theron saw a horse flip sideways, the soldier atop it vanishing beneath the current. Panic erupted.

"Layla!" he roared, but she was already reacting.

"We must go on!" she shouted, voice like thunder. "Go now before it gets worse!" Gods, she was fearless. Her voice viciously sliced through the roar of the river. Even now—drenched, shivering, and death lurking beneath the torrent—she led them. Theron pressed closer, his horse nearly nose-to-tail with hers. The current was a beast clawing at their legs, dragging debris from the woods into the water around them. But they kept moving.

One agonizing moment at a time, they made it across. By the time the survivors reached the far bank, Theron's legs were numb from cold and tension. He spun in his saddle, counting. Eight Graystonian soldiers were missing. Swallowed by the river. Just... *gone*. He saw it on Layla's face, the weight of it. But she didn't crumble, didn't falter. And by the gods, he knew her well enough now to recognize the cracks in her armor. She blamed herself. Theron ached to go to her. To offer warmth, comfort, something. *Anything*. But she stood tall, even soaked and brokenhearted, and issued orders with a voice that didn't waver.

"Run the shoreline!"

Without delay, they scattered, hunting for signs of the missing men. Theron and Kain moved faster than most, their Antonin training making them ghosts in the storm. But it was no use. The river had taken what it wanted. Eventually, all returned, sadly empty-handed. And Layla, standing in the middle of it all, looked smaller somehow. Not weaker—just... more alone.

They kept moving, pressing forward through mud, wind and blistering rain. Theron rode beside her, just close enough to be near if she needed him but just far enough to give her space. However, it was getting dark and they needed shelter. Time out of the negative elements to plan and regroup.

As if the gods themselves offered a reprieve, a manor emerged in the distance, stone walls barely visible through the rain.

Layla turned in her saddle, commanding attention like a born queen. "Sir Edwin. How do you recommend we proceed?"

We could sneak around it through the forest," Edwin offered, "but the terrain may be too dense—and with the weather turning, it'll be even harder off the main path. If it is, we may have to leave the horses.

"Or," Kain said, not bothering to hide his sarcasm, "we knock on the door, kill the noble inside, and warm ourselves by the fire...Just a thought."

Layla shot him a dry glare, then seemed to weigh his words before she gave her final order. "We'll take the manor. Kill any Bartorian soldiers or nobles. Spare the handmaids. They are not our enemy." Theron swallowed a grin. Even after hours in a storm, soaked to the bone, she was sharp, decisive. Gods, she was continually surprising him.

They approached under cover of night, dismounting behind the stables. The horses were quiet, perhaps too exhausted to even protest anymore. The plan was swift and silent—neutralize the guards, secure the manor. Theron moved into position beside Xaden at the door, sword drawn but hidden. Xaden knocked and an older maid answered.

In a blink, Xaden yanked her outside before pinning her against the stone wall. "Scream and you die," he whispered, blade at her neck. Terrified, the woman stuttered out that only she and a few other handmaids remained inside. The guards were at the castle for a celebration. Sir Norsden was gone, the noble of the household.

Theron stepped from the dim alcove and signaled for the others to approach. Layla led them inside with calculated authority. Her guards fanned out, clearing the manor room by room while the rest of the maids cowered together by the kitchen. Theron watched Layla approach them, drenched but radiant. Her voice was calm, reassuring.

"We don't want to hurt you. We only need shelter for the night and a small meal. If you can give us that, we'll leave peacefully come morning." The maids nodded, eyes wide, then hurried to the kitchen.

One lingered. "I can show you some rooms, ma'am," she whispered, eyes on the floor. Layla nodded once, regal as ever. Theron exhaled, tension slowly draining from his shoulders. For tonight, at least, they were safe. But as he watched Layla disappear up the stairs, flanked by

Sparrow and Kain, his heart stayed heavy. She was just within reach yet still felt a thousand miles away...And he had no one to blame but himself.

Layla.

Layla thanked the petite red-headed maid, who looked barely younger than herself, and followed her up the creaking staircase. A few of the Graystonian guards remained downstairs with Xaden and Theron. While Sparrow, Kain, and a couple more soldiers accompanied her. The maid moved quietly, almost timidly, down the hallway, opening room after lavish room, clear signs of a wealthy Bartorian lord. Velvet curtains. Intricate rugs. Chandeliers that swayed gently from the vibrations of thunder outside. At last, they reached the largest chamber, the Lord's own quarters. It had its own fireplace and was nearly double the size of the others. Sparrow stood at the door, his broad form blocking the threshold as Layla stepped inside with the maid.

"Would you like me to start a fire?" the girl asked without meeting Layla's eyes. Layla couldn't help but notice the way she stood—small, cautious, as if waiting for permission to breathe. *Was she this scared of her, or was this submissiveness bred into her by a cruel lord?*

"No. Thank you. I can manage." Layla offered a polite smile. "Where can I find dry clothes?"

The maid stepped toward two separate dressers and motioned, still avoiding her gaze. "Nightgowns here, daywear in this one."

"Thank you. That will be all." Layla nodded. The girl bowed quickly and exited. Sparrow gave Layla a subtle nod before shutting the door behind him, granting her a much-needed moment of solitude.

The stillness instantly pressed in, wrapping around her like a heavy cloak. She leaned against the carved bedpost and exhaled slowly. The ache in her muscles flared now that she'd stopped moving. Her damp gown clung to her skin, making her shiver. She knelt at the hearth and began stacking the wood. Her hands moved by memory, striking flint until the first flickers of flame caught. She cupped her palms around the growing fire, letting the warmth seep in. Finally, something familiar. Something she could control.

When the chill left her fingers, she stood and moved to the dresser the maid had indicated. She rifled through the fine linens and silks, finally settling on a soft nightdress that reminded her of one she had back home. The sight of it tugged at her chest. She would be back there soon. Things would be normal again. *Wouldn't they?* She sighed and reached for the ties of her dress.

"Would you like some help with that?"

Layla jumped and whipped around instinctively. Kain was leaning against the doorframe, his signature grin flickering with mischief in the firelight. She hadn't even heard the door open. Rolling her eyes, she laughed under her breath. Her arms fell loosely to her sides. "Gods, you really have no sense of timing."

"Depends on what we're timing," Kain said smoothly, stepping inside as he unfastened his soaked leather vest. "Any dry clothes in there for me, or are you keeping them all to yourself?"

She narrowed her eyes playfully, tilting her head. "Why do I feel like that question's not entirely innocent?" Kain gave her an exaggeratedly innocent look and then shook out his wet hair like a wolf, spraying droplets across the room. "Kain! Stop that!" Layla shrieked, shielding her face with her hands. Laughter spilled between them like it belonged, easy and real. He grinned, completely unbothered, as he approached.

"I'm freezing, Little Dove. My boys are trying to hibernate somewhere in my ribcage. Help a man out."

Layla blinked. "Your—what?" Her eyes dropped before she could stop herself. His smirk widened. *Shit.* She spun back to the dresser. "Let me just, um, look for something in here for you." She tried to sound casual, tried to control the warmth rising to her face. But then she felt him behind her. His breath ghosted along her neck and she froze. The heat of it licked over her skin, raising goosebumps down the lengths of her arms.

"I need something dry, Dove," he whispered against her ear. "Don't want your soldiers getting jealous." *Jealous?* Confused, she turned sharply and froze. Kain stood right before her now fully naked. A breath caught in her throat. Her eyes dragged over him before she could stop herself—from his wet golden hair to his dangerously carved and inked torso...and lower... much lower. *Gods.* She spun around so fast she nearly knocked over a vase.

"Kain! What the hell!?" She screeched. He laughed, low and unrepentant. She fumbled for a nightshirt and tossed it at him, smacking him in the chest. "Put some clothes on, damn it!" she snapped, her voice cracking somewhere between scandalized and breathless.

The sound of a throat clearing at the door, startled her even more. Layla turned and to her horror, Theron stood there. His expression unreadable. His gaze fixed on her with the sharpness of a drawn blade, unblinking and unrelenting.

Kain, unbothered, strode over and held up the shirt like a peace offering. "Need one too, brother?" Theron didn't move. Didn't blink. Only clenched his jaw tighter. His eyes burned through Layla. Kain just chuckled and strolled out, still entirely too naked. Layla couldn't speak. She couldn't explain it. The hurt in Theron's gaze gutted her. She crossed the room and dropped onto the bed like her body no longer belonged to her.

"I just wanted to check on you..." Theron said quietly, stepping farther into the room. Layla couldn't bring herself to meet his eyes. "The men today... they died protecting you. Protecting your family. They died as heroes, if they..." He paused, choosing his words carefully. "If they even did die."

But his words didn't soothe the ache in her chest. Didn't change the truth that it had been her mission. Her command. Her burden. Her father's voice echoed in her memory—To rule is to carry the weight of others' choices... and their deaths.

She rose to her feet. She had grieved enough for now. Her soldiers needed her. Her people needed her. Her sisters needed her. She would not cower behind stone walls and let sorrow consume her. Not when there was still work to be done. But as she moved toward the door, Theron stepped into her path, lifting a hand to stop her.

"You're dripping water. You'll catch a fever before you save anyone. Change first. Then plan." His voice was steady. Firm but gentle. Layla's defenses cracked just slightly and she reluctantly nodded. He let his hand fall, the tips of his fingers grazing her arm. She tensed at the contact, at how good it felt. He gave her a brief nod and walked out, closing the door behind him.

She stood there, stunned by her own swirling feelings. Then, slowly, she peeled off her wet gown, wrung it out, and hung it near the fire before slipping into the soft blue nightdress. She felt like neither warrior nor princess right now. But feelings were a luxury she could no longer afford. Her sisters needed her—and she would become whatever they needed to be saved.

Layla descended the stairs and paused at the bottom. Nearly all the men were in nightshirts, most of them far too short or frilled for comfort. Their weapons lay awkwardly on laps or beside chairs as they tried to look fierce in this ridiculous attire. She covered her mouth to stifle a laugh. Then the far door flew open.

Kain burst into the hall wearing the most ridiculous women's nightgown she had ever seen—lace, ruffles, and all. His eyes found hers immediately. Furious. Mortified. She couldn't stop herself. Laughter exploded from her lips.

"Hey pretty lady," Xaden crooned, draping an arm around Kain's shoulders. "You free later?" The entire room roared. Layla's laughter shook her shoulders until her eyes watered. But even in that joy, she felt it—that familiar gaze.

Across the room, Theron watched her. A small smile played at his lips. Her laughter faded as her cheeks warmed. He always made her feel so exposed with just a glance.

She dropped her eyes and focused back on Kain, who was now stomping off, presumably in search of something less humiliating to wear. *That's what he gets.* She couldn't help but feel a little bit of pride in the stunt she just pulled on him. Finally, the weight on her chest loosened. Just for a moment. Then, she gathered herself and turned to the group. It was time to plan. Tomorrow, they would face hell. But tonight, they would sleep under stolen roofs, beside warm fires, with weapons close and laughter closer. And Layla Eradellian would be ready for whatever comes.

"At first light, we will carry on to Bartoria," Layla said firmly, straightening her shoulders as her gaze flicked between Sir Edwin and Theron. "Can we continue on the roads, or do we leave the horses behind?" Before either could answer, her mind leapt ahead. "And how far are we from Bartoria? We have to be close… right?"

Sir Edwin glanced at Theron, silently deferring the response. Theron nodded. "We're only a few hours away. If we leave at first light, we'll reach the outskirts by midday," he replied. His voice was steady, authoritative. "With the amount of rain we've had, there's no telling how many roads will be washed out. But we should try with the horses for as long as possible. If we need to abandon them along the way, so be it."

Layla gave a small nod, absorbing the information—but Theron wasn't finished. "If I may…" he added, waiting for her approval. She gestured for him to go on. "Bartoria's outer city is barely guarded. Getting inside will be easy. But the castle…" He hesitated. "We've never infiltrated it. I don't know its weak points. And if the maid was right about a celebration, the guards may be more alert than usual." At that, Layla's brow furrowed. *A celebration?*

As if summoned by her thoughts, a maid emerged from the kitchen carrying a basket of bread. "Maid?" Layla called gently.

The young woman froze mid-step, eyes wide as she turned to face her. "Y-yes, my lady?"

"What celebration is happening at the Bartoria castle?"

"The... wedding, ma'am," the maid answered shakily. "The king is to marry. In two days' time."

Layla blinked. "A wedding?" That made no sense. Not after losing a battle. Not so soon. Unless... he was securing his legacy. "Who is he marrying?"

"I only know what was written in the invitation, ma'am," the maid said, fidgeting with the edge of her apron. "It mentioned a royal wedding. Starting with garden party and royal feast. Then the following morning the official ceremony. All of the northern territories were invited. My lord left just this morning to attend." *A wedding. With all the fanfare of a political summit. That meant new guests. A new opening.*

Layla narrowed her eyes. "And you just happened to read your lord's invitation?"

The maid's eyes widened suddenly, before dropping her head once again. Then with a small shrug, "We're the ones who seal the letters. Press the suits. Ready the horses. We see more than we should."

"Of course you do. Maids always know the secrets." Layla gave a dry smile. "You've been helpful. Thank you," Layla dismissed her with a nod. The maid bobbed a curtsy and fled back to the kitchen. Layla turned to the table of men, who were now all watching her with expectation.

"Well," she said dryly, "looks like we're going to a royal wedding."

The timing was eerie. Fitting. Bartoria had used a celebration to ambush Graystonia. It was only right that she returned the favor. Soon the maids returned, carrying trays of roasted meats, root vegetables, and steaming bread. The scent alone made Layla's stomach grumble, only now realizing how long it had been since her last full meal. Everyone dug in with unspoken urgency. The room filled with the sounds of chewing and satisfied groans. The Antonin warriors, predictably, skipped using the utensils entirely. Layla couldn't stop a small grin from curving her lips as she watched them devour their food like wild animals in silk nightgowns.

Once the plates emptied and everyone began to lean back in their chairs, the planning resumed.

"We can't all go in," Kain said, brushing crumbs from his lap. "Too many of us, too noticeable."

"You'll need us if things go sideways," a Graystonian soldier countered.

"The point is not to fight," Sparrow reminded them. "Stealth is the only way this works."

"They're not just going to hand the princesses over," Xaden muttered. "There'll be a fight."

"We'll fight if we have to," Theron said evenly. "But we go in with the hope that we won't."

"How exactly are we supposed to blend in?" Xaden asked, turning toward Layla. The room fell quiet.

"We'll find proper wedding attire in this manor," she said, her voice steady with command as she informed her decision. "My Graystonian men will stay outside the city limits to guard the escape route and prepare for a swift, loud extraction if things go wrong. They'll be our strength if subtlety fails." She turned her gaze toward the Antonin warriors across the table, men born of wilderness, shaped by silence, and trained to kill like whispers in the dark. "You Antonins, along with Sir Edwin, will come with me into the castle as guests of the wedding." A few brows lifted, but no one spoke. "Your tribe's customs," she continued, "your posture, your poise, they're unfamiliar in Bartoria. That works in our favor. You'll be perceived as nobles or foreign dignitaries. No one will question why you don't speak much or why you keep to the walls. If anything, they'll be too afraid to ask."

Kain smirked at that. Xaden tilted his head, clearly pleased. "Antonins are trained to blend into forests and fortresses alike. You know how to stay quiet. How to kill without a sound. And, if needed, how to vanish. That's what I need inside those walls. Ghosts in silk." She looked around at the others. "If we all went in, we'd draw too much attention. A group this large, this armed, would set off alarms before we ever reached the throne room. But if we move like invited guests, like shadows slipping through candlelight... we may reach the princesses before anyone even knows that we're there." Layla's voice hardened slightly. Every man at the table nodded. Even the ones who clearly hated every part of the plan. They all could at least agree that stealth would get them in, but vengeance would get them out. Layla rose. Fatigue clung to her bones like damp cloth. "Get rest. We'll move out at dawn."

She climbed the stairs slowly, each step heavier than the last. The laughter and planning faded behind her, replaced by the memories of the men they'd lost today. Their faces. Their loyalty. The way they trusted her with their lives. She entered the room and shut the door softly behind her.

The fire still crackled. Her bed was waiting. But so was the weight of command. Layla curled on the mattress, her arms wrapping tightly around her knees, and pressed her face into her hands and cried. Silent tears for the soldiers. For her sisters. For the girl she used to be, the one who thought bravery looked like speeches and crowns.

The door creaked open and Layla jolted upright. Quickly wiping her face with the heel of her hand as Theron stepped inside. His gaze found hers instantly, and even in the flickering low light, she could see the worry there. He crossed the room in two strides, then dropped to one knee before her. Without asking, his hand lifted, warm and steady, his palm cupping her cheek. His thumb brushed the last of her tears away. She closed her eyes. Just for a second, and let herself lean into the comfort. Let herself feel something other than guilt.

"You need to go," she whispered. "Please. I can't..." She opened her eyes slowly, meeting his. She needed him to understand: She was too tired to be angry right now. Too tired to pretend she could hold herself together in front of him. Thankfully, he didn't argue. Just nodded and stood, but didn't step back.

"We don't know this manor. Or these maids," he said softly. "I'll sleep right here. On the floor. Just in case."

Of course he would. Layla sighed, but didn't protest. She shifted toward the head of the bed, pulled the heavy blanket over her body, and reached out to tug the extra pillow from beside her. She held it up in offering. Theron just chuckled. "I'll live," he said, shaking his head, and made a small pallet beside her on the floor.

She listened to the rustle of fabric and the quiet sound of his armor being removed. Then stillness as only the sound of the fire remained. Layla closed her eyes, breathing in the faint scent of smoke, rain, and leather. She was exhausted. But she was safe. Because Theron was here. And for just tonight...that was okay.

ASH AND CARRION ARE
THE SEEDS OF OUR GLORY

By the eternal favor of the Crown, each citizen
is bestowed their breath, their labor, and the
name by which they serve. These are not
possessions, but privileges- a quiet inheritance
of the sovereign's grace. To surrender what was
never truly one's own is the highest form of
loyalty. In such loss, glory is found.

-BY COMMAND OF THE IRON CROWN OF
BARTORIA

Chapter Twenty

Theron.

T heron didn't sleep. Even with Sparrow stationed at the foot of the stairs and the rest of his warriors rotating watch through the night, his body refused to rest. Every creak of the old manor stirred him. Every gust of wind clawing at the shutters made his hand grip for a blade. But more than that, it was *her. Layla.*

Each time he blinked awake, he found his gaze drifting to the bed above him. She lay there curled in the thick covers, her soft breaths steady, her face calm in a way he rarely saw anymore. Watching her sleep was the only thing that eased the war beneath his ribs. He didn't deserve that peace. Still, each time he stoked the fire or shifted to ease the ache in his back from the hard floor, his eyes returned to her. He knew today would change everything. They were marching into the lion's den, and Layla—fiery, stubborn, brave—would never stay behind. He understood now that she would walk straight into danger for her sisters and there was no convincing her otherwise, and that absolutely terrified him.

When the first brush of light ghosted across the distant hills, Theron rose. He stretched, the tension in his spine cracking down his back, then pulled aside the thick curtain to reveal the soft pink edge of dawn. The storm had broken at last. The sky was clear. Quietly, he crossed the room and sat on the edge of the bed, one hand settling on Layla's shoulder. Her skin was warm beneath his palm.

"Layla," he said softly. "It's time." She stirred, groaning lightly, then rolled onto her back. Her lashes fluttered, eyes locking onto his before she winced and shut them again.

"Theron," she murmured, her voice still thick with sleep. "You need to go. I'm fine." He didn't move. She opened her eyes again, this time sharp and guarded. "Theron, go," she repeated, ice laced in her tone. "Send anyone else to worry about me. I'm not yours to worry about anymore." The words hit like a sword's edge. But still, a small, aching smile tugged at his mouth.

He stood and walked to the door, pausing in the frame. Without turning, he said, "I'll always worry about you, Layla." And then he was gone.

Downstairs, the manor was already stirring. Soldiers rearmed, Graystonian warriors donned their gear once again, and maids flitted about laying fruit and bread on the tables. Theron requested wedding attire from one of them, watching the confusion flicker in her eyes before she rushed away. Sparrow met his gaze without needing to be told. He slipped after her, heading up the stairs to ensure Layla remained undisturbed. Theron sighed and sat by the fire, gingerly chewing an apple as his mind already began turning to what came next. How the hell he'd smuggle blades into dress clothes...how they'd find the princesses...how to keep Layla from getting herself killed.

Minutes passed. Then Sparrow, the maid, and Layla returned, arms loaded with garments. The maid laid down a navy dress with delicate white and gold accents. Layla studied it in silence, then turned and ascended the stairs once more, the gown folded carefully over her arm. Theron couldn't help himself. He watched her climb, hoping for something—anything. And just before she disappeared from view, she looked down at him. Her gaze wasn't cold. It wasn't angry. It was... *tender.* His throat tightened. *There it was.* A flicker of hope. And he couldn't ignore it. Without thinking, he grabbed his own dress clothes and sword, and took the stairs two at a time. He stopped at her door. Heart pounding. Then, before he could lose his nerve, he opened it.

Layla stood by the bed, the gown half slipped off one shoulder. She turned, startled, her lips parting as their eyes met. The curve of her bare shoulder, the way the soft morning light kissed her skin, it stole the air from his lungs. She didn't scream. She didn't yell. Her eyes dropped. Slowly. Tracing down his form, then catching on the swelling tension beneath the nightshirt he hadn't yet replaced. When she looked back up, something in her eyes had changed. No hatred. No ice. *Hunger.*

Theron crossed the room in a heartbeat, his hand gliding down her arm, the other grazing the sleeve that taunted him. Her body tensed but she didn't pull away. He bent, lips brushing the tender skin of her shoulder.

"I want you," he whispered, low and raw. She turned slightly, her breath shallow, her eyes drifted to his mouth. Then, their lips crashed—desperate, fevered, starved. The kiss deepened, messy and all-consuming. His hand cupped her breast through the thin shift, feeling the curve of her against his palm. She moaned into his mouth, her body pressing back against his, arching for more. His control was fraying. He wanted her too badly. But as the fire within them raged higher, Layla suddenly pulled back, her fingers trembling slightly. And Theron froze. She looked at him—not with fear, but with conflict. Her lips swollen, her cheeks flushed. But her eyes... her eyes held weight. Theron stepped back, hands falling to his sides.

"I'm sorry," he whispered. "If I could take it all back, every-thing, I would. I never meant to hurt you." Her face softened, but she said nothing. "I know you might not forgive me," he said, voice hoarse. "But I will never stop fighting for you. Never stop protecting you." He took a breath. "I love you, Layla Eradellian."

Silence. He didn't expect a response. He didn't need one. Just needed her to hear it...So he simply bent down and kissed her again—soft this time. A kiss of goodbye. Of apology. Of promise. He helped her steady herself, then turned, retrieved his clothes, and left the room.

Downstairs, the world spun on. Theron dressed in silence, carefully strapping knives beneath sleeves, into boots, along his beltline. He hated the tailored feel of the clothing, hated the vulnerability of it all. But if it got him into the castle, close to Layla and the princesses, it would have to do. His sword would have to be left behind and he despised that most. Then as he looked around. The other Antonin warriors were dressed similarly—strange, stifled versions of themselves, each missing the steel that made them deadly. But they were ready.

Then came her. Layla appeared at the top of the stairs. The navy gown hugged her curves, the golden embroidery catching the morning light. Her hair was braided back from her face, her chestnut curls tumbling over her shoulders like waves of silk. The corset accentuated the rise of her chest, and her poise was straight from a queen's lineage. She wasn't a princess anymore. She was a weapon. Theron's chest ached as he watched her descend. Gods help the kingdom that stood in her way. He loved her. Fiercely. And no matter what came next, he would keep her alive. Even if it meant dying at her side.

Layla.

She didn't know what to think after the bomb he dropped on her before leaving the room. Her mind spun, emotions tangled in knots. Luckily, the day ahead demanded all her focus; she didn't have time to sort through the storm inside her chest. As she descended the stairs to join her men, her eyes involuntarily sought out Theron's. The love and adoration radiating from him were unmistakable. She sighed and quickly looked away. There were sisters to find. Love—and betrayal—would have to wait.

Layla crossed the grand room and gently pushed open the kitchen door to find the maids huddled together. They instantly stood taller, their eyes cast down as if awaiting orders.

"Thank you. We are leaving now. I pray you don't get in trouble for the loss of clothing and food. I hope this will help." She handed them a bundle of coins, offering a small nod before closing the door behind her.

Outside, the crisp morning air greeted them. Autumn had settled in, and the sun peeked over the treetops. One by one, they mounted their horses, ready to ride. They would travel as far as possible by road unless they encountered someone. Her soldiers, those not in Bartorian disguise, would veer into the forest to remain hidden, ready to ambush if needed.

After hours of galloping along the winding dirt road, the sharp breeze cooled Layla's flushed cheeks. She had always loved the fall—crisp air, golden leaves, the sense of change on the wind. But as Theron gradually slowed his pace, she knew they were nearing Bartoria. The breeze faded, replaced by a stillness that clung to the skin, heavy and unnatural. And with it came a tension she could feel in her bones—tightening like a thread pulled taut, ready to snap.

As the city came into view, Layla turned to Sir Edwin. "Have our men stay close to this road, as near to the city edge as possible while hidden in the trees. We need to know where to find them, especially if we need a swift exit. Tell them to give us until morning if it comes to that. We don't know how long it'll take to find my sisters." Sir Edwin nodded and rode ahead to relay her orders. She watched her soldiers veer right, leading their horses into the forest thicket, disappearing from sight. Sir Edwin returned shortly after, falling back in line with the Antonin warriors.

As they crossed into the southern edge of the city, the group slowed to a cautious trot. The narrow, crumbling streets wound between buildings that looked like they might collapse with the next strong wind. The air was thick with smoke, desperation, and the faint scent of rotting food. Layla's gaze swept over gaunt faces peering from behind broken shutters, children with hollow eyes watching them pass in eerie silence. Her grip tightened on the reins.

Xaden and Theron rode several paces ahead, silent sentinels leading the way. Sparrow flanked her left side, his sharp eyes constantly scanning the tree line, while Sir Edwin kept pace on her right with one hand resting near his blade. Behind her, Kain lingered like a ghost, his presence as unmistakable as it was reassuring. She was surrounded—shielded on all sides by men who had fought for her, bled for her, defied orders for her. There was no safer place to be. And yet...

The guilt settled in her chest like a stone. These people watched from the wreckage of their lives as she passed with an armed escort, unable to offer anything more than a solemn glance. She couldn't stop. Couldn't promise salvation. Not yet. But gods, she wanted to. She let the words anchor her as they pressed on, the rhythm of hooves steady, unforgiving.

The city transformed the closer they drew to the castle. Crumbling alleyways gave way to pristine stone homes. Tidy storefronts gleamed with imported wares. Finely dressed citizens lingered at fruit stalls and flower carts, laughing softly, their blissful ignorance cutting sharper than any blade. They were only minutes from a starving district, yet lived as if untouched by suffering. The divide was stark. Revolting. Layla straightened in her saddle, chin high, every inch the princess in disguise.

People nodded politely as the group passed, none the wiser that the riders among them were foreign invaders. And then, just as the castle gates came into view, a cold jolt of panic struck her. They didn't have an invitation. *Shit!*

As they came to a halt before the towering gates, a Bartorian guard stepped forward, his eyes drifting first to Theron. Layla wasn't surprised—Theron carried himself with quiet authority, a commanding presence even in the heart of enemy territory.

"Invitation," the guard demanded, voice rough with suspicion.

Layla tensed. She caught the way the guard's hand hovered near his weapon, the flicker of doubt behind his eyes. Then, almost instinctively, her mother's words surfaced: "Men are ruled by many things, Layla... but desire is always at the helm. Learn when to use it." Thinking fast, Layla turned toward Theron, her mind already racing...

"Honey, I think you gave it to me. Hold on." She addressed Theron loudly enough for the guard to hear as she began patting herself down, feigning panic. "Oh no... I can't seem to find it!" Her hands raked over her dress as she turned to the guard, wide-eyed. "My good sir, would you mind helping me down from my horse so I can look through this dress more thoroughly?" He didn't respond, just walked past Theron toward her. As he lifted her down, her hands rested on his shoulders, positioning her chest inches from his face. While skillfully letting her fingers slide down his arm, her voice becoming soft and flirtatious.

"Oh wow, you're so strong. What a lucky king to have you protecting him." She mused as she resumed patting her sides, pretending to search. Her hands drifted up to her waist, then her chest, grazing over her breasts before she met the guard's eyes again. "Oh no. I must've dropped it on our ride here. And I was so looking forward to seeing you inside later..." She bit her lip, tilting her head. "Maybe for a dance?"

The guard coughed and subtly adjusted himself. "We cannot dance. We are here to guard the sacred house of Bartoria," he muttered stiffly.

She leaned in, her lips brushing his ear. "Well, maybe we don't have to dance then. Just come find me later, and we can do other things." When she pulled back, a smirk had bloomed across his face. He then smugly turned and nodded to the guards at the gate. Without a word, the gate began to open. Layla smiled sweetly, internally rejoicing at her triumph. "Would you be so kind as to help me back onto my horse, my good sir?" The guard obliged, placing his hands on her backside and giving it a firm squeeze as he hoisted her back atop her horse. Her jaw clenched, but she forced that placated smile to remain and waved as they trotted through the gate. She caught Sparrow smirking beside her.

"What? I got us in, didn't I?" she muttered dryly. Sparrow lifted both hands in mock surrender, clearly amused. Layla faced forward again but couldn't help the quick glance toward Theron. His jaw was tight beneath his beard, his gaze fixed straight ahead. She knew he was pissed by his rigid composure. *Of course he hated what he'd just seen.* And just like that, the flicker of triumph she'd felt crumbled... They were never on the same page—not really. He had some idea of who she was supposed to be, how she should act... and no matter what she did, it always seemed to be the wrong version of her. Layla gave an exasperated sigh and faced forward once again.

As they reached the front steps, a row of neatly dressed maids and stable hands stood waiting. Their group dismounted briskly, handed off their reins, and followed a maid up the wide staircase. The grand doors swung open, revealing a castle more beautiful than Layla had expected—soaring arches, polished stone floors, and vibrant tapestries lining every corridor. And yet, with every gilded detail, her anger flared. All this splendor... while the rest of Bartoria was in absolute ruin.

As they made their way through the entry hall, the maid spoke without turning.

"The wedding festivities are in the back courtyard. The ball will be this evening. King Ivar wants everyone to celebrate his soon-to-be wife."

Layla couldn't help but roll her eyes. Of course he did. Annoyance simmered beneath her composed expression, but deep down... there was a flicker of dark satisfaction. He had ruined her Lammas festival, ruined her life and the lives of so many others. Now she would return the favor. Only her revenge would be quiet, calculated, and so exquisitely earned he wouldn't see it coming until it was far too late.

They all stole quick glances down corridors as they passed. The castle was vast. Finding her sisters in this place would be like threading a needle in the dark—slow, dangerous, and one wrong move from bleeding.

Two towering glass doors swung open, spilling music and laughter into the hall. The courtyard beyond teemed with nobles. Jousting matches clashed beside hand-to-hand combat rings, an entertainer juggled gleaming swords, and a lavish spread of food shimmered beneath glasses of champagne catching the afternoon sun.

Layla stopped at the threshold, eyes scanning the battlefield before her as Kain stepped to her right, Theron to her left. Both extended an arm. An Offering. She hesitated only a moment. Then, without a word, she slid her hands through the crooks of their elbows—steady, grounded. Not a choice. Not a question. Just the silent strength she needed, drawn from both, as the weight of what lay ahead settled on her shoulders. Surrounded by the two deadliest men she knew, Layla walked into the lion's den. Not just protected, but empowered.

As they strolled through the crowd, she couldn't help but notice the many women fanning themselves or staring open-mouthed at the Drakaren brothers. Apparently, men like them were rare in Bartoria. If she was being honest, there weren't any like them in Graystonia either. She bit back a smile as they scanned the crowd, hopeful eyes searching for her sisters or the king. Any hint of a way to get to them... After two laps, there was still no sign of either.

Theron leaned in just enough for both her and Kain to hear and whispered, "We're going to have to split up and mingle. We need to find out as much as possible about tonight." Theron's voice was low but firm as he placed his hand over Layla's and slowly pried her fingers from his bicep. She blinked, instantly confused as she dropped her arm. Her other hand still resting delicately on Kain's arm. Theron gave her a small nod—curt, almost apologetic—before turning and walking away into the crowd. As muddled as things were between them, Layla couldn't deny that she didn't like watching him walk away. It unsettled her, more than she was ready to admit.

"Come on, Little Dove," Kain murmured beside her, his breath brushing her ear. "We'll see him again shortly. Let me teach you how to mingle."

Layla scoffed at the assumption, "I know how to mingle."

"From what I saw, you know how to let a man grab your ass, but can you actually *mingle*?" he teased. "Guess we'll find out." His voice was light, mocking even but she didn't miss the flash in his eyes, the flicker of tension in his jaw. Something about the way he said it wasn't just sarcasm. She opened her mouth to fire back, but he tightened his arm around hers, pulling her snug to his side. "Not now, Dove. You can yell at me in private later. Or do whatever else you want me to do. I'm flexible." He wiggled his eyebrows as that familiar grin slid into place. Layla let out a soft huff, irritated by him and by herself for hating how easily he could fluster her.

They made their way toward the sword-fighting ring, pausing near a well-dressed couple who appeared too preoccupied with the match to notice their arrival. Kain tilted his head, watching the dueling men with theatrical interest.

"You know, darling," he said just loudly enough to be over-heard, "I do wonder why the King isn't out here enjoying these delightful festivities. Seems a shame to miss it."

Layla clasped her hands together with a breathy giggle, doing her best impression of a naive, overeager guest. "I was just saying the same! The castle is stunning—I can't wait to see how the rest of the day unfolds."

A nearby woman turned slightly, clearly eager to contribute. "Oh, the King won't be out today," she offered with a knowing tone. "He's still handling the aftermath of the battle. But he'll be at the wedding feast tonight."

"Truly?" Layla gasped, eyes wide with feigned delight. "That's wonderful! We were overjoyed to receive an invitation. I mean, who doesn't love a wedding?"

"Oh, absolutely!" the woman gushed, her eyes glittering. "Plus we're all hoping Prince Leif wins the auction in the morning. Of course, no one really wants a southern brat in the kingdom—but securing rights to that fertile land? Goodness, wouldn't that make this the perfect weekend?"

Layla's stomach clenched. *Wait... what?* The words echoed—impossible, incomprehensible. Her sisters. Being auctioned off. Sold to the highest bidder like cattle. Her mind reeled, the ground seemed to tilt beneath her feet. Air caught in her throat, shallow and sharp, and for a terrifying heartbeat, she couldn't tell if she was breathing at all. A dull ringing filled her ears as the world narrowed and blurred at the edges. Her limbs felt weightless, like they belonged to someone else. Kain's arm was still tucked through hers, solid and steady—but even that felt far away. Distant. Unreachable. Her entire reality had cracked open in an instant, and all she could do was try not to shatter with it.

Without hesitation, Kain turned her toward him, his hand gently sliding up to her cheek as he tilted her face up to find his. Those piercing emerald eyes burrowed deep into hers. His voice was soft, intimate as he spoke, "Have I told you how beautiful you look today?" The words washed over her, a startling contrast to her spiraling panic. She tried to look away, but he caught her chin between his fingers. "Don't hide, Dove." His voice lowered to a sensual murmur. "You're the most beautiful thing I've ever seen." His eyes held hers as he leaned closer. Her heart thundered, *was he going to kiss her? Was she going to let him?*

Just when her lips parted in confusion or maybe anticipation, he veered to her ear instead. "You better now? Thought I was going to lose you there for a second." Her entire body went rigid. *Of course.* It was a distraction. An act. Anger and humiliation burned through her. She ripped her arm free and stormed away.

"Woah, woah, what's wrong?" Kain called, easily catching up with her.

She spun to face him, chest heaving. "You know what you did!"

He froze at her tone before his eyes narrowed in harrowing recognition. "What exactly did I do that was so upsetting, *Layla*?" Her name. He'd never used it before. Not like that. The seriousness in his voice stopped her anger cold. She stared at him, breath caught, her temper suspended by uncertainty. Then she yanked her arm away again and walked off, unwilling to confront whatever just passed between them. "Yeah," Kain muttered behind her, "that's what I thought."

They continued to move through the crowd in silence for another hour. Layla refused to play into whatever game Kain was attempting. Refused to think about the way his fingers brushed hers when they passed too close or the heat of his body every time he leaned in to whisper something harmless, yet dangerously charming. She refused. Or so she kept reminding herself.

Finally, they stopped near the champagne table. Kain reached to offer her a glass, but Layla's attention was caught by two noblewomen standing just behind the tiered crystal display. The women spoke in hushed tones, but their sharp-edged words carried easily enough.

"I don't care if that stupid Graystonian bitch is pretty," one of the women sneered, swirling her drink so hard it nearly spilled. "If we win the auction, imagine what Yssra could do with all that land... we would have it all." Layla's stomach twisted violently. Her hands clenched at her sides, nails biting crescent moons into her palms. Burning indignation surged up her spine, hot and blinding—And without thinking, she reached for Kain's hand. Her fingers found his and locked tight, as if anchoring herself to something real. Something solid. Something *hers* in a room full of vultures, already circling.

"Just breathe, Little Dove," he whispered, barely turning toward her. His voice was a steadying force, low and warm against the noise. "We'll save them before anything happens. I promise." She forced her eyes to his, grounding herself in their quiet fierceness. His certainty helped her remember who she was, who she'd fought to become and what they were here to do. But the women's voices carried on, barbed with entitlement and ignorance.

"Frankly, I'm shocked Redmore even bothered to send delegates," the second woman said coolly, adjusting the delicate lace cuff of her glove. "Everyone knows they don't have the coin to place a serious bid."

"Please," the first scoffed, swirling her drink with a smirk. "You could say the same about Velastra." She gave a sharp laugh. "Honestly, I'd stomach anyone winning but Xantar. I don't trust anything that slithers out of those gods-forsaken mountains."

The second woman let out a bitter laugh. "All that snow, and somehow it still manages to hide every secret ever whispered. No one knows what they're planning up there." Layla's heart stuttered. She glanced sideways at Kain, wondering if he'd caught it too. *He had*. His eyes were already on her, unreadable now. The mention of Xantar darkened his expression, if only briefly.

"Let's go find the others," she said under her breath, her tone sharp with purpose. "It's time to update the plan." Kain nodded and slipped his hand from hers, but not before brushing a thumb once across her knuckles, subtle and comforting. And then they were gone, slipping into the crowd like silk drawn through fingers.

As they turned toward the jousting arena. Layla's gaze swept the crowd—then stopped, fixating on a scene ahead. Theron. Standing *much* too close to a woman. One hand planted above her shoulder against a column. He was smiling. Laughing. *Flirting*. The sight sucker-punched her. She hadn't even known Theron *could* smile like that. *Had he ever looked at her that way?* Her blood boiled and on top of that, she knew she didn't need to look to feel Kain's eyes on her.

"Don't say a damn word, Kain."

"Wouldn't dream of it," he replied smoothly, though she didn't miss the faint smirk tugging at his lips.

Just then, Theron looked up and their eyes clashed. She watched in stewing anger as he turned to the woman, whispered something, and stepped back. The moment shattered as quickly as it formed. Theron approached, the smile gone, replaced by that stoic mask she knew all too well.

"We've got some information," Kain said before the tension could boil over.

"So do I," Theron replied, eyes never leaving Layla's.

"Let's find the others. Figure out our next move," Kain interjected, breaking the standoff. Theron nodded, and they began walking. Layla fell into step between them, barely containing the blaze of anger seething inside her—every step beside him a battle not to explode.

Theron leaned in. "It didn't mean anything," he said under his breath. "I was just trying to get information." Layla said nothing, her fists clenched so tight her nails dug into her palms. "Layla," he tried again, quieter this time. "I was trying to help *you*."

She spun to face him, her voice low and venomous. "So much for *never* hurting me again." Theron's shoulders sank just enough for her to notice. She turned away and kept walking. Her sisters needed her. The mission mattered. Love, betrayal, confusion—all of it could wait. For now.

BY FLAME, BY ROOT, BY GOD AND STAR—
CAELERIA SHALL RISE, OR PERISH WHOLE.

THE LAW OF THE DEAD

The dead belong to the gods. Disturb them not.
Grave-robbing, necromancy, or binding souls is
an affront to Lapetic, and such defilers are
hunted by both men and monsters alike.

- THE HIGH LAWS OF CAELERIA

Chapter Twenty-One

Theron.

As they approached the others, the guilt settled heavier on Theron's shoulders with every step. The woman had thrown herself at him, and he'd made the calculated decision to flirt back. It had seemed the easiest way to draw out information without raising alarm. Easier than slitting a throat in broad daylight he thought. But now, he wasn't so sure.

The look on Layla's face when she saw them together had gutted him. He didn't know where he stood with her after that morning, but after this? He had the sinking feeling he'd just made it worse.

"We haven't found out much, other than the King won't be making an appearance until tonight," Xaden said as they rejoined the group.

Kain stepped forward, his voice rougher than usual. "It's not just a wedding," he said. "This entire weekend is about his wedding, yes—but

301

also... an auction." The entire group stilled in confusion and wary anticipation. Even the air seemed to hold its breath.

"He's selling the princesses," Kain continued grimly. "To the highest bidders from the northern kingdoms. The auction is scheduled for morning." He glanced down at Layla as he said it, and for a rare moment, the teasing gleam in his eyes was gone—replaced with something raw. Something close to heartbreak.

A stunned silence settled over the group like a storm cloud. Sparrow muttered a curse under his breath. Edwin's fists clenched at his sides. Even Xaden stiffened, his brows knitting in barely contained vehement disapproval. But Theron just watched the shift in Kain—how he stood nearer to Layla than before, how his hand hovered close to hers, seemingly ready if she needed him. Protective even. It needled something deep inside Theron and he swallowed it like poison.

"Tonight's the wedding feast, I guess more of a ball really," Theron said, forcing his voice to steady. "A woman I spoke with owns a clothing shop just outside the main square. She mentioned it's unattended. Accessible. We'll use the festivities as cover to search the castle." His gaze drifted to Layla, but she didn't look at him. Didn't look at anyone. Just stared past them, eyes distant, jaw clenched. But he could feel it—the heat radiating off her in waves. Not quiet anger. Not grief. This was a blazing, unforgiving wrath.

"Do we have coin for this little shopping spree?" Xaden asked with a half-smile, trying to cut the tension.

"Nope," Theron said with a shrug, letting a smirk tug at his mouth as he turned toward the exit. Flirting with that woman had worked. She'd told him enough to confirm her shop would be empty and unguarded for days. They wouldn't be spending anything. He only hoped Layla would see that the tactic, however painful, had been necessary.

They swept the courtyard one last time with their eyes, but no hidden doors or dungeon entrances revealed themselves. As they moved to exit, castle maids awaited to escort them down the halls. Clearly, Bartoria wasn't taking chances, definitely no wandering guests. Theron made mental notes of every turn, every visible door. The other warriors did the same, subtly cracking doors as they passed, memorizing the layout. This wasn't how he liked to operate. Blind. Without a map, without certainty. He wasn't used to sneaking around in layered costumes and pretending to smile. He missed his sword in his hand. Missed the simplicity of combat.

They left their horses at the castle—the shop wasn't far, and drawing attention now could cost them everything. As they approached the row of storefronts, Theron spotted it immediately: tall windows trimmed in gold leaf, expensive fabrics draped artfully behind the glass. That had to be the one.

He gave Sparrow a quick nod, and the two of them circled around to the alley behind it. Nestled between stone and overgrown brush sat a narrow window—low to the ground and half-obscured. Perfect. Without a word, Theron shrugged off his coat, then his shirt and wrapping the fabric around his fist. With one sharp punch, the glass gave way with a muted crack. From the front, the others raised their voices, mimicking drunken laughter to cover the sound.

Too broad to fit through the opening himself, Theron steadied Sparrow by the hips and helped guide him through the jagged frame. Swiftly throwing his stuff back on, he reached the others around front A few tense seconds later. Just as they heard a click of the front lock echoing from inside. The door creaked open, and one by one, they slipped inside—unseen and unheard.

"Sit. Rest. Sir Edwin and I will find proper attire," Layla ordered without glancing at Theron. He watched as she tore through the racks with clear purpose, though her movements were clipped and sharp. She was still furious. Taking a deep breath, he walked over to her.

"Layla," he said gently, stopping behind her. She didn't turn. Didn't flinch or give any other indication that she was going to acknowledge his presence. "I'm sorry," he said softly, just loud enough for her to hear. "I was only trying to get information quickly, without drawing attention." With that, she spun around, fire scorching her eyes.

"Well, you certainly got *her* attention," she snapped, before spinning back to the clothes. "You know what? It doesn't matter. Do what you want Theron. I don't care."

"I care," he whispered, leaning down until his lips hovered just above the curve of her ear. He heard her breath catch. Saw the moment she froze as he went on. "I never want to hurt you, Layla."

"Then stop." Her voice was quiet, breaking slightly at the edges. She turned and walked away without another word. Theron stood there a moment longer, his heart pounding, before exhaling hard and walking back to join the others. With every misstep, every glance she didn't give him, every word left unsaid—he felt it sinking in. He didn't belong at her side anymore. But gods, it still tore him apart not to be there.

A while later, Layla and Sir Edwin emerged with clothing for each of them. Theron muttered his thanks as he took the bundle and looked it over. The pants were manageable, fitted but close enough to his leathers that he wouldn't complain. The shirt, however, felt like a noose around his throat. High-collared, stiff, and strangling. The vest and coat were even worse—tight in the arms, heavy on the back. When he saw the two long flaps hanging behind him, he turned to Sir Edwin with a flat stare.

"It's a tailcoat. High fashion for a royal ball," Sir Edwin offered, clearly uncomfortable under Theron's glare. Theron said nothing. Just kept glaring. *This had to be a joke.*

They all dressed in the center of the shop as Layla slipped behind a curtain to change. Theron found himself staring at it longer than he should have. He wanted to follow her. Apologize again. Kiss her until she remembered how much he cared. But he stayed put. She needed space and maybe he deserved the silence.

Grumbling filled the room as the men all tried to shove themselves into their constricting layers. The outfits were similar in cut and color, with minor variations. Theron wore a crisp white shirt, black vest, and black tailcoat. No one had deep enough pockets for their knives, so they began sliding them into their sleeves and waistbands. Kain's complaints were the loudest.

"I feel like a fucking peacock," he muttered, tugging at his vest.

"Get over it," Theron snapped. "We'll be out of it in a few hours. Then you can set it on fire for all I care." He was fidgeting with his own vest hem as he spoke, the material foreign and stiff. Attempting but failing at concealing his fury and frustration with everything, especially himself.

"Are you ready, My Lady?" Sir Edwin's voice drew Theron's attention and when he turned, it hit him like a blow to the chest. Layla stood in gold. Her gown shimmered with each step, cascading down in elegant folds. The corset hugged her perfectly, accentuating her waist and curves. The sleeves flowed like silk waterfalls, brushing the floor. Her hazel eyes sparkled, framed by the rich chestnut waves of her hair. Theron's breath caught in his throat. She didn't look like a warrior now—she looked like a goddess draped in gold, descending not to walk among mortals, but to remind them they were never worthy of her.

"Yes. I am." Layla's voice was calm, confident. She glanced at him once—just once—and then looked away. Theron's stomach clenched.

"Get your jaw off the floor," Xaden muttered, stepping beside him. "Time to save her sisters. Then you can focus on her again." Theron straightened, forcing the ache in his chest to harden into purpose. Xaden was right. Layla wasn't his to love right now, but she was his to protect. And he'd see this mission through, even if it killed him.

Layla.

As they crossed the dirt road from the shop back to the castle steps, Layla's heart thundered in her chest. They were so close. Her sisters were somewhere beyond those walls, maybe only a hallway away and yet still impossibly out of reach. She needed to see them. To know they were still whole. *Still alive..* Layla forced herself to take steady, subtle breaths, trying to cage the panic tightening in her chest.

"I've got you."

Layla looked up to see Kain's arm extended, the warmth of his body close, steady, unshakable. She slipped her arm into his without a second thought, grateful for the quiet strength as he pulled her closer.

"What if…" she began, her voice faltering as fear clawed its way up her throat. "What if we can't get to them? What if there are too many guards? Too much—"

"Then we'll kill them all." He said it so matter-of-factly that it stole the breath right out of her. There was no fear in him, no hesitation. Just absolute certainty. "Every last one of those Bartorian bastards will die if needed. We will get your sisters back." Layla gave a small nod, letting the weight of his conviction bolster her. His arm locked around hers like a shield. She could do this. They could do this.

As they stepped back within the castle walls, the grand hall they had previously walked had been roped off, redirecting them to a side corridor. Two male attendants opened towering double doors ahead, revealing a ballroom bursting with candlelight, laughter, and clinking goblets. The scent of roasted meats and sweet perfumes swept over her as Kain guided her in. Almost instantly, Layla felt the eyes.

She tensed, her grip tightening around Kain's arm. A chill ran down her spine as dozens of eyes turned their way. "Why are they staring?" she hissed, the words barely escaping her lips. For a breathless moment, dread coiled in her gut—terrified that somehow, the entire room had recognized them. That their ruse had collapsed before it even began.

"Breathe, Dove," Kain murmured, then leaned closer. "They're staring at you." She blinked at him, utterly confused. His lips curved in a smug smile as he let his gaze drag down the length of her golden gown.

"Yeah sure," she muttered, releasing his implication and proceeding to roll her eyes.

"You think I'm joking," he replied, eyes twinkling. "Every woman here wants to be you and every man wants to bed you in that dress." She scoffed under her breath, but heat crept up her neck all the same.

Kain led her through the ballroom with exaggerated ease, pointing out tapestries and entertainers as they casually scouted exits and weak points. Their charade gave them time to memorize the space without drawing suspicion. At the front of the ballroom was a long, elevated table—lavish and half-filled. Two ornate chairs sat empty in the center. King Ivar and his bride-to-be, no doubt. Just as the thought crossed her mind, trumpets blared.

The crowd parted as the ballroom doors opened once again. King Ivar strode in, basking in the attention like an animal in heat. He wore a navy tailcoat embroidered in gold, his ivory pants stiffly pressed, and a golden cape draped over one shoulder like a badge of vanity. Layla's stomach twisted at the very sight of this monster.

"My people and friends from the North," he called out, voice booming. "Thank you for attending the celebrations this weekend!" A round of cheers erupted. "I hope you enjoyed the courtyard festivities e arlier....Now tonight we feast and dance...Then tomorrow, the real event begins!" He raised his goblet high. "I am thrilled to gift one of my northern neighbors the precious fertile treasure of the South" More cheers erupted and Layla's stomach dropped. "Now sadly, my bride-to-be is feeling bashful, so we may see her later. But allow me to give you a preview of what you'll be bidding on in the morning!" The ballroom hushed.

Doors burst open, and a procession of soldiers entered. Layla pushed up on her toes, peering over heads and then she saw her. *Aerilynn.* Her sister looked fragile as she shivered in a tattered ballgown. Bruises marred her porcelain skin, her hair a mess of tangled curls. Layla's vision tunneled in response. Her body screamed to move, to run to her sister, to fight and tear apart anyone who got in her way but Kain's grip tightened on her arm.

The King grabbed Aerilynn's hips and barked, "Look at these childbearing hips! She is ready for you!" Cheers. Laughter. Layla wanted to scream. To throw her blade and cut out the King's throat where he stood.

"Stay with Theron and Eddy," Kain whispered suddenly. He slipped from her side and vanished into the crowd with Xaden and Sparrow. Theron appeared at her elbow almost immediately, guiding her arm into his.

"What's happening?" She choked out, torn between helplessly watching her sister and wanting answers.

"I'll explain soon. I promise." His hand covered hers, steady and strong. She tried to bolt forward as guards began pulling Aerilynn back out through the doors. Theron held her firm. "Just wait. Trust me." And so she did. Barely.

When the crowd dispersed again, Theron pulled her toward the dance floor. "What are you doing?" she snapped under her breath. He turned, bowed, and offered his hand. When she didn't move, he stepped forward, spun her into him, and began to dance. "Theron—what the hell—"

He pulled her close, one hand steady at her waist, and lowered his voice as he guided her across the floor—away from the walls, away from listening ears. "Kain and the others are following the guards to find where your sisters are being kept. Sir Edwin's in position for a distraction. Once we have eyes on their location, we'll act. We've got them, Layla." She blinked at him, stunned. The words cut through the panic like a blade through fog. She nodded and let herself lean into his hold, her head resting on his shoulder as he continued to lead her gently around the floor.

As the music faded, they made their way to the bar and pretended to sip champagne. "This isn't the time," Theron said quietly, "but I want to tell you something." She warily turned to fully look at him. "You look beautiful tonight. Always—but especially tonight." The words hit harder than they should. She looked down, face flushing. She hated that her body still reacted to him.

"Thank you," she whispered.

He stepped closer, brushing a kiss against her cheek. She leaned into it for the briefest moment before straightening, trying to keep her composure. But something shifted. Theron's body tensed. His shoulders squared and jaw tightened with visible strain, prompting Layla to slowly turn around to see what was causing his alarm. And what she discovered, shocked her to her very core.

King Ivar stood directly before her, his hand outstretched. "May I have this dance?"

The room spun but Layla placed her hand in his with forced grace anyway, and curtseyed. "My King."

Daring to glance behind her, she saw Theron's face—dark and murderous.

King Ivar led her to the center of the dance floor, his hand resting far too low on her back as he did. "I noticed you the moment I walked in," he purred.

Layla forced a smile. "Isn't this a ball in honor of your bride?"

"She's bashful. I, however, am not." His hand dropped lower as he spoke. "Don't worry," he whispered in her ear. "If your husband minds, he can watch. Or my men can entertain him while we're busy." Revulsion crawled up her spine. She could barely breath, she wanted to vomit and kill all at the same time. But using every ounce of strength she could muster, she attempted to calm her breathing and plaster that damned practiced smile on her face. But she was struggling. She was failing. It was too hard. This was too hard. He had taken so much from her...

"May I cut in?"

Relief slammed into her chest at the sight of Kain. But just as quickly, it was chased by sharp-edged worry. Of course he would show up like this. Fearless. Defiant. Infuriating.

"We aren't finished," King Ivar growled, voice rising with authority. Kain took a single step forward, eyes fixed on the king's. Calm. Unshaken. Dangerous.

"I think you are," he said, quiet but cutting—like a blade pressed to the throat. King Ivar blinked, then let out a sharp laugh. He clapped

Kain on the shoulder, not in mockery, but with the grudging admiration of a man who knew strength when he saw it.

"Bold. Sharp. I like that. I could use someone like you in my guard."

"I'm good. Thanks," Kain said flatly. Not cocky. Just aware of exactly how much power he carried.

The King just grinned and sauntered away. "I hope to see you later," he added, eyes raking her chest. Layla nearly gagged at the sight. But Kain swiftly took her hand and waist, pulling her back into a dance and away from the vile man.

"Are you okay?" He asked, his voice calm but with what sounded like a hint of concern. She nodded, barely, before the reason why they were even hear came slamming back into her head.

"Where's Aerilynn and Ciana?!"

"We followed the guards. Theron's already heading in."

"But why didn't you get them?"

"Look. I am very good with a bow. The best, really. But I know my hand-to-hand and blade skills are no match for Theron's. There were many guards, and we figured this situation called for the best. Theron reluctantly agreed.... Plus, from the looks of it, he was about to kill the King in the middle of this ballroom. So, it was good timing to make a little switch." Kain explained, his characteristic sarcastic charm dripping from every word. But Layla knew him well enough by now to sense it—he was holding something back. There was more he wasn't saying. She could see it in the slight shift of his jaw, the way his eyes didn't quite meet hers. But she also knew better than to push. There was no point. Kain would tell her when he felt she needed to know... or not at all. As infuriating as that was.

She nodded slowly, realization dawning. *Theron was going to save her sisters* . She could feel it deep in her chest—he would die before coming back without them. He was not the same man who had blindly followed his mother's order to slaughter her family just days ago.

Her heart gave a small, involuntary leap at the thought. A flicker of something too dangerous to name.

ASH AND CARRION ARE
THE SEEDS OF OUR GLORY

All that endures within the realm- be it soil,
silver, station, or blood- exists beneath the
shadow of the Throne. To be entrusted with its
keeping is a mark of favor. To relinquish it when
called is the duty of the loyal. The will of the
Crown is not to be contested, for what it
reclaims was never lost.

-BY COMMAND OF THE IRON CROWN OF
BARTORIA

Chapter Twenty-Two

Theron.

Theron moved in silence behind Xaden and Sparrow, their footsteps ghosting across the cold stone floor. Veiled gloom clung to the walls, and every turn of the corridor felt carved from the breathless hush of war. The weight of urgency bore down on him, each step tight with purpose. Layla's sisters were close. And if even one hand had touched them in violence—he would paint these halls red.

Xaden signaled with two fingers and stopped at the edge of the corridor. They crept to the archway before them and peered around it's stone frame. Four guards stood posted in front of a staircase descending into the depths—the same stairwell where Xaden had seen Aerilynn dragged not long ago.

Theron's gaze sharpened. No words were needed. With a flick of his hand, the plan was in motion.

He slung an arm over Sparrow's shoulders and staggered forward, laughing like a drunken fool. Xaden followed close behind, grin wide and steps unsteady. They weaved toward the guards with perfect chaos—every sway and stumble a practiced misdirection. Assassins cloaked in folly, moving like fools with blades hidden behind their smiles.

"Halt! Who goes there?" barked one of the guards, hand already drifting to his weapon.

"Who goes where?" Theron slurred, blinking in exaggerated confusion. "Oh no! I lost her—she was right here! Blonde, big... ya know." He flailed his arms dramatically, nearly toppling over in the process.

One of the guards groaned, clearly unimpressed. "You've got three seconds to turn around before I draw."

"Wait—wait," Xaden slurred, stumbling into the wall with theatrical clumsiness. "She said she was gonna show us the royal wine cellar..." The nearest guard stepped forward, sighing as he moved to usher them away. It was all they needed.

In a blink, Theron's hand shot up, grabbing the man by the jaw and twisting violently. The sharp crack of vertebrae echoed through the hall. Before the others could register the kill, Xaden slammed a knife up under a second guard's chin, piercing straight into the brain. Sparrow whirled and buried his own blade beneath the third guard's ribs. The fourth reached for his sword- but it was too late. Theron was already behind him, slicing his throat clean with a single motion. Four guards. Six seconds. No alarms.

They quickly dragged the bodies into a dark supply room, leaving a streak of blood Theron didn't bother worrying about. If anyone found it, they wouldn't live long enough to raise the alarm. Without a word, they grabbed the discarded swords and descended the stairwell in a tight formation—Theron at the front, sword already drawn, his approach was as noiseless as falling ash. A dull orange glow flickered from the room below, along with the low murmur of voices. He paused at the final step, every sense honed on what waited ahead.

"Fifteen, maybe more," Xaden whispered behind him.

Theron nodded, eyes like ice. "We take them all."

Then he stepped into the dungeon without hesitation.

This was what he'd been built for—what generations of duty, blood, and silence had carved into his bones. And as he moved into the flickering dark, he unleashed everything they had forged him into. The warrior whose blade was not merely his own, but death's will given form, here to claim without mercy.

A wave of noise swept over him—guards drinking, laughing, gathered in front of a heavy iron cell. All fifteen heads turned as Theron lunged, slicing across the chest of the nearest man before he could draw his blade. At once, the entire room erupted in chaos. Steel flashed. Shouts rose. Blood sprayed. Xaden and Sparrow exploded into motion behind him, blades cutting with surgical precision. Theron ducked under a wild swing and drove his elbow into a guard's throat, then spun and slashed another across the belly. His body moved on instinct—fluid, practiced, deadly. Three men attacked at once. Theron pivoted, parried one, kicked another into the wall, then ran the third through with a snarl. He didn't stop, wouldn't until the last guard was no longer breathing.

Another guard charged him. Theron grabbed the man's arm mid-swing, twisted, disarmed him, and used his own sword to slice him from shoulder to hip. A roar of pain was cut short as Sparrow buried a dagger in the man's neck.

Another man's shriek erupted behind Theron, Xaden had flung a broken chair leg through a guard's eye. Blood pooled at Theron's feet as the bodies piled higher. None of them—*none*—were a match for an Antonin armed with steel and driven by rage.

When the final man collapsed, choking on his own blood, silence settled over the chamber like a shroud. Only the harsh breath of three warriors remained. Then Theron turned to the cell where Aerilynn sat inside, curled in the corner like a trapped deer, her eyes wide with terror. Her gown was tattered, streaked with filth and torn in places that made Theron's stomach twist. Bruises marked her arms and collarbone. But she was alive. *But where was the other sister?*

Xaden rushed to the wall and ripped down the ring of keys. The lock clicked open and Sparrow slipped inside, kneeling.

"Aerilynn," Sparrow said gently. "It's okay. Layla sent us. You're safe now." She didn't speak—just stared, eyes wild and shaking. Slowly, with clear hesitation, she reached out and took Sparrow's hand. He pulled her to her feet with care.

"Can you walk?" A small nod.

Theron stepped closer, his voice lower but urgent. "Where's Ciana? Is she down here too?" Aerilynn's lips parted, but no sound came out. Her eyes simply flooded with more fear. Theron's jaw tightened. He tried again, softer this time. "Is Ciana trapped somewhere else in the castle?"

She shook her head—just once. But it was enough. The tears in her eyes said the rest.

The men exchanged a glance. No words were needed. They needed to get Aerilynn to safety, then regroup. They would find Ciana next, before it was too late.

They moved in tight formation up the stairwell. Every step, every breath, every turn was calculated. When they passed the blood smear from earlier—still undisturbed—Theron knew no one had found it. No alarm. No reinforcements waiting to swarm and shatter their stealth. Good. They pressed on, pausing only when necessary. Near the ballroom entrance, Theron spotted a large, dust-covered storage room—unused and cloaked in shadow. Perfect.

"In here," he whispered, opening the door and scanning the hall behind them. "Stay until I return with Layla."

Aerilynn still hadn't let go of Sparrow's hand, clinging to it like a lifeline. Theron lingered only a second, making sure the door sealed tight behind them, leaving the two warriors and Aerilynn cloaked in dimness. Then he turned toward the ballroom, straightened his ridiculous tailcoat, and slipped back into the crowd unnoticed.

He needed to find Layla—not just to show her that Aerilynn was safe, but because the plan had to shift. Ciana was still missing, and they were running out of time.

He spotted her instantly as he slid discreetly back into the ballroom. Her golden gown shimmered under the chandeliers as she danced with Kain. As if he could feel Theron's presence from across the vast room, Kain's gaze lifted and zeroed in on Theron instantly. A single tilt of his head was all that was needed and Theron watched as Kain leaned down and whispered something to Layla a moment later. Her head whipped around, scanning the crowd before spotting Theron. Her eyes widened in what he could only interpret as a flicker of both fear and hope before she gripped Kain's arm, the two of them weaving through the crowd. Theron also noticed Sir Edwin began closing in from the flank—likely sensing a shift in the plan or reading the unspoken signal. No words. Just motion.

"This way," Theron muttered when they all reached him, guiding them swiftly out and into the hallway. His eyes swept behind them for watchers before he shut the ballroom door and strode to a stop before the storage room. He silently opened it, peaking in before allowing Layla to step through. She froze only for an instant.

"Aerilynn." The name fell from Layla's lips like a prayer as he watched her take in the sight of her sister, alive and safe, though barely. In the next second, Layla was running. She collapsed into her sister's arms and broke. The room filled with only the sound of tears and sob-choked gasps. The kind of sound born from days of torment, fear, and endless not-knowing. Theron stood still, letting the moment wash over him—until a slight movement pulled his attention. Sir Edwin had caught sight of Aerilynn, recognition flickering in his eyes. One princess safe. He gave a brief nod, but the grim line of his mouth spoke volumes. More remained to be done. Without a word, he turned and slipped back through the door to resume his post outside, guarding the path for what came next.

Layla clutched Aerilynn like she'd never let go again. "Thank you," she whispered to Sparrow and Xaden, tears still falling, her sister still wrapped in her arms. "Thank you both."

When she finally pulled back, she turned to Kain and hugged him hard. "Thank you." He looked surprised but held her gently. Then she turned to Theron. Her eyes shimmered. Her chest rose and fell with shaky breath as she stepped forward. Time stilled as he held his breath looking down at her. And then she hugged him. Hard. And Theron's heart stuttered. His arms went around her instinctively, holding her to him like she was the only real thing in the world. She smelled like lavender and candle smoke and something wholly *hers*.

"Thank you, Theron," she whispered. He closed his eyes. When she finally stepped away, smiling through the tears, she turned back to Aerilynn. But her brow creased with confusion.

"Wait... Where's Ciana?" The room went still. Layla's gaze flicked from Xaden to Sparrow to Theron. Then finally, to Aerilynn—whose face crumpled as fresh tears fell. And that's when Layla knew. Her body tensed. One sister was safe. But one... One was still gone.

Layla.

Layla stared at her sister, her voice tense with urgency. "Aerilynn... where is Ciana?" Aerilynn's gaze dropped to the floor, clearly avoiding Layla's gaze now. Layla stepped closer. "Aerilynn!" she hissed, her tone sharpening. "Tell me now—where is she?"

Aerilynn let out a shaky breath, still looking at the ground between them. "A few days ago, the Bartorian guards brought us here. We overheard them joking about how the King planned to sell us off to the highest bidder. They said marrying us would give their heirs claim to Graystonia, claim to Serelai's blessings... and that we'd fetch a fortune..."

Layla felt bile rise in her throat. "But once we arrived," Aerilynn continued, voice cracking, "everything changed. The King saw Ciana and... decided he wouldn't sell her at all. He wanted her for himself." Layla's stomach twisted.

"Aerilynn," she said, already bracing herself, "what are you saying?"

"This ball..." Aerilynn whispered. "It's *her* wedding feast. The King is marrying *her*. *Tomorrow*." The words hit Layla like a mortar shell—silent at first, then detonating through her chest with brutal force. Her breath caught as she turned to Theron, whose jaw had gone rigid, eyes burning with the same fury she felt erupting inside her.

"We have to find her. Now." Layla's voice was raw, trembling with urgency. "We cannot let that wedding happen... Once they realize Aerilynn is missing, they'll lock down the castle—Ciana will vanish behind walls we won't be able to reach. We have to move. Now."

"We'll get her," Theron said, his voice low and resolute, lethal calm coiled beneath each word. Layla heard him—she did—but the panic was still clawing its way up her throat, tightening its grip. But before it could fully take hold, Sparrow stepped forward, cutting clean through her spiraling thoughts and anchoring her back to the present.

"Let me get Aerilynn out now before the alarm is raised," he offered quietly, already understanding what was unspoken. Just in case... they couldn't risk losing both sisters.

Layla turned to him, eyes burning. "You make sure she gets out," she said, voice cracking with ferocity. "Even if the rest of us fall, you get her home."

"I swore I'd protect you. I swear the same to her." Layla knew he would. He hadn't left her side even after it was no longer his duty. She knew that she could trust him to do the same for Aerilynn.

Xaden stepped up beside him. "I'll go too. If things go sideways, I'll make the noise."

Layla frantically nodded, grateful for these warriors before she turned to Aerilynn and gripped her shoulders. "You can trust them. I'll come for you after we get Ciana. I promise."

"No! Layla, please don't leave me again!" Aerilynn sobbed, latching onto her. Layla held her tightly, swallowing the lump in her throat.

"I came for you, didn't I?" Layla said firmly. "Now trust these men. They'll get you out safely before anyone realizes you're gone. But you have to go. Now. Please." Her voice was low, urgent—unyielding.

Aerilynn didn't answer right away, and Layla felt her own breath hitch. But then—finally—her sister gave a small, reluctant nod. Hesitant, but it was enough. Layla saw the shift in her eyes: the quiet surrender, the unspoken trust. Aerilynn didn't want to leave, not without her. But she understood. She trusted Layla to make the impossible call, to carry the weight and see it through. And gods, that trust burned like a brand in her chest.

Aerilynn wrapped her arms around her once more, holding tight before stepping back with red-rimmed eyes. "I love you," she said, barely above a whisper, as Sparrow took her hand and guided her away. Xaden moved behind them, silent as a promise not yet spoken.

Sir Edwin slipped into the room, and they quickly brought him up to speed on the news about Ciana. His jaw tightened, but he didn't waste time on shock or outrage—only strategy.

"If she's truly the bride," he said after a beat, "she'll have to make an appearance. When she does, we track her—just like the others did with Aerilynn."

Layla nodded, barely breathing. It wasn't much, but it was something. *It had worked before—why not again?* What Sir Edwin said made sense. They couldn't keep waiting in this room; the longer they stayed, the greater the chance someone would find them all huddled where they clearly didn't belong. At least out there, they had a plan. A chance.

She straightened. "Then we watch. And when she shows—we move."

They righted their ridiculous attire and slipped back into the ball-room. Layla took her place between Theron and Kain. Her gaze snapped to the throne-like chair beside King Ivar that was still empty. Her stomach dropped again. That seat... it was Ciana's. Theron gently slid his hand into hers. The warmth grounded her and she clutched it like a lifeline.

"The King's still staring at you," Kain whispered on her other side.

Layla glanced up. Ivar's eyes were pinned to her—dark, possessive, entitled.

Her lip curled. "If he looks at me like that again, I'll claw his eyes out and shove them down his royal throat."

Kain let out a low, amused whistle. "There's the dove with talons."

She didn't smile. Not this time.

The blare of trumpets split the air, sharp and jarring. Layla's heart jolted, a stuttering beat against her ribs. She rose onto her toes, eyes sweeping the crowd in frantic search—until they found her. *Ciana.*

She stepped into the ballroom flanked by Bartorian guards, each step as poised as it was forced. Her gown was a deep navy trimmed in ivory and gold, elegant and stately, her hair intricately braided with gilded threads that caught the torchlight like a crown. To anyone else, she looked the part of a queen. But Layla saw past the illusion.

Her sister's mouth was drawn tight, tension rippling down her neck with every step. Her shoulders were squared in defiance, but her eyes—gods, her eyes—burned with silent wrath and barely contained terror. And King Ivar? He watched her approach with grotesque satisfaction, his smile a curling mockery of triumph as Ciana was led to the throne beside him like a prize on display.

"She's perfect, isn't she?" King Ivar boomed to the crowd. "My bride-to-be! Feast your eyes, nobles of the North!" Cheers erupted. "I mean, look at that rack!" he crowed, waving a hand at Ciana's chest. The room roared with laughter and whistles. Layla's anger built like thunder in her chest. Her nails dug into Theron's hand. He held on tighter in response, anchoring her.

"Ciana, stand! Let them admire you properly!" Ivar barked. Ciana rose without a word. Tall. Proud. Unflinching. Ivar stepped behind her and slid a hand around her waist—then upward, groping her breast in full view of everyone in the ballroom. "Let me show you more of my prize!" he howled as the crowd surged with laughter. Layla shook with violent, white-hot rage and stepped forward instinctively but Theron caught her.

No," he whispered in her ear, wrapping her tightly in his arms. She fought him, thrashing in his grip, but he didn't release her.

She knew she couldn't cause a scene. Couldn't lunge for the vile king and stop this horrific display—this grotesque parade of her sister—without dooming them all. If she acted now, none of them would make it out alive. *But gods, how was she supposed to just stand there?* Her instincts screamed to protect Ciana, to put herself between her sister and that monster, to claw his eyes out for daring to touch her. Yet logic—cold, brutal logic—held her in place like chains around her throat. Her body quivered against Theron's hold, eyes pinned on Ciana, a consuming fire burning so hot it nearly drowned her.

Across the ballroom, Kain stood like a statue. His gaze fixed on the King, eyes black with rage. It wasn't a glare she saw—but a vow. A promise etched in fury.

Layla's eyes flicked to him, and she remembered what he'd whispered to her earlier, just before they stepped into this gilded nightmare. And something in her—something fragile and fraying—steadied.

"Every last one," she breathed, the words almost reverent. "Starting with him."

Kain would do it. Of that, she was certain. And the calm that settled over her was as sudden as it was sure. So she inhaled slowly, grounding herself. Then, whispered softly to Theron, "I'm okay." He hesitated, eyes scanning her face, before finally loosening his hold.

Her moment of vengeance-laced reprieve was short-lived. With grotesque flair, the King lifted a blade and sliced down the back of Ciana's gown. The laces fell apart like severed sinew. Layla's jaw clenched so tightly, she was certain something would snap.

Ciana stepped free of the tattered gown, now left standing in a nearly sheer ivory shift that did nothing to shield her from the leering eyes around the room. The crowd erupted—jeering, howling like beasts scenting blood. Then Ivar placed his hand on her again. Possessive. Violating. As he laughed, deep and cruel. As if this public humiliation were nothing more than theater for his amusement.

The King laughed, dark and vile. "The rest of the view," he shouted, raising his goblet high, "is just for me!" He drained it in one gulp and hurled it to the marble with a shatter. The crowd roared in approval.

Layla couldn't breathe. Her hand had latched onto Theron's arm without realizing it, fingers digging in so tight she knew she'd leave bruises. But she couldn't loosen her grip. Couldn't look away. Her sister—stripped, displayed, degraded—and there was nothing she could do without risking all of them.

She didn't realize she was crying until Theron's thumb gently brushed beneath her eye, grounding her with the smallest touch. *How in the hell were they going to get Ciana out of this?*

ASH AND CARRION ARE
THE SEEDS OF OUR GLORY

To preserve unity, peace, and the sanctity of the realm, no voice shall rise against the Crown. Words that breed unrest, challenge the law, or cast doubt upon Bartoria's sovereign right shall be deemed treasonous. Let it be known: order is preserved through obedience, and loyalty is proven silence.

-BY COMMAND OF THE IRON CROWN OF
BARTORIA

Chapter Twenty-Three

Theron.

Theron was ready to spill blood. He couldn't tear his eyes from the King—not when Ivar had the gall to humiliate Ciana like that, to touch her with lecherous hands in front of a roaring crowd. The same rage that once surged in battle now coiled like a viper in his chest. And Layla... Layla was barely holding it together. He could feel it in the tremor of her fingers. In the way she gripped his arm like a tether to keep herself from lunging across the ballroom. The guilt, the helplessness, the white-hot rage—it surged through him. He would kill Ivar. He didn't know how or when. Only that the bastard would pay for what he'd done—slowly, brutally, and without mercy.

The King finally collapsed into his seat, laughing hoarsely as he gestured toward Ciana like a drunk displaying his spoils. Theron didn't move. Couldn't. The weight of restraint pressed against every muscle. He looked down at Layla—her eyes were fixed on her sister, wide with urgency, desperation etched in every line of her face. She was barely keeping herself upright. And still, she didn't break. She didn't run. She waited—burning with the need to act, to save. So he would act for her. Somehow. Now. Before the last thread holding her together snapped.

"Come with me," he murmured. "Let's dance." Layla blinked at him, confused, resisting his gentle tug. He nodded toward Ciana, then back to Layla. "Trust me." Realization dawned and she nodded.

They stepped into the swirl of dancers. Theron pulled her close and twirled her with practiced ease. They blended seamlessly into the chaos, gliding among silk and satin and drunken nobles. He kept one eye on Ciana the entire time. She endlessly just stared ahead, distant and cold. Theron gritted his teeth, this wasn't working. He racked his brain, then had another idea.

"Follow my lead," he whispered. He spun Layla, then lifted her high above his head, slowly rotating her so Ciana would have a clear view of Layla. Layla wrapped her arms around him as he held her suspended a moment longer, then gently brought her back down. Her smile was radiant, even if forced. Once grounded, she instantly glanced over her shoulder at Ciana's direction. Theron followed her gaze.

Thank the gods, Ciana was now staring at them, mouth slightly open, eyes wide. Layla pressed a finger to her lips. Ciana closed her mouth, sitting straighter. Alert now. Theron exhaled and pulled Layla off the floor towards where Kain was waiting.

"Washroom?" Layla mouthed toward her sister. Ciana subtly shook her head, barely perceptible. *Damn.* Layla turned to him and Kain, searching for another way. Another idea. Theron's mind raced.

"Dance," he said. "See if she can get up and dance."

Layla nodded and turned back. "Dance?" she mouthed. Ciana gave the faintest shrug. *Maybe.* Maybe was hope. They had hope. Theron exhaled sharply, the tightness in his chest easing just enough to function again. He gently pulled Layla off the floor, guiding her back toward where Kain waited. Now, all they could do was wait—anxiously, breath held—for Ciana to make her move. She would have to ask Ivar for permission to dance. And they had to pray he'd say yes.

As they waited, Layla glanced between the two brothers, needing a break from the panic chewing at her nerves. "Okay," she whispered, breathless, "but seriously—how do you two know these dances? And not just know them, but actually pull them off without looking like idiots?"

Kain smirked. "Wedding rituals."

"Wedding—what?"

"Our ceremonies," Theron muttered, not quite looking at her. "They have traditional dances. All of them do."

Layla blinked at him. "You're telling me that Antonin wedding ceremonies involve ballroom choreography?"

Kain rolled his eyes. "It's not ballroom, Dove. We don't exactly have marble floors and gilded ceilings. Try packed dirt and a drunken choir of uncles shouting in the wrong key."

"And who," she asked suspiciously, "taught you charming savages to waltz like nobles?" Both warriors grimaced at the same time.

Kain muttered, "Illyada."

Layla blinked. "Illyada?"

"She said," Theron gritted out, "'No son of a king will be caught bumbling around like a donkey with two broken legs.'"

"Once we were of age to participate, she made us practice for weeks," Kain added dryly. "With her barking orders, whacking our ankles with a stick if we missed a step. Zero mercy." Layla burst out laughing, the sound breathless and brief but real. "So let me get this straight. You two learned to dance... from a terrifying tribal warrior woman... in the dirt... for weddings?"

"Exactly," Kain said, completely straight-faced. "Romantic as hell." Theron only grunted. And for a fleeting moment, the weight in her chest loosened.

King Ivar finally returned to Ciana's side, laughing loudly with his nobles. His wine glass nearly empty once again. They watched as Ciana casually leaned in. The King looked irritated at first, then gave a bark of laughter and rolled his eyes. He promptly stood and they watched as Ciana followed suit. The guards stepped forward, but he waved them off and escorted her to the dance floor himself.

Theron's hands curled into fists. *Now what?* He knew Layla was about to suggest they go out next, but Kain stepped in.

"I've got this," he said, already moving toward her. Theron met his eyes, he saw something darker than mischief there. Something resolved.

So he nodded tightly and stepped back. He watched as Kain led Layla out to the center of the dance floor. They danced fluidly, casually. Theron tensely stared after them. When the song ended, Kain led Layla straight toward the King and Ciana. Theron's heart leapt into his throat. *What the fuck is he doing?!* Theron began blindly charging out into the dance floor. He had no plan other than to get Layla the hell away from that king.

He saw Ivar's eyes narrow as he turned towards whomever was interrupting his dance with Ciana, until they landed on Layla. Then they sparkled with desire. Theron's fists clenched as he was attempting to navigate the crowd to get to them. Ivar stepped forward, smirking then dismissing Kain before quickly pulling Layla against him as they danced away. Kain bowed smoothly to Ciana and began dancing with her instead. Kain saw the anger, the force of nature Theron had just become nearing them and subtly held up his hand behind Ciana, indicating for Theron to stop. *To wait.* Theron immediately slowed to a stop. Anger radiating from him. Theron could hardly breathe. His pulse thundered as he watched Ivar touch Layla's waist, his hand sliding lower, whispering who-knows-what in her ear. She wore a mask of flirtation, a smile that didn't reach her eyes. Rage surged beneath his skin, barely leashed. But he held his position, watching every step, every expression. When the dance ended, the King released Layla with a kiss to her hand before swaggering back to the table. Kain was quickly at her side before wordlessly leading Layla back towards where Theron now waited.

"Are you okay?" Theron asked immediately, his voice low and tight.

She waved him off, eyes focused on Kain. "Kain—what did she say?"

"She's fine," Kain assured them. "No one's hurt her, just..." He paused, jaw tightening. "Just public humiliation, threats towards Aerilynn to keep her in line. She's staying in a room across from the King's. No weapons, no furniture—just a bed. They've stripped it bare so she can't defend herself or cause any trouble." Theron's blood ran cold at this admission.

He looked between Layla and Kain. "That means it's extremely well guarded. And once they realize Aerilynn's missing..."

"They'll seal the castle," Kain finished grimly.

Theron's thoughts swirled. They were running out of time. Running out of options. And Layla was still here. He looked at her—really looked. Pale. Angry. Yet beautiful and resolute. His chest constricted with a tight ache he couldn't breathe past.

He reached for her shoulders gently. "Layla..." She stiffened at his tone and he swallowed hard. "You should leave. Go with Kain and Sir Edwin now. I'll stay. I'll get Ciana out."

Her eyes snapped to his, full of fire and hurt. "Absolutely not."

"Layla—"

"No!" she hissed. "I am not leaving my sister behind. I don't care what happens to me. You can't force me to run away." He closed his eyes, pained. He'd known she'd say that. Still, it gutted him.

"I just..." he rasped, his voice hoarse. "I can't bear it if something happens to you." Praying she could feel his sincerity

She softened and took a ragged breath before looking up at him. She gently brushed her fingers against his cheek. "I know." Then turned her attention back toward the ballroom, toward her sister.

"Will you get me a glass of champagne?" she asked, her voice low. "My nerves are frayed, and we need clear heads to plan what comes next." Theron lingered for a breath, then gave a quiet nod. He let his fingers linger on her shoulder for a moment longer before stepping away. If it were up to him, he'd steal her away and never look back. But it wasn't up to him. And now... now they would have to outwit a king before the volatility inside him exploded.

Layla.

As Theron disappeared into the crowd, Layla's throat tightened with guilt. Her heart warred between loyalty and desperation, but she shoved the guilt down like broken glass. *Later.* She could feel guilty later.

Now, she had to act. She turned toward Kain and Sir Edwin, pasting a sugary smile across her face. "Kain, could you please excuse Sir Edwin and me for a moment?" Kain didn't so much as blink. His smirk said it all.

"Not on your life, Dove. You may fool my brother, but you don't fool me. What little scheme are you spinning behind those deceptively sweet eyes?" Her smile dropped. Gods, he knew her too well. The urge to scream at him—*just trust me*—bubbled in her chest, but she swallowed it.

Instead, she met his eyes, defiant. "I might have an idea. But you're not going to like it."

Kain tilted his head, amused. "Obviously. You just sent Theron off on a wild goose chase, which tells me this plan of yours is reckless, probably idiotic, and absolutely going to put you in danger." Layla narrowed her eyes. She hated how right he was.

Still, she powered forward. "The King's... fondness for me has been made painfully clear. Tonight, he invited me to his bed." She saw Sir Edwin stand up even straighter somehow. But Kain—Kain didn't move. His entire body went still, a terrible silence bleeding from him. The green in his eyes seemed to vanish as a darker storm rolled in. Layla couldn't look at him as she continued.

"I wouldn't actually... I mean—I *won't*. I don't think I could even..." Her voice cracked slightly, but she pushed on. "But if we let the guards believe I'm going to him willingly, I can find his chamber. Find hers. Get to Ciana before he even arrives." With a small gulp, she finally looked back up and met Kain's eyes. They were bottomless. Haunted. And furious.

Sir Edwin cleared his throat first, stepping in like a buffer between emotional warheads. "My Lady. I will carry out your wishes... but I must raise a few concerns." His voice was measured but uneasy. "What if the king is already there? What if the guards stop you or worse? And even if you reach her room, there's no guarantee you won't be caught trying to cross back or escape with Lady Ciana." Layla nodded slowly, absorbing the logic but pushing past it.

"I understand. And I appreciate your concern, truly. But I'm not helpless. I have a dagger. I know how to use it. I just need to get to her. If I can reach her, I can lead her out. You'll be waiting as close as possible if anything goes wrong... We'll move fast." The moment the words left her lips, she knew how naïve they sounded. *But what choice did she have?*

Kain still hadn't spoken. When he finally did, his voice was tightly controlled like a fuse barely keeping its flame. "And if Ivar's already there?" His jaw flexed hard. "If he walks in while you're trapped in that gods-forsaken room with no way out, *then what*, Layla?" Her throat tightened. Tears burned her eyes without permission.

"Then I do whatever I have to," she whispered. "Because that's my sister. And she deserves to be saved, no matter what it costs me." She blinked the tears away and straightened her shoulders. "This is the best option we have. The only one. I'm doing this with or without your help."

Kain raked both hands through his hair, muttering something vicious under his breath as he turned away from her. He stood like that for a long moment. Then his shoulders dropped. He looked back at her, his expression raw and sharp. "I'll help you," he said quietly, voice like the calm before a massacre. "But if something goes wrong, Layla, if one hand touches you, I swear I'll kill every man in this castle." There was no jest in his voice. Just steel.

Layla's heart twisted in a strange, bittersweet knot. Somehow, that violent promise meant more to her than any vow of protection ever could.

"Kill away."

ASH AND CARRION ARE
THE SEEDS OF OUR GLORY

As loyalty is given, so it is passed. The service of
the parent binds the child; the child's worth
reflects the blood from which it came. Let it be
known: the debts of devotion are inherited, and
the blessings of the Crown fall only on those
whose line remains unbroken in its allegiance.

-BY COMMAND OF THE IRON CROWN OF
BARTORIA

Chapter Twenty-Four

Layla.

Theron returned, glass of champagne in hand. Layla did her best to steady her fingers before he could see the tremble. She forced herself to smile, to look calm. But she wasn't, not even close. He stopped in front of her and gently placed his hand beneath her elbow. His touch was tender, but his eyes burned with intensity.

"I have a plan, Layla," he said, voice low, urgent. "It'll work. It has to." She tilted her head, giving him her full attention, though her pulse was a war drum in her ears. "When the ballroom clears," Theron continued, "the king will likely escort Ciana out himself. If we can watch closely, track which direction they take her, we'll know where she's being kept. Then we hide. Wait for the castle to fall quiet. After midnight, when the halls are thinner, we move. No fighting unless we must. No risk to you."

Layla's stomach twisted. She understood why Theron was hesitating—why he hadn't suggested a direct pursuit. Ciana was kept close to the King, surrounded by guards. There would be no way for the men to trail her her discreetly like they had with Aerilynn without raising suspicion. If they tried, they'd alert the entire damned kingdom. And Theron... he wouldn't want Layla fighting her way through that kind of chaos. He knew she wouldn't willingly stay behind, so he was stalling—trying to find a plan that didn't involve risking her life. It was noble. It was infuriating. And it was flawed.

By midnight, someone would realize Aerilynn was gone. Then the castle would shift. Doors would be locked. Guards would double. Ciana would be surrounded, unreachable. This was the only chance. But she couldn't tell him that. Not when he looked at her like that—so certain, so desperate to protect her from everything except the truth. So instead, she gave him what he needed. She smiled.

"That sounds..." She hesitated, forcing her voice into something soft and agreeable, "reasonable." Layla dropped her eyes before the guilt could show in them. "It's safer. And we'll know more if we're patient... I trust you, Theron." The relief on his face was like a blade in her ribs. He nodded, exhaled, and gave her shoulder a tight squeeze, the kind that said he was grateful she wasn't fighting him. That she was letting him protect her.

He turned away to look back toward Ciana. And Layla—Layla swallowed the rising tide of shame. She was lying to him. Because they didn't have until midnight. And she couldn't lose Ciana. Her eyes darted toward Kain and Sir Edwin. Kain was already watching her. Not with suspicion. Not judgement. Just... understanding. A quiet, knowing look. He gave the smallest nod. *Her plan was still on.*

"Eddy," Kain said casually, "why don't you take another walk around the perimeter. Just make sure we're not missing anything." Sir Edwin glanced at Kain, then to Layla, and something in her face must have told him the truth. He gave a curt bow, then slipped into the crowd. Layla turned her face back toward the ballroom, her lips still curved, her heart pounding, her hands quivering just beneath the surface. The lie was in motion. And it had to work.

Layla impatiently waited for them to escort Ciana out of the ballroom. Her fingers quivered against the stem of her glass, barely able to fake another polite sip. They had a plan. Gods, she prayed it would be enough. She had already mouthed to Ciana—*we're coming*. But now the waiting, the pretending, the stillness... it was excruciating.

Kain and Theron stayed close, ever her shadows, while Sir Edwin was still discreetly across the ballroom, ready to light the signal fire. A single flare that would serve as the distraction, pulling attention from both the King and Theron so that Layla could slip away. It would force Theron to stay behind, waiting for her return with Ciana. Kain would follow her stealthily, get as close as possible, a hidden sword if needed. It was a desperate plan, fragile as glass and built on the thinnest thread of timing. One misstep, one second too late, and everything would collapse.

Layla tilted her chin, inhaled slowly, and made a silent plea to the stars—for just one night of luck. And then it began.

Two guards crossed the ballroom and flanked Ciana. Layla's breath caught as her sister cast a fleeting glance in her direction. She gave the smallest nod. Layla returned it, her eyes wide with silent promise. *We're coming*.

As Ciana disappeared through the grand doors, Layla gripped the edge of the table. Almost time. Every muscle in her body was tense, ready to snap. Theron reached for her hand and gave it a reassuring squeeze. She looked up at him, heart heavy. So much had passed between them in so little time. She didn't know what they were anymore, what they ever even were. But this wasn't the time.

"Layla..." Theron began, voice low, burdened with too much unsaid.

She stopped him gently, she could see it etched throughout his face. "You don't have to apologize again. I understand." His mouth parted, as if to argue, but the words caught—lodging behind clenched teeth and regret. "No, really. You did what your queen commanded. I should've never asked you to disobey. You barely knew me, and I expected you to choose me. That wasn't fair."

"It was fair, Layla," he said, voice rough, laced with desperation and confusion. "Hurting you... it's the last thing I ever want to do."

Her heart twisted. She reached up and rested a hand over his chest, grounding them both with the simple, steady pressure.

"I know," she whispered. "I believe you."

He pressed a kiss to her forehead, arms wrapping around her in a reluctant, almost breaking embrace. She held on tightly—because she knew what was coming. Knew what she was about to do... and that if it went wrong, it would break him. Then, at the edge of the ballroom, a flicker. Smoke.

Layla stepped back just as Theron's head snapped toward the commotion. A cluster of guards rushed to stamp out a small fire—Sir Edwin's signal. It worked. Theron's attention shifted, even if only for a heartbeat. That was all she needed. The distraction had begun.

In one fluid motion, Layla turned and slipped away to the same side doors Ciana had disappeared behind. Her pulse thundered in her ears, nerves crackling like a live wire beneath her skin. There was no room for second thoughts. Only forward.

As Layla neared the doors, a guard stepped in her path.. "Turn around. You're not permitted here."

Mustering every ounce of false bravado, Layla slipped into the role she knew the king would underestimate—a ditsy, forgettable girl with wide eyes and no spine. She blinked up at the guard, twirling a strand of hair with exaggerated bashfulness.

"Oh... but the King requested I meet him," she said sweetly, leaning in like she was sharing some scandalous gossip. "You know... tonight."

The guard stared, unimpressed. She dropped her gaze demurely, voice softening to a whisper. "He... requested I meet him in his chambers."

That did it. The guard grunted, muttered a curse, and signaled his partner. The doors creaked open. One of them fell in step behind her,

About the Author

escorting her up the staircase in silence. She didn't dare glance back. If Theron had seen her... it was already too late.

They reached the top, a long corridor with ornate doors stretching in either direction. Her escort stopped before two massive double doors. *The King's chambers.* Across the hall, another door. *Ciana's.* Layla locked that location into her mind, then turned back just as the guard opened the royal doors and gestured her inside. She expected him to turn and leave, but he didn't. Instead, he stepped inside and closed the door behind him. Layla's stomach dropped as panic surged, but she forced a smile and strode farther into the room as she tried to figure out what to do. She racked her brain, then her eyes landed on his sword. A quick and bad plan, but a plan none the less developed.

"Oh wow!" She said suddenly, her voice high and sweet. "That's a beautiful sword! May I see it?" The guard frowned, lifting a hand to stop her. *Too late.* Layla lunged, one hand grabbing his wrist, the other driving her hidden dagger into his throat. He gurgled violently, clutching at the hilt, but the blade was deep and sure. He dropped to his knees, blood spraying down his chest, and crumpled.

Shaking, Layla dragged him into the washroom. Her arms burned with the effort, but adrenaline fueled her. She yanked her dagger free, wiped the blade clean with quick, practiced hands, and shut the door behind him with a soft thud. *Almost there.*

She turned toward the double doors, chest tight, fingers curling around the handle. *If I can just make it across the hall...* But the knob twisted beneath her grip and she jerked back, startled. The door creaked open—And King Ivar stepped into view. Layla's breath instantly vanished.

"Ah," he grinned, eyes narrowing as he closed the door behind him. "You came after all." She swallowed hard, tucking the blade into the folds of her dress, hiding the unsteadiness in her hands. He prowled closer, eyes devouring her. "I knew you would. You're just like all the others."

Layla forced a simper as bile racked up her throat. "I thought I'd... please you, my King."

He chuckled—low, wicked. "Oh, you will."

Ivar motioned to the velvet couch near the hearth as he sauntered across the room, pouring two glasses of amber liquor with deliberate ease. His eyes never left her—dark with lust, devouring her like a feast already promised.

He returned, drink in hand, and lowered himself beside her with all the smugness of a king certain of his prize. Layla accepted the glass with unsteady fingers and lifted it to her lips, only pretending to sip. The sharp fumes alone made her stomach twist.

So... where does that husband of yours think you've run off to?" Ivar drawled, his voice dripping with venomous amusement. "Does he know his precious little prize snuck away to warm my bed instead?"

She forced a smile. "He doesn't need to know."

King Ivar leaned in, his breath rancid as he murmured, "Then let's not waste time." He rose abruptly, yanking her to her feet by the elbow. "Undress." Layla went rigid. "I said—undress." The playful mockery vanished from his voice, replaced by a cold, commanding edge.

When she didn't obey fast enough, he snarled, drew a dagger from his belt, and began slashing through her gown. Steel tore through silk. The fabric fluttered to the floor in ribbons, pooling around her ankles. Until only her thin shift remained.

"Now that's more like it," Ivar purred, eyes glinting. "Now take it off."

Tears burned at the corners of her eyes, but she didn't let them fall. Her mind screamed, but her body obeyed. *Endure. Live. Save Ciana.*

She reached for the thin straps of her shift, letting them slide down her shoulders. As the fabric slipped lower, so did her hands—graceful, deliberate—until they reached the shredded heap of her gown at her feet...And the hidden blade within it. Fingers closing around the hilt, she moved in one swift, fluid motion and threw.

The dagger sliced through the air—silent, deadly—aimed for his throat. But he moved. Faster than she ever could've anticipated. The blade caught his ear, carving a bloody line before embedding deep into the wall behind him. He roared, sounding more beast than man. Before Layla could react, he ripped the dagger free and lunged. His hand fisted in her hair, yanking her forward before slamming her against the bedpost. Her skull cracked hard against the wood, white-hot pain exploding behind her eyes.

"You fucking bitch!" King Ivar snarled, slamming her back onto the bed with enough force to knock the air from her lungs. She struggled, kicked, clawed—but he was too strong, her limbs no match against his bulk. He pinned her with one knee to her stomach, pressing the flat of his knife against her throat. The metal was icy, unforgiving as she felt it cutting into the delicate skin. Forcing her to now hold perfectly still or chance swift death. His other hand roamed with grotesque familiarity, pawing over her waist, her hips, her chest.

"You think you're brave?" he growled into her ear. "You think you're untouchable? I'll show you what it means to be powerless." He licked a slow, wet strip up her cheek. Layla choked back a sob, bile rising in her throat. The sheer violation, the animalistic glee in his touch, sent a fresh wave of nausea through her. Her shift tore with an ugly rip, the sound louder than the thunder of blood in her ears. Cold air swept across her skin, making her flinch. The sound of King Ivar's grunts as he hastily ripped at the laces of his pants before they hit the stone floor sent ice down her spine. *Endure. Live. Save Ciana.* Her mind clung to the words like a lifeline, a prayer she screamed inside while her body froze in terror.

He grabbed her by the hair again as he roughly forced her stomach down against the bed, his weight pressing her into the mattress. Her arms thrashed even with the the tip of the blade at the side of her throat. She couldn't help the instinct to get away. To not allow this to happen. Her nails clawing at the bedding, but he was stronger—drunk with power, heavy with malice.

He snarled against her ear. "I'll make sure you never forget this." She whimpered, her breath coming in shallow gasps, her body shaking uncontrollably as he shoved himself into her. Tears streamed down her cheeks, burning her skin with their helplessness. She couldn't see him, but she could feel everything: his hands, his cruelty, his intent as he was forcing himself on her again and again. *Endure. Live. Save—*

A deafening crash shattered the air. The sound of a door exploding off its hinges, wood splintering and flying across the room. And then, in an instant, the world shifted.

"What the fu—" The King's final words gurgled in his throat, cut short by a sickening, wet sound. Layla didn't have time to scream before his full weight collapsed onto her back, slamming the air from her lungs.

She buckled beneath him, her arms pinned under the dead weight of a man she hated more than death itself. Then—silence.

Her eyes cracked open just in time to see it. His head, detached from his body, lay sideways on the bed beside her. Eyes glassy, lips parted in a frozen snarl of ferocity. Layla's breath caught. Her scream never came as she was overtaken with absolute shock. Then the weight was gone. Yanked off of her in a blur.

Strong hands gripped her shoulders and flipped her gently onto her back. *Theron*. She didn't think, didn't breathe, didn't even register the wetness on her cheeks before she lunged into his chest, arms locking around his neck. In the safety of his arms, Layla sobbed—guttural, shaking sobs that ripped through her like a tidal wave. Her fists curled into his dress shirt as she pressed her face into his throat, as if she could disappear into him and never come back.

"It's okay, Layla. I've got you. It's okay now," Theron whispered, voice cracking as he rubbed circles into her back. His arms wrapped around her with a desperate tenderness, like if he let go, she might shatter, but she already had. Minutes passed—how many, she couldn't say—before she finally began to breathe again. The violent shudders dulled to a quiet ache. Her body loosened just enough to pull away, only far enough to see his face.

"I'm so sorry we weren't here sooner," he said, voice thick with guilt as he cupped her cheek, eyes swimming with pain and rage.

"How did you even...?" Layla blinked, eyes foggy with tears, as she turned her head toward the splintered doorway. Sir Edwin and Kain stood like sentinels in the flickering candlelight, weapons bloodied and waiting, eyes scanning the hall. Her heart leapt at the sight of them.

"Of course you didn't follow my orders," she whispered through a ragged laugh, tears still streaking her cheeks.

Kain's eyes met hers. Despite the fury behind them, his expression softened as a crooked, knowing smile curved his lips. "We do have a history of ignoring your better judgment, Dove."

Theron helped her sit up, still cradling her protectively. But urgency returned fast. "I'm sorry to ask, but... can you move? We don't know how long we've got before the rest of the guards follow the blood trail we left," he said, glancing over his shoulder toward the corridor. Layla nodded instinctively, but the motion halted as a wave of awareness crashed over her. She was utterly naked.

"Oh Gods," she gasped, face igniting with shame as she snatched the blood-specked blanket from Theron's hands and yanked it over her chest. Her eyes flicked around the room, her shredded gown like torn silk and carnage at her feet. Her stomach twisted anew at the thought of what they must have seen, what she looked like when they entered.

Theron turned his head, giving her space, as he reached for a fresh cloth to wipe the blood off her arms. "Don't worry," he said gently. "You're safe now, that's what matters." Layla barely nodded, her cheeks still blazing. She hadn't even realized the tears had returned until Kain appeared beside her, holding out what remained of her shift.

"Dove," he said, voice light but eyes deadly serious. "We can talk about this whole... view... later, or we can go rescue your sister now. Dealer's choice." He winked. The tension snapped—replaced by that familiar spark of indignation that only Kain could ignite.

Layla snatched the shift from his hand and jabbed a finger at him. "Turn around."

349

He chuckled, turning on command. "My eyes are sealed."

She pulled the shift over her head, still shaking slightly, and stood on unsteady legs between the two Drakaren brothers. Her slip clung to her, sheer and with a long tear up the side, but it was all she had. There was no time to care. As she reached for the small blanket to wipe the blood from her arms, her gaze fell to the shredded gown at her feet—and she made her decision. *Let them see. Let the world know exactly what the King had tried to take... and the fate he earned in return.* She was still standing. Battered, bloodied—but unbroken. And now, she would save her sister.

So... is someone going to tell me how?" Layla's voice cracked as she spoke, breath hitching while she scrubbed at her arms with shaking hands. The blood only smeared, refusing to disappear. She'd learned something tonight—a decapitated corpse collapsing on top of you left more blood than she ever could've imagined. Her gaze flicked between the three men standing around her, each one stained nearly as badly as she was.

"The minute I turned and saw you were gone..." Theron's voice broke, his jaw clenched tight with fury and guilt. His eyes held hers like he was afraid to let go. "Kain told me. He told me everything."

Her head snapped toward Kain. He didn't flinch under her scrutiny. He stood tall, arms crossed over his blood-slick chest, wearing that damned smirk like a crown. Like he'd do it all again without hesitation. Layla shot him a glare sharp enough to slice. Theron continued, stepping slightly in front of her. "We followed as quickly, and as quietly, as we could. But the quiet part didn't last." She looked at them again—really looked. The blood. The torn clothes. The bruises already blooming beneath their armor. Her lips parted in horror.

"Oh..." It was all she could manage.

"You led the way," Kain said simply, as if describing a pleasant walk. "We just cleaned up behind you."

Layla blinked. "Cleaned up...?"

"I told you," Kain added with a raise of his brows. "I'd probably have to kill everyone with that brilliant plan of yours." There was no regret in his voice. No hesitation. Just brutal honesty. Her jaw fell open. They had *slaughtered* their way to her. Risked everything—for *her*. For *Ciana*. Gods, *how many had they faced?*

Theron stepped closer, gently placing his hands on her shoulders, grounding her. "You ready?" Layla swallowed hard and nodded once. Her body still shook, but the fire in her chest was burning again. Rage. Resolve. Love. Sir Edwin was still at the doorway. Kain took position beside him, knives at the ready. Theron gripped Layla's wrist and pulled her close behind him, sword now in his other hand. The tension in the air was suffocating but they were as ready as they would ever be.

Sir Edwin swiftly glanced down the hall. "Clear! Go—now!" Kain darted across the hall like lightning. The bolt on the door clanged under his hands. Layla's heart thundered in her chest. *Click.* Ciana's door flew open with a crash. *We're here, Ciana. We've got you.*

By blood we are born, and by blood we rise.
Varyn, God of Blood and Valor, watches all
who bear the mark of the warrior. To serve
with courage is to walk beneath his gaze. To fall
with honoris to earn his favor. But to flee the
call, to betray the fight, is to be cast from
Ondurin and denied his glory. Let every blade
drawn, every wound endured, and every
sacrifice made be offered in his name- so that
when death comes, it finds us worthy.

- FROM THE OATHBOUND LAW OF THE
ANTONIN FLAME

Chapter Twenty-Five

Theron.

Theron led Layla across the corridor like a shield, every nerve in his body strung tight. Kain slipped through the doorway first, blade drawn, eyes sharp and scanning. Sir Edwin remained in the hall outside, sword raised, listening. Ready to give warning if so much as a whisper of boots echoed their way. But Layla didn't wait for the all-clear. She tore free from Theron's grasp and darted around him, feet silent against the cold stone. Her bloodied slip clung to her body as she launched herself onto the bed.

"Ciana," she breathed, voice cracking. Her sister was seated stiffly in the center of the mattress, arms wrapped tightly around herself. The room was cold and bare. Nothing but some sheet and pillow, no furniture, no coverings, no comfort. A cell dressed up like a bedroom.

At the sound of her name, Ciana flinched violently. But as soon as her eyes landed on Layla's face, everything broke. Joy cracked through terror. She scrambled forward and the sisters clung to one another like a dam against a raging river. Layla buried her face in Ciana's shoulder as Ciana wept openly. There was no time, but they held each other like they might never get the chance again.

"Are you okay?" Layla asked, voice shaking, panic rising despite herself.

"Yes. I—yes. Gods, what happened to you?" Ciana touched the blood on her sister's temple, her throat, her shoulder.

"Doesn't matter. We're getting you out of here."

"There's no way," Ciana said hopelessly. "The window's sealed. The drop's too long." Theron stepped to the glass. Two stories. Maybe more. His bloodied hand pressed against the pane.

"We've done worse," he muttered.

Sir Edwin slipped inside and shut the door behind him, his voice low and urgent. "We've got company. They're close."

"It doesn't lock from the inside," Ciana whispered, almost apologetically.

"We won't be here long enough to need it," Theron answered. His eyes swept the room once, landing on the bed. "Layla. Kain. Sheets. Now. Tie them tight." He tore off his ruined shirt, wrapping the fabric around his already-bleeding fist.

They quickly yanked the linens free, tying knots fast but strong.. Ciana joined in, hastily helping. Kain secured the first end around the bedframe as Layla raced the rest to Theron. He took them without a word and looked to Sir Edwin.

"You're first. Clear the landing then help the girls down."

The young commander nodded briskly and moved to the window. Theron breathed once, then punched through the glass. It shattered with a thunderous crash, shards spraying outward. Wind roared into the room. Cold air, sharp and biting, replaced the still heat of fear.

"Go!" Theron commanded. Sir Edwin moved. He climbed to the sill, gripped the rope of sheets, and slid down into the dark. Seconds passed.

"Clear!" he shouted from below. Theron turned, gripped Ciana by the waist, and lifted her to the ledge. Her whole body was shaking viciously.

"Hand over hand," he instructed gently. "Don't rush. Sir Edwin's down there. He'll catch you if you slip."

"I can't—"

"Yes, you can."

She gave a shallow nod, eyes wide with terror, but began her descent anyway. Her foot slipped immediately and she let out a scream. Theron instinctively lunged, catching her wrists, ignoring the glass biting into his forearms as he dragged her back to the sill.

"Look at me," he ordered, holding her gaze with pure steel. "You. Can. Do. This." Ciana nodded again. This time, steadier. And she began to climb down.

"Layla. Go." Theron turned to her, urgency in his voice. Just then, a loud thud slammed against the door. Then another.

Theron lunged to brace the door beside Kain, muscles straining as another brutal crash hit the other side. Dust rained from the frame, the hinges groaning. The Bartorians were here, and they were out of time.

And then he saw her.

Layla stood by the open window, frozen. Her eyes fixed on the chaos, wide and shining. And in that split second, he knew—she realized it too. They weren't all getting out.

Then she moved. Before he could call out, she ran to him, and her lips crashed against his—fierce, breathless, final. His arms closed around her instinctively, holding her like he could stop time. Like he could shield her from this with just his body and will alone. And Gods, he didn't want to let her go.

She pulled back just slightly, her hand on his jaw, eyes burning into his soul. "Theron..." she whispered, a promise and a plea wrapped in his name. And he knew—whatever happened next, she was about to do something reckless. Something brave. Something that might tear him in two.

"I'll find you," he said. "Just go." But she didn't and he knew that she wouldn't.

"Take her!" Theron snapped, eyes locking on Kain. Kain turned, stunned.

"Get her out. That's an order. You keep her safe, no matter what."

He could never leave any other man to give their life for him—let alone Kain. Despite everything, despite the chaos and bitterness and wounds between them, he was still his family. His blood. His little brother. And Theron would never ask someone to do what he wasn't willing to do himself. If someone had to stay behind, it would be him. No hesitation. No regret.

Kain clenched his jaw, understanding the weight of what Theron had just said. What he was asking. With a grim nod, he seized Layla.

"No! Don't—don't you leave him!" she screamed, thrashing in his arms. "Kain, let me go! Theron!"

"You either climb or I throw you out the window," Kain growled, dragging her bodily to the sill. Another crash shook the door. He was holding it with every ounce of strength the gods had given him but wood cracked. Layla's eyes met Theron's one last time. He mouthed it again: *Go.* Tears streaming, he watched as she gripped the makeshift rope and reluctantly began her descent. Kain a wall not allowing her to attempt to come back in. Then—*RIP.* The sheet tore where it caught on the jagged glass and the rope gave way.

"LAYLA!" Theron screamed. He watched in horror as Kain dove, his torso nearly all the way out the window. His body going taut as the glass visibly shredded his torso.

"I got her!" he gritted out, "I got her!"

Theron turned back to look at the giant splinter in the door behind him. Then with another loud crash, the hinges buckled, and the wood splintered more. He pressed his full weight into it, blood dripping from his arms, knowing what was coming. But he didn't care. They were getting out. If he had to hold the whole castle back to buy them that chance, so be it.

Layla.

Holding onto Kain with every ounce of strength she had left, Layla dangled in the air, her limbs trembling, vision blurring with tears. Pain was etched deep into Kain's face as he looked down at her, blood streaming down his arms.

"Just let me go!" she pleaded, her voice raw, cracking. "I'll be okay. Please, go help him. He needs you!" She knew it was a lie. She wouldn't be okay. But if it bought Theron a second longer, she would say anything. *Anything.*

Kain's gaze flicked upward toward the shattered window, where she knew chaos raged unseen. The sound of boots pounding and steel clashing echoed down to them. *The guards had got in.* They'd breached the room. Theron was fighting them alone.

Kain's jaw clenched at something he saw. Then without a word he yanked her up with a sudden, desperate heave and wrapped his arms around her. Layla let out a gasp just as Kain launched himself out the ledge and they fell. The wind screamed in her ears as her scream caught in her throat. Then—A sickening thud. Not her into the ground, but Kain. She had landed on Kain's body.

"Kain?" Her voice was a breath, a prayer. "Kain!" She scrambled off him. Blood pooled fast beneath the back of his head, soaking his pale blond hair into a crimson mat. "No, no, no—please," she whispered, kneeling beside him, cupping his face. "You can't do this. Not you too. Please!" His face was deathly pale and slack. His chest unmoving, and for a moment, the world shattered.

"Kain!" she screamed. "Kain, wake up!" She was pleading over him. Tears pooling down her face as she begged all the gods to save him. To bring him back.

After what felt like eternity, she watched in utter relief as his eyelids fluttered. A broken groan escaped his lips. Layla sobbed out a breath, half-laughing, half-choking as she touched his cheeks. "Oh, thank the Gods..."

"I think that's the first time you've said 'please,' Dove," he rasped, wincing as his bloodied lips twitching into a faint smirk.

With her help, he quickly started to get up, but he staggered, nearly collapsing again.

"Kain, your head—"

"I'll live," Kain muttered, though the blood soaking through his hair told a different story. He swayed again, and Layla tightened her grip around his waist, steadying him as best as she could. Then his voice dropped, rough with something more painful than injury.

"We need to go. Theron…" Layla's breath caught as she turned to look at him. Kain's eyes flicked upward to the shattered window above, then back to hers, guilt etched across his face like a wound. "They broke through. They… they stabbed him, Layla. I saw it. He… I'm so sorry."

The words didn't land all at once. They crashed into her slowly—like waves, each one heavier than the last, until they dragged her under. *Stabbed. Theron. Her Theron.*

"No," she whispered. Her knees buckled, and for a heartbeat she sagged beneath Kain's weight. She turned her eyes upward, staring through the darkness at the fractured window above. He would be there. *He had to be.* He was strong enough to survive it, he always was. She half-expected to see his silhouette in that frame, his voice calling her name like it always had when she lost herself. But the window remained dark. The broken shards still clung to the sill like teeth. There was no movement. No silhouette. No sign of him. He was gone.

And yet—there was no time to fall apart. No time to cry, or scream, or collapse in the dirt like every part of her wanted to. Not while Kain was half-dead in her arms, bleeding from his head, limping on a ruined ankle and shredded abdomen.. Not while Ciana was still waiting for her in the trees. So she ripped her gaze from the window and swallowed her scream. Shoved it down so deep she didn't know if she'd ever be able to pull it out again.

"Come on," she rasped, wrapping her arm tighter around Kain's waist, taking as much of his weight as she could. His breath hitched as he stumbled, the pain clearly worsening. His steps were uneven, barely coordinated. His blood smeared across her skin like ink as she dragged them forward. Each footfall was agony. Not just from the terrain. But from the truth. *She was walking away from Theron.* From the man who'd died saving them. From the man she hadn't even had time to say goodbye to. She blinked hard, fighting back the hot sting of tears as she half-dragged Kain into the dark tree line.

He had done this—for her. For her sister. For all of them. And now he was gone. But she would come back. She swore it on every God she could name. She would come back for him—even if all that remained was blood, armor and dust. She would not leave him behind forever.

But right now... she had to keep the living alive.

Kain let out a weak groan beside her, and she held him tighter. "One step at a time," she whispered, mostly to herself now. "Just... one more step."

Just as they broke into the tree line, a voice called out. "Lady Layla?" Sir Edwin emerged from the darkness with Ciana.

"Sir Edwin, Ciana. Kain is badly injured." Layla breathed, her voice strained. "We have to get to Aerilynn and everyone else and get out now."

Sir Edwin's expression faltered as he dove to Kain's other side. "And Theron?" Layla shook her head, unable to speak. The grief threatened to drown her again.

"I'm so sorry, My Lady..." After a brief pause, he solemnly looked away and pointed. "This way," he said gently. "They're waiting just beyond the ridge."

As they moved through the thick canopy, where moonlight barely touched the forest floor, Layla kept glancing back. Every step away felt wrong. Like her heart was still trapped in that terrible castle. At last, they emerged to the sound of familiar voices. Xaden stood, sword drawn, Sparrow kneeling beside Aerilynn, who still clung tightly to his hand. Their Graystonian guards were scattered in a wide perimeter, keeping alert. Relief washed over the group like a breath held too long—Antonins exhaled in silent thanks, the Graystonians nodded in quiet respect, the success of the mission heavy in their eyes. But the moment cracked as Xaden's gaze swept past them and his brow furrowed. His voice cut through the fragile stillness like a blade:"Where's Theron?"

Kain slumped heavily against her now. "We... we killed the King. In the escape, Theron took a sword to the heart holding off the guards...." He paused, "he saved us all." Her lip quivered at the admission. She couldn't believe it. She wouldn't.

"What if he survived?" Layla's voice cracked, broken with panic. "What if they missed his heart? We should go back. Please, someone help me go back and save him."

"No," Kain said firmly, voice like stone as he stepped out of his friends grip. "He didn't die so you could throw your life away. There is no saving him, Layla. He's gone. Now we have to go. Now." His tone left no room for doubt. For argument. But still—she couldn't believe it.

"But—"

Xaden stepped forward, steadying her with a hand on her shoulder, gentle but unyielding. His eyes met hers with a rare flicker of softness. "He died as he lived. Standing between the innocent and a blade. He was struck protecting the escape... and he bought you the time to get out." Layla's breath hitched.

"He's not gone, not really," Xaden added. "He's in Ondurin now—feasting with Varyn, probably already challenging some poor bastard to a spar between rounds of ale." A faint, respectful smile touched his mouth, more solemn than amused. "That's not a tragedy, Layla. That's an honor. That's the warrior's reward."

She wanted to scream, to collapse, to deny every word—but the conviction in Xaden's voice, the quiet reverence, made something deep in her chest fracture instead.

Then—Kain's knees buckled and his eyes rolled back.

"Kain!" Layla's scream ripped through the trees as he collapsed beside her, crashing to the earth like a warrior struck down mid-charge. She dove after him, catching his weight just before it hit the ground fully. But he was heavy—too heavy. Blood poured down his back, soaking through his dress clothes, through her fingers, through her soul.

No. No. No.

She didn't know there was anything left inside her to break. But there was. Seeing him like that shattered it. The last tether of hope. The final flicker of strength. Layla dropped to her knees, hands frantically pressing to his chest, his face, his throat. "Kain?! No! Look at me—look at me!" she begged. "Please... stay with me. Please." *Nothing.* No groan. No flicker of pain. No infuriating smirk. Just blood. Everywhere.

"HELP ME!" She shrieked, her voice unrecognizable. "Some-one—please!"

Sparrow was already moving, Xaden just behind him, but they weren't fast enough. No one was. She cradled Kain to her chest, her fingers shaking as she ran them through his blood-soaked hair, her sobs ragged and relentless. She kissed his temple. His jaw. Anything to wake him.

"Don't do this. Don't you dare leave me too," she whispered. "Not you. Not now." he sky above blurred, her tears falling fast and hot as if the heavens wept with her. First Theron. Now Kain. She rocked him in her arms like she could hold his soul in place. But it was slipping. And she could feel it. And all around them, the forest stood still, as if the entire world had stopped to grieve.

Please, not both of them.
Not tonight.
Not like this.

Epilogue

Layla.

It had been a month since Layla was carried out of Bartoria in Sparrow's arms, half-conscious and soaked in blood. A month since the night that shattered her, that ripped away the last piece of the woman she had just begun to become. She returned to Graystonia alive—but something in her had not survived.

A month since her heart had been shredded by the loss of Theron... and nearly torn again when Kain collapsed before her, blood pouring from his head as she screamed for him to live. The image haunted her. The moments blurred together now—blood, steel, smoke, and the suffocating terror that she might lose both of them in a single night. One she had lost forever. The other she had dragged back from the brink with desperate hands and prayers she never knew she believed in.

Autumn had settled over the kingdom like a shroud. The skies were heavy with ash-colored clouds, and the once-verdant trees now stood cloaked in dying amber and rust. The wind carried the scent of scorched wood and damp earth- an omen of the winter and war to come. And yet inside the palace, nothing seemed to change.

Everything looked the same as it had before. Gilded hallways, polished marble, warm hearths. As if the kingdom had simply paused and waited for them to return. But the stillness was a lie. Because the storm was coming—and they all felt it. They were preparing for war. A bigger war than any of them had dared to imagine.

The rumors spread like fire through dry brush—Bartoria was not weakened. It was enraged. Killing King Ivar had not severed the snake's head; it had revealed three more. He had been nothing but a puppet, a mask for something far more calculated and sinister. His death hadn't broken their armies—it had emboldened them. Strengthened their resolve. Now the North stirred with fury, preparing for all-out war. Sir Charles, still unaccounted for, had vanished without a trace, and Layla could feel his betrayal like an old wound that refused to close. The man who helped destroy her father... was still out there. Still breathing. But Layla had no power to hunt him. Her mother made certain of that.

After weeks confined to bed, her wounds stitched and monitored daily, Queen Raynera finally emerged from recovery—steadier than before, and twice as cold. She did not rule, not truly. As Queen Regent, her power was borrowed, temporary—meant only to fill the void until Layla married and a king could be crowned. But what she could do, she did with ruthless efficiency. Whatever warmth had once softened her edges was gone now, replaced by a chilling resolve.

Peace was an illusion, and Raynera knew it. So she poured herself into diplomacy, securing fragile alliances with the southern kingdoms of Myriamis, Elarith, and the newly splintered remnants of the Antonin people. She navigated court like mist behind the throne, holding a crown she could never wear, desperate to place it on a man strong enough to hold their crumbling realm together.

So each time Layla tried to step into the war councils, she was turned away. Each time she requested to brief the generals—eager to share everything she'd learned in the forests and manor halls of Antonin and Bartoria—she was told to rest. To recover. To stay out of matters too grave for a woman. Avenging her father, hunting Sir Charles, even speaking Theron's name aloud was met with clipped warnings and disapproving glances. Her role, she was told, was not on the battlefield. It was in the drawing room. At fittings. In courtship.

Her duty, her mother reminded her, was singular and absolute:

Finalize a marriage.

Secure a strong king.

Remain silent.

She had endured two enemy kingdoms. Fought through fire, steel, and ruin. Survived a slave collar and the hands of a king who tried to break her. She had crossed burning forests, spilled blood in the dark, and saved the royal women of her realm when no one else could. But none of that mattered here. Here, she was not a warrior or a survivor. She was a daughter. A symbol. A womb. Her voice was a whisper. Her wrists, too delicate. Her future—already written by men who hadn't bled for it.

And so, as the adrenaline of survival faded and the palace doors closed to her, Layla broke.

Not all at once—but piece by piece, with every door shut in her face, with every dismissive glance from the men who'd never seen what she had. She let the weight of it all crush her. Her father, gone. Theron, lost. Kain, barely alive. The kingdom bleeding. And she—shooed from every room that mattered, her voice drowned beneath silk and tradition.

Her mother's words echoed again like a death sentence:

Finalize a marriage.

Secure a strong king.

Remain silent.

If this was her true purpose—if this was all she was allowed to be—*then what was left to fight for?* And so she let herself become the thing they demanded: quiet, obedient, ornamental. A shell of the woman she had once been. Because if she could not choose her future, could not seek revenge, could not even speak the names of those she had loved and lost— Then none of it mattered.

No longer was she the girl sneaking daggers into the courtyard, secretly dreaming of being something more.

And so, when Queen Raynera summoned her weeks later to announce that the kingdom could wait no longer for a king—that Layla would fulfill her duty through marriage—Layla didn't protest. She didn't cry or beg, she simply nodded. Because that's what daughters did. That's what princesses were trained for. To accept that their lives did not belong to them. That their worth was measured in alliances and heirs. That they were vessels of power, not power itself.

Even though Theron's face haunted her when she closed her eyes. His voice echoed in the hollow spaces where her heart used to be. He had given everything to save her—his sword, his kingdom, his life....She would now wed a stranger for peace. She told herself she was lucky. That most women never got even a taste of the life she had lived, the passion, the drive. Even if only for a few bloody, burning days.

So she buried the memories with the woman she had been for a fleeting moment—free, wild, strong. Then easily, too easily, she became the shell the kingdom needed. She put on the gowns. The crown. The smile. She walked the halls like a ghost of herself. Head high, back straight, her grief folded neatly behind her eyes where no one could see it. Where no one cared to look.

Because the leaves were falling. The wind was sharpening. And the realm was holding its breath for the war to come.

And Layla? She had no choice but to endure. That was what queens did. Even if it meant burying the only pieces of herself she had ever truly been proud of.

Kain.

The sharp bite of autumn wind sliced through Kain's coat, tousling his blond hair and stinging the scar that now curved across his right temple. His breath rose in faint, white clouds before him, curling like smoke between the trees. Normally, he loved this season—the fire-hued leaves, the crisp tang of the air, the quiet hush before winter's descent. But not this time, he didn't fucking care about anything else, especially not a damned leaf. Not when every step brought him closer to her.

A fucking month. An entire gods-damned month since he'd seen her face, heard her voice, felt her breath stir against his skin. And it had been torture. Agonizing, silent torture. He'd survived a cracked skull, near blood loss, and a warlord's wrath, but it was the distance from her that had nearly broken him.

Technically, he was here under orders, as the newly named liaison between the Antonin Tribe and Graystonia Kingdom. Queen Okteria hadn't argued when Kain had offered himself up for the negotiations. She definitely didn't want to be the one to deal with all of the political bullshit, but she also knew it was important, vital even. A continent wide war was coming and for the first time in centuries and whether they liked it or not, they needed alliances to have a chance at winning it.

But Kain didn't give a damn about whatever the hell the title was. He took the job for one reason: So he could see her again. Not that she ever had to know that. Let her believe it was duty. Let her believe it was strategy. But the truth, buried somewhere beneath the armor and the posturing, was far more raw. He just needed to know she was alive. *Whole. Real.*

Beside him, Sparrow emerged from the woods, his own breath fogging the air as they crested the rise. The capital came into view at last, its familiar gray stone walls rising against the slate-colored sky, flags snapping in the wind. A month ago, this city had felt like an enemy. Now... it felt like a second heartbeat.

"Still standing," Sparrow muttered, a low whistle escaping him. "Guess that counts for something." Kain didn't answer. He was too focused. Too tightly wound. They passed through the outer perimeter easily, Graystonian guards greeting them not with suspicion, but with nods. Respect. Camaraderie. It was strange. And yet... earned.

The castle gates yawned wide before them, flanked by torchlight and the faint crunch of leaves underfoot. The seasons were changing faster than anyone had planned. Winter was closing in. And with it, the war they'd all feared had grown far bigger than any of them could have imagined. Allies were no longer a luxury. They were a necessity.

As they approached the steps, servants rushed out to meet them, collecting their packs, ushering them toward the open archway of the great hall. Warmth spilled out—firelight dancing across high stone walls, banners rustling gently from the vaulted ceiling. And then he saw her.

Layla stood at the far end of the corridor, a pale blue gown clinging to her frame, her chestnut curls falling in soft waves down her back, kissed golden by the hearth light. She was facing away at first, speaking quietly to someone near the hearth. But then, as if she sensed something shift, she turned. Her eyes found his instantly. And Kain forgot how to breathe. She looked... different. Still achingly beautiful, still burning like a flame behind her eyes but quieter somehow. More distant. A version of Layla wrapped in silk and silence, the wildness he remembered buried beneath a veneer of composure. But when her gaze locked with his, something inside her cracked, just enough. Her mouth curled into the softest, saddest smile he had ever seen. Not the sharp smirk she used to wield like a blade. Not the amused grin that danced during their verbal duels. This smile... was weary. Grateful. Real. And it undid him completely.

He didn't care that the castle was watching. He didn't care that they were expected to discuss battle lines and treaty clauses. Not when she was standing right there, breathing, whole. Not after everything they had lost. She was here. He was here. And Kain swore by every god that had ever existed—nothing would keep him from her again.

Acknowledgements

To my husband- yes, you already got the dedication, but you also survived months of plot rants, late-night typing fury, and endless complaints about the lack of coffee. You wrangled our tiny tornadoes for entire weekends so I could chase a scene that I couldn't let go of, and you even read my rough draft on the side of a mountain like a legend. So here's your second crown. You've earned it. Barely.

To Alex Palmer- my sounding board, hype woman, and the fiercest story ally I could ask for. You've read this book more times than anyone should ever have to, from the cringe-worthy first draft to the polished final version- and somehow, you never ran. I've bombarded you with screenshots, plot holes, and wild theories at all hours, and you've answered every one with excitement, wisdom, and way too much patience. You're almost as invested in this story as I am (which is both impressive and mildly concerning). Thank you for being everything I needed and more. I can't wait for more fantasy balls, ridiculous gowns, and stories yet to come.

To my family- Mom, Dad, and my beautiful sisters- thank you for answering the phone that one random day when I blurted out, "I think I'm going to write a book." You didn't laugh or blink. You supported me from the start, offering endless encouragement, thoughtful feedback, and the kind of patience only blood relatives are legally bound to give. To my sisters: thank you for enduring the voice memos, ramblings, and plot twists I couldn't keep to myself.

And Dad...I know you probably wish I'd written something wholesome and gone by a mysterious pen name like *A.G. Storm*. But here we are. Your daughter writes smut- under her real name. Try not to make eye contact with the neighbors or employees who decide to pick up a copy.

To Bryanna Beverlin- thank you for being the best listening ear a girl could ask for. You didn't just deal with me, my chaos, and my wild toddlers...you also dealt with my husband, and honestly, that deserves its own medal. Your support, your constant cheering, and the way you endlessly help keep my family functioning gave me the space to finish this book.. I can't begin to express how grateful we are to have you in our lives. And the fact that you love this genre? That's just the cherry on top. You are truly one of the kindest souls I know, and I am cheering for you in every step life takes you.

To Mandi Ann- thank you for your incredible feedback, sharp insight, and unwavering encouragement. You helped me stretch this story beyond what I thought it could be, guiding it into places I hadn't even imagined. Your edit recommendations didn't just refine the words- they revealed the heart of the heart of the story. I'm so grateful our paths crossed.

And to you- the reader. You made it. Through the chaos, the drama, the heartbreak, the slow burns, the smut...all of it. I don't know what that says about you, but I love it. Thank you for giving this story your time, your heart, and your imagination. Whether you laughed, cried, blushed or cursed at the characters (hopefully all of the above), I'm endlessly grateful you chose to take this journey with me. Here's to fierce heroines, morally grey men, and stories that stay with us long after the final page.

About the Author

Alexia Gray is a lifelong lover of all things magical, romantic, and just a little dangerous. Raised on fairy tales and fantasy novels, she's spent years dreaming up enchanted worlds and star-crossed lovers. Love of the Bladed Dove is her debut romantasy novel, blending epic stakes with slow-burn passion. When she's not writing, Alexia can be found getting lost in fantasy book series, or chasing toddlers. She lives in small town Missouri with her novel-worthy husband and two wild boys.